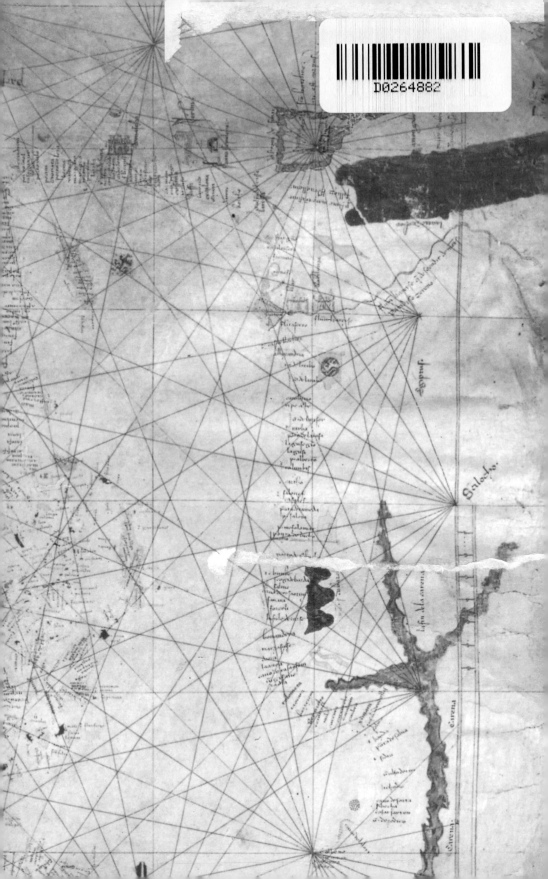

BAUDOLINO

ALSO BY UMBERTO ECO

Umberto Eco

BAUDOLINO

Translated from the Italian by
William Weaver

SECKER & WARBURG
LONDON

Published by Secker & Warburg 2002

2 4 6 8 10 9 7 5 3 1

Copyright © 2000 RCS Libri S.p.A.
English translation copyright © 2002 by Harcourt, Inc.

Endpapers: portolan chart attributed to Angelino Dulcert,
Add. MS. 2591 from the British Library, London

First published in Great Britain in 2002 by Secker & Warburg
Random House, 20 Vauxhall Bridge Road,
London SW1V 2SA

Random House Australia (Pty) Limited
20 Alfred Street, Milsons Point, Sydney,
New South Wales 2061, Australia

Random House New Zealand Limited
18 Poland Road, Glenfield,
Auckland 10, New Zealand

Random House South Africa (Pty) Limited
Endulini, 5A Jubilee Road, Parktown 2193, South Africa

The Random House Group Limited Reg. No. 954009
www.randomhouse.co.uk

A CIP catalogue record for this book
is available from the British Library

ISBN 0 436 27603 8 (Hardback)
ISBN 0 436 20604 8 (Trade paperback)

Printed and bound in Great Britain by Clays Ltd, St Ives PLC

BAUDOLINO

1

Baudolino tries his hand at writing

Rattisbon Anno ~~Dommini~~ Domini mense decembri mclv Cronicle of Baudolino of the fammily of Aulario.

I Baudolino son of ~~Galiaudo~~ Gagliaudo of the Aulari with a head that looks like a lion halleluia gratias to the Allmighty may he forgive me

ego habeo facto the greatest stealing of my life, I mean from the cabbinet of the Bishop Oto I have stollen many pages that may belong to the Immperial Chancellor and I have scraped clean almost all of them excepting where the writing would not come off et now I have much parchmint to write down what I want which is my own story even if I don't know to write Latin.

if they find out the pages are gone God knows the Hell they will raze et may be theyll think it was some spy of the Roman bishops who hate the Emperer Fredericus

but may be nobody cares in the chancellery they write and write even when theres no need and whoever finds them (these pages) ~~can shove them up his~~ ... wont do anything about them

ncipit prologus de duabus civilitatibus historiae AD mcxliii conscript saepe multumque volvendo mecum de rerum temporalium motu ancipitq these lines were allready here before and I couldnt scratch them away so I leave them

if they find these pages now Ive writen on them not even a chancelor will understand them because this lingua here is what they talk at la Frescheta but noboddy knows to write it down

but even if its a langwadge noboddy understands they can tell right away its me because everyboddy says we Frescheta people talk a lingua no Kristian ever heard so I have to hide these pages well

Jesù writing is hard work all my fingers ake allready

my father Galiaudo always use to say I must have a gift of Santa maria of Roboreto because since I was a little pup if someboddy say just ~~quinkue~~ five V words I could do their talk right off whether they came from Terdona or from Gavi and even from Mediolanum where they talk stranger than dogs, anyway even when I met the first Alamanni in my life who were laying siege seige seege to Terdona, all Toische and nasty and they say rousz and Myn got, before the day was over I was saying rousz and Myn got too and they woiud would say to me Kint go find us a pretty Frouwe and we'll do fiki fiki even if she doesn't wan to just tell us where she is and we'll grab her fast

whats a Frouwe I said and they said a womman a feemale du verstan and with theiur hands they made like big tits because in this siege we were kinmd of scarce on women, the ones in Terdona are in the town and when we enter just leave it to us but the wommen outside the town don't show their faces and then they set to cursing with words that gave even me goosebumps

lousy shitty Hunns, you needn't think I'm going to tell you where the Frouws are, I'm no informer, keep jerking off

mamma mia, they like to killed me

kill or necabant, now I'm writing Latin almost, not that I understand Latin even if I learned to read from a Latin librum and when they talk

2

Latin to me, I understand but its the writing I don't know how you write the words

Goddamm I never know if it's equus or equum and I always get it wrong while for us a horse is always a chivaus and I never get it wrong because nobody writes Horse in fact they dont write anything because they dont know how to read

but that day things went all right and the germanns didn't harm a hair of my head because just then some milites arrived yelling come on come on we're attacking again and then Hell broke loose and I couldnt think with the cavalry going this way and the foot soldeiers going that way with their banners and trumpets blowing and wooden towers tall as the trees of Burmia moving like carts with bowmen and fundibulari on them and others carrying ladders and all these arrows raining down on them like hail and the others flinging stones with a kind of big Spoone and they whistled over my head like the iaculi that the Derthonesi threw from the walls, what an uproar!

and I hidd myself for a good two hours under a bush saying sancta virgine help me then everything calmed down and some men ran by me speaking like people from Pavia and yelling they'd killed so many Derthonesi that it looked like a lake of Blood and they were very happy because now the Derthonesi would find out what it meant to side with the Mediolanenses

since those alamanns with the Frouwe business were coming back, may be not so many, because the Derthonesi hadnt exakly been idle I said to myself I better cleer out

so I walked and walked and got home when it was almost day and told the whole story to my father Galiaudo who said you big booby getting mixed up with seiges and the like one of these days you'll get a pike up your ass that stuff is all for the lords and masters so let them stew in their own juice because we have the cows to worry about and we're serious folk forget about Frederick, first he comes then he goes then he comes back and it adds up to fuckall

3

anyway Terdona didnt fall because they never got the fort. And it went on right up to the end of my story when the Allamanns cut off the water and so instead of drinking their own piss they told Frederick they were his men, he let them come out but first he burned the city and then chopped it to pieces like what the men of Pavia did because they're dead set against the Derthonesi here non est like the Alamans who all love one another and are as close as my crossed fingers but here at Gamondio if we see someone from Bergolio it makes our balls spin

but now back to my storey of when I was in the Frescheta woods there specially when theres real fog when you cant see the tip of your nose and things appear all of a sudden and you dont see them coming then I have visions like that time when I saw the unicorn and the other time when I saw Saint Baudolino who spoke to me and said sonofawhore youre going to Hell because the unicorn story goes like this everybody knows that to hunt a unicorn you have to put a girl whose still a virgin at the foot of a tree and the animal smells the virgin smell and comes and puts his head in her lap so I took Bergolio's Nena who had come with her father to buy my fathers cow and I said to her come into the woods with me and we'll hunt the unicorn then I put her under the Tree because I was sure she was a virgin and I said to her sit still like this and spread your legs to make room for the animal's head and she asked spread like this and I said there right there and I touched her and she began making some noises like a nanny goat dropping a kid and I lost my head and had something like a napocalips and afterwards she wasnt pure like a lily any more and she said o my god now how will we make the unicorn come and just then I heard a voice from Heaven said that the unicorn qui tollis peccata mundis was me and I started jumping around the bushes and crying hip heee frr frr because I was happier than a real unicorn because I had put my horn in the virgin's lap and this was why Saint Baudolino had called me son et setera but then he forgave me and I caught site of him other times but only if there is plenty of fog or if it isnt bright like to scorch everything.

but when I told my father Galiaudo that I saw Saint Baudolino he hit me on the back thirty times with a stick saying O Lord this had to happen to me, a son who sees things and cant even milk a cow either I bust his head with my stick or I give him to one of those men who visit the fairs making an African monky dance and my sainted mother shouted at me goodfornothing your the worst all what have I done to make the Lord give me a son who sees saints and my father Galiaudo said its not true he sees saints hes a wors liar than Judass and he makes things up to get out of working

I am telling this story because if I dont you wouldnt undertstand what happened that evening with the fog so thick you could cut it with a knife and it was already april but in our Parts theres fog even in august and if your not from those Parts you get lost between Burmia and Frescheta especially if there isnt a saint to take you by the bridle and there I was heading for home when I saw right in front of me a baron on a horse all covered with iron

it was the baron covered with iron not the horse and with a sword he looked like the King of Arragon

and I like to died Mamma mia you want to bet this really is Saint Baudolino whose here to take me to Hell but he said Kleine kint Bitte and I caught on that he was an Alaman lord lost in the wood because of the fog and he couldnt find his friends and it was almost night and he showed me a Coin and I had never seen Money before and he was happy I could answer in his language and in Diutsch I said to him if you keep straight youll end in the swamp sure as sunshine

may be I shouldnt have said sunshine with that fog you could cut with a Knife but he understood all the same

and then I said I know the Germanes come from a country where its always Spring and maybe the seeders of Lebanon grow there but here in the Palea theres fog and in this fog there are some bastards roming around who are still the grandsons of the grandsons of the Ayrabics who fought against Charlemain and theyre a bad bunch and when they see a

5

stranger they hit him in the face with a club and they steal even the hair on his head ergo if you come to my fathers hut youll find a bowl of hot broth and some straw to sleep on in the stable then tomorrow morning at daybreak Ill show you the road specially if you have that Coin gratias benedicite we're poor folk but honest

so I took him to my father Galiaudo who started yelling you damn fool whats got into your head you told my name to a stranger whose with those people theres no telling maybe hes even a vassal of the marquis of Monferrato and hes going to ask me for a tithe de fructibus and de hay and leguminibus or a tax on the cattle now we are ruined and he was about to reach for his stick

I told him the Gentleman was an Alaman et non from Mon Ferrato and he said all the worse but when I told him about the Coin he calmed down because the Marengo people have heads hard as a bulls but sly as a horse and he understood that he could make something out of this and he said to me you speak all laangwidges so say these things to him

Item: we are poor folk but honest

Ive already told him that

all the same its better to repeat it and item thanks for the Coin. But theres also the matter of the hay for the horse item besides the hot soup I can add a piece of cheese and some bread and a jug of the good stuff item he can sleep where you sleep by the fire and tonight you go to the stable item show me the Coin and I want a Genovine solido and then fiat like one of the family because for us Marengo folk the guest is sacred

the Gentleman said haha you are smart you Marincum folk but a negotio est un negotio I will give you two of these Coins and you wont ask for a Genovine solido because with a Genovine solido I can kauf your house and all your stock but take this and be quiet because youre still making a profit my father kept quiet and took the two Coins that the Gentleman dropped on the table because the Marengo folks heads are hard but sly and he ate like a wolf (the gentleman) or rather like two (wolfs) then while my father and my mother went off to sleep after breaking their backs all day while I was out in the Frescheta the herre said

6

this wine is good I'll drink a bit more here by the fire so mine kint *tell me how it is that you speak my langwidge so well*

ad petitionem tuam frater Ysingrine carissime primos libros chronicae meae missur

ne humante pravitate

heres another place I couldnt scrape off

now to go back to my story of that Alaman lord who wanted to know how it was that I spoke his lingua and I told him that I have the gift of tongues like the Apossles and the gift of Vision like the Madalenes because I walk in the wood and I see Saint Baudolino riding a unicorn milk-colored like his twisted Horn just where horses have what for us would be a Nose

but a horse doesn't have a Nose other wise underneath there would be a beard like that Gentleman had who had a fine beard the color of a copper pan where as the other Alamans I had seen had yellow hair even in their ears

and he said well well you see what you would call a unicorn and maybe you mean the Monokeros but where did you learn that there are unicorns in this world and I told him I had read it in a book that the Frescheta hermit had and with his eyes so wide he looked like an owl he said What You know how to read too

Lordamercy I said now Ill tell you the Story

so the story went like this there was a holy hermit near Bosco who every so often the people took him a fat hen or a hare and he would pray over a written book and when people go by he hits his chest with a Stone but I say its a clod id est all dirt so he doesnt hurt himself so much anyway that morning we took him two eggs and while he was reading I said to myself one for you and one for me like good Christians if only he doesnt see me but I don't know how he managed but he caught me by the Neck and I said to him diviserunt vestimenta mea and he started laughing and said you know something youre a smart puerulus come here every day and Ill teach you to read so he taught me my written Letters to the tune of raps on my head. only later when we were friends he began saying what a handsome sturdy youth you are with a Lions head but show me how strong your arms are and whats your chest like let me touch here where the Legs begin to see if your sound then I figured out where he was heading and I hit him with my knee on the balls I mean the Testicules and he bent double saying Godamighty Im going to tell the Marengo people your possessed by the devil so theyll burn you alive and I say all right but first I will tell how I saw you at night sticking it in the belly of a Whitch. And then we'll see who they think is possessed and then he said no wait I was just joking and wanted to see if you had the fear of God lets say no more about it come tomorrow and I'll start teaching you to write because reading is one thing that costs nothing you just have to look and move your lips but if you write in a book you need paper and ink and the inkwell that alba pratalia arabat et nigrum semen seminabat because he always spoke Latin

and I said to him when you learn to read then you learn everything you didnt know before. But when you write you write only what you know allready so patientia Im better off not knowing how to write because the ass is the ass

when I told this to the Alaman gentleman he laughed like a Lunnatic and said Goot Kint those hermits are allesammt Sodomiten but tell me tell me what else you saw in the wood but thinking he was one of those that wanted to take Terdona like the troops of Federicus Imperator I said to myself Id better satisfy him and maybe hell give me another Coin and I told him that two nights before Saint Baudolino had appeared to me and said that the Emperor makes a victory at Terdona because Fridericus was the one and only lord of all Longobardia including Frescheta

then the gentleman said you Kint have been sent by Heaven would you like to come to the imperial Camp and say what Saint Baudolino said and I said that if he wanted I would say also that Saint Baudolino said that Saints Peterandpaul would come to the siege and lead the imperial troops and he said Ach wie Wunderbar for me just Peter by himself would be enough

8

Kint *come with me and your fortune is made*

illico or almost illico anyway the next morning that gentleman says to my father that hes going to take me with him to a place where I will learn to read and write and may be Ill become a Ministerial

my father Galiaudo didnt know what this meant but he understood that he would be getting rid of one who ate more than he was worth and he wouldnt suffer any more when I went roming. But he thought that may be this gentleman one of those men who go to the fairs and the marketplaces with a Monky and may be he would lay his hands on me and he didnt like that idea but that gentleman said he was a grand comes palatinus and among the Alamans there werent any Sodomiten

what are these sodomiten my father asked and I explained theyre kypioni shit he said kypioni are everywhere but when the Gentleman pulled out another five Coins after the two of the night before then he forgot everything and said son go then and maybe this is a piece of luck for you and may be for us too since one way or another these Alamans are always around our partts and this means you can come and see us now and then and I said I swear I will and I was ready to leave but I still felt a lump in my throat because I saw my mother crying like I was going off to die

et so we left and the Gentleman told me to take him to where the Castrum of the imperials was and I said thats easy you just follow the sun that is go where it comes from

and as we were going and could already see the tents a company of horsemen arrived all decked out and when they see us they fall on their knees and lower their pikes and their banners and raise their swords why what can this be I asked myself and they started yelling ~~Chaiser~~ Kaisar *here and Keiser there and* Sanctissimus Rex *and they kissed that gentlemans hand and my jaw almost fell off because my mouth was open so wide like an oven because it was only then I understood the gentleman with the red beard was the emperor Fridericus in flesh and blood and I had been telling him madeup stories all night like he was any old asshole*

now he'll have them cut off my head I say to myself but still I cost

9

him VII coins and if hed wanted to cut my head off he would of done it last night gratis et amoredei

et he said dont be afraid of anything its all right Im bearing news of a great Vision little puer tell us all the vision you had in the wood and I drop down like I had the falling sickness and my eyes open wide and theres foam on my mouth and I yell I saw I saw and I tell the whole storey of Saint Baudolino who made the prophecy to me and they all praise ~~Dominnus~~ Domine Deus and say Miraculo miraculo gottstehmirbei

and with them there were also the messengers of Terdona who hadnt yet decided whether to surrender but when they heard me they lay flat on the ground and said if even the saints were against them then they better surrender because it couldnt go on anyway

et then I saw the Derthonesi who were all coming out of the City men women and children et vetuli too and they were crying while the alamans carried them away like they were beeccie that is berbices and sheep everywhere and the people of Pavia who cheered and entered Turtona like lunnatics with faggots and hammers and clubs and picks because tearing a city down to the ground was enough to make them come

et towards evening I saw on the hill a great smoke and Terdona or Derthona was just about gone and this is how war is as my father Galiaudo says its an ugly animal war is

but better them than us

et in the evening the Emperor comes back all happy to the Tabernacula and gives me a slap on the cheek like my father never did and then he calls a gentleman who turned out to be the good canon Rahewinus and tells him he wants me to learn to write and the abacus and even gramar which then I didnt know what it was but now slowly I learn and my father Galiaudo never immagined such a thing

what a great thing to be a man of learning and who would ever have thought it

gratis agimus ~~domini dominus~~ I mean thanks to the Lord

all the same writing a story makes you sweat even in winter also Im afraid because the lamp has gone out and as the man said my thumb akes

2

Baudolino meets Niketas Choniates

"What's this?" Niketas asked, after he had turned the parchment over in his hands and tried to read a few lines.

"It's my first attempt at writing," Baudolino answered, "and ever since I wrote it—I was fourteen, I think, and was still a boy of the woods—I've carried it with me like an amulet. After I had filled many other parchments, sometimes day by day, I felt I was alive only because in the evening I could tell what had happened to me in the morning. Then I was content with those monthly ledgers, a few lines, to remind me of the main events. And I said to myself, when I was further on in years—now, for example—on the basis of these notes I would compose the *Gesta Baudolini*. So in the course of my journeys I carried with me the story of my life. But in the escape from the kingdom of Prester John . . ."

"Prester John? Never heard of him."

"I'll tell you more about him—maybe even too much. But as I was saying: During the escape I lost these pages. It was like losing life itself."

"You will tell me what you remember. I receive scraps of events, fragments of actions, and I extract a story from them, woven by a design of Providence. In saving my life you have given me what little future remains to me and I will repay you by giving you back the past you have lost. . . ."

"But maybe my story has no meaning."

"There are no stories without a meaning. And I am one of those men who can find it even where others fail to see it. Afterwards the story becomes the book of the living, like a blaring trumpet that raises from the tomb those who have been dust for centuries. . . . Still it takes time, you have to consider the events, arrange them in order, find the connections, even the least visible ones. But we have nothing else to do; your Genoese friends say we must wait until the fury of those dogs has calmed down."

Niketas Choniates, former court orator, supreme judge of the empire, judge of the Veil, logthete of secrets or—as the Latins would have said—chancellor of the basileus of Byzantium as well as historian of many Comneni and Angelus emperors, regarded with curiosity the man facing him. Baudolino had told him that the two of them had met at Gallipoli, in the days of the emperor Frederick, but if Baudolino had been there, he had been surrounded by many other ministerials, whereas Niketas, who was negotiating in the name of the basileus, had been far more visible. Was Baudolino lying? No matter: it was he who had saved Niketas from the fury of the invaders, brought him to a safe place, reunited him with his family, and was now promising to take him out of Constantinople. . . .

Niketas observed his rescuer. In appearance now he seemed not so much a Christian as a Saracen. Face burned by the sun, a livid scar that ran the length of his cheek, a crown of still-tawny hair, which gave him a leonine demeanor. Niketas would soon be even more amazed to learn that this man was over sixty years old. His hands were thick, when he held them clasped on his lap the gnarled knuckles were striking. Peasant's hands, made more for the spade than the sword.

And yet he spoke fluent Greek, not spitting saliva the way foreigners usually did, and Niketas had, only briefly, heard him address some of the other invaders in a hirsute language of their own, which sounded swift and harsh; this was a man who could use it offensively. For that matter Baudolino had told him the night before that he possessed a gift: he had only to hear two people speaking any language and in no time he was able to speak as they did. A singular gift, which Niketas had believed granted only to the apostles.

Living at court—and at *that* court—had taught Niketas to evaluate people with calm distrust. What struck him about Baudolino was that, whatever the man said, he would glance furtively at his interlocutor, as if warning him not to take him seriously. A tic admissible in anyone, except perhaps in one from whom you are expecting a truthful account, to be translated into history. But Niketas was curious by nature. He loved to listen to the stories of others, and not only concerning things unknown to him. Even things he had seen with his own eyes, when someone recounted them to him, seemed to unfold from another point of view, as if he were standing on the top of one of those mountains in ikons, and could see the stones as the apostles on the mountains saw them, and not as the faithful observer did, from below. Besides, he liked questioning the Latins, so different from the Greeks, firstly because of their totally new languages, each different from the other.

Niketas and Baudolino were seated opposite each other, in the little chamber of a tower, with double windows on three sides. One side revealed the Golden Horn and the Pera shore opposite, with the tower of Galata emerging from its procession of hamlets and hovels, from the second pair they could see the canal of the port debouching into the Strait of Saint George, and finally the third pair faced west, and from it all Constantinople should have been visible. But on this morning the delicate color of the sky was darkened by the thick smoke of the palaces and basilicas consumed by the fire.

It was the third fire to strike the city in the last nine months: the first had destroyed storehouses and the stores of the court, from the Blachernae palace to the walls of Constantine, the second had devoured all the warehouses of the Venetians, the Amalfitan merchants, the Pisans and the Jews, from Perama almost to the shore, sparing only this Genoese quarter almost at the foot of the Acropolis, and now the third fire was raging on all sides.

Down below, there was a veritable river of flame, arches were crashing to the ground, palaces were collapsing, columns were shattered, the fiery globes that rose from the heart of that conflagration consumed the more distant houses, then the flames that had capriciously fed that inferno returned to devour whatever they had previously spared. Above, dense clouds rose, still ruddy at their lower edge with the reflection of the fires, but of a different color, whether through a trick of the rising sun's rays or because of the nature of the spices, the lumber, or other burning material that engendered them. Further, depending on the direction of the wind, from different points in the city, aromas arrived, of nutmeg, cinnamon, pepper, and saffron, mustard or ginger—the world's most beautiful city was burning, yes, but like a brazier of scented condiments.

Baudolino had his back to the third window, and he seemed a dark shadow haloed by the double glow of the day and of the fire. Niketas half-listened to him, while at the same time his mind returned to the events of the previous days.

By now, on this morning of Wednesday, 14th of April of the year of Our Lord 1204—or six thousand seven hundred and twelve since the beginning of the world, as the date was usually calculated in Byzantium—for two days the barbarians had definitively been in possession of Constantinople. The Byzantine army, so glittering with its armor and shields and helmets when on parade, and the imperial guard of English and Danish mercenaries, armed with their awful two-edged hatchets, who until Friday had fought bravely and held off the enemy, on Friday gave way, when the enemy finally breached the walls. The victory was so sudden that the victors themselves paused, timorous, towards evening, expecting a counterattack, and to

14

keep the defenders at bay, set the new fire. But on Tuesday morning the whole city realized that, during the night, the usurper Alexius Ducas Murzuphlus had fled inland. The citizens, now orphaned and defeated, cursed that thief of thrones whom they had fêted till the night before, just as they had flattered him when he had strangled his predecessor, and now did not know what to do. (Cowards, cowards, cowards, how shameful, Niketas lamented at the scandal of that surrender.) They had gathered in a great procession, with the patriarch and priests of every rank in ritual garb, the monks blathering about mercy, ready to sell themselves to the new potentates as they had always sold themselves to the old ones, holding up crosses and images of Our Lord, their shouts and cries loud as they moved towards the conquerors, hoping to mollify them.

What folly! To hope for mercy from those barbarians, who had no need to wait for the enemy to surrender before doing what they had been dreaming of for months: destroying the most extensive, most populous, richest, noblest city in the world, and dividing the spoils. The immense weeping procession was facing unbelievers of enraged mien, swords still red with blood, stamping horses. As if the procession had never existed, the sack began.

Dear Christ, Our Lord! What horrors and tribulations we suffered! But how and why had not the roar of the sea, the dimming or total obscuring of the sun, the moon's red halo, the movements of the stars, forewarned us of this final disaster? Thus Niketas cried, on Tuesday evening, moving with bewildered steps in what had been the capital of the last Romans, on the one hand seeking to avoid the infidel hordes, and on the other finding his path blocked by ever-new fires, in despair because he could not take the street to his house, fearing meanwhile some of that rabble might be threatening his family.

Finally, towards night, not daring to cross the gardens and the open spaces between Saint Sophia and the Hippodrome, he had run to the temple, seeing the great doors open, and never supposing that the barbarians' fury would come to profane even that place.

But just as he entered, he went white with horror. That vast space was sown with corpses, among which enemy horsemen, foul drunk, were wheeling their mounts. In the distance the rabble was shattering with clubs the silver, gold-edged gate of the tribune. The splendid gate had been bound with ropes to uproot it so it could be dragged off by a team of mules. One drunken band was cursing and prodding the animals, but their hoofs slipped on the polished floor. The soldiers, first with the flat of their swords, then with the tips, incited the poor animals, who in their fear loosed volleys of dung; some mules fell to the ground, breaking their legs, so that the whole area around the pulpit was a gruel of blood and feces.

Groups of that vanguard of the Antichrist were stubbornly attacking the altars. Niketas saw some of them rip open a tabernacle, seize the chalices, fling to the ground the sacred Hosts, using their daggers to pry loose the gems that adorned the cup, hiding them in their clothes, then throwing the chalice into a general pile, to be melted down. Snickering, some took from their saddlebags flasks filled with wine, poured it into the sacred vessel and drank, mimicking the celebrant's actions. Worse still, on the main altar, now stripped, a half-naked prostitute, drunk on liquor, danced with bare feet on the table of the Eucharist, parodying the sacred rites, while the men laughed and urged her to remove the last of her clothing; she gradually undressed, dancing before the altar the ancient and lewd dance of the cordax, until finally she threw herself, with a weary belch, on the seat of the Patriarch.

Weeping at what he saw, Niketas hurried towards the back of the temple, to the monument the pious populace called the Sweating Column—which, in fact, produced a mystical and continuous transpiration—but it was not for mystical reasons that Niketas wanted to reach it. Halfway there, he found his path blocked by two enormous invaders—to him they seemed giants—who were shouting at him in an imperious tone. It was not necessary to know their language to understand that his courtier's dress had led them to presume he was

16

laden with gold, or else could tell them where gold was hidden. At that moment Niketas felt he was doomed because, as he had already seen in his breathless race through the streets of the invaded city, it was not enough to show that you were carrying only a few coins, or to deny having a treasure hidden somewhere: dishonored nobles, weeping old gentlemen, dispossessed possessors were tortured to make them reveal where they had hidden their wealth, and killed if, now having none, they were unable to reveal it, and left on the ground when they did reveal it, after having undergone so many and such terrible tortures that, in any event, they died while their tormentors lifted a stone, broke through a fake wall, knocked down a false ceiling, and rummaged with rapacious hands amid precious vessels, soft silks and velvets, stroking furs, sifting gems and jewels through their fingers, sniffing pots and sacks of rare spices.

So Niketas saw himself dead, mourned the family he had lost, and asked God Almighty to forgive him his sins. And it was at that moment that into Saint Sophia came Baudolino.

He appeared as handsome as Saladin, on a bedecked horse, a great red cross on his chest, sword drawn, shouting "Gods belly! By the Virgin! 'sdeath! Filthy blasphemers, simonist pigs! Is this any way to treat the things of Our Lord?" and then he flattened all those profaners red-crossed like himself, but with the difference that he was enraged, not drunk. Reaching the whore sprawled on the patriarchal seat, he bent over, grabbed her by the hair, and began dragging her in the mules' dung, shouting at her horrible things about the mother who had borne her. Around him, all those whom he intended to punish were either so drunk or so intent on removing gems from every object holding any that they were unaware of what he was doing.

Doing it, he arrived at the two giants who were about to torture Niketas. He looked at the wretched man pleading for mercy, let go of the prostitute's hair, and, as she fell, now lamed, to the ground, said, in excellent Greek: "By all twelve of the Magi! Why, you are Master Niketas, minister of the basileus! What can I do for you?"

17

"Brother in Christ, whoever you may be," Niketas cried, "free me from these Latin barbarians who want me dead, save my body and you will save my soul!" Of this exchange of Oriental vocalism, the two Latin pilgrims had understood little and they sought an explanation from Baudolino, who seemed one of their company, expressing themselves in Provençal. And in excellent Provençal, Baudolino shouted that this man was the prisoner of Count Baudoin of Flanders, at whose command he was seeking him, and *per arcana imperii* that two miserable sergeants like themselves would never understand. The two were stunned for a moment, then decided that arguing would only be a waste of time when they could seek other treasures without any effort, and they went off towards the main altar.

Niketas did not bend to kiss the feet of his savior. He was already on the ground, and too distraught to behave with the dignity his rank required. "O my good lord, thank you for your aid. This means that not all Latins are wild beasts with faces distorted by hatred! Not even the Saracens acted this way when they reconquered Jerusalem, when Saladin was content with a handful of coins to guarantee the safety of the inhabitants. How shameful for all Christendom, brothers against armed brothers, pilgrims who were to recover the Holy Sepulcher but have allowed themselves to be halted by greed and envy, and are destroying the Roman empire! O Constantinople, Constantinople! Mother of churches, princess of religion, guide of perfect opinions, nurse of all learning, now you have drunk from the hand of God the cup of fury, and burned in a fire far greater than that which burned the Pentapolis! What envious and implacable demons have poured down on you the intemperance of their intoxication, what mad and odious Suitors have lighted your nuptial torch? O mother, once clad in gold and imperial purple, now befouled and haggard. And robbed of your children, like birds imprisoned in a cage, we cannot find the way to leave this city that was ours, nor the strength to remain here, but instead, sealed within many errors, we roam like vagrant stars!"

"Master Niketas," Baudolino said, "I have been told that you Greeks talk too much and about everything, but I didn't believe it went this far. At the moment, the question is how to move our ass out of here. I can offer you safety in the Genoese quarter, but you have to tell me the fastest and most secure route to the Neorion, because this cross on my chest protects me but not you. The people here have all lost their reason; if they see me with a Greek prisoner they'll think he has some value and they'll take him away from me."

"I know a good way, but it doesn't follow the streets," Niketas said, "and you'd have to leave your horse behind...."

"So be it," Baudolino said, with an indifference that amazed Niketas, who did not yet know at what a cheap price Baudolino had acquired his charger.

Niketas, helped to his feet, took Baudolino by the hand and furtively approached the Sweating Column. He looked around, surveyed the vast temple; the pilgrims, seen in the distance, were moving like ants, bent on dilapidation, paying no attention to the two of them. At the column he knelt and thrust his fingers into a somewhat loose crevice in a slab of the pavement. "Help me," he said to Baudolino. "If we both try, we may be able to do it." And indeed after some effort the slab was raised, disclosing a dark opening. "There are some steps," Niketas said. "I'll go first because I know where to set my feet. Then you close the stone over your head."

"Then what do we do?"

"We climb down," Niketas said. "Then we'll find a niche, and in it are some torches and a flint."

"What a fine city this Constantinople is, so full of surprises," Baudolino remarked as he descended the winding stair. "Too bad these pigs will not leave a stone upon a stone."

"These pigs?" Niketas asked. "But aren't you one of them?"

"Me?" Baudolino was amazed. "Not me. If it's this clothing you refer to, I borrowed it. When they entered the city I was already inside the walls. But—where are the torches?"

"Don't worry. Just a few more steps. Who are you? What's your name?"

"Baudolino of Alessandria—not the city in Egypt, but the one they now call Caesarea, or maybe they don't even call it that and it's been burned down like Constantinople. I'm from up in the mountains, in the north, near Mediolanum. You know it?"

"I know about Mediolanum. Once its walls were destroyed by the king of the Alamans. Later our basileus gave them some money to help rebuild them."

"Indeed, I was with the emperor of the Alamans before he died. You met him when he was crossing the Propontis, almost fifteen years ago."

"Frederick. Old Copper Beard. A great and most noble prince, clement and merciful. He would never have done what these . . ."

"When he conquered a city, he wasn't so tenderhearted."

Finally they were at the foot of the steps. Niketas found the torches, and the two men, holding them high above their heads, proceeded down a long passage, until Baudolino saw the very belly of Constantinople, where, almost directly beneath the greatest church in the world, another basilica extended, unseen, a forest of columns stretching infinitely into the darkness like so many trees of a lacustrine wood, rising from the waters. Basilica or abbatial church, completely upside down, because even the light, which gently licked capitals that faded into the shadows of the very high vaults, came not from rose windows or vitrages, but from the watery pavement, which reflected the moving flames of the visitors.

"The city is pierced by cisterns," Niketas said. "The gardens of Constantinople are not a gift of nature but an effect of art. You see? Now the water comes only up to our knees because almost all of it has been used to put out the fires. If the conquerors destroy the aqueducts, then everyone will die of thirst. Usually you can't move on foot here; you need a boat."

"Does this passage arrive at the port?"

20

"No, it stops well before; but I know other passages and stairs that connect it with other cisterns and other tunnels, so that even if we can't reach the Neorion we can walk underground to the Prosphorion. However," he added, in anguish, as if he were just remembering another errand, "I can't come with you. I will show you the way, but then I have to turn back. I have to save my family, who are hiding in a little church behind Saint Irene. You know"—he seemed to be apologizing—"my palace was destroyed in the second fire, the one in August."

"Master Niketas, you're mad. First, you bring me down here, making me abandon my horse, when—even without you—I could have reached the Neorion through the streets. Second, you believe you can reach your family before being stopped by another pair of sergeants like those I found you with. Even if you succeeded, then what would you do? Sooner or later someone will root you out, and if you do collect your family and set off, where will you go?"

"I have friends in Selymbria," Niketas said, puzzled.

"I don't know where that is, but to reach it you first have to get out of the city. Listen to me: you're no good to your family. On the other hand, where I will take you, we'll find some friends, Genoese who decide which way the wind blows in this city. They're used to dealing with Saracens, Jews, monks, the imperial guard, Persian merchants, and now with these Latin pilgrims. They're smart people; you tell them where your family is and tomorrow they'll bring them to where we are. I don't know how they'll do it, but do it they will. They would do it in any case for me, since I'm an old friend, and for the love of God, but all the same they're Genoese, and if you give them a little present, so much the better. Then we'll stay there till things calm down. A sack normally doesn't last more than a few days. You can trust me, I've seen plenty of them. Afterwards, you can go to Selymbria or wherever you like."

Deeply moved, Niketas thanked him. And as they resumed their way, he asked why Baudolino was in the city if he wasn't a pilgrim.

"I arrived when the Latins had already landed on the opposite shore, with some other people . . . who are no longer with us. We came from very far away."

"Why didn't you leave the city? You would have had time."

Baudolino hesitated before answering. "Because . . . because I had to stay here in order to understand something."

"Have you understood it?"

"Unfortunately, yes. But only today."

"Another question: why are you devoting yourself so to me?"

"What else should a good Christian do? But, actually, you're right. I could have freed you from that pair and then let you go off on your own, and instead here I am, sticking to you like a leech. You see, Master Niketas, I know that you are a writer of stories, just as Bishop Otto of Freising was. But when I knew Bishop Otto, I was only a boy and I had no story, I wanted to know only the stories of others. Now I might have a story of my own, though I've lost everything I had written down about my past and, what's more, when I try to recall it, my thoughts become all confused. It's not that I don't remember the facts, but I'm not able to give them a meaning. After everything that's happened to me today I have to talk to somebody, or else I'll go crazy."

"What happened to you today?" Niketas asked, plowing ahead in the water. He was younger than Baudolino, but his life as a scholar and courtier had made him fat, lazy, and weak.

"I killed a man. It was the man who almost fifteen years ago assassinated my adoptive father, the best of kings, the emperor Frederick."

"But Frederick drowned, in Cilicia!"

"So everyone believed. But he was assassinated. Master Niketas, you saw me wield my sword in anger this evening in Saint Sophia, but I must tell you that in all my life I had never shed anyone's blood. I am a man of peace. This time I had to kill: I was the only one who could render justice."

"You will tell it all to me. But first tell me how you arrived so providentially in Saint Sophia to save my life."

22

"As the pilgrims were beginning their sack of the city, I was entering a dark place. When I came out, it was nearly nightfall, an hour ago, and I found myself near the Hippodrome. I was almost trampled to death by a crowd of Greeks in flight, screaming. I ducked into the doorway of a half-burned house, to let the crowd pass, and when they had gone by I saw the pilgrims pursuing them. I realized what was happening, and in an instant this great truth flashed into my mind: that I was, true, a Latin and not a Greek, but, before these infuriated Latins could realize that, there would no longer be any difference between me and a dead Greek. No, it cannot be, I said to myself, that these men will want to destroy the great city of Christendom now that they have finally conquered it. . . . I reflected that when their ancestors entered Jerusalem at the time of Godfrey of Bouillon, and the city became theirs, they killed everybody: women, children, domestic animals, and it was thanks only to a mistake that they did not also burn down the Holy Sepulcher. True, they were Christians entering a city of infidels, and even on my own journey I had seen Christians massacre each other for a word. Everyone knows how for years our priests have been quarreling with your priests over the question of *Filioque*. And finally, it's simple: when a warrior enters a city, all religion is irrelevant."

"What did you do then?"

"I left the doorway and, sticking close to the walls, I reached the Hippodrome. There I saw beauty wither and become dire. You know? After I arrived in the city, I used to go over there to gaze at the statue of that maiden, the one with the shapely feet, arms like snow, and red lips that smile, and those breasts, and the robe and the hair that danced so in the wind that when you saw her from a distance you couldn't believe she was made of bronze: she seemed living flesh. . . ."

"The statue of Helen of Troy. But what happened?"

"In the space of a few seconds I saw the column on which she stood bend like a tree sawed at the root, and fall to the ground in a great cloud of dust, the body shattered, the head a few steps from me, and only then did I realize how big that statue was. The head—you couldn't have embraced it with both arms, and it was staring at me sideways, like a person lying down, with the nose horizontal and the lips vertical, which, forgive me the expression, looked like those lips women have between their legs; and the pupils had fallen out of the eyes, and she seemed suddenly to have gone blind, Holy God, like this one here!" And he leaped backwards, splashing in all directions, because in the water the torch had suddenly illuminated a stone head, the size of ten human heads, which was propping up a column, and this head was also reclining, the mouth even more vulvular, half-open, with many snakes like curls on the head, and a mortiferous pallor of old ivory.

Niketas smiled: "That has been here for centuries. These are Medusa heads, from I don't know where, and they're used by builders as plinths. It doesn't take much to scare you...."

"I don't scare. The fact is: I've seen this face before. Somewhere else."

Seeing Baudolino upset, Niketas changed the subject: "You were telling me they pulled down the statue of Helen—"

"If only that were all.... Everything, every statue between the Hippodrome and the Forum—all the metal ones anyway. They climbed on top of them, wound a rope or a chain around the neck, and from the ground, pulled them down with two or three pairs of oxen. I saw all the statues of charioteers come down, a sphinx, a hippopotamus and a crocodile from Egypt, a great she-wolf with Romulus and Remus attached to the teats, and the statue of Hercules—that, too, I discovered, was so big that the thumb was like the chest of a normal man.... And also that bronze obelisk with those reliefs, the one topped by the little woman who turns according to the winds...."

"The Companion of the Wind. What a disaster! Some works were by ancient pagan sculptors, older even than the Romans. But why? Why?"

"To melt them down. The first thing you do when you put a city

24

to the sack is melt down everything you can't carry off. They've set up melting pots everywhere, and you can imagine—with all these fine houses in flames, they're like natural foundries. And you also saw those men in the church; they can't go around showing they've stolen the pyxes and the patens from the tabernacles. Melt everything down: and quickly! A sack," Baudolino explained, like a man who knows a trade well, "is like a grape harvest: you have to divide the tasks. There are those who press the grapes, those who carry off the must in the tuns, those who cook for the others, others who go to fetch the good wine from last year.... A sack is a serious job—at least if you want to make sure that in the city not a stone remains on a stone, as in my Mediolanum days. But for that you'd really want the Pavians; they knew how to make a city disappear. These men here have everything to learn. They pulled down the statue, then sat on it to have a drink, then another man arrived dragging a girl along by the hair and shouting that she was a virgin, and they all had to stick in a finger to see if it was worth it.... In a proper sack you have to clean the place out immediately, house by house, and the fun comes afterwards; otherwise the smartest get all the best stuff. Anyway, my problem was that with people like this I didn't have time to explain that I too was born in the Monferrato region. So there was only one thing to be done. I crouched behind the corner until a knight came into the alley, so drunk he seemed not to know where he was going and was letting his horse carry him. I had only to yank his leg, and he fell down. I took off his helmet, and I dropped a stone on his head...."

"You killed him?"

"No. It was friable stone, barely hard enough to leave him unconscious. I took heart because he began vomiting up some purplish liquid. I took off his coat of mail and his shirt, his helmet, weapons, I took his horse, and rode off through the streets until I arrived at the portal of Saint Sophia. I saw them going in with mules, and a group of soldiers passed me carrying off the silver candelabra with their chains as thick as your arm, and they were talking like Lombards.

When I saw that destruction, that wickedness, that greed, I lost my head, because the ones wreaking that ruin were men from my land, devout sons of the pope of Rome...."

Their torches were sputtering as the two of them talked, but soon they climbed from the cistern into the dead of night and, by way of deserted alleys, they reached the tower of the Genoese.

They knocked at a door, and someone came down; they were welcomed and fed with rough cordiality. Baudolino seemed to be at home among these people, and he promptly recommended Niketas to them. One man said: "That's easy, we'll take care of it. Go and sleep now." He said this with such confidence that not only Baudolino but Niketas himself passed a serene night.

3

Baudolino explains to Niketas
what he wrote as a boy

The next morning Baudolino collected the cleverest of the Genoese: Pevere, Boiamondo, Grillo, and Taraburlo. Niketas told them
where his family could be found, and the men set off. Niketas then
asked for some wine and poured a cup for Baudolino. "See if you like
this. It's a resinous wine that many Latins find disgusting; they say it
tastes of mold." Assured by Baudolino that this Greek nectar was his
favorite drink, Niketas settled down to hear his story.

Baudolino seemed eager to talk, as if to free himself from things
he had been keeping inside since God knows when. "Here, Master
Niketas," he said, opening a leather bag he carried around his neck
and handing him a parchment. "This is the beginning of my story."

Niketas tried to decipher the words, and though he could read
Latin letters he could understand nothing.

"What is this?" he asked. "I mean—what language is this written in?"

"I don't know what language. Let's begin this way, Master Niketas. You have an idea of where Ianua is—Genoa, I mean—and
Mediolanum, or Mailand, as the Teutonics or Germanics say, the Alamans, as your people call them. Well, halfway between these two
cities there are two rivers, the Tanaro and the Bormida, and between

27

the two there is a plain that, when it isn't hot enough to cook eggs on a stone, there is fog, when there isn't fog, there's snow, when there isn't snow, there's ice, and when there isn't ice, it's cold all the same. That's where I was born, in a place called the Frascheta Marincana, which is also a swamp between the two rivers. It's not exactly like the banks of the Propontis."

"I can imagine."

"But I liked it. The air keeps you company. I have done much traveling, Master Niketas, maybe even as far as Greater India...."

"Are you sure?"

"No, I don't really know where I got to. It was the place where I saw some men with horns and others with their mouth on their belly. I spent weeks in endless deserts, on plains that stretched as far as the eye could see, and I always felt like a prisoner of something that surpassed the powers of my imagination. In my parts, when you walk through the woods in the fog, you feel like you're still inside your mother's belly, you're not afraid of anything, and you feel free. Even when there's no fog, when you're walking along and you're thirsty, you break off an icicle from a tree, and you blow on your fingers because they're covered with *gheloni*—"

"What are these... these *gheloni*? Something that makes you laugh?"

"No, no, I didn't say *gheloioi*! Here in your country there isn't even a word for it, so I had to use my own. They are like sores that form on your fingers, and on your knuckles, because of the great cold, and they itch, and if you scratch them, they hurt."

"You talk as if you had a pleasant memory of them."

"Cold is beautiful."

"Each of us loves his native land. Go on."

"Well, once upon a time the Romans were there, the ones from Rome, who spoke Latin, not the Romans you claim to be today, you Greek-speakers, that we call Romei or Greculi, excuse the term. Then the empire of those Romans disappeared, and in Rome only the pope

28

was left, and all through Italy you saw different people who spoke different languages. The people of Frascheta speak one language, but in Terdona, nearby, they speak a different one. Traveling in Italy with Frederick, I heard some very sweet languages, compared to our Frascheta language, which isn't really a language, more like a dog's yawping. But nobody writes in that language, because they still do that in Latin. So when I was scrawling on this parchment, I was maybe the first to try to write the way we talked. Afterwards I became a man of letters and I wrote in Latin."

"But . . . what are you saying?"

"As you can see, living among educated people, I knew what year it was. I was writing in Anno Domini 1155. I didn't know my age: my father said twelve; my mother thought it was thirteen, maybe because all she had gone through, trying to bring me up in the fear of God, made the time seem longer to her. When I started writing I was certainly going on fourteen. Between April and December I'd learned how to write. I applied myself ardently, after the emperor had taken me away with him, setting myself to work in every situation: in the camp, under a tent, leaning against the wall of a destroyed house. On slabs of wood mostly, once in a great while on parchment. I was already becoming accustomed to living like Frederick, who never stayed in the same place more than a few months, always and only in winter, and for the rest of the year on the march, sleeping every night in a different place."

"Yes—but what is your story?"

"At the beginning of that year I was still living with my father and mother, a few cows and a vegetable patch. A hermit of those parts had taught me to read. I roamed around the forest and the swamp. I was an imaginative boy, I saw unicorns, and in the fog (I said) Saint Baudolino appeared to me. . . ."

"I've never heard the name of such a saint. Did he really appear to you?"

"He's a saint from our parts; he was bishop of Villa del Foro.

Whether or not I saw him is another question. Master Niketas, the problem of my life is that I've always confused what I saw with what I wanted to see."

"That happens to many people."

"Yes, but with me, whenever I said I saw this, or I found this letter that says thus and so (and maybe I'd written it myself), other people seemed to have been waiting for that very thing. You know, Master Niketas, when you say something you've imagined, and others then say that's exactly how it is, you end up believing it yourself. So I wandered around Frascheta and I saw saints and unicorns in the forest, and when I came upon the emperor, without knowing who he was, I spoke to him in his language. I told him that Saint Baudolino had said he would conquer Terdona. I said that to please him, but it suited him for me to say it to everybody, and especially to the delegates from Terdona, so they would be convinced that even the saints were against them. That's why he bought me from my father. It wasn't so much for the few coins, but because it was one less mouth to feed. And so my life was changed."

"You became his footman?"

"No, his son. At that time Frederick hadn't yet become a father. I believe he took a liking to me, I told him things others didn't say out of respect. He treated me like I was his own, he praised me for my first scrawls, the first sums I could do with my fingers, for the things I was learning about his father, and his father's father. . . . Sometimes he confided in me things that perhaps I wouldn't understand."

"And did you love this father more than your blood father, or were you dazzled by his regality?"

"Master Niketas, until then I had never asked myself if I loved my father, Gagliaudo. I took care only to stay out of range of his kicks or his club, and that seemed to me normal for a son. I did love him, but I realized that only when he died. Before, I don't think I ever embraced my father. I would go and cry on my mother's bosom, poor woman, but she had so many animals to tend that she had little time

30

to console me. Frederick was an impressive figure of a man, with a red-and-white face, not leathery like the faces of my neighbors, with flaming beard and hair, and long hands, slender fingers, neatly tended nails. He was confident and he inspired confidence, he was good-humored and decisive and he inspired good-humor and decision, he was courageous and he inspired courage. . . . I was the cub, he the lion. He could be cruel, but with those he loved he was very gentle. I loved him. He was the first person who listened to what I said."

"He used you as his *vox populi*. . . . A wise ruler does not lend an ear only to his courtiers, but tries to understand how his subjects think, too."

"Yes, but I no longer knew who I was or where I was. After I met the emperor, the imperial army overran Italy twice between April and September, proceeding like a snake from Spoleto to Ancona, from there to Apulia, then again in Romagna, and on towards Verona and Tridentum and Bolzano, finally crossing the mountains and return-ing to Germany. After having spent twelve years confined between two rivers, I had finally been flung into the center of the universe."

"So it must have seemed to you."

"I know, Master Niketas, that the center of the universe is your city here, but the world is vaster than your empire, and there's even Ultima Thule and the land of the Hibernians. True, compared to Constantinople, Rome is a pile of ruins and Paris is a muddy village, but even there something happens every now and then. In many vast, vast regions of the world people don't speak Greek, and there are those who, when they want to agree with something, say *oc*."

"*Oc*?"

"*Oc*."

"Strange. But do go on."

"I will. I saw all of Italy, new lands and new faces, dress I'd never seen before, damasks, embroidery, golden cloaks, swords, armor; I heard voices that I strained to imitate day after day. I remember only vaguely when Frederick received Italy's iron crown in Pavia, then the

31

descent towards what they called *Italia citeriore,* the long journey along the Francigene way, the emperor meeting Pope Hadrian at Sutri, the coronation in Rome..."

"But this basileus of yours, this emperor, as you call him, was he crowned in Pavia or in Rome? And why in Italy, if he's the basileus of the Alamans?"

"One thing at a time, Master Niketas. For us Latins things aren't as simple as they are for you Romei. In your country someone gouges out the eyes of the current basileus, and he becomes basileus himself, everybody agrees, and even the patriarch of Constantinople does what the new basileus tells him, otherwise the basileus gouges out his eyes too."

"Now don't exaggerate."

"Exaggerate? Me? When I got here they told me right away that the basileus, Alexis III, ascended the throne because he'd blinded the legitimate ruler, his brother Isaac."

"Doesn't anybody ever eliminate his predecessor and seize the throne in your country?"

"Yes, but they kill him in battle, or with some poison, or with a dagger."

"You see? You people are barbarians. You can't imagine a less bloody way of managing questions of government. And besides, Isaac was Alexis's brother. Brother doesn't kill brother."

"I understand. It was an act of benevolence. That's how we do things. The emperor of the Latins—who hasn't been a Latin himself since the days of Charlemagne—is the successor of the Roman emperors—the ones of Rome, I mean, not those of Constantinople. But to make sure he's emperor, he has to be crowned by the pope, because the law of Christ has swept away the false law, the law of liars. To be crowned by the pope, the emperor also has to be recognized by the cities of Italy, and each of them kind of goes its own way, so he has to be crowned king of Italy—provided, naturally, that the Teutonic princes have elected him. Is that clear?"

Niketas had long since learned that the Latins, though they were barbarians, were extremely complicated, hopeless when it came to fine points and subtleties if a theological question was at stake, but capable of splitting a hair four ways on matters of law. So for all the centuries that the Romei of Byzantium had devoted to fruitful discussions bent on defining the nature of Our Lord, while never questioning the power that still came directly from Constantinople, the Occidentals had left theology to the priests of Rome and had spent their time poisoning one another and trading hatchet blows to decide if there was still an emperor and who he was, achieving the admirable result of never having a genuine emperor again.

"So then, Frederick had to have a coronation in Rome. It must have been a solemn occasion. . . ."

"Only up to a point. First, because Saint Peter's in Rome, compared to Saint Sophia, is a hut, and a rather run-down hut at that. Second, because the situation in Rome was very confused; in those days the pope was sealed up in his castle, close to Saint Peter's, and on the other side of the river, the Romans seemed to be the masters of the city. Third, because it wasn't clear whether the pope was spiting the emperor, or vice versa."

"What do you mean?"

"I mean that if I listened to the princes and bishops of our court, they were furious at the way the pope was treating the emperor. The coronation was supposed to take place on a Sunday, and they held it on Saturday. The emperor was supposed to be anointed at the main altar, and Frederick was anointed at a side altar, and not on the head, as they had done in the past, but between his arms and shoulder blades, not with the chrism but with the oil of the catechumens. Perhaps you don't understand the difference—nor did I in those days— but at court they were all glowering. I was expecting Frederick, too, to be mad as a bull, but instead he was all deference towards the pope, while the pope's face was grim, as if he had sealed a bad bargain. I asked Frederick straight out why the barons grumbled and he didn't, and he told me I had to understand the value of liturgical symbols, where a mere nothing can change everything. He needed to have a coronation, and it had to be complete with the pope, but it shouldn't be too solemn, otherwise it would mean he was emperor only thanks to the pope, whereas he was already emperor by the will of the Germanic princes. I told him he was sly as a weasel, because it was as if he had said: See here, Pope, you're merely the notary, but I've already signed papers with the Almighty. He burst out laughing and slapped my head, saying smart boy, you always find the right way to express things. Then he asked me what I had been doing in Rome those days, because he had been so taken up with the ceremonies he'd lost sight of me. I saw the ceremonies you were taken up with, I said. The fact is that the Romans—the Romans of Rome, that is—didn't like that business of the coronation in Saint Peter's, because the Roman senate wanted to be more important than the pope, and they wanted to crown Frederick on the Capitoline. He refused, because if he then went around saying he had been crowned by the people, not only the Germanic princes but also the kings of France and England would say: Fine anointment this, by the holy rabble. Whereas if he could say he was anointed by the pope, they would all take him seriously. But the matter was even more complicated, and I realized that only later. For some time the Germanic princes had been talking about the *translatio imperii*, which was like saying that the hereditary line of the Roman emperors had passed to them. Now if Frederick had himself crowned by the pope it was like saying that his right was recognized also by the vicar of Christ on earth, and he would be what he was even if he lived, so to speak, in Edessa or Ratisbon. If he had himself crowned by the senate and by the Roman *populusque*, it was like saying the empire was still there, without any *translatio*. Smart thinking, as my father Gagliaudo used to say. At that point, surely, the emperor wasn't going to put up with it. That's why, as the great coronation banquet was taking place, the Romans in a fury crossed the Tiber and killed not only a few priests, which was everyday stuff, but also two or three imperials. Frederick flew into a rage, interrupted the banquet, and had them all killed then and there, after which there were more corpses than fish in the Tiber, and by nightfall the Romans understood who was master. To be sure, as festivities go, it wasn't a great festivity. This was what caused Frederick's bad humor towards those communes of *Italia citeriore,* and that's why when he arrived before Spoleto at the end of July, he demanded they pay for his sojourn there, and the Spoletini made a fuss. Frederick got even madder than he had in Rome, and carried out a massacre that makes this one in Constantinople seem like child's play. . . . You have to understand, Master Niketas, an emperor has to act like an emperor and forget about feelings. . . . I learned many things in those months; after Spoleto there was the meeting with the envoys of Byzantium at Ancona, then the return to ulterior Italy, to the foot of the Alps, which Otto called the Pyrenees, and that was the first time I saw the tops of mountains covered with snow. Meanwhile, day after day, Canon Rahewin introduced me to the art of writing."

"A hard introduction, for a boy."

"No, not hard. It's true that, if I didn't understand something, Canon Rahewin would hit my head with his fist, but that had no effect on me, not after the blows of my father. For the rest, everyone hung on my lips. If I felt like saying I had seen a sea siren—after the emperor had brought me there as one who saw saints—they all believed me and said good boy, good boy."

"This must have taught you to weigh your words."

"On the contrary, it taught me not to weigh them. After all, I thought, whatever I say is true because I said it. . . . When we were heading for Rome, a priest by the name of Corrado told me about the mirabilia of that urbs, the seven automata of the Lateran, which stood for the individual days of the week, each of them with a bell that announced a revolt in a province of the empire; and about the bronze statues that moved on their own, and about a place filled with enchanted mirrors. . . . Then we arrived in Rome, and that day, when they were killing each other along the Tiber, I took to my legs and wandered through the city. As I walked, I saw only flocks of sheep among ancient ruins, and under the arcades some poor people who spoke the language of Jews and sold fish. As for mirabilia, not a sign, except for a statue of a man and a horse in the Lateran, and even that didn't seem to me anything special. Yet, on our return journey, when they were all asking me what I had seen, what could I say? That in Rome there were only sheep among the ruins and ruins among the sheep? They would never have believed me. So I told of the mirabilia that I had been told about and I added a few of my own ... for example, that in the Lateran palace I had seen a reliquary of gold studded with diamonds and inside it were the navel and the foreskin of Our Lord. They were all devouring my words, and they said too bad in those days we had to kill the Romans and weren't able to see all those mirabilia. So for all the years I've been hearing others talk about the wonders of the city of Rome, in Germany, in Burgundy, and even here, it is only because I had told about them."

Meanwhile the Genoese had come back, dressed as monks, ringing their little bells and preceding a troop of creatures wrapped in lurid whitish sheets, which covered even their faces. These people were the pregnant wife of Master Niketas, with her youngest in her arms, and the other sons and daughters, very young and pretty girls, some other relations, and a few servants. The Genoese had brought them through the city as if they were a band of lepers, and even the pilgrims had kept well out of their way as they passed.

"How could they take you seriously?" Baudolino asked, laughing. "The lepers maybe ... but you men, even in those robes, don't look anything like monks!"

"With all due respect, the pilgrims are a bunch of dickheads," Taraburlo said. "And besides, after all the time we've been here, we also know what Greek we need. We repeated *kyrieleison pighè pighè*, in a low voice, all together, like a litany, and they stepped back, some

36

made the sign of the cross, some made the horns sign to ward off the evil eye, and some touched their balls."

A manservant brought Niketas a box, and Niketas withdrew to the back of the room to open it. He returned with some gold coins for our hosts, who uttered extravagant blessings and insisted that, until he left, he was the master here. The sizable family had been divided among some nearby dwellings, along somewhat filthy alleyways, where no Latin would ever think of searching for loot.

Now content, Niketas called Pevere, who seemed the most authoritative of the hosts, and said that, if he had to remain in hiding, he was unwilling to give up his habitual pleasures. The city was burning, but in the port merchant ships continued to arrive, and fishermen's boats, but they now had to stop in the Golden Horn, unable to unload their goods at the storehouses. With money, it was possible to purchase cheaply the things necessary to a comfortable life. As for a proper cuisine, among the relatives just rescued was his brother-in-law Theophilus, who was an excellent cook; they had only to ask him what ingredients he needed. And so, towards afternoon, Niketas was able to offer his host a dinner worthy of a logothete. A fat kid, stuffed with garlic, onion, and leeks, covered with a sauce of marinated fish.

"More than two hundred years ago," Niketas said, "there came to Constantinople, as ambassador from your king Otto, a bishop of yours, one Liudprand, who was the guest of our basileus Nicephorus. It was not a happy encounter, and we learned later that Liudprand had set down an account of his journey, in which we Romei were described as sordid, crude, uncivilized, shabbily dressed. He could not bear even our resinous wine, and it seemed to him that all our food was drowned in oil. But there was one thing he described with enthusiasm, and it was this dish."

The kid tasted exquisite to Baudolino. And he went on answering Niketas's questions.

———

37

"So, living with an army, you learned to write. And you already knew how to read."

"Yes, but writing is harder. And in Latin. Because, if the emperor had to curse some soldiers, he spoke Alaman, but if he was writing to the pope or to his cousin Jasomirgott, he had to do it in Latin, and the same with every document of the chancellery. I had to struggle to write down the first letters, I copied words and sentences without understanding what they meant, but by the end of that year I knew how to write. Still, Rahewin hadn't yet had time to teach me grammar. I could copy but I couldn't express myself on my own. That's why I wrote in the language of Frascheta. But was that really the language of Frascheta? I was mixing memories of other speech that I had heard around me, the words of the people of Asti, and Pavia, Milan, Genoa, people who sometimes couldn't understand one another. Then later, in those parts we built a city, with people who came from here and from there, all united to build a tower, and they spoke in the same, identical way. I believe it was a bit the way I had invented."

"You were a nomothete," Niketas said.

"I don't know what that means, but maybe I was. In any case, the later pages were already in fair Latin. I was by then in Ratisbon, in a quiet cloister, entrusted to the care of Archbishop Otto, and in that peacefulness I had many, many pages to leaf through....I learned. You will notice, among other things, that the parchment is clumsily scraped, and you can even glimpse parts of the text underneath. I was really a rogue. I was robbing my teachers; I had spent two nights scraping away what I believed was ancient writing, to make space for myself. The nights following, Bishop Otto was in despair because he could no longer find the first version of his *Chronica sive Historia de duabus civitatibus* that he had been writing for more than ten years, and he accused poor Rahewin of having lost it on some journey. Two years later he determined to rewrite it, and I acted as his scribe, never daring to confess to him that I had been the one who scraped away the first version of his *Chronica*. As you say, justice does exist, because

I then lost my own chronicle, only I didn't have the courage to write it over. But I know that, as he rewrote, Otto changed some things...."

"In what sense?"

"If you read Otto's *Chronica*, which is a history of the world, you see that he—how should I put it?—did not have a good opinion of the world and of us human beings. The world had perhaps begun well, but it had grown worse and worse; in other words, *mundus senescit*, the world grows old, we are approaching the end.... But in the very year that Otto began rewriting the *Chronica*, the emperor asked also that his feats be celebrated, and Otto began writing the *Gesta Friderici*, which he didn't then finish because he died just over a year later, and Rahewin continued the work. You can't narrate the feats of your sovereign if you're not convinced that with him on the throne a new era begins, that this, in other words, is a *historia iucunda*...."

"One can write the history of one's own emperors without renouncing severity, explaining how and why they advance towards their ruin."

"Maybe you can do that, Master Niketas, but not the good Otto; and I'm only telling you how things went. So that holy man on the one hand was rewriting the *Chronica*, where the world went badly, and on the other the *Gesta*, where the world could only become better and better. You will say he contradicted himself. If it were only that. What I suspect is that in the first version of the *Chronica* the world went even worse, and so as not to contradict himself too much, as he gradually went on rewriting the *Chronica*, Otto became more indulgent towards us humans. This is what I caused by scraping away the first version. Maybe, if that had remained, Otto wouldn't have had the courage to write the *Gesta*, and since it's thanks to the *Gesta* that in the future they will say what Frederick did and didn't do; if I hadn't scraped away the first text, in the end Frederick wouldn't have done everything we say he did."

"You," Niketas said to himself, "are like the liar of Crete: you tell me you're a confirmed liar and insist I believe you. You want me to believe you've told lies to everybody but me. In all my years at the court of these emperors I have learned to extricate myself from the traps of masters of deceit far more sly than you.... By your own confession, you no longer know who you are, perhaps because you have told too many lies, even to yourself. And you're asking me to construct the story that eludes you. But I'm not a liar of your class. In all my life I have questioned the stories of others in order to extract the truth. Perhaps you're asking me for a story that will absolve you of having killed someone to avenge the death of your Frederick. You are building, step by step, this story of love for your emperor, so that it will then be natural to explain why it was your duty to avenge him— assuming that he was killed, and that he was killed by the man you have killed."

Then Niketas looked outside. "The fire is reaching the Acropolis," he said.

"I bring bad luck to cities."

"You believe you are omnipotent. That is a sin of pride."

"No. If anything, it's an act of mortification. All my life, no sooner did I approach a city than it was destroyed. I was born in a land sown with hamlets and a few modest castles, where I heard itinerant merchants sing the beauties of the *urbis Mediolani,* but what a city was, I didn't know. I had never gone even to Terdona, whose towers I could see in the distance, and Asti and Pavia I thought were at the confines of the Earthly Paradise. Afterwards, all the cities I encountered were about to be destroyed or had already been burned to the ground: Terdona, Spoleto, Crema, Milan, Lodi, Iconium, and then Pndapetzim. And the same will happen to this one. Could I be—how do you Greeks say it?—a polioclast, fated to bear the evil eye?"

"Don't punish yourself."

"You're right. At least once, I saved a city. My own. I saved it with a lie. Do you think that one good deed is enough to ward off the evil eye?"

"It means there is no destiny."

Baudolino remained silent for a moment. Then he turned and looked at what had been Constantinople. "All the same, I feel guilty. The men who are doing that are Venetians, and people of Flanders, and above all the knights of Champagne and of Blois, of Troyes, Orleans, Soissons, not to mention my own people of Monferrato. I would rather see this city destroyed by the Turks."

"The Turks would never do that," Niketas said. "We're on excellent terms with them. It's the Christians we have to guard against. But perhaps your people are the hand of God, who has sent you for the punishment of our sins."

"*Gesta Dei per Francos,*" Baudolino said.

4

Baudolino talks with the emperor and falls in love with the empress

In the afternoon Baudolino resumed his narrative, more tersely, and Niketas decided not to interrupt him any more. He was in a hurry to see the story grow, to arrive at the point. He had not realized that Baudolino, as he was narrating, had not yet reached the point of his life, and that he was narrating precisely in order to reach it.

Frederick had entrusted Baudolino to Bishop Otto and to his assistant, Canon Rahewin. Otto, of the great family of Babenberg, was the emperor's maternal uncle, even though he was barely ten years Frederick's senior. A very learned man, Otto had studied in Paris with the great Abélard, then he had become a Cistercian monk. At a very young age he had been raised to the dignity of bishop of Freising. It was not that he had devoted much energy to this great city, but, as Baudolino explained to Niketas, in Western Christianity, the offspring of noble families were named bishop of this or that place without having actually to go there, and it sufficed for them to enjoy the income.

Otto was not yet fifty, but he seemed a hundred, always a bit sickly, crippled on alternate days by pains now in a hip, now in a shoulder, affected by gallstone, and a bit bleary-eyed thanks to all his reading and writing, which he did both in the sun's light and by that of a candle flame. Highly irritable, as is often the case with the gouty, the first time he spoke to Baudolino he said to him, almost snarling: "You've won over the emperor by telling him a pack of lies. Isn't that so?"

"Master, I swear it isn't," Baudolino protested.

Otto replied: "A liar who denies is confirming. Come with me. I'll teach you what I know."

Which shows that, in the final analysis, Otto was a goodhearted man and had become fond of Baudolino because he found him receptive, capable of retaining in his memory everything he heard. But he realized that Baudolino proclaimed loudly not only what he had learned but also what he had invented.

"Baudolino," he would say to him, "you are a born liar."

"Why do you say such a thing, master?"

"Because it's true. But you mustn't think I'm reproaching you. If you want to become a man of letters and perhaps write some Histories one day, you must also lie and invent tales, otherwise your History would become monotonous. But you must act with restraint. The world condemns liars who do nothing but lie, even about the most trivial things, and it rewards poets, who lie only about the greatest things."

Baudolino profited from these lessons of his master's, and as for his being a liar, he also began to realize, little by little, the extent of Otto's lying, seeing how he contradicted himself passing from the *Chronica sive Historia de duabus civitatibus* to the *Gesta Friderici*. Whereupon Baudolino decided that if he wanted to become a perfect liar, he also had to listen to the talk of others, to see how people persuaded one another in turn on this or that question. For example, on the subject of the Lombard cities he had heard various dialogues between the emperor and Otto.

"How can they be such barbarians? There's a reason why in the past their kings wore a crown of iron!" Frederick was outraged. "Has no one ever taught them that respect is due the emperor? Baudolino, do you realize? They practice *regalia*!"

"And what *reglioli* are they, my good father?" The others all laughed, and Otto most of all, because he still knew the Latin of ancient times, the proper language, and he knew that the *regaliolus* is a little bird.

"*Regalia, regalia, iura regalia,* Baudolino, you blockhead!" Frederick cried. "They are the rights due to me, such as appointing magistrates, collecting levies on the public roads, on the markets, and on the navigable rivers, the right to mint money, and ... and ... and what else, Rainald?"

"And the income from fines and sentences, from the appropriation of estates without legitimate heir or through confiscation for criminal activities or through having contracted an incestuous marriage, and the percentages of the earnings of mines and salt works. And fisheries, percentages of the treasures excavated from public land," continued Rainald of Dassel, who would shortly be named chancellor and thus the second person of the empire.

"There. And these cities have appropriated all of my rights. But they lack any sense of what is just and good! What demon so clouded their minds?"

"My dear nephew and emperor," Otto interjected, "you are thinking of Milan, of Pavia and Genoa as if they were Ulm or Eu. The cities of Germany were all born at the command of a prince, and from the beginning they have recognized themselves in the prince. But for these cities it is different. They arose while the Germanic emperors were engaged in other matters, and they have grown and taken advantage of the absence of their princes. When you speak to the inhabitants about the podestà, the governor that you would like to impose on them, they feel this *potestatis insolentiam* is an intolerable yoke, and they have themselves governed by consuls whom they themselves elect."

"But don't they like to have the protection of princes and share in the dignity and glory of an empire?"

"They like that very much, and for nothing in the world would

44

they deprive themselves of this advantage. Otherwise they would fall prey to some other monarch, perhaps the emperor of Byzantium or perhaps the sultan of Egypt. But the prince must remain distant. You live surrounded by your nobles, so perhaps you are not aware that in their cities relations are different. They do not recognize the great vassals, lords of field and forest, because fields and forests belong to the cities—except perhaps for the lands of the marquess of Monferrato and a few others. Mind you, in the cities young men who practice the mechanical arts—who could never set foot in your court—administer, command, and are sometimes raised to the dignity of knight."

"So the world is upside down?" the emperor cried.

"My good father"—Baudolino held up a finger—"why, you are treating me as if I were one of your family, and yet yesterday I was sleeping on straw. What of that?"

"It means that, if I wish, I will make you a duke, because I am the emperor and I can ennoble anyone by my decree. But it does not mean that anybody can ennoble himself on his own! Don't they understand that if the world is turned upside down, they are also hastening towards their own ruin?"

"It seems they don't, Frederick," Otto replied. "These cities, with their way of governing themselves, are now the places through which all wealth passes. Merchants gather there from all over, and their walls are more beautiful and solid than those of many castles."

"Whose side are you on, uncle?" the emperor shouted.

"Yours, my imperial nephew, but for this very reason it is my duty to help you understand the strength of your enemy. If you insist on obtaining from those cities that which they don't want to give you, you will waste the rest of your life besieging them, defeating them, and seeing them rise again, more proud than before, in the space of a few months; and you will have to cross the Alps to subdue them once more, whereas your imperial destiny lies elsewhere."

"Where would my imperial destiny lie?"

"Frederick, I have written in my *Chronica*—which through some

45

inexplicable accident has disappeared and now I must set myself to rewriting it, may God punish Canon Rahewin, who is responsible for its loss—that, some time ago, when the supreme pontiff was Eugene III, the Syrian bishop of Gabala, who visited the pope with an Armenian delegation, told Eugene how in the Extreme Orient, in lands very close to the Earthly Paradise, there is the prospering realm of a *Rex Sacerdos*, the Presbyter Johannes, a king certainly Christian, even though a follower of the heresy of Nestor, and whose ancestors are those Magi, also kings and priests, but depositaries of very ancient wisdom, who visited the infant Jesus."

"And what is the connection between me, emperor of the holy and Roman empire, and this Priest John, may the Lord long keep him king and priest down there wherever the devil he may be, among his Moors?"

"You see, my illustrious nephew, that you say 'Moors' and think as the other Christian kings do, while they exhaust themselves in the defense of Jerusalem—a most pious enterprise, I won't deny that, but let's leave it to the king of France, since in any case the Franks now command in Jerusalem. The destiny of Christianity, and of every empire that wants to be holy and Roman, lies beyond the Moors. There is a Christian realm beyond Jerusalem and the lands of the infidel. An emperor capable of joining the two reigns would reduce the infidel empire and the empire of Byzantium itself to a pair of abandoned islands, lost in the vast sea of his glory!"

"Fantasies, dear uncle. Let's keep our feet on the ground, if you please. And let's get back to those Italian cities. Explain to me, dearest uncle, why, if their condition is so desirable, some of them become my allies against the others, instead of uniting, all together, against me."

"Not yet, at least," Rainald prudently remarked.

"I repeat," Otto explained, "they don't mean to deny their position as subjects of the empire. That's why they seek your help when another city oppresses them, as Milan does Lodi."

"But if the condition of being a city is the ideal, why does each try to oppress its neighboring city, as if it wanted to engulf that territory and transform it into a realm?"

Then Baudolino spoke up, with his wisdom as local informant. "My dear father, the question is why not only the cities but also the hamlets beyond the Alps feel the greatest pleasure in screw—ouch!" (Otto also used pinching as an educational tool.) ". . . I mean to say, one likes to humiliate the other. That's how it is in our parts. You may hate the foreigner, but most of all you hate your neighbor. And if the foreigner helps us harm our neighbor, then he's welcome."

"But why?"

"Because people are wicked, as my father always said, but the people of Asti are worse than Barbarossa."

"And who is Barbarossa?" The emperor Frederick was furious.

"You are, dear father; that's what they call you there, and for that matter I don't see anything bad about it, because your beard really is red, and the name suits you well. And if they wanted to say that your beard was the color of copper, would Copperbeard suit you? *Barbadirame*? I would love and revere you all the same if your beard were black, but since it's red, I don't see why you should make such a fuss about being called Barbarossa. What I wanted to say, if you hadn't got angry about the beard, is that you should be calm, because, in my opinion, they'll never join all together against you. They're afraid that if they win, one city will become stronger than the others. And so they prefer you, provided you don't make them pay too much."

"Don't believe everything Baudolino tells you." Otto was smiling. "The boy's a liar by nature."

"No, sir," Frederick replied. "When he talks about Italy, the boy as a rule says things that are absolutely right. For example, now he teaches us that our only chance, with the Italian cities, is to divide them as much as possible. Only then you never know who's with you and who's against you!"

"If our Baudolino is right," Rainald of Dassel said, sneering, "whether they're with you or against you doesn't depend on you, but on the city they want to harm at that moment."

Baudolino felt a little sorry for this Frederick, so big and grand and powerful, who couldn't accept the reasoning of his subjects. And to think that he spent more time on the Italian peninsula than in his own lands. He, Baudolino said to himself, loves our people and doesn't understand why they betray him. Maybe that's why he kills them like a jealous husband.

In the months after their return Baudolino had had few opportunities to see Frederick, who was preparing a diet at Ratisbon, then another at Worms. He had to maintain the friendship of two quite fearsome relatives, Henry the Lion, to whom he had finally given the dukedom of Bavaria, and Henry Jasomirgott, for whom he had actually invented a dukedom of Austria. Early the next spring, Otto announced to Baudolino that in June they would all be leaving for Herbipolis, where Frederick was happily to be married. The emperor had already had a wife, from whom he had been separated a few years before, and now he was about to wed Beatrice of Burgundy, who brought him as her dowry that county, as far as Provence. With such a dowry, Otto and Rahewin thought the marriage was inspired by material interest, and in this spirit Baudolino, supplied with new clothing as the auspicious occasion demanded, was prepared to see his adopted father on the arm of a Burgundian spinster more appealing on account of the possessions of her ancestors than for any personal beauty.

"I was jealous, I confess," Baudolino said to Niketas. "After all, I had only recently found a second father, and now he was being taken away from me, at least in part, by a stepmother."

Here Baudolino paused, displaying some embarrassment; he ran a finger over his scar, then he revealed the terrible truth. He arrived at the wedding and discovered that Beatrice of Burgundy was a twenty-year-old maiden of extraordinary beauty—or at least so she seemed to him, who, once he had seen her, was unable to move a muscle, as he looked at her wide-eyed. Her hair was a tawny gold, the face was lovely, the mouth small and red as a ripe fruit, teeth white and neatly aligned, erect of posture, a demure gaze, clear eyes. Her smooth speech was modest, the body slender. She seemed to dominate in her dazzling grace all those surrounding her. She knew how to appear (supreme virtue in a future queen) submissive to her husband, whom she apparently feared as a master, but she was his mistress in making clear to him her own will as his wife, with such graceful manners that her every wish was promptly taken as a command. If one then needed to add something further in her praise, it was said she was versed in letters, skilled at making music, and sweet in singing it. Thus, Baudolino concluded, being called Beatrice, she was truly beatified.

It took little time for Niketas to understand that the youth had fallen in love with his stepmother, but—since he was falling in love for the first time—he didn't yet know what was happening to him. To fall in love for the first time is a devastating, unbearable event for any peasant enamored of a milkmaid with pimples; so imagine what it can mean for a peasant to fall in love for the first time with a twenty-year-old empress with skin as white as milk.

Baudolino realized immediately that what he was feeling represented a kind of theft with respect to his father, and he tried to convince himself that, because of the stepmother's young age, he was seeing her as a sister. But then, even if he had studied little moral theology, he became aware that it was not even licit for him to love a sister—at least not with the tremors and the intensity of passion that the sight of Beatrice inspired in him. He bowed his head, blushing, and just then Beatrice, to whom Frederick was introducing his little Baudolino (a strange and beloved imp of the Po plain, as he was saying), tenderly extended her hand and stroked him first on the cheek and then on the head.

Baudolino was about to lose consciousness; he felt the light failing around him and his ears rang like the Easter bells. He was awakened by the heavy hand of Otto, who struck his nape and muttered: "On your knees, jackass!" He remembered that before him stood the holy Roman empress and also the queen of Italy, and he bent his knees, and from that moment on he behaved like the perfect courtier, except that at night he was unable to sleep and, instead of rejoicing at this inexplicable road to Damascus, he wept for the intolerable ardor of his unknown passion.

Niketas looked at his leonine interlocutor, appreciating the delicacy of his expression, the restrained rhetoric in an almost literary Greek, and asked himself what sort of creature he was facing, capable as he was of using the language of rustics when he spoke of farmers, and that of kings when he spoke of monarchs. Can he have a soul, Niketas wondered, this character who can bend his narrative to express different souls? And if he has different souls, through which mouth, as he speaks, will he tell me the truth?

5

Baudolino gives Frederick some wise advice

The next morning the city was still covered with a single cloud of smoke. Niketas savored some fruit, moving about the room in a restless manner, then asked Baudolino if he could send one of the Genoese to seek out a man named Architas, who would cleanse his face.

Just look at this, Baudolino said to himself: the city is lost, people are getting their throats cut in the streets, only two days ago this man risked losing his entire family, and now he wants someone to shave him. Obviously the people of the palace in this corrupt city are accustomed to such things—faced with such a man, Frederick would have sent him flying out of the window.

Later Architas arrived, with a basket of silver instruments and phials of the most unexpected scents. He was an artist, who first softened your face with hot cloths, then covered it with emollient creams, smoothed it, freed it of every impurity, and finally covered the wrinkles with cosmetics, lightly treating the eyes with bistre, making the lips delicately rosy, depilating the ears, to say nothing of what he did to the chin and the head. Niketas sat with closed eyes, stroked by those knowing hands, cradled by the voice of Baudolino, who continued telling his story. It was actually Baudolino who interrupted himself every now and then to discover what that master of beauty was doing, for example, when he took a lizard from a pot, chopped off its head and tail, almost minced the rest, and set this paste to cook in a little pan of oil. What a question! It was the decoction meant to keep alive the few hairs that Niketas still bore on his pate and make them shiny and perfumed. And that phial? Why, it contained essences of nutmeg or cardamom, or rose water, each to restore vigor to a part of the face; that thick honey was to strengthen the lips, and this other one, whose secret he could not reveal, was to harden the gums.

In the end Niketas was splendid, as a judge of the Veil should be and a logothete of the secrets, and as if reborn, he shone in his own light on that wan morning, against the frowning background of Byzantium smoldering in agony. And Baudolino felt a certain embarrassment in telling about his adolescent life in a monastery of Latins, cold and inhospitable, where Otto's health obliged the youth to share meals composed of boiled vegetables and insipid broth.

That year Baudolino had to spend little time at court (where, when he had to be there, he wandered around shyly, yearning at the same time to encounter Beatrice, and all was torment). Frederick first had to settle things with the Poles (*Polanos de Polunia,* wrote Otto, *gens quasi barbara ad pugnandum promptissima*). In March he convened a new diet at Worms to prepare for another descent into Italy, where Milan, as usual, with her allies, was becoming more and more unruly, then a diet at Herbipolis in September, and one in Besançon in October; in short, he seemed possessed. Baudolino for the most part remained in the abbey of Morimond with Otto, continued his studies with Rahewin, and acted as copyist for the bishop, who was increasingly frail.

When they arrived at that book of the *Chronica* that tells of Presbyter Johannes, Baudolino asked what it meant to be a Christian *sed Nestorianus.* Were these Nestorians then a bit Christian and a bit not?

"My son, in plain words Nestorius was a heretic, but we owe him much gratitude. You should know that in India, after the preaching of the apostle Thomas, it was the Nestorians who spread the Christian religion. Nestorius committed only one error, but a very grave one, concerning Jesus Christ Our Lord and his most holy mother. You see, we firmly believe that there exists a single divine nature and that nevertheless the Trinity, within the unity of this nature, is composed of three distinct persons, the Father, the Son, and the Holy Ghost. But we believe further that in Christ there was a sole person, the divine one, and two natures, the human and the divine. Nestorius on the contrary sustained that in Christ there are, indeed, two natures, human and divine, but there are also two persons. So Maria had begotten only the human person and could not thus be called the mother of God, but only the mother of Christ the man, not *Theotokos,* or God-bearer, she who has begotten God, but at most *Christotokos.*"

"Is it bad to think that?"

"It's bad and it isn't...." Otto became impatient. "You can still love the Blessed Virgin even if you consider her as Nestorius did, but it is certain that you are paying her less honor. And besides, the person is the individual substance of a rational being, and if in Christ there were two persons, were there then two individual substances of two rational beings? Where would this all end? Would we be saying that Jesus one day reasoned in one way and the next day in another? This said, it isn't that Presbyter Johannes is a perfidious heretic, but it would be well for him to enter into contact with a Christian emperor who would make him appreciate the true faith, and since he is surely an honest man, he could only be converted. However, it is certain that if you don't set yourself to studying a bit of theology, you will never understand these things. You are quick-witted, Rahewin is a good teacher as far as reading and writing go, and doing sums, and learning a few rules of grammar; but trivium and quadrivium are a different matter. To arrive at theology you should study dialectics, and these are things you cannot learn here at Morimond. You must go off to some *studium,* one of those schools that exist only in the great cities."

"But I don't want to go to a *studium,* whatever that is."

"When you understand what it is, you'll be pleased to go. You see, my son, everyone is accustomed to saying that the human community is based on three forces: warriors, monks, and peasants, and this may have been true until yesterday. But we live in new times, in which the man of learning is becoming equally important, even if he is not a monk but a man who studies law, philosophy, the movement of the stars, and many other things, and who doesn't always give an account of what he is doing to his bishop or to his king. And these *studia,* which are slowly growing up in Bologna and in Paris, are places where learning is cultivated and transmitted, and learning is a form of power. I was a pupil of the great Abélard, may God have mercy on this man who sinned greatly but also suffered and expiated. After his misfortune, when through a bitter vendetta he was robbed of his virility, he became a monk, an abbé, and lived apart from the world. At the peak of his glory he was a master in Paris, worshiped by his students, and respected by the mighty precisely because of his learning."

Baudolino told himself he would never leave Otto, from whom he continued to learn so many things. But before the trees had blossomed for the fourth time since Baudolino had met him, Otto was reduced to a shadow of himself by malarial fevers, pains in all his joints, fluxions of the chest, not to mention gallstone. Numerous physicians, including some Arabs and some Jews, and therefore the best that a Christian emperor could offer a bishop, had tormented his now fragile body with countless leeches, but—for reasons that those pillars of wisdom were unable to explain—after almost all his blood had been extracted, he was worse than if they had left him with it.

Otto first called Rahewin to his bedside, to entrust to him the continuation of his account of the feats of Frederick, assuring him that it was easy: he should narrate the events and put in the emperor's mouth speeches drawn from the texts of the ancients. Then he summoned Baudolino. "*Puer dilectissime,*" he said to him, "I am going away. You might even say I am going back, and I'm not sure which expression is the more appropriate, since I am not sure whether my story of the two cities is more true or the story of the feats of Frederick...." ("You must understand, Master Niketas," Baudolino said, "the life of a boy can be marked by the confession of a dying teacher who can no longer distinguish between two truths.") "It's not that I am content to go away, or back, as it so pleases the Lord, and if I were to question his decrees, there's the risk he might strike me dead at this very instant, so it's best to take advantage of the little time he is granting me. Listen. You know how I have tried to make the emperor understand the reasoning of the cities beyond the Alps. The emperor can do nothing but subject them to his rule. However, there are many ways to acknowledge submission, and perhaps a way can be found other than the way of siege and massacre. So you, who have the emperor's ear, and who are still a son of those lands, must try to do your best to reconcile the demands of our lord with those of your cities, so that the smallest possible number of people may die, and that finally all may be content. To do this you must learn to use your reason properly, and I have asked the emperor to send you to study in Paris. Not in Bologna, where they concern themselves only with law; a rogue like you should never stick his nose into the Pandects, because with the law there can be no lying. In Paris you will study rhetoric and you will read the poets; rhetoric is the art of saying well that which may or may not be true, and it is the duty of poets to invent beautiful falsehoods. It would also be well for you to study a bit of theology, but without trying to become a theologian, because there must be no joking with the things of Almighty God. Study enough so that you will afterwards cut a fine figure at court, where you will surely become a ministerial, which is the highest rank the son of peasants can aspire to; you will be like a knight, the peer of many nobles, and you will be able to serve faithfully your adoptive father. Do all this in memory of me, and Jesus forgive me if, without meaning to, I have used his words."

Then he emitted a rattle, and lay immobile. Baudolino was about to close Otto's eyes, believing he had heaved his last sigh, but suddenly the older man reopened his mouth and whispered, exploiting his final breath: "Baudolino, remember the kingdom of the Presbyter Johannes. Only in seeking it can the oriflammes of Christianity go beyond Byzantium and Jerusalem. I have heard you invent many stories that the emperor has believed. So then, if you have no other news of that realm, invent some. Mind you, I am not asking you to bear witness to what you believe false, which would be a sin, but to testify falsely to what you believe true—which is a virtuous act because it compensates for the lack of proof of something that certainly exists or happened. I beseech you: there is surely a Johannes, beyond the lands of the Persians and the Armenians, beyond Baktu, Ecbatana, Persepolis, Susa, and Arbela, descendant of the Magi.... Press Frederick to the East, because from there comes the light that will illuminate him as the greatest of all kings.... Take the emperor out of that mire that stretches between Milan and Rome.... He could remain trapped in it until his death. Keep clear of a kingdom even where a pope rules. He will always be only half an emperor. Remember, Baudolino... Presbyter Johannes... the way to the East..."

"But why are you saying this to me, master, and not to Rahewin?"

"Because Rahewin has no imagination, he can recount only what he has seen, and at times not even that, because he doesn't understand what he has seen. But you can imagine what you haven't seen. Oh, why has it become so dark?"

Baudolino, who was a liar, told him not to worry, because night was falling. Just as noon was striking, Otto exhaled a hiss from his now hoarse throat, and his eyes remained open and fixed, as if he were looking at his Prester John enthroned. Baudolino closed his teacher's eyes, and shed honest tears.

Saddened by Otto's death, Baudolino went back to Frederick for a few months. At first he consoled himself with the thought that, seeing the emperor again, he would also see the empress. He saw her, and was saddened still more. We must not forget that Baudolino was approaching his sixteenth year and if, before, his falling in love might have seemed a boyish perturbation, of which he himself understood very little, now it was becoming conscious desire and complete torment.

Rather than remain at court and languish he always followed Frederick into the field, and he had witnessed things he was far from liking. The Milanese destroyed Lodi for the second time, or, rather, first they sacked it, taking away livestock, forage, and goods from every household; then they drove all the citizens outside the walls, telling them that if they didn't clear out to Hell and gone, every last one of them would taste the sword: women, old people, and children, including babes still in the cradle. The citizens of Lodi abandoned in the city only their dogs, and went off into the countryside, on foot, under the rain, even the nobles, who had been deprived of their horses, and the women with infants at their breast, and at times they fell by the wayside, or rolled brutally into the ditches. They took refuge between the Adda and the Serio; there they managed to find only some hovels where they slept, piled one upon another.

This in no way placated the Milanese, who came back to Lodi, imprisoning the very few who had refused to leave. They cut down all the vines and the trees and then set fire to the houses, destroying also most of the dogs.

These are not things that an emperor can tolerate, hence Frederick once again went down into Italy, with a great army made up of men from Burgundy, Lorraine, Bohemia, Hungary, Swabia, France, and any other imaginable place. First of all, he founded a new Lodi at Montegezzone, then he encamped before Milan, enthusiastically supported by the people of Pavia and Cremona, Pisa, Lucca, Florence and Siena, Vicenza, Treviso, Padua, Ferrara, Ravenna, Modena, and more, all allied with the empire to humiliate Milan.

And Milan was truly humiliated. By the end of the summer the city had capitulated and, in an effort to save it, the Milanese subjected themselves to a ritual that humiliated Baudolino himself, though he had no feelings for Milan. The defeated passed in a sad procession, all barefoot and in sackcloth, including the bishop, with the men-at-arms wearing their swords hung around their neck. Frederick, at this point his magnanimity returning, gave the humiliated the kiss of peace.

"Was it worth it," Baudolino asked himself, "to act so overbearing with Lodi, and then have to humble themselves like this? Is it worth living in these lands where everyone seems to have made a vow of suicide, and one side helps the other kill themselves? I want to leave." In reality, he also wanted to get away from Beatrice, because finally he had read somewhere that distance can cure the love illness (and he had not yet read other books where, on the contrary, it is said that distance is precisely that which fans the flames of passion). So he went to Frederick to remind him of Otto's advice and to have himself sent to Paris.

He found the emperor sad and wrathful, pacing back and forth in his chamber, while in one corner Rainald of Dassel was waiting for him to calm down. At a certain point Frederick stood still, looked into Baudolino's eyes, and said: "You are my witness, boy, that I am bending every effort to bring all the cities of Italy under a single law, but, every time, I have to start over again from the beginning. Is my law perhaps wrong? Who can tell me my law is right?"

And, as if instinctively, Baudolino said: "Sire, if you start thinking that way, you'll never reach an end, whereas, on the contrary, the emperor exists for this very reason: he isn't emperor because he has the right ideas, but his ideas are right because they come to him, and that's that."

Frederick looked at him, then said to Rainald: "This boy expresses things better than the whole pack of you! If these words were simply turned into good Latin, they would seem wondrous!"

"*Quod principi plaquit legis habet vigorem*: that which pleases the prince has the strength of law," Rainald of Dassel said. "Yes, it sounds very wise, and definitive. But it would have to be written in the Gospel, otherwise how could all be persuaded to accept this beautiful idea?"

"We clearly saw what happened in Rome," Frederick said. "If I have myself anointed by the pope, I admit *ipso facto* that his power is superior to mine; if I grab the pope by the throat and fling him into the Tiber, I become a scourge of God worse even than poor Attila.... Where the devil can I find someone who will define my rights without claiming to be above me? Such a person doesn't exist in the world."

"Perhaps a power such as that doesn't exist," Baudolino then said to him, "but the knowledge exists."

"What do you mean?"

"When Bishop Otto told me what a *studium* is, he said that these communities of masters and students operate independently: the students come from all over the world and it doesn't matter who their sovereign is, and they pay their teachers, who are therefore dependent entirely on their pupils. This is how things work with the masters of law in Bologna, and this is how it is also in Paris, where in earlier times the masters taught in the cathedral schools and hence were dependent on the bishop, until one fine day they went off to teach on the Mountain of Saint Geneviève, and they attempt to discover the truth without listening either to the bishop or to the king."

"If I were their king I'd show them a thing or two. But even if this were the case?"

"It would be the case if you made a law by which you acknowledge that the masters of Bologna are truly independent of every other power, whether yours or the pope's or any other sovereign's, and they are in the service only of the Law. Once they are invested with this dignity, unique in the world, they will affirm that—in accord with true reason, natural enlightenment, and tradition—the only law is the Roman and the only person representing it is the holy Roman emperor—and that naturally, as Master Rainald has said so well—*quod principi plaquit legis habet vigorem.*"

"And why would they say that?"

"Because, in exchange, you give them the right to say it, and that is no small thing. So you are content, they are content, and, as my father Gagliaudo used to say, you are both in an iron-clad barrel."

"They wouldn't agree to anything like that," Rainald grumbled.

"Yes, they would." Frederick's face brightened. "I tell you they will agree. Only, first, they have to make that declaration, and then I'll give them independence. Otherwise everyone will think that they did it to repay a gift from me."

"If you ask me, even if you do turn the process around, if someone wants to say it was prearranged, they'll say so anyway," Baudolino remarked skeptically. "But I'd like to see anyone stand up and say the doctors of Bologna aren't worth a dried fig, when even the emperor has gone humbly to ask their opinion. At that point, what they have said is Gospel."

And so it happened, that same year, at Roncaglia, where for the second time a great diet was held. For Baudolino it was above all a great spectacle. As Rahewin explained to him—so he wouldn't believe that everything he saw was simply a big circus with banners flapping on all sides, standards, colored tents, merchants, and mountebanks—Frederick, along one side of the Po, had a typical Roman camp reconstructed, to remind everyone that his dignity derived from Rome. In the center of the camp stood the imperial tent, like a temple, and it was encircled by the tents of feudal lords, vassals, and vavasours. On Frederick's side were the archbishop of Cologne, the bishop of Bamberg, Daniel of Prague, Conrad of Augusta, and many others. On the other side of the river, the cardinal legate of the Apostolic See, the patriarch of Aquileia, the archbishop of Milan, the bishops of Turin, Alba, Ivrea, Asti, Novara, Vercelli, Terdona, Pavia, Como, Lodi, Cremona, Piacenza, Reggio, Modena, Bologna, and others, more than can be remembered. Seated in this majestic and truly universal assembly, Frederick opened the discussion.

In brief (Baudolino said, so as not to bore Niketas with the masterpieces of imperial, judicial, and ecclesiastical oratory), four doctors of Bologna, the most famous, pupils of the great Irnerius, were invited by the emperor to express an unchallengeable doctrinal opinion on his powers. And three of them, Bulgarus, Jacopus, and Hugo of Porta Ravegnana, expressed themselves as Frederick wished: namely, that the right of the emperor was based on Roman law. Only a certain Martinus was of a different opinion.

"And Frederick had then to gouge out his eyes," Niketas commented.

"Oh, not at all, Master Niketas," Baudolino replied, "You Romei gouge out the eyes of this man or that and you have no idea where the law stands any more, forgetting your great Justinian. Immediately afterwards, Frederick promulgated the *Constitutio Habita*, with which the autonomy of the Bologna *studium* was recognized, and if the *studium* was autonomous, then Martinus could say what he wanted and not even the emperor could touch a hair of his head. For if he had, then the doctors were no longer autonomous, and if they weren't autonomous then their opinion was worthless, and Frederick risked passing for a usurper."

All right, Niketas thought, then Master Baudolino wants to suggest to me that he was the founder of the empire, and that if he simply uttered an ordinary sentence, such was his power that it became truth. Let's hear the rest.

Meanwhile the Genoese had come in bearing a basket of fruit, because it was midday, and Niketas had to have refreshment. They said the sack was continuing, and it was best to remain in the house. Baudolino resumed his story.

Frederick had decided that, if a boy still almost beardless produced such acute ideas, who could say what would happen if the boy were actually sent to study in Paris? He embraced Baudolino affectionately, urging him to become truly learned, since he himself, with his duties of government and his military operations, had never had time to cultivate his mind properly. The empress had taken her leave of him with a kiss on the forehead (we can only imagine Baudolino's ecstasy), saying to him (that prodigious woman, though she was a great lady and a queen, knew how to read and write): "Write to me, tell me about yourself, about what happens to you. Life at court is monotonous. Your letters will be a comfort to me."

"I will write, I swear," Baudolino said, with an ardor that should have aroused the suspicions of those present. None of them became suspicious (who notices the excitement of a boy about to go to Paris?), except perhaps Beatrice. In fact, she looked at him as if she were seeing him for the first time, and her very white face was covered with an immediate flush. But Baudolino, with a bow that obliged him to look at the ground, had already left the hall.

6

Baudolino goes to Paris

Baudolino arrived in Paris a bit late: in those schools, students entered before they were fourteen, and he was two years older. But he had already learned so many things from Otto that he allowed himself to miss some of the lessons in order, as will be seen, to do other things.

He had set off with a companion, the son of a knight from Cologne, who preferred to devote himself to the liberal arts rather than to the army, not without causing his father some pain, but supported by his mother, who vaunted his precocious poetic gifts, whence Baudolino, if he had ever known the youth's name, soon forgot it. He called him the Poet, and so did all the others who met him later. Baudolino soon discovered that the Poet had never written a poem, but had only declared his wish to write some. Since he constantly recited the poems of others, in the end even his father became convinced that his son should follow the Muses and allowed him to leave, putting in his pocket barely enough to keep him alive, in the completely mistaken notion that the small amount necessary to live in Cologne would be more than enough for life in Paris.

Immediately upon his arrival, Baudolino, who could hardly wait to obey the empress, wrote her some letters. In the beginning he

believed he would allay his ardor by fulfilling that request, but he realized how painful it was to write without being able to tell her what
he truly felt, inditing letters perfect and seemly, in which he described
Paris, a city rich in beautiful churches, where one breathed fine air,
the sky was vast and serene, except when it rained, but never more
than once or twice a day, and for someone who came from virtually
eternal fog, it was a place of eternal spring. There was a winding river
with two islands in the middle, and the water was very good to drink,
and just beyond the walls balmy spaces stretched away, such as the
meadow next to the abbey of Saint Germain, where they spent beautiful afternoons playing ball.

He told her of his troubles in the early days, when he had to find
a room, to share with his companion, without letting the landlords
cheat him. At a dear price they had found a fairly spacious room,
with a table, two benches, shelves for books and a trunk. . . . There was
a high bed with an ostrich-feather comforter, and a low bed on
wheels with a goose-down cover, which in the daytime was concealed
beneath the bigger one. The letter did not say that, after a brief hesi-
tation over the assignment of the beds, it was decided that every evening the two roommates would play chess for the more comfortable
bed, because at court chess was considered an unseemly game.

Another letter told how they awoke early because lessons began at
seven and lasted until late afternoon. They fortified themselves with
a good ration of bread and a bowl of wine, before going to listen to
their masters/teachers in a kind of stable, where, seated on the sparse
straw on the ground, they were colder than they would have been
outside. Beatrice was moved and urged him not to be frugal with the
wine, otherwise a youth feels listless the whole day, and to hire a servant, not only to carry the books, which are very heavy and to carry
them oneself is unworthy of a person of rank, but also to buy the
wood and light the fire in the room betimes, so that it would be good
and warm in the evening. And for all these expenses she sent forty solidi of Susa, enough to buy an ox.

The servant had not been hired and the wood had not been bought, because at night the two featherbeds were fine; the sum had been spent more wisely, inasmuch as the evenings were passed in taverns, which were splendidly heated and permitted some refreshment after a day of study, and some pinching of bottoms of the serving wenches. And further, in those places of merry repose, like the Ecu d'Argent, the Croix de Fer, Les Trois Chandeliers, between one mug and the next, they restored their vigor with pork or chicken pies, a pair of pigeons or a roast goose or, if they were poorer, with tripe or mutton. Baudolino helped the Poet, who was penniless, to live not by tripe alone. But the Poet was a costly friend, because the amount of wine he drank made that Susa ox grow thinner before their very eyes.

Omitting these details, Baudolino went on to write of his masters and the fine things he was learning. Beatrice was very sensitive to these revelations, which whetted her own appetite for knowledge, and she read and reread the letters in which Baudolino told her about grammar, dialectics, rhetoric, and of arithmetic, geometry, music, and astronomy. But Baudolino felt more and more cowardly, because, writing to her, he remained silent about what most oppressed his heart and about all the other things he did, which cannot be told to a mother or to a sister, or to an empress or, still less, to the beloved woman.

Mostly the students played ball, true, but they also brawled with the people of the Abbey of Saint Germain, or among students of different origin, Picards against Normans, for example, and they traded insults in Latin, so that anyone could understand you were offending him. These were all things frowned upon by the Great Provost, who sent his bowmen to arrest the most unruly. Obviously, at this point the students forgot their differences and all together fell to exchanging blows with the bowmen.

No men in the world were more easily corrupted than the bowmen of the provost. So if a student was arrested, they all had to dig into their purses to persuade the bowmen to set him free. This made the pleasures of Paris even more costly.

Second, a student who has no amorous affairs is derided by his fellows. Unfortunately, the most inaccessible thing for the students was women. There were very few female students to be seen, and there were legends still circulated about the beautiful Héloïse, who had cost her lover the cutting off of his pudenda, even if it was one thing to be a student, hence by definition ill-famed and yet tolerated, and another to be a professor, like the great and unhappy Abélard. Mercenary love was expensive, and so they had to rely on the occasional tavern wench or some common woman of the neighborhood, but in that quarter there were always more students than females.

Unless they managed to assume an idle air and ribald look while strolling on the Ile de la Cité, and thus succeed in seducing ladies of higher station. Much desired were the wives of the butchers of La Grève, who, after an honored career in their trade, no longer slaughtered cattle but governed the meat market, behaving like gentlemen. With a husband born quartering oxen, who had achieved comfort late in life, the wives were alert to the fascination of the more handsome students. But these ladies wore sumptuous dresses decorated with fur, and silver and bejeweled belts, which made it difficult at first sight to distinguish them from grand prostitutes who, though the laws forbade it, usually dressed in the same fashion. This exposed the students to some unfortunate misunderstandings, for which they were all the more derided by their friends.

If a student succeeded in winning a real lady, or indeed a virtuous maiden, sooner or later husbands and fathers would find out, and there would be a fight, sometimes with weapons; and someone died or was wounded, almost always the husband or father, and then there was more brawling with the bowmen of the provost. Baudolino hadn't killed anyone, and in general he also stayed well away from brawls, but with one husband (and butcher) he had had to deal. Ardent in love but cautious in matters of war, when he saw the husband enter the room, swinging one of those hooks used to hang slaughtered animals, Baudolino immediately tried to jump out the window. But, as he was judiciously calculating the distance before making the leap, he had had time to receive a slash on the cheek, thus decorating forever his face with a scar worthy of a man-at-arms.

On the other hand, even winning working-class women was not an everyday occurrence and demanded long sieges (at the expense of lessons), and whole days spent observing from the window, which generated boredom. Then dreams of seduction were abandoned, and the youths threw water down on the passersby, or they used the women as targets, firing peas with a slingshot, or they even taunted teachers who went past below, and if these grew angry, the students would follow them, in a body, to their house, throwing stones at the windows because, after all, it was the students who paid them and thus had earned some rights.

Baudolino, in fact, was telling Niketas what he had not told Beatrice, namely, that he was becoming one of those clerics who studied the liberal arts in Paris, or jurisprudence in Bologna, or medicine in Salerno, or sorcery in Toledo, but in no place learned good behavior. Niketas did not know whether to be shocked, amazed, or amused. In Byzantium there were only private schools for the sons of well-to-do families, where, from their earliest years, they learned grammar and read pious works and the masterpieces of classical culture; after the age of eleven they studied poetry and rhetoric, they learned to compose on the literary models of the ancients; and the rarer the terms they used, and the more complex their syntactical constructions, the more readily they were considered for a bright future in the imperial administration. But afterwards, either they became sages in a monastery or they studied things such as law or astronomy from private masters. Still, they studied seriously, whereas it seemed that in Paris the students did everything except study.

Baudolino corrected him. "In Paris we worked very hard. For example, after the first years, we were already taking part in debates, and in debate you learn to posit objections and to move on to the determination, that is, to the final solution of a question. And you mustn't think that the lessons are the most important things for a student, or that the tavern is only a place where they waste time. The good thing about the *studium* is that you learn from your teachers, true, but even more from your fellows, especially those older than you, when they tell you what they have read, and you discover that the world must be full of wondrous things and to know them all— since a lifetime will not be enough for you to travel through the whole world—you can only read all the books."

Baudolino had been able to read many books with Otto, but he hadn't realized that there could exist as many in the world as there were in Paris. They were not at everyone's disposal, but through good luck, or, rather, through good attendance at his lessons, he had come to know Abdul.

"To explain the connection between Abdul and the libraries, I have to go back a little, Master Niketas. While I was following a lesson, always blowing on my fingers to warm them, and with my bottom freezing, because the straw didn't offer much protection against that floor, icy like all of Paris on those winter days, one morning I noticed a boy near me who, by the color of his face, seemed a Saracen, except that he also had red hair, which you don't find among Moors. I don't know if he was following the lesson or pursuing his own thoughts, but he was staring into space. Every so often he would shiver and pull his clothing around him, then he would return to looking into the air, and at times he would scratch something on his tablet. I craned my neck, and I realized that half of what he wrote looked like those fly droppings that are the Arabs' alphabet, and for the rest he wrote in a language that seemed Latin but wasn't, and it even reminded me of the dialects of my land. Anyway, when the lesson was over, I struck up a conversation; he reacted politely, as if he had been wanting for some time to find a person to talk with; we made friends, we went walking along the river, and he told me his story."

———

The boy's name was Abdul, a Moor's name, in fact, but he was born of a mother who came from Hibernia, and this explained the red hair, because all those who come from that remote island are like that, and according to report, they are bizarre, dreamers. His father was Provençal, of a family that had settled overseas after the conquest of Jerusalem, fifty some years before. As Abdul tried to explain, those Frankish nobles had adopted the customs of the peoples they had conquered. They wore turbans and indulged in other Turkeries, they spoke the language of their enemies, and were within an inch of following the precepts of the Koran. For which reason a half-Hibernian, with red hair, could be called Abdul and could have a face burned by the sun of Syria, where he was born. He thought in Arabic, and in Provençal he told the ancient sagas of the frozen seas of the north, which he had heard from his mother.

Baudolino immediately asked him if he was in Paris to become a good Christian again and speak as one should, namely, in proper Latin. As to his reasons for coming to Paris, Abdul remained fairly reticent. He spoke of a thing that had happened to him, something fairly upsetting apparently, a kind of terrible ordeal to which he had been subjected while still a boy, so that his noble parents had decided to send him to Paris to save him from some unknown vendetta. Speaking of this, Abdul turned grim, blushing as much as a Moor can blush, his hands trembling, and Baudolino decided to change the subject.

The youth was intelligent, and after a few months in Paris he spoke Latin and the local vernacular. He lived with an uncle, canon of the abbey of Saint Victoire, one of the sanctuaries of learning of that city (and perhaps of the whole Christian world), with a library richer than that of Alexandria. And that explains how, in the months that followed, thanks to Abdul, Baudolino and also the Poet gained access to that repository of universal learning.

Baudolino asked Abdul what he was writing during the lesson, and his companion said that the notes in Arabic concerned certain things that the teacher said about dialectics, because Arabic is surely the language best suited to philosophy. As for the other things, they were in Provençal. He was reluctant to speak of it and evaded the questions for a long time, but with the air of one who with his eyes asks only to be questioned further; and finally he translated. They were some verses, and they said more or less : *O my love, in your distant land—my heart aches for you. . . . O my flowered curtain, O my unknown, O my companion.*

"You write verses?" Baudolino asked.

"I sing songs. I sing what I feel. I love a distant princess."

"A princess? Who is she?"

"I don't know. I saw her—or rather it's as if I saw her—in the Holy Land when I was a prisoner . . . in other words, while I was experiencing an adventure I haven't yet told you about. My heart burst into flame, and I vowed eternal love to that lady. I decided to dedicate my life to her. Perhaps one day I will find her, but I fear its happening. It is so beautiful to languish for an impossible love."

Baudolino was about to say to him: some fool you are, as his father used to say, but then he remembered that he too languished for an impossible love (even if he had undoubtedly seen Beatrice, and her image was the obsession of his nights), and he was touched by the fate of his friend Abdul.

This is how a great friendship begins. That same evening Abdul turned up at the room of Baudolino and the Poet, with an instrument that Baudolino had never seen, shaped like an almond, with many taut strings, and letting his fingers stray over those strings, Abdul sang:

> When the flow of the fountain
> Runs clear and, as always,
> The dog rose blossoms,
> And the nightingale on the bough
> Sings its soft and varied song
> And refines its sweet singing,
> My song accompanies it.

O, my love in your distant land,
My heart aches for you
Nor will I find medicine
If I do not answer your summons,
In the warmth of your wool,
O my flowered curtain,
O my unknown, O my companion.

I cannot have you near
And in the fire I burn and yearn.
Never have I seen a Christian maid
Who existed, God willing,
Nor Jew, nor Saracen maid,
Superior to your beauty.
Who wins your love?

At evening and at morn,
O my love, I call you;
My mind turns insane,
My yearning clouds the sun.
Already, as if by a thorn, I am stung
By that pain that heals me,
And a tear bathes me.

The melody was sweet, the chords awoke unknown or dormant passions, and Baudolino thought of Beatrice.

"Dear Christ," the Poet said, "why can't I write verses that beautiful?"

"I don't want to become a poet. I sing for myself, nothing else. If you like, I will give them to you," Abdul said, also touched now.

"Oh, yes," the Poet replied, "but if I translate them from Provençal into German, they turn to shit...."

Abdul became the third member of that band, and when Baudolino tried not to think of Beatrice, that damned Moor with the red hair would take his accursed instrument and sing songs that made Baudolino's heart ache.

> If the nightingale amid the leaves
> Bestows love and demands it,
> And his companion replies,
> And already mingles her song
> With his, and the rivulet from the brook
> With the happiness of the meadow
> Feels joy in its heart.

> In friendship melts my soul,
> And greater benefice does not claim
> Than the love that she returns
> And that is promptly perceived
> In my ailing heart, sick
> With aching savor.

Baudolino told himself that one day he too would write songs for his faraway empress, but he did not clearly know how it was done, because neither Otto nor Rahewin had ever mentioned poetry to him, unless it was when they taught him some sacred anthem. For now at least he took advantage of Abdul to gain access to the library of Saint Victoire, where he spent long mornings stolen from his lessons, pondering, his lips parted, over the fabulous texts, not the manuals of grammar, but the stories of Pliny, the romance of Alexander, the geography of Solinus, and the etymologies of Isidore.

He read of distant lands, where crocodiles live, great aquatic serpents that, when they have eaten a man, weep, move their upper jaw and have no tongue; the hippopotami, half man and half horse; the leucochrocan beast, with the body of an ass, the behind of a stag, the breast and thighs of a lion, horse's hoofs, a bifurcated horn, a mouth stretching to the ears from which an almost human voice emerges, and in the place of teeth, a single bone. He read of lands where there lived men without knee joints, men without tongues, men with huge ears that sheltered their body from the cold, and the skiapods, who run very swiftly on a single foot.

Since he could not send Beatrice songs not of his own composition (and even if he had written some, he would not have dared), he decided that, as one sends his beloved flowers or jewels, he would make her a gift of all the wonders that he was acquiring. So he wrote her of lands where honey trees and flour trees grow, of Mount Ararat, from whose peak, on clear days, you can glimpse the remains of Noah's ark, and those who have scaled it say they touch with their finger the hole through which the devil escaped when Noah recited the Benedicite. He told her of Albania, where men are whiter than elsewhere, and have hair sparse as a cat's whiskers; of a country where if one turns to the east he casts his shadow to his own right; and of another inhabited by people of the greatest ferocity, who go into deepest mourning when children are born, but hold a great festivity when people die; of lands where enormous mountains of gold rise, guarded by ants the size of dogs, and where the Amazons live, warrior women who keep their men in a neighboring region; if they bear a son they send him to his father or else they kill him, if they bear a female they remove her breast with a searing iron; if she is of high rank, they remove the left breast so that she can carry a shield, if of low degree, the right breast so that she can draw a bow. And finally he told her of the Nile, one of the four rivers springing from the Earthly Paradise, which runs through the deserts of India, goes underground, emerges near Mount Atlas, then empties into the sea after crossing Egypt.

But when he came to India, Baudolino almost forgot Beatrice, and his mind turned to other fancies, because he had got it into his head that in those parts there had to be, if there ever had been, the kingdom of that Presbyter Johannes of whom Otto had told him. Baudolino had never ceased to think of Johannes: he thought of him every time he read about an unknown country, and even more when on the parchment varicolored miniatures appeared of strange beings, like horned men, or pygmies, who spend their lives fighting cranes. He thought of this so much that, to himself, he now spoke of Prester John as if he were a family friend. And hence to discover where he was became for Baudolino a matter of the greatest moment and, if Johannes was nowhere, still an India had to be found where he could be placed, because Baudolino felt bound by an oath (though none had been sworn) to the beloved dying bishop.

Of Prester John he had spoken to his two companions, who were immediately attracted by the game and communicated to Baudolino any vague and curious information they found, leafing through codices, that might waft an aroma of India's incenses. Abdul suddenly had the idea that his distant princess, if she had to be distant, should conceal her splendor in that most distant land of all.

"Yes," Baudolino replied, "but where do you go to reach India? It shouldn't be far from the Earthly Paradise, and thus east of the Orient, just where the land ends and the Ocean begins. . . ."

They had not yet begun the course of lessons in astronomy, and on the question of the earth's shape their ideas were hazy. The Poet was still convinced that it was a long, flat expanse, at the ends of which the waters of the Ocean poured down, God knows where. To Baudolino, on the contrary, Rahewin had said—though with some skepticism—that not only the great philosophers of antiquity, or Ptolemy, father of all astronomers, but also Saint Isidore had asserted that the earth was a sphere; indeed, Isidore had such Christian assurance of this that he had even established the breadth at the equator: eighty thousand stadia. However, Rahewin cautiously added that it was equally true that certain Fathers, like the great Lactantius, had recalled that according to the Bible the earth had the shape of a tabernacle, and therefore land and sky together should be seen as an ark, a temple with its fine dome and its floor, a large box, in other words, not a ball.

Prudent man that he was, Rahewin held to what Saint Augustine had said, that maybe the pagan philosophers were right and the earth was round, and the Bible had mentioned tabernacle in a figurative sense, but the fact of knowing how it was shaped did not help resolve the one serious problem of every good Christian, namely, how to save one's soul, and therefore devoting even just a half hour to ponder the shape of the earth was a total waste of time.

"That seems right to me," said the Poet, who was in a hurry to go to the tavern, "and it's useless to seek the Earthly Paradise, because it must have been a marvel of hanging gardens, and it has remained un-inhabited since the time of Adam, nobody has taken the trouble to reinforce the terraces with hedges and palisades, and during the flood it must all have slid down into the Ocean."

Abdul, on the contrary, was absolutely certain that the earth was a sphere. If it were just a flat expanse, he argued with undoubting severity, my gaze—which my love makes very acute, like that of all lovers—would be able to glimpse far, far away, some sign of the presence of my beloved, but instead the curve of the earth conceals her from my desire. And he ransacked the library of Saint Victoire to find maps that he then reconstructed summarily, from memory, for his friends.

"The earth is in the center of the great chain of the Ocean, and it is divided by three great bodies of water: the Hellespont, the Mediterranean, and the Nile."

"Just a moment: where's the Orient?"

"Up here, naturally, where there's Asia, and at the far end of the Orient, just where the sun rises, is the Earthly Paradise. To the left of Paradise there's Mount Caucasus, and nearby the Caspian Sea. Now bear in mind: there are three Indias: an India Major, which is very hot, just to the right of Paradise; a Northern India, beyond the Caspian Sea, another here, in the upper left, where it is so cold that the water turns to crystal, and where there are the peoples of Gog and Magog,

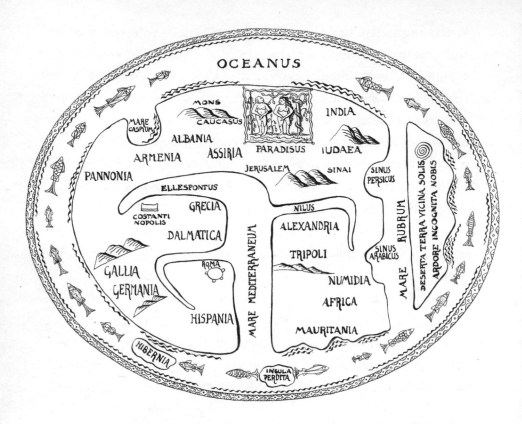

whom Alexander the Great imprisoned inside a wall; and finally a Temperate India, close to Africa. An Africa you see in the lower right-hand corner, where the Nile flows, and where the Arabian Sea opens and the Persian Gulf, just on the Red Sea, beyond which there is desert land, very close to the sun of the equator and so hot that no one can venture there. To the west of Africa, near Mauretania, are the Isles of the Blest or the Lost Isle, which was discovered many centuries ago by a saint from my country. Below, to the north, is the land where we live, with Constantinople on the Hellespont, and Greece, and Rome, and in the extreme north the Germanians and the Hibernian Island."

"But how can you take such a map seriously," the Poet snickered, "when it shows the earth flat, and you claim it's a sphere?"

"What kind of argument is that?" Abdul was indignant. "Could you depict a sphere in such a way that you could see everything on it?

A map must serve to point out the way, and when you walk, you see the earth flat, not round. Besides, even if it's a sphere, all the part underneath is uninhabited, and occupied by the Ocean, for if anybody were to live there he'd be living with his feet up and his head down. So to depict the upper part, a circle like this is enough. But I want to examine better the maps of the abbey, also because in the library I met a cleric who knows everything about the Earthly Paradise."

"Of course. He was there when Eve was giving the apple to Adam," the Poet said.

"You don't have to be in a place in order to know everything about it," Abdul replied. "Otherwise sailors would be more learned than theologians."

This, Baudolino explained to Niketas, showed how, ever since their first years in Paris, when they were still almost beardless, our friends had begun to be gripped by this story, which so many years later would take them to the far ends of the earth.

7

Baudolino makes the Poet
write love letters and poems to Beatrice

In the spring, Baudolino discovered that his love was growing greater and greater, as happens to lovers in that season, and it was not allayed by the squalid encounters with maids of no importance, indeed in comparison it grew gigantic, because Beatrice, besides the advantages of grace, intelligence, and royal anointment, had also the advantage of absence. The fascination of absence was a question with which Abdul never ceased tormenting him, spending whole evenings stroking his instrument and singing more songs, until, fully to appreciate them, Baudolino had by now also learned Provençal.

> And when the days are long in May
> How sweet to hear the distant birdsong,
> Because, since this journey first began,
> I recall forever that distant love.
> In my pain I bow my head
> Nor does song ease me more, and the hawthorn...

Baudolino dreamed. Abdul despairs of seeing one day his unknown princess, he said to himself, O happy he! Worse is my suffering, for surely I will have to see my beloved again one of these days, and I haven't the good fortune never to have seen her, but rather the misfortune of knowing who and what she is. But if Abdul finds consolation in telling his grief to us, why should I not find the same in telling my life to her? In other words, Baudolino sensed that he could discipline the throbbing of his heart by writing down on paper what he felt, and so much the worse if the object of his love would be deprived of these treasures of tenderness. So, late in the night, while the Poet was sleeping, Baudolino wrote.

"*The star illuminates the pole, and the moon colors the night. But my guide is a sole star and if, when the shadows have been dispelled, my star rises from the East, my mind will ignore the shadows of sorrow. You are my radiant star, who will dispel the night, and light itself without you is night, whereas with you night is splendid radiance.*"

And he went on: "*If I feel hunger, only you sate me; if I feel thirst, only you quench it. But what am I saying? You refresh, but do not satiate. Never have I been sated with you, nor shall I ever be. . . .*" And then: "*So great is your sweetness, so wondrous your constancy, so ineffable the tone of your voice, such the beauty and the grace that crown you, that it would be a great offense to attempt to express them in words. May the fire that consumes us grow always, and with new fuel, and the more it remains hidden, the more it will flare up and deceive the envious and the treacherous, so that the question will ever remain: which of us two loves the more, and so between us there will always be joined a beautiful duel in which both are victorious. . . .*"

The letters were beautiful, and rereading them, Baudolino trembled, and was ever more enchanted by a creature capable of inspiring such ardor. At a certain point he could no longer accept not knowing how Beatrice would have reacted to such sweet violence, and he decided to impel her to reply. Trying to imitate her hand, he wrote:

"*To the love that rises from the heart of my heart, that is more sweetly fragrant than any perfume, she who is yours body and soul, for the thirsting flowers of your youth, wishes the freshness of an eternal*

happiness.... *To you, my happy hope, I offer my faith, and with all de-*
votion I offer myself, for as long as I may live...."

"*Oh,*" he immediately replied to her, "*be well, for in you lies all my*
health, in you are my hope and my repose. Even before I am fully awake,
my soul finds you again, preserved within itself...."

And she answered, boldly: "*From that first moment when we saw*
each other, I have loved you before all others; preferring you, I have
wanted you; wanting you, I have sought you; seeking you, I have found
you; finding you, I have loved you; loving you, I have desired you; desir-
ing you, I have set you in my heart above all else ... and I have savored
your honey ... I greet you, my heart, my body, my only joy...."

This correspondence, which lasted for some months, gave, first,
refreshment to Baudolino's exacerbated soul, then a replete happiness, and finally a kind of blazing pride, because the lover had not realized how the beloved could love him so much. Like all those in love,
Baudolino became vain, like all those in love, he wrote that he wanted to
enjoy jealously with his beloved their shared secret, but at the same time
he insisted that the whole world be informed of his joy, and be stunned
by the immeasurable loving nature of the woman who loved him.

So one day he showed the correspondence to his friends. He was
vague and reticent about the manner and identity of this exchange.
He did not lie; indeed he said he was showing those letters precisely
because they were the fruit of his imagination. But the other two believed that, only and precisely in this instance, he was lying, and they
envied his lot all the more. In his heart Abdul attributed the letters to
his princess, and he agonized as if he had received them himself. The
Poet, who made a show of attaching no importance to this literary
game (though it gnawed at his heart that he himself had not written
such beautiful letters, provoking replies even more beautiful), and
having no one with whom to fall in love, had fallen in love with the
letters themselves—which, as Niketas remarked with a smile—was
not surprising, since in youth we are prone to fall in love with love.

Perhaps to find new themes for his songs, Abdul jealously copied the letters, to reread them at night in Saint Victoire. Then one day he realized that someone had stolen them from him, and he feared that by now some dissolute canon, after having lubriciously spelled them out at night, had thrown them among the thousand manuscripts of the abbey. Shuddering, Baudolino locked his correspondence in his trunk, and from that day on he wrote no further missives, so as not to compromise his correspondent.

Having, in any case, to release his adolescent fervor, Baudolino then took to writing verses. While in the letters he had spoken of his wholly pure love, in these new writings he practiced that tavern poetry with which the clerics of the period vaunted their dissolute and carefree life, not without some melancholy reference to their wasting of it.

Wishing to give Niketas evidence of his talent, he recited a few hemistichs:

> *Feror ego veluti—sine nauta navis,*
> *ut per vias aeris—vaga fertus avis...*
> *Quidquit Venus imperat—labor est suavis,*
> *quae nunquam in cordibus—habitat ignavis.*

Realizing that Niketas did not clearly understand the Latin, he made a rough translation: "I am derelict like a ship without a helmsman, like a bird along the pathways of the sky.... But what pleasant toil it is to obey the commands of Venus, unknown to common souls."

Baudolino showed these and other verses to the Poet, who flushed with envy and shame, and wept, confessing the aridity that dried up his imagination, cursing his impotence, shouting that he would have preferred not to know how to penetrate a woman than to find himself so incapable of expressing what he felt inside—and that it was exactly what Baudolino had expressed so well, making the Poet wonder if his friend had not read his heart. Then he observed how proud his father would be if he were able to compose such beautiful verses, for one day or another he would have to justify to his family and to the world the acquired nickname of Poet, which, while it flattered him, made him feel a *poeta gloriosus*, a braggart, who steals a dignity that is not his.

Seeing him in such despair, Baudolino pressed the parchment between the youth's hands, offering him the poems so he could display them as his own. A precious gift, because it so happened that Baudolino, to have something new to tell Beatrice, had actually sent her the verses, attributing them to his friend. Beatrice had read them to Frederick. Rainald of Dassel, a lover of literature, though always taken up with palace intrigues, heard them and said he would like to have the Poet in his service. . . .

In that same year Rainald was raised to the lofty office of archbishop of Cologne; and to the Poet the notion of becoming official poet to an archbishop and thus, as he put it, half-joking and half-swaggering, the archpoet, did not displease him, not least because he had very little desire to study; the paternal funds in Paris never sufficed, and he had got the idea—not mistaken—that a court poet ate and drank all day long without a thought for anything else.

But to be a court poet you have to write poems. Baudolino promised to write at least a dozen for him, but not all at once. "You see," he said, "great poets are not always diarrhoic, sometimes they're styptic, and those are the greater ones. You must seem tormented by the Muses, able to distill only one couplet every now and then. With the ones I'll give you, you can keep going for quite a few months, but allow me some time, because while I'm not styptic, I'm not diarrhoic either. So postpone your departure and send a few verses to Rainald, to whet his appetite. For the present it's a good idea for you to introduce yourself with a dedication, a eulogy of your benefactor.

He thought about it all one night, then gave the Poet some verses for Rainald:

> *Presul discretissime—veniam te precor,*
> *morte bona morior—dulci nece necor,*
> *meum pectum sauciat—puellarum decor,*
> *et quas tacto nequeo—saltem chorde mechor.*

Which is to say: "Most noble bishop, forgive me, for I face a happy death and am consumed by such a sweet wound: maidens' beauty pierces my heart, and those whom I cannot touch, I possess at least in my thoughts."

Niketas remarked that Latin bishops found pleasure in things that were not very holy, but Baudolino told him that he should first understand what a Latin bishop was: it was not required that he necessarily be a sainted man, especially if he was also chancellor of the empire. And second, who Rainald was: a little bit bishop and very much chancellor, certainly a lover of poetry, but still more inclined to use a poet's talents also for his own political ends, as he would subsequently do.

"And so the Poet became famous thanks to your verses."

"That's right. For almost a year the Poet sent Rainald letters overflowing with devotion, accompanying verses that I wrote for him from time to time. Finally Rainald insisted that this unusual talent should join him at any price. The Poet set off with a good provision of verses, enough to supply him for at least a year, however styptic he might seem. It was a triumph. I've never understood how anyone can be proud of a fame received as alms from another, but the Poet was content."

"Speaking of amazement: I ask myself what pleasure you can have felt, seeing your creations attributed to someone else. Isn't it atrocious that a father should give away, as alms, the fruit of his loins?"

"The fate of a tavern poem is to pass from one mouth to another: it is happiness to hear it sung, and it would be egoism to want to exhibit it only to increase one's own glory."

"I don't believe you're that humble. You are happy to have been once again the Prince of Falsehood, and you flaunt it, just as you hope that one day someone will find your love letters among the jumble of papers in Saint Victoire and attribute them to God knows whom."

"I don't mean to seem humble. I like making things happen, and to be the only one who knows they are my doing."

"The question doesn't change, my friend," Niketas said. "Indulgently, I suggested you wanted to be the Prince of Falsehood, and now you make me realize you would like to be God Almighty."

8

Baudolino in the Earthly Paradise

Baudolino was studying in Paris but he kept abreast of what was happening in Italy and in Germany. Rahewin, obeying the orders of Otto, had continued writing the *Gesta Friderici*; but, having now reached the end of the fourth book, he had decided to stop, because it seemed to him blasphemous to exceed the number of the Gospels. He left the court, satisfied, his duty done, and was dying of boredom in a Bavarian monastery. Baudolino wrote him of his free access to the endless library of Saint Victoire, and Rahewin asked him to indicate a few rare treatises that could enhance his knowledge.

Sharing Otto's opinion of the poor canon's scant imagination, Baudolino considered it useful to nourish it a bit. After sending him a few titles of codices he had seen, he also mentioned others of his own invention, such as *De optimitate triparum* of the Venerable Bede, an *Ars honesti petandi*, a *De modo cacandi*, a *De castramentandis crinibus*, and a *De patria diabolorum*—all works that provoked the amazement and the curiosity of the good canon, who hastened to ask for copies of these unknown treasures of learning. A service that Baudolino would have done him willingly, to heal his remorse for the parchment of Otto that he had scraped, but he simply did not know what to copy, and he had to invent the excuse that those works were, indeed, in the abbey of Saint Victoire, but were in odor of heresy and the canons would not allow anyone to see them.

"Then I learned," Baudolino said to Niketas, "that Rahewin had written to a Parisian scholar, begging him to ask the Victoriens for those manuscripts, but the scholars obviously found no trace of them. They accused their librarian of negligence, and the poor man had to swear that he had never seen them. I imagine, in the end, some canon, to put matters right, really did compose those texts and I hope that someday someone will come upon them."

Meanwhile, the Poet kept him informed of the exploits of Frederick. The Italian communes were not keeping faith with all the oaths they had sworn at the Diet of Roncaglia. According to the pacts, the unruly cities were to demolish their walls and destroy their war machines; but instead the citizens pretended to fill in the moats around the cities, and the moats were still there. Frederick sent envoys to Crema, to enjoin them to act quickly, and the people of Crema threatened to kill the imperial envoys, who would really have been killed if they hadn't run off. Then to Milan they actually sent Rainald and a Palatine count, to name the podestà, because the Milanese could not claim to acknowledge the imperial rights and then elect their consuls on their own. And there, too, both envoys nearly lost their skins, and they were no ordinary messengers, but the chancellor of the empire and one of the counts of the Palace! Still not content, the Milanese besieged the castle of Trezzo and put the garrison in chains. Finally, they again attacked Lodi, and when they touched Lodi, the emperor flew into a blind rage. And so, to set an example, he lay siege to Crema.

In the beginning the siege proceeded according to the rules of a war among Christians. The Cremasques, helped by the Milanese, made some good sorties and captured many imperial prisoners. The Cremonese (who in their hatred of Crema were then siding with the empire, along with Pavia and Lodi) built very powerful war machines— which had cost the life of more besiegers than of besieged, but that is the way things went. There were fine clashes, as the Poet recounted with gusto, and everyone recalled how the emperor made the Lodigiani give him two hundred empty hogsheads, which were then filled with earth and wood the Lodigiani had brought in more than two thousand wagons, so that it was possible to pass with the *magli,* the so-called cats, to hammer at the walls.

But when they attacked with the greatest of the wooden towers, one built by the Cremonesi, and the besieged began catapulting so many stones that the tower risked collapse, the emperor lost his head in his great fury. He ordered some Crema and Milanese prisoners brought, and had them bound to the front and sides of the tower. He thought that the besieged, seeing before them their brothers, cousins, sons, and fathers, would not dare shoot. He failed to calculate the great fury of the Cremasques—both those on the walls and those bound outside them. It was the latter who shouted to their brothers not to give in, and those on the walls, clenching their teeth, tears in their eyes, executioners of their own kin, continued assailing the tower, killing nine of their people.

Milanese students arriving in Paris swore to Baudolino that some children had also been tied to the tower, but the Poet assured him that the rumor was false. The fact remains that at this point even the emperor was affected, and ordered the other prisoners to be untied. But Cremasques and Milanese, maddened by their comrades' end, brought Lodigiani and Alaman prisoners from the city, placed them on the ramparts, and killed them in cold blood before Frederick's eyes. He then ordered two Crema prisoners carried below the walls and, below the walls, he tried them as perjurers and traitors, sentencing them to death. The Crema leaders sent word that if Frederick hanged their men, they would hang any men of his they were still holding hostage. Frederick replied that he would like to see them do that, and he hanged the two prisoners. The only reply of the Crema men was to hang *coram populo* all their hostages. Frederick, who by now had lost the power of reason, had all the Cremaschi he still held brought out, ordered a forest of gallows to be raised before the city, and was about to hang them all. Bishops and abbots rushed to the scene of the torture, begging him, who should be the fountainhead of mercy, not to emulate the wickedness of his enemies. Frederick was touched by this intervention, but he could not take back his assertion, hence he decided to execute at least nine of those unfortunates.

Hearing these things, Baudolino wept. He was by nature a man of peace, and the idea that his beloved adoptive father had stained himself with such crimes convinced him to remain in Paris to study and, in a very obscure way, without his realizing it, persuaded him that it was not unlawful to love the empress. He resumed writing letters, more and more impassioned, and replies that would make a hermit yearn. Only now he no longer showed anything to his friends.

Still feeling guilty, he resolved to do something for the glory of his master. Otto, as a sacred bequest, had left him the task of bringing Prester John forth from the shadows of hearsay. So Baudolino devoted himself to the search for the Priest, unknown, and yet, as Otto had testified, surely notorious.

Having completed the years of trivium and quadrivium, Baudolino and Abdul had been educated in disputation, so first of all they asked themselves: Does a Prester John really exist? But they began asking themselves this question in circumstances that Baudolino was reluctant to explain to Niketas.

After the Poet left, Abdul now lived with Baudolino. One evening coming home, he found Abdul alone, singing a beautiful song, in which he dreamed of meeting his distant princess, but as she drew closer, he seemed to be receding. Baudolino wondered whether it was the music or the words, as the image of Beatrice, which had appeared to him with the song, faded from his gaze into the void. Abdul sang, and never had his singing seemed so seductive.

The song came to an end. Abdul fell back, exhausted. For a moment Baudolino feared the boy was going to faint. He bent over him, but Abdul raised a hand, as if in reassurance, and laughed softly for no reason. His whole body trembled, as if he had a fever. Still laughing, Abdul asked to be left alone; he would calm down, he knew well what was happening. Pressed by Baudolino's questions, he finally decided to confess his secret.

"Listen, my friend. I have eaten a little green honey, just a little. I know it's a diabolical temptation, but sometimes I need it, to sing. Listen, and don't reproach me. In early childhood in the Holy Land I heard a marvelous and terrible story. It was said that not far from Antioch there lived a race of Saracens, dwelling among the mountains in a castle that only the eagles could reach. Their lord was named Aloadin and he inspired the greatest fear in the Saracen princes, and in the Christian as well. In fact, in the center of his castle, according to the story, there was a garden full of every kind of fruit and flower, where little canals flowed, filled with wine or milk or honey and water, and all around danced maidens of incomparable beauty. In the garden only certain youths could live, whom Aloadin had ordered abducted, and in that place of delights he trained them only to pleasure. And I say pleasure because, as I heard my elders whisper—and, disturbed, I would blush—those maidens were generous and ready to satisfy those guests, procuring them ineffable joys, also debilitating, I imagine. So, naturally, those who entered that place would never want to leave it, not at any price."

"No fool, your Aloadin, or whatever he was called." Baudolino smiled as he passed a moist cloth over his friend's brow.

"You think that," Abdul said, "because you don't know the whole story. Some fine morning one of these youths woke up in a sordid, sun-filled yard, where he found himself in chains. After a few days of suffering, he was brought into Aloadin's presence; he threw himself at the master's feet, threatening suicide and imploring to be restored to the delights without which he could no longer live. Aloadin then revealed to the youth that he had fallen into disfavor with the prophet and could regain favor only if he declared himself willing to carry out a great mission. Aloadin gave him a golden dagger and told him to set forth, to journey to the court of a certain lord, Aloadin's enemy, and kill him. In this way the youth would gain what he wished, and if he were to die in the enterprise, he would be raised into Paradise, in every way identical with the place from which he had been excluded, or if anything, still better. And this is why Aloadin had very great power and frightened all the princes in the region, whether Moors or Christians, because his messengers were prepared for any sacrifice."

"Then," Baudolino commented, "better one of these fine taverns in Paris, and their girls, whom you can have without paying a forfeit. But what does this story have to do with you?"

"This. When I was ten years old I was carried off by Aloadin's men. And I remained there for five years."

"And at the age of ten you enjoyed all those maidens you're telling me about? And then you were sent to kill somebody? Abdul, what are you saying?" Baudolino was worried.

"I was too little to be admitted immediately to the company of the happy youths, so I was assigned as a servant to a eunuch of the castle who supervised their pleasures. But hear what I discovered: for five years I never saw any gardens, because the youths were always chained all together in that sun-baked yard. Every morning the eunuch took from a certain cupboard some silver pots that contained a paste as thick as honey, but of a greenish color; he passed in front of each of the prisoners and fed him that substance. They tasted it and began to recount to themselves and to the others all the delights listed in the legend. You understand? They spent the day with eyes open, smiling, blissful. Towards evening they felt tired, they began to laugh, sometimes softly, sometimes raucously, then they would fall asleep. So, as I slowly grew, I understood the deceit to which they were subjected by Aloadin: they lived in chains, with the illusion that they were living in Paradise, and rather than lose this bliss, they became the instruments of their master's vengeance. If they returned safe from their missions, they were put in chains again, but they began again to see and feel the dreams produced by the green honey."

"And you?"

"One night, while the others were sleeping, I sneaked into the place where they kept the silver pots of green honey, and I tasted it. Taste, did I say? I gulped down two spoonfuls and I began to see wondrous things...."

"Did you feel you were in the garden?"

"No. Maybe the others dreamed of the garden because, when they arrived, Aloadin told them about the garden. I believe the green honey makes you see what you want from the bottom of your heart. I found myself in the desert, or, rather, in an oasis, and I saw a splendid caravan arriving, the camels all decked with plumes, and a host of Moors with colored turbans, beating on drums and clashing cymbals. Behind them, on a baldachin carried by four giants, there she was, the princess. I can't tell you what she was like, she was so . . . how can I say it? . . . so dazzling that I recall only the dazzle, a dazzling splendor...."

"But what was her face like? Was she beautiful?"

"I didn't see her face; she was veiled."

"But . . . then whom did you fall in love with?"

"With her, because I couldn't see her. In my heart, here—you understand?—there was an infinite sweetness, a languor that has never since died. The caravan moved off towards the dunes, and I realized that the vision would never again return. I told myself that I should have followed that creature, but towards morning I began to laugh, with what I believed was joy, while it was the effect of the green honey when its power dies. When I woke the sun was already high, and the eunuch almost caught me still dozing in that place. Since then I have told myself that I should have fled, to find again the distant princess."

"But you realized it was only the effect of the green honey..."

"Yes, the vision was an illusion, but what I now felt inside was not; it was true desire. When you feel it, it's not an illusion. It's real."

"But it was the desire of an illusion."

"By then I wanted never to lose that desire. It was worth devoting my life to it."

Abdul eventually managed to find an avenue of escape from the castle, and to rejoin his family, who had by then given him up for lost. Concerned about the revenge of Aloadin, Abdul's father sent him away from the Holy Land, to Paris. Before fleeing from Aloadin, Abdul had seized one of the pots of green honey, but, as he explained to Baudolino, he had never tasted it again, for fear that the cursed substance would carry him back to that same oasis, to relive infinitely his ecstasy. He was not sure he could bear the emotion. At this point the princess was with him, and nobody could take her away from him. Better to dream of her as a goal than to possess her in a false memory.

Then, as time went on, to find strength for his songs, in which the princess appeared, present in her distance, he had ventured to taste the honey, just barely, on the tip of a spoon, only enough to sense the flavor on his tongue. He had some ecstasies of brief duration, and this is what he had done that evening.

Abdul's story fascinated Baudolino, and he was tempted by the possibility of having a vision, however brief, in which the empress would appear. Abdul could not deny him that taste. Baudolino sensed only a slight torpor, and the desire to laugh. But he felt his mind stimulated, and, curiously, not by Beatrice, but by Prester John. So he asked himself if the true object of his desire was not that inaccessible realm, more than the mistress of his heart. So it had been that night. Abdul, almost free of the effect of the honey, and Baudolino, slightly inebriated, had resumed discussing the Priest, posing for themselves the question of his existence. And as it seemed that the virtue of the green honey was to make tangible that which has never been seen, they decided the Priest did exist.

He exists, Baudolino decided, because there are no reasons opposing his existence. He exists, Abdul agreed, because a cleric had told him that, beyond the land of the Medes and the Persians, there are Christian kings who fight the pagans of those regions.

"Who is this cleric?" Baudolino asked eagerly.

"Boron," Abdul replied. And so it was that the next day they went out to find Boron.

He was a cleric of Montbéliard, who, a vagrant like his similars, was now in Paris (and a regular visitor to the library of Saint Victoire), and tomorrow he would be God knows where, because he seemed to pursue a plan of his own of which he never spoke with anyone. He had a great head with a mop of hair and eyes reddened from all his reading by lamplight, but he truly seemed an ark of learning. He fascinated them at this first meeting—in a tavern naturally—asking them subtle questions on which their teachers would have spent days and days of disputation. Can sperm freeze? Can a prostitute conceive? Does the sweat of the head stink more than that of other parts of the body? Do the ears flush when one feels shame? Does a man grieve more over the death of a beloved or over her marriage? Must nobles have drooping ears? Do the mad worsen during the full moon? The question that fascinated them most was that of the existence of the vacuum, on which Boron considered himself wiser than any other philosopher.

"The vacuum," Boron said, his tongue already thick, "does not exist, because nature has a horror of it. The fact that it does not exist is evident for philosophical reasons, because if it did exist it would be either substance or accident. It is not material substance, because otherwise it would be body and would occupy space, and it is not incorporeal substance, because otherwise, like the angels, it would be intelligent. It is not accident, because accidents exist only as attributes of substances. In the second place, the vacuum does not exist for physical reasons: take a cylindrical vessel..."

"But why," Baudolino interrupted, "are you so interested in demonstrating that the vacuum does not exist? What does the vacuum matter to you?"

"It matters. Yes, it matters. Because the vacuum can be either interstitial, that is, between one body and another in our sublunar world, or else extended, beyond the universe that we see, closed by the great sphere of the celestial bodies. If that were so, there could perhaps exist, within that vacuum, other worlds. But if it is demonstrated that the interstitial vacuum does not exist, all the more reason why the extended vacuum cannot exist."

"But what do you care whether other worlds exist?"

"I care. It matters. Because if they did exist, Our Lord should have sacrificed himself in each of them and in each he should have consecrated the bread and the wine. And hence the supreme object, which is testimony and evidence of that miracle, would not be unique, and there would be many copies of it. And what value would my life have if I did not know that, somewhere, there is a supreme object to be found again?"

"And what would this supreme object be?"

Here Boron tried to truncate the discussion. "That's my business," he said, "things that are not good for the ears of the profane. Let us speak of something else. If there were so many worlds there would have been so many first humans, so many Adams and so many Eves, who have committed original sin infinite times. And therefore there would be so many Earthly Paradises from which they were driven. Can you think that something sublime, like the Earthly Paradise, could exist in so many copies, as there exist so many cities with a river and a hill like that of Saint Geneviève? Only one Earthly Paradise exists, in a remote land; beyond the realm of the Medes and the Persians."

They had come to the core of the discussion, and they told Boron of their speculations about Prester John. Yes, Boron had heard a monk talk about this question of the Christian kings of the Orient. He had read the account of a visit, many years ago, by a patriarch of the Indies, to Pope Calixtus II. It told of the effort the pope had to make to understand his visitor, thanks to the extreme difference of language. The patriarch described the city of Hulna, where a river flows that originates in the Earthly Paradise, the Physon, which others call the Ganges; and where, on a mountain outside the city, stands the sanctuary containing the body of the apostle Thomas. This mountain was inaccessible because it rose in the center of a lake, but for eight days every year the waters of the lake withdraw, and the good Christians of the region can go and worship the body of the apostle, still intact as if he were not dead, but, rather, as the text described him, with a star's shining face, red hair falling to his shoulders, a beard, and garments that seemed just sewn.

"But nothing tells us that this patriarch is Prester John," Boron concluded cautiously.

"No, of course not," Baudolino replied, "but it tells us that for a long time there has been talk about some distant region, blessed and unknown. Listen to me: in his *Historia de duabus civitatibus,* my beloved Bishop Otto reported that a certain Hugo of Jabala once said that John, after defeating the Persians, tried to go to the aid of the Christians in the Holy Land, but was forced to stop on the banks of the Tigris because he had no vessels to carry his men across. So John lives beyond the Tigris. Am I right? But the great thing is that everyone must have known this even before Hugo spoke of him. Let's reread carefully what Otto wrote, and he did not write at random. Why should this Hugo have to explain to the pope the reasons John had been unable to assist the Christians of Jerusalem; why should Hugo have to justify John? Obviously because in Rome there were those already nursing this hope. And when Otto says that Hugo mentions John, he adds *sic enim eum nominare solent,* as they generally called him. Why did he use this verb in the plural? Clearly not only Hugo but also others *solent,* are accustomed to, and hence already in those days that was what they called him. Further, Otto writes how Hugo affirms that John, like the Magi from whom he was descended, wanted to go to Jerusalem, but then Otto doesn't write that Hugo asserts John did not succeed, but, rather, that *fertur,* it is reported, and that some, others, in the plural, *asserunt*, assert that he did not succeed. We are learning from our masters that there is no better proof of the truth," Baudolino concluded, "than the continuity of the tradition."

Abdul whispered in Baudolino's ear that perhaps Bishop Otto also occasionally took a little green honey, but Baudolino jabbed an elbow into his ribs.

"I still don't understand why this priest is so important to you," Boron said, "but if he has to be sought, it must not be along a river that comes from the Earthly Paradise, but, rather, in the Earthly Paradise itself. And on this point I would have many things to say...."

Baudolino and Abdul tried to press Boron to tell them more about the Earthly Paradise, but Boron had abused the hogsheads of Les Trois Chandeliers, and said he could no longer remember anything. As if they had had the same thought and without saying a word to each other, the two friends grasped Boron under the armpits and carried him to their room. There, Abdul, though with some parsimony, offered their guest a touch of green honey, on the tip of a spoon, and they shared another drop. Boron, after remaining stunned for a moment, looking around as if unable to grasp precisely where he was, began to see something of Paradise.

He spoke, and he told of a certain Tugdalus, who seemed to have visited Hell and Paradise. The nature of Hell was not worth talking about, but Paradise was a place filled with charity, joy, gaiety, honesty, beauty, holiness, harmony, unity, charity, and eternity without end, defended by a golden wall beyond which you could discern many chairs decorated with precious stones, with men and women seated there, young and old, dressed in silken stoles, their faces glowing like the sun, with hair of purest gold, and all singing Alleluia, reading from a book illuminated with golden letters.

"Now," Boron said sensibly, "to Hell all can go, you have only to wish it, and sometimes those who have been there come back to tell us something of it, in the form of incubus or succubus, or some other troubling vision. But can you really believe that someone who has seen these things has been admitted to the Heavenly Paradise? Even if that had happened, no living person would have the immodesty to recount it, because there are some mysteries that a modest and virtuous person should keep to himself."

"God grant that never on the face of the earth such a person, corroded by vanity, appear," Baudolino commented, "to prove unworthy of the trust the Lord has bestowed on him."

"Now then," Boron said, "you must have heard the story of Alexander the Great, who arrived on the shore of the Ganges and supposedly reached a wall that followed the course of the river but had no gate, and after three days of sailing he saw in the wall a little window, at which an old man was looking out. The travelers asked that the city pay a tribute to Alexander, king of kings; but the old man replied that this was the city of the blest. It is impossible that Alexander, great king but a pagan, had arrived at the celestial city, and therefore what he and Tugdalus had seen was the Earthly Paradise. What I see at this moment..."

"Where?"

"There." And he pointed to a corner of the room. "I see a place where meadows extend, lovely and green, decked with flowers and scented grasses, while all around a sweet odor wafts, and, breathing it, I feel no more desire for food or for drink. There is a most beautiful lawn, with four men of venerable aspect, crowns of gold on their heads and palm fronds in their hands...I hear singing, I sense a balsamic aroma, O my God, I taste in my mouth a sweetness as of honey....I see a church of crystal, with an altar in its midst from which flows water white as milk. The church, from the north, seems a precious stone, on its austral side it is blood-colored, to the west white as snow, and above it shine countless stars more splendid than those in our sky. I see a man with hair white as snow, beplumed as a bird, his eyes almost indiscernible, covered as they are by snowy, drooping lashes. He points out to me a tree that never ages and cures of any ill one who sits in its shade, and another with leaves all the colors of the rainbow. But why am I seeing these things this evening?"

"Perhaps you have read of them somewhere, and the wine has brought them to the surface of your soul," Abdul said then. "That virtuous man who came from my island, Saint Brendan, sailed the seas to the farthest confines of the earth, and discovered an island all covered with ripe grapes, some blue, some purple, others white, with seven miraculous fountains and seven churches, one of crystal, another of garnet, the third of sapphire, the fourth of topaz, the fifth of ruby, the sixth of emerald, the seventh of coral, each with seven altars and seven lamps. And before the church, in the middle of a square, rose a column of chalcydon with, at its top, a turning wheel covered with rattles."

"Ah, no, mine is not an island." Boron flared up. "It's a land close to India, where I see men with ears larger than ours, and a double tongue, so that they can speak with two people at once. And many crops: it seems they grow spontaneously...."

"Of course," Baudolino glossed, "we must remember that according to Exodus the people of God were promised a land dripping with milk and honey."

"Let's not confuse things," Abdul said. "In Exodus it's the Promised Land, promised after the fall, whereas the Earthly Paradise was the land of our forefathers before the fall."

"Abdul, this isn't a *disputatio*. Here it's not a question of identifying a place where we will go, but of understanding the nature of the ideal place where each of us would like to go. It's obvious that if such marvels existed and still exist, not only in the Earthly Paradise but also on islands where Adam and Eve never set foot, the kingdom of Prester John must be very similar to those places. We are trying to understand what a kingdom of abundance and virtue is like, where falsehood does not exist, nor greed nor lust. Otherwise why should one be drawn to it as to the supreme Christian kingdom?"

"But there must be no exaggerating," Abdul wisely insisted. "Otherwise nobody would believe in it any more: I mean, nobody would believe any more that it is possible to go so far."

He said "far." Shortly before, Baudolino believed that, in imagining the Earthly Paradise, Abdul had forgotten, for one evening at least, his impossible passion. But no. He thought of it still. He was seeing the Paradise, but in it he was looking for his princess. In fact, he murmured, as the honey's effect slowly faded: "Perhaps one day we will go *langan li jorn long en mai,* you know, in May when the days are long...."

Boron began to laugh softly.

"There, Master Niketas," Baudolino said, "when I was not prey to the temptations of this world, I devoted my nights to imagining other worlds. A bit with the help of wine, and a bit with that of the green honey. There is nothing better than imagining other worlds," he said, "to forget the painful one we live in. At least so I thought then. I hadn't yet realized that, imagining other worlds, you end up changing this one."

"Let's try for the present to live serenely in this one, where the divine will has placed us," Niketas said. "Now that our incomparable Genoese have prepared for us some delicacies of our cuisine. Taste this soup of different varieties of fish, from fresh water and from the sea. Perhaps you have good fish also in your parts, though I imagine that your intense cold does not allow them to grow plentifully, as in the Propontis. We season the soup with onions cooked in olive oil, with fennel, and herbs, and two glasses of dry wine. You pour it on these slices of bread, and then you put in some *avgolemenos,* which is this sauce of egg yolks and lemon juice, diluted in a hint of broth. I believe that in the Earthly Paradise Adam and Eve ate like this. But before original sin. Afterwards, perhaps they resigned themselves to eating tripe, as in Paris."

9

Baudolino upbraids the emperor and seduces the empress

Baudolino, among his not very rigorous studies and his fantasies on the garden of Eden, had now spent four winters in Paris. He was eager to see Frederick again and, even more, Beatrice, who in his giddy spirit had now lost every earthly feature and had become an inhabitant of Paradise, like Abdul's distant princess.

One day Rainald asked the Poet to provide an ode to the emperor. The Poet, desperate, tried to gain time by saying to his master that he was awaiting proper inspiration, then sent off to Baudolino a request for help. Baudolino wrote an excellent poem, *Salve mundi domine,* in which Frederick was set above all other kings, and which said that his yoke was most sweet. But unwilling to entrust it to a messenger, he decided to return to Italy, where meanwhile many things had happened, which he had difficulty summing up for Niketas.

"Rainald had devoted his life to creating an image of the emperor as lord of the world, prince of peace, source of all law and subject to none, at the same time *rex et sacerdos,* like Melchizedek, and therefore he could not avoid conflict with the pope. Now, at the time of the siege of Crema, Hadrian, the pope who had crowned Frederick in Rome, died, and the majority of the cardinals elected Cardinal

Bandinelli as Alexander III. For Rainald this was a calamity, because with Bandinelli it was cats and dogs, and the new pope would not yield on the question of papal supremacy. I don't know what Rainald schemed, but he managed to ensure that some cardinals and people of the senate elected a different pope, Victor IV, whom he and Frederick could maneuver as they wished. Naturally Alexander III immediately excommunicated both Frederick and Victor, and it did not suffice to say that Alexander was not the true pope and thus his excommunication was worthless, because on the one hand the kings of France and England were inclined to recognize him, and on the other hand for the Italian cities it was an unexpected boon to find a pope who said that the emperor was a schismatic and hence no one owed him obedience. Further, news arrived that Alexander was plotting with your basileus Manuel, seeking support from an empire greater than Frederick's. If Rainald wanted Frederick to be the sole heir of the Roman empire, he had to find the visible proof of a lineage. That's why he had also set the Poet to work."

Niketas had some trouble following Baudolino's story, year by year. Not only did it seem to him that his narrator was a bit confused about what had happened before and what had happened after, but he also found that Frederick's exploits were repeated, always the same, and he could no longer understand when the Milanese had taken up arms again, when they had again threatened Lodi, or when the emperor had again come down into Italy. "If this were a chronicle," he said to himself, "it would suffice to take any page at random and you would find there the same deeds. It's like one of those dreams where the same story keeps recurring, and you long to wake up."

In any case it seemed to Niketas that for two years now the Milanese had created trouble for Frederick with spiteful acts and skirmishes, and the following year the emperor, with the support of Novara, Asti, Vercelli, the marquess of Monferrato, the Marquess Malaspina, the count of Biandrate, with Como, Lodi, Bergamo, Cremona, Pavia, and some others, had again laid siege to Milan. One fine spring morning Baudolino, now twenty, bearing his *Salve mundi domine* for the Poet, and his correspondence with Beatrice, which he would not leave in Paris at the mercy of thieves, arrived at the walls of that city.

"I hope that Frederick behaved better in Milan than at Crema," Niketas said.

"Even worse, according to what I heard on arriving. He had had the eyes gouged out of six prisoners from Melzo and Roncate, whereas with one Milanese he had torn out a single eye, so that the man could lead the others back to Milan, but in compensation he had cut off that prisoner's nose. And when he captured men trying to deliver provisions to Milan, he had their hands cut off."

"So you see? He also gouged out eyes."

"But with common people, not with lords, the way your rulers do. And they were his enemies, not his relatives!"

"Are you justifying him?"

"Now I am. Not then. Then I was outraged. I didn't want even to meet him. But I had to go and pay him homage; I couldn't avoid it."

The emperor, on seeing him after such a long time, was about to embrace him with great joy, but Baudolino was unable to control himself. He drew back, wept, said the emperor was wicked, that he couldn't claim to be the source of justice if he then acted unjustly, that he was ashamed of being his son.

If anyone else had said such things to him, Frederick would have ordered not only his eyes gouged and his nose cut off, but also his ears severed. Instead, he was impressed by Baudolino's ire; and he, the emperor, tried to justify himself. "It's rebellion, rebellion against the law, Baudolino, and you were the first to tell me that I am the law. I cannot pardon, I cannot be good. It is my duty to be merciless. You think I like it?"

"Yes, you like it, my father. Did you have to kill all those people two years ago at Crema and mutilate these others in Milan, not in battle, but in cold blood, for a question of pride, a vengeance, an affront?"

"Ah, you follow my actions as if you were Rahewin! Then let me tell you it was not a question of pride: it was an example. It's the only way to subdue these disobedient sons. Do you think that Caesar and Augustus were more clement? It's war, Baudolino; do you know what that is, you who act the great scholar? Do you, in Paris, realize that when you return here I will want you at court among my ministers, and perhaps I will even make you a knight? And do you think you will ride with the holy Roman emperor and not soil your hands? Does blood revolt you? Then tell me so and I'll have you made a monk. Then you'll have to be chaste, mind you, though I've been told stories about you in Paris that make it hard for me to see you as a religious. Where did you get that scar? I'm amazed that you have it on your face and not on your ass!"

"Your spies may have told you stories about me in Paris, but I, with no need of spies, have heard on all sides a fine story about you at Adrianople. Better my stories with Parisian husbands than yours with the Byzantine monks."

Frederick stiffened, and turned pale. He knew very well what Baudolino meant (the youth had heard it from Otto). When Frederick was still duke of Swabia, he had taken up the cross and participated in the second expedition to go to the aid of the Christian reign in Jerusalem. And as the Christian army was advancing, with great difficulty, near Adrianople, one of his noblemen, who had become separated from the expedition, was attacked and killed, perhaps by local bandits. There was already great tension between Latins and Byzantines, and Frederick took the incident as an affront. As at Crema, his wrath became uncontrollable; he attacked a nearby monastery and slaughtered all the monks.

The episode had remained a blot on Frederick's name; everyone pretended to forget it, and even Otto, in his *Gesta Friderici*, remained silent about it, mentioning instead immediately afterwards how the young duke escaped a violent flood not far from Constantinople—a sign that heaven had not revoked its protection. Frederick's pallor turned to a flush, he seized a bronze candlestick and flung himself on Baudolino as if to kill him. He barely restrained himself, lowering the weapon when he had already seized the youth by his coat, and said to him through clenched teeth: "By all the devils of Hell, never repeat what you have said." Before leaving the tent, he turned for an instant: "Go and pay homage to the empress, then back to your milksop clerics in Paris."

"I'll show you if I'm a milksop, I'll show you what I can do," Baudolino muttered, leaving the field. He did not know what he could do, yet he felt hatred towards his adoptive father and wanted to harm him.

Still furious, he reached Beatrice's quarters. He dutifully kissed the hem of her dress, then her hand. She was surprised by the scar, and asked anxious questions. Nonchalantly, Baudolino answered that there had been a brawl with some highway thieves. Such things happen when you travel the world. Beatrice looked at him with admiration, and it must be said that this twenty-year-old, with his leonine face made even more virile by the scar, was by now what you would call a fine figure of a knight. The empress bade him be seated and invited him to tell her of his latest deeds. As the empress, smiling, went on with her embroidery, sitting under a pretty canopy, he crouched at her feet and talked, on and on, not even knowing what he was saying, simply to calm his tension. Little by little, as he spoke, he noticed, glancing up, the beautiful face, and he felt again all the ardor of those years—multiplied a hundred times over—until Beatrice said to him, with one of her most seductive smiles: "You haven't written as much as I ordered you to, or as often as I would have wished."

Perhaps she said it with her usual sisterly solicitude, perhaps she wanted only to animate the conversation, but for Baudolino anything Beatrice said was at once balm and toxin. With trembling hands, he drew from his bosom his letters to her and hers to him and, holding them out to her murmured: "No. I have written, and very often, and you, my Lady, have answered me."

Beatrice did not understand. She took the pages, began to read them in a low voice in order better to decipher that double calligraphy. Baudolino, two paces from her, wrung his hands, sweating, told himself he was mad, that she would send him away, calling her guards. He wished he had a weapon to plunge into his heart. Beatrice continued reading, and her cheeks grew increasingly flushed, her voice trembled as she spelled out those inflamed words, as if she were celebrating a blasphemous Mass. She stood up, once, twice she seemed to sway. Twice she waved off Baudolino, who had risen to support her. Then in a faint voice she said only: "Oh, child, child, what have you done?"

Baudolino stepped closer, to take those pages from her hand, all atremble; she reached out to stroke the back of his neck; he turned his head aside because he was unable to look into her eyes; she stroked his scar with her fingertips. To avoid that touch, too, he again moved his head, but by now she had come closer, and they found themselves nose to nose. Baudolino put his hands behind his back, to prohibit himself an embrace, but now their lips had touched, and after touching they parted slightly, so for an instant, only one instant of the very few that the kiss lasted, through their parted lips their tongues also met.

As that swift eternity ended, Beatrice drew back, now white, as if ill, and, fixing Baudolino's eyes, harshly, she said to him: "By all the saints in Paradise, never do again what you have done."

She said this without wrath, almost without emotion, as if she were about to faint. Then her eyes became moist and she added, sweetly: "I beg you!"

Baudolino knelt, almost grazing the ground with his forehead, and left, with no conscious direction. Later he realized that in a single instant he had committed four crimes: he had offended the majesty of the empress, he had stained himself with adultery, he had betrayed the trust of his father, and he had given way to the insidious temptation of revenge. "Revenge, why?" he asked himself. "If Frederick had not committed that massacre, had not insulted me, and I had not felt

hatred in my heart, would I still have done what I did?" In trying not
to reply to this question, he realized that, if the answer were what he
feared, then he would have committed the fifth and most horrible of
sins: he would have indelibly besmirched the virtue of his idol only to
satisfy his rancor; he would have transformed the meaning of his existence into a sordid weapon.

"Master Niketas, this suspicion has accompanied me for many
years, even if I could never forget the heartrending beauty of that
moment. I was ever more in love, but this time with no hope, not
even in my dreams. Because if I wanted any kind of forgiveness, her
image had to vanish from my dreams, too. After all, I said to myself
during many long, sleepless nights, you have had everything, and you
can desire nothing else."

Night was falling on Constantinople, and the sky was no longer
reddening. The fire by now was dying out, and only on some city hills
could you see a glow, not of flames but of embers. Niketas meanwhile had ordered two cups of honeyed wine. Baudolino sipped it,
his eyes lost in the void. "It's wine from Thasos. Sweet, isn't it?" Niketas asked. "Very sweet," Baudolino replied, as he seemed to be thinking of other things. Then he set down the cup.

"That same evening," he concluded, "I forever renounced judging Frederick, because I felt more guilty than he. Is it worse to cut off
the nose of an enemy or to kiss the mouth of your benefactor's wife?"

The next day he went and asked his adoptive father's forgiveness
for the harsh words he had said, and he blushed on realizing that it was
Frederick who felt remorse. The emperor embraced him, apologizing
for his wrath, and saying that he preferred, to the hundred flatterers he
had around him, a son like this, capable of telling him when he was
wrong. "Not even my confessor has the courage to tell me that," Frederick said, smiling. "You are the only person I trust."

Baudolino began paying for his crime, with burning shame.

10

Baudolino finds the Magi and canonizes Charlemagne

Baudolino arrived at Milan when the Milanese were at the end of their strength, partly because of their internal arguments. In the end, they sent delegations to agree on the surrender, and the conditions were still those established by the Diet of Roncaglia, which meant that after four years, and with so many dead and such devastation, they were right where they had been four years earlier. But it was a surrender more shameful than the preceding one. Frederick would have liked again to grant his pardon, but Rainald, implacable, fanned the flames. A lesson had to be taught, which no one would ever forget, and the other cities had to be satisfied, those that had fought alongside the emperor, not out of love for him but out of hatred for Milan.

"Baudolino," the emperor said, "this time you mustn't oppose me. There are times when an emperor must do what his counselors want." And he added, lowering his voice: "That Rainald frightens me more than the Milanese."

So he ordered Milan erased from the face of the earth, and had everyone, men and women, sent out of the city.

The fields surrounding the city now teemed with Milanese roaming aimlessly about. Some sought refuge in neighboring cities, others remained encamped below the walls, hoping that the emperor would pardon them and allow them to go back inside. It was raining, the refugees shivered with cold during the night, the children fell ill, the men by now were disarmed, huddled along the edge of the roads, shaking their fists at the heavens, for it was wiser to curse the Almighty than the emperor, since the emperor had his men patrolling and demanding explanations for any violent lamentation.

Frederick had first tried to annihilate the rebel city by setting it on fire; then he had thought it better to leave the matter in the hands of the Italians, who hated Milan more than he did. He assigned the Lodi forces the task of destroying the whole quarter at the eastern gate known as Porta Renza, the Cremonesi were to destroy Porta Romana, the Pavese should raze to the ground Porta Vercellina, and the Comasques should destroy Porta Comacina, while the men of Seprio and Martesana should reduce Porta Nuova to a single ruin. The task greatly pleased the men of those cities, who indeed had paid the emperor much money to enjoy the privilege of settling with their own hands their scores with defeated Milan.

The day after the beginning of the demolition, Baudolino ventured inside the girdle of the walls. In certain places nothing could be seen, except a great dust cloud. Entering the cloud, he could discern here a group of men, who had tied heavy ropes to a façade, pulling in unison until it collapsed; there, expert masons on the roof of a church swinging their picks until the roof was gone, and then with great mallets breaking the walls, or uprooting the columns by inserting wedges at their base.

Baudolino spent a few days wandering through the convulsed streets; he saw the spire of the main church crumble, the most beautiful and mighty of all Italy. The most zealous were the Lodigiani, who sought only revenge: they were the first to demolish their assigned area, then they rushed to assist the Cremonesi in leveling Porta Romana. But the Pavesi seemed the most expert. They struck no random blows, and they controlled their rage: they scraped away the mortar wherever the stones were joined together, or else they dug at the foot of the walls until the rest collapsed.

In short, for anyone who did not understand what was going on, Milan seemed a merry workplace, where everyone labored with alacrity, praising the Lord. Except that it was as if time ran backwards: it seemed that from the void a new city was rising, when instead an ancient city was returning to dust and bare earth. Absorbed in these thoughts, Baudolino, on Easter day, when the emperor had decreed great celebrations in Pavia, hastened to discover the *mirabilia urbis Mediolani* while Milan still existed. So he happened to pass a splendid basilica still intact, and to see in the vicinity some Pavesi who were completing the demolition of a little palace, hard at work even on this holy day of obligation. He learned from them that this was the basilica of Sant'Eustorgio, and that the following day they would devote their attentions to it: "It's too beautiful to be left standing, isn't it?" one of the destroyers said to him persuasively.

Baudolino entered the nave of the basilica, cool, silent, and empty. The altars and the side chapels had already been demolished. Some dogs had arrived from God knows where to find this welcoming place, and had made it their inn, pissing at the base of the columns. Beside the main altar a cow roamed, moaning. She was a handsome animal, and Baudolino was led to ponder the hatred that drove the destroyers of the city to overlook such appetizing booty in their haste to level the city.

In a side chapel, beside a stone sarcophagus, he saw an old priest emitting sobs of despair, or, rather, chirps like a wounded animal; his face was whiter than the white of his eyes, and his wasted body twitched at every lament. Baudolino tried to help, offering him the flask of water he was carrying. "Thank you, good Christian," the old man said, "but now I can only wait for death."

"They won't kill you," Baudolino said to him. "The siege is over, the peace has been signed. Those men outside want only to knock down your church, not take your life."

"And what will my life be without my church? This is heaven's just punishment, because in my ambition, many years ago, I wanted my church to be the most famous and most beautiful of all, and I committed a sin."

What sin could that poor old man have committed? Baudolino asked him.

"Years ago an Oriental traveler suggested I buy from him the most splendid relics of Christianity, the uncorrupted bodies of the three Magi."

"The Magi? All three of them? Intact?"

"Three, Magi, and intact. They seem alive; that is, I mean they seem barely dead. I knew it couldn't be true, because the Magi are spoken of in only one Gospel, the Gospel of Matthew, and he says very little about them. He doesn't say how many there were, where they came from, whether they were kings or wise men.... He says only that they reached Jerusalem following a star. No Christian knows what their origin was or where they returned to. Who could have found their grave? For this reason I never dared tell the Milanese I was concealing this treasure. I was afraid that, out of greed, they would seize the opportunity to attract the faithful from all Italy, gaining money from a false relic...."

"Therefore you didn't sin."

"I sinned because I kept them hidden in this consecrated place. I kept waiting for a sign from heaven, and it did not come. Now I don't want these vandals to find them. They might divide up the treasure to confer an extraordinary dignity on some of the very cities that today are destroying us. Please, get rid of every trace of my past weakness. Seek help, come before evening and take away these dubious relics. With little effort you can surely win Paradise, and to me that seems no small thing."

"You see, Master Niketas, I remembered then that Otto had spoken to me about the Magi in connection with Prester John. To be sure, if that poor old priest had displayed them as if they had appeared from nowhere, nobody would have believed him. But does a relic, to be true, have to date back to the saint or to the event of which it was part?"

"No, of course not. Many relics that are preserved here in Constantinople are of very suspect origin, but the worshiper who kisses them perceives supernatural aromas wafting from them. It is faith that makes them true, not they who make faith true."

"Precisely. I also thought that a relic is valid if it finds its proper place in a true story. Outside the story of Prester John, those Magi could have been the trick of some rug merchant; within the true story of John they became genuine testimony. A door is not a door if it does not have a building around it; otherwise it would be only a hole—no, what am I saying?—not even a hole, because a void without something surrounding it is not a void. I understood then that I had the story in which the Magi could have a meaning. I thought that if I said something about Prester John to the emperor to lure him to the Orient, having the confirmation of the Magi, who surely came from the Orient, would support my argument. These poor three kings were asleep in their sarcophagus, letting the Pavesi and the Lodigiani tear to pieces the city that unwittingly housed them. They owed it nothing, they were only there in transit, as at an inn, waiting to go elsewhere; after all, they were rovers by nature—hadn't they set out from God knows where to follow a star? It was up to me to give those three bodies a new Bethlehem."

Baudolino knew that a good relic could change the fate of a city, cause it to become the destination of uninterrupted pilgrimage, transform a simple church into a shrine. Who might be interested in the Magi? Rainald came to mind: he had been given the archbishopric of Cologne, but he had still to go there for his official consecration. To enter one's own cathedral with the three Magi would be a great deed. Was Rainald looking for symbols of imperial power?

Here he had, within reach, not one but three kings, who had also been priests.

He asked the old man if he could see the bodies. The priest required Baudolino's help, because they had to shift the lid of the sarcophagus until they had uncovered the box in which the bodies were kept.

It was hard work, but it was worth it. O wonder! The bodies of the three kings seemed still alive, even though the skin had dried and become like parchment. But it had not darkened, as happens with mummified bodies. Two of the Magi had faces almost milky, one with a great white beard down to his chest, the beard still intact even if stiffened, like spun sugar; the second was beardless. The third was the color of ebony, not because of the passing of time, but because he must have had dark skin while still alive: he seemed a wooden statue, and even had a kind of crack in his left cheek. He had a short beard and a pair of fleshy lips, bared to reveal only two teeth, feral and white. All three were staring, their great, dazed eyes wide, the pupils glistening like glass. They were enfolded in cloaks, one white, one green, and one purple, and from the cloaks trousers emerged, in barbarian style, but of pure damask embroidered with rows of pearls.

Baudolino quickly returned to the imperial encampment, and rushed to speak with Rainald. The chancellor realized at once the value of Baudolino's discovery, and said: "It must all be done in secret, and quickly. We can't carry away the box; it would be too noticeable. If someone else here were to be aware of what you have found, he wouldn't hesitate to steal it from us, to take it to his own city. I'll have three coffins made, of plain wood, and during the night we'll carry them outside the walls, saying they contain the bodies of three dear friends fallen in the siege. There will be just you, the Poet, and a servant of mine. Then we'll leave them where we put them, without haste. Before I can take them to Cologne, authentic documentation will have to be produced, regarding the origin of the relics and of the Magi themselves. Tomorrow you will return to Paris, where you know learned people, and you will find out whatever you can about their story."

During the night the three kings were carried to a crypt in the church of San Giorgio, outside the walls. Rainald wanted to see them, and he then exploded in a series of imprecations unworthy of an archbishop: "With these breeches? And this cap that looks a jester's!"

"Lord Rainald, apparently this is how they dressed then, the wise men of the Orient. Years ago I was in Ravenna and I saw a mosaic where on the robe of the empress Theodora the three Magi are depicted more or less like this."

"Exactly. Things that can convince the Greeklings of Byzantium. But can you imagine me presenting myself in Cologne with the Magi dressed like buffoons? We must change their clothes."

"How?" the Poet asked.

"How? I've allowed you to eat and drink like a feudal lord for writing two or three verses a year, and you don't know how to dress those who first adored Our Lord Jesus Christ? Dress them the way people imagine they were dressed, like bishops, like a pope, an archimandrite. Do it!"

"The cathedral and the bishopric have been sacked. Maybe we can recover some holy vestments. I'll try," the Poet said.

It was a terrible night. The vestments were found, and also something resembling three tiaras, but the problem was to strip the three mummies. While the faces seemed still alive, the bodies—except the hands, totally desiccated—were reduced to a framework of withes and straw, which came apart at every attempt to remove the clothing. "No matter," Rainald said, "once the box is in Cologne, nobody will open it. Put some sticks inside, anything that will keep them straight, the way you do with scarecrows. With all due reverence, mind you."

"Dear Lord Jesus," the Poet complained, "even in my most

113

drunken state would I ever have imagined I'd be sticking anything up a Magi's ass?"

"Shut up and dress them," Baudolino said. "We're working for the glory of the empire." The Poet let out some horrible blasphemies, but the Magi finally looked like cardinals of the Holy Roman Apostolic Church.

The next day Baudolino set forth on his journey. In Paris, Abdul, who knew a great deal about matters of the Orient, put him in touch with a canon of Saint Victoire, who knew even more.

"Eh, the Magi!" he said. "Tradition refers to them constantly, and many of the Fathers have spoken of them, but three of the Gospels are silent on the subject, and the quotations from Isaiah and other prophets are unrevealing: some have read them as referring to the Magi, but they could have been referring to something else. Who were they? What were their real names? Some say Hormizd of Seleucia, king of Persia; Jazdegerd and Peroz, kings of Sheba. Others say Hor, Basander, Karundas. But according to other, highly credible authors, they are called Melkon, Gaspar, and Balthasar, or else Melco, Caspare, and Fadizzarda. Or even Magalath, Galgalath, and Saracin. Or perhaps Appelius, Amrus, and Damascus..."

"Appelius and Damascus are beautiful; they suggest distant lands," Abdul said, looking vaguely into space.

"And why not Karundas?" Baudolino rebutted. "We're not here to find three names that please you; we want three real names."

The canon continued: "I would tend towards Bithisarea, Melichior, and Gastapha: the first was king of Godolia and Sheba; the second, king of Nubia and Arabia; the third, king of Tharsis and the island of Egriseula. Did they know one another before undertaking the journey? No; they met in Jerusalem and miraculously recognized one another. But some say they were wise men who lived on Mount Victorial or Mount Vaus, from whose peak they studied the signs in the heavens, and to Mount Victorial they returned after the visit to

Jesus, and later they joined the apostle Thomas to evangelize the Indies, except that they were twelve, not three."

"Twelve Magi? Isn't that too many?"

"Even John Chrysostom says as much. According to others, their names would be Zhrwndd, Hwrmzd, Awstsp, Arsk, Zrwnd, Aryhw, Arthsyst, Astnbwzn, Mhrwq, Ahsrs, Nsrdyh, and Mrwdk. But you have to be careful, because Origen says that there were three of them, like the sons of Noah, and three like the three Indias from which they came."

"There may well have been twelve Magi," Baudolino remarked, "but in Milan three were found, and we have to construct an acceptable story based on three. Let's say they were called Balthasar, Melchior, and Caspar, which seem to me names more easily pronounced than those awful sneezes our venerable master emitted just now. The problem is: how did they arrive in Milan."

"It doesn't seem a problem to me," the canon said, "since they did arrive there. I'm convinced that their grave was found on Mount Victorial by Queen Helen, the mother of Constantine. A woman capable of finding the True Cross would also have been able to discover the true Magi. And Helen took the bodies to Constantinople, to Saint Sophia."

"No, no. Otherwise the emperor of the Orient will want to know how we took them away from him," said Abdul.

"Never fear," said the canon. "If they were in the basilica of Sant'Eustorgio, surely that sainted man had brought them there, when he set out from Byzantium to occupy the bishop's seat in Milan at the time of the emperor Mauritius, and long before Charlemagne lived in our land. Eustorgio couldn't have stolen the Magi, so he must have received them as a gift from the basileus of the empire of the Orient."

With such a well-constructed story, Baudolino returned at the year's end to Rainald, and reminded him that, according to Otto, the Magi were surely ancestors of Prester John, whom they had invested

115

with their dignity and function. Whence came the power of Prester John over all three Indias, or at least over one of them.

Rainald had completely forgotten those words of Otto, but on hearing mention of a priest who ruled over an empire, a king with priestly functions, pope and monarch at the same time, he was now convinced he had put Alexander III in difficulties: the Magi kings and priests; king and priest John: what a wondrous figure, allegory, augury, prophecy, herald of that imperial dignity that Rainald, step by step, was creating around Frederick!

"Baudolino," he said at once, "I'll deal with the Magi now; you must think about Prester John. From what you tell me, for the moment we have only rumors, and that's not enough. We need a document that will attest to his existence, that says who he is, where he is, how he lives."

"And where will I find that?"

"If you can't find it, make it. The emperor has allowed you to study, and this is the moment to put your talents to use. And to win yourself knighthood, just as soon as you have ended your studies, which, if you ask me, have gone on too long."

"You understand, Master Niketas?" Baudolino said. "Now Prester John for me had become a duty, not a game. And I was to seek him no longer in memory of Otto, but to obey an order of Rainald's. As my father, Gagliaudo, used to say, I've always been contrary by nature. If I'm ordered to do something, I promptly lose any desire to do it. I obeyed Rainald and went immediately back to Paris, but it was to avoid having to encounter the empress. Abdul had resumed writing songs, and I noticed the pot of green honey was now half empty. I talked to him again about the adventure of the Magi, and he strummed his instrument and chanted: *Let no one be amazed if I, you know—love her who will never see me—my heart knows no other love—except for what I have never seen—nor can any other joy make me laugh—and I know not what good will come to me—ha, ha.* Ha ha, I gave up arguing with him about my plans and, as far as Prester John was concerned, for about a year I did nothing more."

"And the Magi?"

"Rainald took the relics to Cologne two years later, but he was generous. Some time back he had been provost of the cathedral of Hildesheim, and so before sealing the remains of the kings in their box in Cologne, he had a finger cut from each one and sent them, as a donation, to his old church. However, in that same period, Rainald had to resolve other problems, and not small ones. Just two months before he could celebrate his triumph in Cologne, the antipope, Victor, died. Almost everyone heaved a sigh of relief: this would automatically put things back in order, and perhaps Frederick would have a reconciliation with Alexander. But it was that schism that kept Rainald alive. You understand, Master Niketas? With two popes he counted for more than with one pope. So he invented a new antipope, Paschal III, organizing a parody of a conclave with a few ecclesiastics he collected practically off the street. Frederick wasn't convinced. He said to me—"

"You had gone back to him?"

Baudolino sighed. "Yes, for a few days. In that same year the empress had borne Frederick a son."

"What did you feel?"

"I realized I had to forget her definitively. I fasted for seven days, drinking only water, because I had read somewhere that it purifies the spirit, and in the end provokes visions."

"Is that true?"

"Very true. But the visions were of her. Then I decided I had to see that baby, to establish the difference between the dream and the vision. So I went back to court. More than two years had gone by since that magnificent and awful day, and since then we had never seen each other. I told myself then that, even if I couldn't resign myself to loving Beatrice as a mother, I would consider that child a brother. But I looked at that little thing in the cradle, and I couldn't dispel the thought that, if matters had gone just a little differently, he could have been my son. In any case I still risked feeling incestuous."

Frederick meanwhile was troubled by quite different problems. He said to Rainald that half a pope was scant guaranty of his rights, that the Magi were all well and good, but they weren't enough, because having found the Magi did not necessarily mean being descended from them. The pope, lucky man, could trace his origins back to Peter, and Peter had been designated by Jesus himself, but what could the holy and Roman emperor do? Trace his origins to Caesar, who was, after all, a pagan?

Baudolino then pulled out the first idea that came into his head, namely, that Frederick could have his origins date back to Charlemagne. "But Charlemagne was anointed by the pope: so we're back where we started," Frederick replied.

"Unless you have him made a saint," Baudolino said. Frederick admonished him to think before he uttered nonsense. "It's not nonsense," replied Baudolino, who had not so much thought as visualized the scene that his idea could engender. "Listen: you go to Aix-la-Chapelle, to Charlemagne's tomb, you have his remains exhumed, you put them in a fine reliquary in the midst of the Palatine Chapel and, in your presence, with a suite of loyal bishops, including Master Rainald, who as archbishop of Cologne is also the metropolitan of that province, and with a bull from Pope Paschal that legitimizes you, you proclaim Charlemagne saint. You understand? You proclaim saint the founder of the holy Roman empire, once he is a saint he is superior to the pope, and you, as his legitimate successor, are of the race of a saint, freed from any authority, even that of one who claims to excommunicate you."

"By Charlemagne's beard!" Frederick said, the hairs of his own beard bristling with excitement. "Did you hear that, Rainald? As always, the boy's right!"

And so it happened, even though not until the end of the following year, because certain things require time if they are to be prepared properly.

Niketas observed that as an idea it was insane, and Baudolino answered that, nevertheless, it had worked. And he looked at Niketas with pride. It's only natural, Niketas thought; your vanity is boundless, you have even made Charlemagne a saint. From Baudolino anything could be expected. "And after that?" he asked.

"While Frederick and Rainald were preparing to canonize Charlemagne, little by little I realized that neither he nor the Magi were enough. All four of them were safely in Paradise; at least the Magi surely were, and we could hope for Charlemagne as well, otherwise at Aix-la-Chapelle we'd made a fine mess. But still it took something more, here on this earth, where the emperor could say, Here I am, and this sanctions my power. And the only thing the emperor could find on this earth was the kingdom of Prester John."

11

Baudolino constructs a palace for Prester John

On the Friday morning, three of the Genoese—Pevere, Boiamondo, and Grillo—came to confirm what could very clearly be
seen even from a distance: the fire had gone out, as if by itself, because nobody had taken much trouble to fight it. But this did not
mean they could now venture into Constantinople. On the contrary,
enabled to move more easily through the streets and squares, the pilgrims had intensified their search for wealthy citizens, and amid the
still-warm ruins they demolished what little remained standing,
searching for those treasures that had eluded the first looting. Niketas
sighed, disconsolate, and asked for some Samos wine. He also wanted
them to toast for him, in just a hint of oil, some sesame seeds that he
could chew slowly between sips, and then he asked also for some wal-
nuts and pistachios, the better to follow the story that he invited Baudolino to continue.

One day the Poet was sent by Rainald on some mission to Paris,
and he took advantage of the occasion to return to the delights of the
taverns with Baudolino and Abdul. He also met Boron, but those
fantasies about the Earthly Paradise seemed to hold little interest for
him. The years spent at court had changed him, Baudolino noted. He

had hardened; he never ceased clinking cups gaily, but he seemed to control himself, to shun excess, to remain on his guard, like someone lying in wait for his prey, ready to spring.

"Baudolino," he said one day, "you are wasting time. What was to be learned here in Paris, we have learned. But all these great doctors would shit in their pants if tomorrow I presented myself at a dispute in full ministerial regalia, with a sword at my side. At court I have learned a few things: if you are with great men, you also become great; great men in reality are very small; power is everything, and there is no reason why one day you could not seize it yourself, at least in part. You must know how to wait, of course, but not let your opportunity escape."

However, he promptly pricked up his ears when he heard that his friends were still talking about Prester John. When he had left them in Paris that story still seemed a fantasy of bookworms, but in Milan he had heard Baudolino speak of it to Rainald as of something that could become a visible sign of the imperial power, at least as much as the rediscovery of the Magi. The enterprise, in that case, would interest him, and he began taking part in it as if he were constructing a war machine. The more they talked about it, the more it seemed to him that the land of Prester John, like an earthly Jerusalem, was being transformed from a place of mystical pilgrimage to a land of conquest.

So he reminded his comrades that, after the Magi business, the Priest had become far more important than before: he had to be presented truly as *rex et sacerdos*. As king of kings he had to have a palace compared to which those of the Christian sovereigns, including the basileus of the Constantinople schismatics, would seem hovels, and as priest he had to have a temple compared to which the churches of the pope were shacks. He had to be given a worthy palace.

"There is a model," Boron said, "and it is the Heavenly Jerusalem as the apostle John saw it in the Apocalypse. It must be girded by high walls, with twelve gates, like the twelve tribes of Israel, to the south three gates, to the west three gates, to the east three gates, and to the north three gates...."

"Yes," the Poet jested, "and the Priest enters one and goes out the other, and when there is a storm they all slam at once; I can imagine the drafts. In a palace like that you would never find me, not even dead...."

"Let me continue. The foundations of the walls are of jasper, sapphire, chalcedony, emerald, sardonix, sard, chrysolite, beryl, topaz, chrysoprase, hyacinth, and amethyst; and the twelve gates are twelve pearls, and the forecourt is pure gold, transparent as glass."

"Not bad," Abdul said, "but I think the model must be the Temple of Jerusalem, as the prophet Ezekiel describes it. Come with me tomorrow morning to the abbey. One of the canons, the learned Richard of Saint Victoire, is trying to reconstruct the design of the Temple, since the text of the prophet is at times obscure."

"Master Niketas," Baudolino said, "I don't know if you've ever studied the measurements of the Temple."

"Not yet."

"Well, don't, because it's enough to drive you crazy. In the Book of Kings it says that the Temple is sixty cubits wide, thirty high, and twenty deep, and that the porch is twenty wide and ten cubits deep. In Chronicles, however, it is said that the porch is one hundred twenty cubits high. Now, if it were twenty wide, one hundred twenty high, and ten deep, not only would the porch be four times higher than all the Temple, but it would also be so flimsy that it would fall down at a mere breath. The problem, however, arises when you read the vision of Ezekiel. Not one measurement holds up, and so a number of pious men have admitted that Ezekiel had indeed had a vision, which is a bit like saying he had drunk too much and was seeing double. Nothing wrong with that, poor Ezekiel (he also had a right to his fun), but then that Richard of Saint Victoire reasoned as follows: if everything, every number, every straw in the Bible has a spiritual meaning, we must clearly understand what it says literally, because it's one thing to say, for the spiritual meaning, that something is three long and another's length is nine, since these two numbers have different mystical meanings. I can't describe to you the scene when we went to hear Richard's lecture on the Temple. He had the Book of Ezekiel before his eyes, and he was working with a tape to demonstrate all the measurements. He drew the outline of what Ezekiel had described, then he took some sticks and little slabs of soft wood, and, with the help of his acolytes, he cut them and tried to put them together with nails and glue.... He tried to reconstruct the Temple, and he reduced the measurements proportionally. What I mean is that where Ezekiel said one cubit, he had a finger's width cut. ... Every two minutes the whole thing collapsed. Richard became angry with his helpers, saying they had let go of the stick, or hadn't put on enough glue; they defended themselves, saying that he was the one who had given them the wrong measurements. Then the master corrected himself, saying that perhaps the text said *porta*, but in this case the word meant porch, otherwise there would be a door almost as big as the whole Temple; at other moments he reversed himself, and said that when two measurements didn't agree it was because the first time Ezekiel was referring to the dimension of the whole building and the second to the measurement of one part. Or else sometimes it said cubit but it meant geometric cubit, which is equal to six ordinary cubits. In other words, it was amusing for a few mornings to follow that sainted man as he racked his brains, and we burst out laughing every time the Temple came apart. To keep him from noticing, we pretended to pick up some fallen object, but then a canon realized we were always dropping things, and he sent us away."

In the days that followed, Abdul suggested that, as Ezekiel after all belonged to the people of Israel, perhaps others of his faith could shed some light. When his companions, shocked, said that it was not right to read the Scriptures while asking advice of a Jew, since notoriously that treacherous race altered the text of the sacred books to remove every reference to the coming of Christ, Abdul revealed that some of the greatest masters in Paris took advantage at times, though in secret, of the learning of the rabbis, at least for those passages where the coming of the Messiah was not involved. As luck would have it, in those very days, the Saint Victoire canons had invited to their abbey one such man, still young but of great reputation: Solomon of Gerona.

Naturally Solomon was not staying at Saint Victoire: the canons had found him a room, dark and fetid, in one of the shabbiest streets of Paris. He was, indeed, a young man, even though his face seemed haggard from meditation and study. He expressed himself in good Latin, but in an almost incomprehensible fashion, because he had a peculiar mouth: in the whole left side he had all his teeth, upper and lower, from the central incisor, but no teeth on the right side. Though it was morning, the darkness of the room obliged him to read with a burning lamp, and on the arrival of his visitors, he put his hands on a scroll he had before him as if to prevent others from peering at it— a futile precaution, because the scroll was written in Hebrew characters. The rabbi tried to apologize because, he said, that was a book that Christians rightly execrated, the ill-famed *Toledot Jeschu,* in which it was said that Jesus was the son of a courtesan and a mercenary, a certain Pantera. But the Saint Victoire canons themselves had asked him to translate a few pages, because they wanted to understand the extent of the Jews' perfidy. He said that he would undertake the task willingly because he also considered the book too severe, inasmuch as Jesus was surely a virtuous man, even if he had had the weakness to consider himself, wrongly, the Messiah, but perhaps he had been deceived by the Prince of Darkness, and even the Gospels admitted that the Prince had come to tempt him.

He was questioned about the form of the Temple according to Ezekiel, and he smiled: "The most alert commentators on the sacred text have not succeeded in establishing the exact structure of the Temple. Even the great rabbi Solomon ben Isaac admitted that, if you

124

follow the letter of the text, there is no understanding where the northern external chambers are, where they begin to the west, and how far they stretch to the east, and so on. You Christians do not understand that the sacred text is born from a Voice. The Lord, *ha-qadoch baruch hu,* that the Holy One, may his name always be blessed, when he speaks to his prophets, allows them to hear sounds, but does not show figures, as you people do, with your illuminated pages. The voice surely provokes images in the heart of the prophet, but these images are not immobile; they liquefy, change shape according to the melody of that voice, and if you want to reduce to images the voice of the Lord, blessed always be his name, you freeze that voice, as if it were fresh water turning to ice that no longer quenches thirst, but numbs the limbs in the chill of death.

"Canon Richard, to understand the spiritual meaning of each part of the Temple, would like to reconstruct it, as a master mason would do, and he will never succeed. Visions are like dreams, where things are transformed one into another, not like the images of your church, where things remain always the same."

Then Rabbi Solomon asked why his visitors wanted to know what the Temple was like, and they told him of their search for the kingdom of Prester John. The rabbi showed great interest. "Perhaps you do not know," he said, "that our texts also tell us of a mysterious kingdom in the Far East, where the scattered ten tribes of Israel still live."

"I have heard these tribes spoken of," Baudolino said, "but I know very little of them."

"It is all written. After the death of King Solomon, the twelve tribes into which Israel was then divided fell to fighting. Only two, that of Judah and that of Benjamin, remained loyal to the house of David, and ten whole tribes went north, where they were defeated and enslaved by the Assyrians. Of them nothing more was heard. Esdras says that they went towards a land never inhabited by man, in a region called Arsareth, and other prophets have announced that one day they would be found and would make a triumphal return to Jerusalem. Now, one of our brothers, Eldad of the tribe of Dan, more than a hundred years ago, arrived at Qayrawan, in Africa, where a community of the Chosen People exists, saying that he came from the kingdom of the ten lost tribes, a land blessed by heaven, where life is peaceful, never troubled by any crime, where truly the streams flow with milk and honey. This land has remained separated from every other country because it is defended by the river Sambatyon, which is as wide as the shot of the mightiest bow, but it is without water, and only sand and stones flow there furiously, making a noise so horrible that it can be heard even at the distance of a day's march, and that inanimate matter flows there so rapidly that anyone wishing to cross the river would be swept away by it. That stony course stops only at the beginning of the Sabbath, and only on the Sabbath can it be crossed, but no son of Israel could violate the Sabbath day of rest."

"But Christians could?" asked Abdul.

"No, because on the Sabbath a hedge of flames makes the banks of the river inaccessible."

"Then how did that Eldad reach Africa?" the Poet asked.

"This I do not know, but who am I to dispute the decrees of the Lord, the Holy One be he ever blessed? Men of little faith, Eldad may have been borne by an angel. The problem for our rabbis, who immediately began arguing about that account, from Babylon to Spain, was rather something else: if the ten lost tribes had lived by the divine law, their laws should have been the same as Israel's, whereas according to Eldad's story they were different."

"But if the kingdom Eldad tells of was the realm of Prester John," Baudolino said, "then its laws would truly be different from yours, but similar to ours, even better!"

"This is what divides us from you gentiles," Rabbi Solomon said. "You have the freedom to practice your law, and you have corrupted it, so you seek a place where it is still observed. We have kept our law intact, but we haven't the freedom to follow it. In any case, you should know that it would also be my desire to find that kingdom, because it could be that our ten lost tribes and the gentiles live there in peace and harmony, each free to follow his own law, and the very existence of that prodigious kingdom would be an example to all the children of the Almighty, may his Holy Name be always blessed. And further, I must tell you I would like to find that kingdom for another reason. According to what Eldad said, the Holy Language is still spoken there, the original language that the Almighty, blessed always be his name, had given to Adam, and which was lost with the construction of the tower of Babel."

"What folly," Abdul said. "My mother always told me that the language of Adam was reconstructed on her island, and it is the Gaelic language, composed of nine parts of speech, the same number as the nine materials from which the tower of Babel was built: clay and water, wool and blood, wood and mortar, pitch, linen, and bitumen. It was the seventy-two sages of the school of Phenius, who constructed the Gaelic language, using fragments of all the seventy-two tongues born after the confusion of tongues, and for this reason Gaelic contains what is best in every language, and since the Adamitic language has the same form as the created world, so each noun in it expresses the essence of the very thing it denotes."

Rabbi Solomon smiled indulgently. "Many nations believe that theirs is the language of Adam, forgetting that Adam could speak only the language of the Torah, not of those books that tell of false and lying gods. The seventy-two languages born after the great confusion are ignorant of fundamental letters: for example, the gentiles do not know the letter Het and the Arabs are unaware of Peh, and hence such languages resemble the grunting of swine, the croaking of frogs, or the cry of the crane, because they belong to peoples who have abandoned the true way of life. The original Torah, at the moment of the creation, was before the Almighty, always may his name be blessed, written like black fire upon white fire, not in order of the written Torah as we read it today, and which was manifested only

127

after Adam's sin. For this reason every night I spend hours and hours spelling out, with great concentration, the letters of the written Torah, to confuse them, to make them spin like the wheel of a mill, and thus cause to reappear the original order of the eternal Torah, which preexisted creation and had been given to the angels by the Almighty, blessed be his name always. If I knew that a distant kingdom exists where the original order is preserved, as well as the language that Adam spoke with his creator before committing his sin, I would gladly devote my life to seeking it."

As Solomon said these words, his countenance was illuminated by such a light that our friends asked themselves if it were not worth having him share in their future discussions. It was the Poet who found the decisive argument: the fact that this Jew wanted to find in the kingdom of Prester John his language and his ten tribes should not disturb them. Prester John had to be so powerful that he could govern even the lost tribes of the Jews, and there seemed to be no reason why he should not also speak the language of Adam. The chief question was, first of all, how to construct that kingdom, and to that end a Jew could be as useful as a Christian.

Nevertheless, they still had not decided what John's palace should be like. They resolved the question some nights later, the five of them in Baudolino's room. Inspired by the genius of the place, Abdul made up his mind to reveal to his new friends the secret of the green honey, saying that it could help them not to imagine but, rather, to see Prester John's palace directly.

Rabbi Solomon said at once that he knew far more mystical methods to provoke visions, and that at night he had only to murmur the multiple combinations of the letters of the secret name of the Lord, spinning them on his tongue, until a whirl of thoughts and of images was born, whereupon he plunged into a blissful exhaustion.

The Poet at first seemed suspicious, then he determined to try, but, wishing to temper the property of the honey with that of wine, in the end he lost all restraint and raved better than the others.

Having reached the proper state of intoxication, and helping himself with a few unsteady lines that he drew on the table, dipping his finger into the jar, he suggested that the palace had to be like the one the apostle Thomas had had built for Gondophorus, king of the Indians: ceilings and beams of Cyprus wood, roof of ebony, and a dome surmounted by two golden apples, on each of which gleamed two carbuncles, so that the gold shone during the day by the light of the sun and the gems at night in the glow of the moon. Then he stopped relying on his memory and on the authority of Thomas, and began seeing doors of sardonyx mixed with horns of the cerastes, which prevent passersby from introducing poison into the building, and windows of crystal, tables of gold on columns of ivory, lights nourished with balsam, and the king's bed of sapphire, to preserve chastity, because—the Poet concluded—this John may be a king all right, but he is also a priest and so, as for women, nothing doing.

"It seems beautiful to me," Baudolino said, "but for a king who rules over such a vast land, I would also put, in some hall, those automata that I've heard existed in Rome, that gave warning when one of the provinces was in revolt."

"In the Priest's kingdom, I don't believe," Abdul remarked, "that there can be revolts, because peace and harmony reign there." However, the idea of the automata appealed to him, because everyone knows that a great emperor, whether Moor or Christian, had to have automata at court. So he saw them, and with wonderful hypotyposis he made them visible also to his friends: "The palace stands on a mountain, and it's the mountain that is made of onyx, with a peak so smooth that it shines like the moon. The temple is round, its dome is of gold, and the walls, too, are of gold, encrusted with gems so rutilant that they produce warmth in winter and coolness in summer. The ceiling is encrusted with sapphires that represent the sky and carbuncles that represent the stars. A gilded sun and a silvered moon— these are the automata—travel through the heavenly vault, and mechanical birds sing every day, while at the corners four bronze angels accompany them with their trumpets. The palace rises over a hidden well, in which teams of horses move a grindstone, making it turn according to the changes of the seasons, so that it becomes the image of the cosmos. Beneath the crystal floor fish swim, and fabulous marine creatures. However, I have heard talk of mirrors from which you can see all the things that happen. One would be most useful, for John, to survey the extreme confines of his realm...."

The Poet, by now thinking in terms of architecture, began drawing the mirror, explaining: "It will be set very high, and can be reached by ascending a flight of one hundred twenty-five steps of porphyry...."

"And alabaster," Boron suggested, who until then had been silently cherishing the effect of the green honey.

"All right, we'll add alabaster. And the highest steps will be of amber and panther."

"What's this panther? The father of Jesus?" Baudolino asked.

"Don't be foolish. Pliny mentions it: it's a multicolored stone. But actually the mirror rests on a single pilaster. Actually, no, it doesn't. This pilaster supports a plinth on which stand two pilasters, and these support a base on which stand four pilasters, and so the pilasters increase until on the central base there are sixty-four. These support a base with thirty-two pilasters, which support a base with sixteen pilasters, and so they diminish until you come to a single pilaster that supports the mirror."

"Listen," Rabbi Solomon said, "with this pilaster business the mirror will fall down the moment you set it on its base."

"You shut up: you're as false as the soul of Judas. For you it's fine when your Ezekiel sees a temple and we know nothing about its form; if a Christian mason comes and tells you it couldn't stand up, you answer that Ezekiel heard voices and wasn't paying attention to the figures, so then I have to make only mirrors that will stand on their feet? All right, I'll also put twelve thousand armed guards around the mirror, at the base of the column, and they'll see that it stands up. All right?"

"All right, all right, it's your mirror," Rabbi Solomon said, conciliatory.

Abdul followed this talk, smiling, his eyes lost in empty space, and Baudolino realized that in the mirror Abdul would have liked to glimpse at least the shadow of his distant princess.

"In the days that followed we had to make haste because the Poet had to leave again, and he didn't want to miss the rest of the story," Baudolino said to Niketas. "But by now we were on the right track."

"On the right track? But this Priest was, in my opinion, less credible than the Magi dressed as cardinals and Charlemagne amid the heavenly host...."

"The Priest would become credible if he made himself known, with a personal letter to Frederick."

12

Baudolino writes the letter of Prester John

The decision to write a letter of Prester John was inspired by a story that Rabbi Solomon had heard from the Arabs of Spain. A sailor, Sindbad, who lived in the time of the caliph Harun-al-Rashid, was shipwrecked one day on an island, along the line of the equinox, where both day and night last exactly twelve hours. Sindbad said he had seen many Indians on the island, and so the island was close to India. The Indians took him into the presence of the prince of Sarandib. This prince moved only on a throne, mounted on an elephant, eight cubits high, and on either side, in double file, marched his vassals and his ministers. He was preceded by a herald with a golden javelin, and behind him came a second herald with a golden mace, an emerald at its apex. When the prince descended from the throne to continue on horseback, he was followed by a thousand horsemen dressed in silk and brocade, and yet another herald preceded him, crying that a king was arriving who possessed a crown such as Solomon had never had. The prince granted Sindbad audience, asking him many questions about the kingdom from whence he came. Finally the prince asked him to bear a letter to Harun-al-Rashid, written on sheepskin parchment with ultramarine ink, which said: "I send you the greeting of peace, I, prince of Sarandib, before whom stand a thousand elephants, and in whose palace the battlements are made of jewels. We consider you a brother and we beg you to send us a reply. And we beg you to accept this humble gift." The humble gift was an enormous ruby goblet, its bowl adorned with pearls. This gift and that letter increased throughout the Saracen world the veneration of the name of the great Harun-al-Rashid."

"That sailor of yours was surely in the kingdom of Prester John," Baudolino said. "Though in Arabic they call it by a different name. But he lied in saying that the Priest sent letters and gifts to the caliph, because John is Christian, even if a Nestorian, and if he had sent a letter, it would have been to the emperor Frederick."

"Then let's write that letter ourselves," the Poet said.

In seeking any information that could enhance their construction of Prester John's kingdom, our friends encountered Kyot. He was a young native of Champagne, who had just returned from a journey in Brittany, his spirit still aflame with stories of errant knights, wizards, fairies, and spells, which the inhabitants of those lands tell in the evening around the fire. When Baudolino mentioned to him the wonders of Prester John's palace, the youth cried out: "Why, in Brittany I heard tell of such a castle, or almost! It's where the Grasal is kept!"

"What do you know about the Grasal?" Boron asked, turning suspicious immediately, as if Kyot had laid a hand on something that was his property.

"Well then," Baudolino said, "I see that this object means a lot to both of you. What is it? As far as I know, a grasal, or gradalis, is some kind of bowl."

"Bowl? Bowl!" Boron smiled indulgently. "More of a chalice." Then, as if making up his mind to reveal his secret, he went on: "I'm amazed you haven't heard of it. It is the most precious relic of all Christianity, the cup in which Jesus consecrated the wine at the Last Supper, and in which later Joseph of Arimathea collected the blood that flowed from the ribs of Christ on the cross. Some say that the name of that cup is the Holy Grail, others say it is Sangreal, royal blood, because he who possesses it becomes one of the chosen knights, of the same lineage as David and Our Lord."

"Grail or grasal?" the Poet asked, immediately alert, hearing of something that could confer some kind of power.

"We don't know," Kyot said. "Some also say Graal. And it may not necessarily be a bowl. Those who have seen it do not recall the shape; all we know is that it is an object endowed with extraordinary powers."

"Who has seen it?" the Poet asked.

"Surely the knights who guarded it in Broceliande. But every trace of them has also been lost, and I have met only people who tell of them."

"It would be better if they told about that thing less and tried to learn more," Boron said. "That boy's been to Brittany, he's barely heard it mentioned, and he's already looking at me as if I wanted to steal from him what he doesn't have. That's how it is with everybody. You hear talk of the Grasal, and you think you'll be the one to find it. But I've spent five years in Brittany, and in the islands beyond the sea, without telling stories, only to find—"

"And did you find it?" Kyot asked.

"The problem wasn't to find the Grasal, but to find the knights who knew where it is. I traveled, I asked questions, I never encountered them. Maybe I wasn't one of the chosen. And here I am, rummaging among parchments, hoping to uncover a clue that escaped me while I was roaming in those forests. . . ."

"Now why are we here talking about the Grasal?" Baudolino said. "Whether it's in Brittany or in those islands, it doesn't concern us, because it has nothing to do with Prester John." No, Kyot said, because where the castle is and the nature of the object it houses have never been clear, but among the many stories he had heard there was one according to which one of those knights, Feirefiz, had found it and given it to his son, a priest who was to become king of India.

134

"Nonsense," Boron said. "Would I then have searched for years in the wrong place? Who told you the story of this Feirefiz?"

"Any story can be valid," the Poet said, "and if you follow Kyot's you might find your Grasal. But for the moment the question is not to find it, but to establish if it's worth connecting to Prester John. My dear Boron, we're not seeking a thing; we're seeking someone who will tell us about it." Then he turned to Baudolino. "What do you think? Does Prester John possess the Grasal? Is that the source of his great distinction, and could he transmit that distinction to Frederick, making him a gift of it?"

"And could it be the same ruby cup that the prince of Sarandib had sent to Harun-al-Rashid," suggested Solomon, who in his excitement had begun to speak through the toothless side of his mouth. "The Saracens honor Jesus as a great prophet; they could have discovered the cup, and then Harun might, in turn, have given it to the Priest...."

"Splendid," the Poet said. "The cup as harbinger of the reconquest of what the Moors had held as unjust possessors. Better than Jerusalem!"

They decided to try. During the night Abdul managed to remove from the scriptorium of Saint Victoire a parchment of great value, never scraped. It lacked only a seal to make it seem the letter of a king. In that room meant for two people, which now housed six around a rickety table, Baudolino, his eyes closed, dictated as if inspired. Abdul wrote, because his calligraphy, which he had learned in the Christian kingdoms beyond the sea, could suggest the way an Oriental would write Latin letters. Before beginning, he had proposed, so that all would be suitably clever and inventive, emptying the pot of the remaining green honey, but Baudolino objected: this evening, they had to have clear minds.

They promptly asked themselves if the Priest should not write in his Adamic language, or at least in Greek, but it was decided that a king like John probably had at his service secretaries who knew every language, and out of respect for Frederick, he would write in Latin. Also because, Baudolino added, the letter was intended to amaze and convince the pope and the other Christian princes, and therefore it had, first of all, to be comprehensible to them. They set to work.

The Priest Johannes, by the power and grace of God and of Our Lord Jesus Christ, master of all those who rule, to Frederick, holy and Roman emperor, wishing him good health and perpetual enjoyment of the divine benediction . . .

It has been announced to our majesty that you held in great esteem our Excellency and that word of our greatness has reached you. Also we have learned from our emissaries that you wish to send us some pleasing and entertaining gift, to delight our clemency. Gladly we accept the gift, and through our ambassador we send you a token, on our part, as we desire to know if you follow, as we do, the true faith, and if you believe completely in Our Lord Jesus Christ. In the breadth of our munificence, if you desire something that can procure for you pleasure, inform us, either by a word to our messenger or by a sign of your affection. Accept in exchange . . .

"Stop a moment," Abdul said. "This could be the point where the Priest sends Frederick the Grasal!"

"Yes," Baudolino said, "but these two nitwits Boron and Kyot haven't yet managed to tell us what it is!"

"They've heard so many stories, they've seen so many things, maybe they don't remember everything. That's why I suggested the honey: we have to encourage the flow of ideas."

Yes, perhaps Baudolino, who was dictating, and Abdul, who was writing, could limit themselves to wine; but the witnesses, or the sources of the revelation, had to be stimulated with green honey. And thus after a few moments Boron, Kyot (stupefied by the new sensations he was experiencing), and the Poet, who had now developed a taste for the honey, were seated on the floor with foolish smiles engraved on their faces, raving like so many hostages of Aloadin.

"Oh, yes," Kyot was saying, "there is a great hall, and torches that illuminate it with a brightness beyond anything imaginable. An attendant appears grasping a spear of such whiteness that it shines in the glow of the fireplace. From the tip of the spear comes a drop of blood and it drips on the hand of the attendant. Then two other attendants arrive with honey-gold candelabra, in each of which at least ten candles are alight. The candles pale, as do the moon and the stars when the sun rises. The Grasal is made of purest gold, studded with extraordinary precious stones, the rarest that exist on land or in the sea.... And now another maiden enters, carrying a silver dish...."

"So what's this damn Grasal like?" the Poet cried.

"I don't know. I see only a light...."

"You see only a light," Boron said, "but I see more. There are torches illuminating the hall, true, but now thunder is heard, a terrible shaking, as if the palace were collapsing. A great darkness falls.... No, now a ray of sunlight illuminates the palace, seven times brighter than before. Oh, the Holy Grasal is entering, covered with a cloth of white velvet, and as it enters, the palace is filled with the perfumes of all the spices of the world. Gradually, as the Grasal moves around the table, the knights see their plates fill with all the foods they could desire...."

"But what's this Grasal like? Devil take it!"

"Don't curse. It's a cup."

"How do you know if it's under a velvet cloth?"

"I know because I know," Boron said stubbornly. "They told me."

"May you be damned through the centuries and tormented by a thousand demons! You seem to have a vision, and then you tell us what you've been told and can't see? Why, you're worse than that asshole Ezekiel, who didn't know what he was seeing because those Jews never look at pictures and only hear voices!"

"Please, you blasphemer!" Solomon interjected. "Not just for my sake: the Bible is a holy book also for you, you loathesome gentiles!"

"Calm yourselves," Baudolino said. "Now listen to this, Boron. We'll assume that the Grasal is the cup that held the wine Our Lord blessed. How could Joseph of Arimathea collect the blood from the crucified Christ if, when he takes Jesus down from the cross, our Savior was already dead, and, as you know, the dead don't bleed?"

"Even dead, Jesus could work miracles."

"It wasn't a cup," Kyot interrupted, "because the man who told me the story about Feirefiz also revealed that it was a stone fallen from the sky, *lapis ex coelis,* and if it was a cup it's because it was carved from this celestial stone."

"Then why wasn't it the tip of the spear that pierced the holy bosom?" the Poet asked. "Didn't you say earlier that you saw an attendant carrying a bleeding spear? Well, what I see is not one but three attendants, each with a spear from which blood is streaming. . . . And then a man dressed like a bishop with a cross in his hand, borne on a chair by four angels, who put him down before the silver table where the spear now lies . . . Then two maidens carrying a charger with a man's severed head on it, bathed in blood. And then the bishop who is officiating over the spear: he raises the Host, and in the Host the image of a babe can be seen! The spear is the portentous object, and it is a sign of power because it's a sign of strength!"

"No, the spear drips blood, but the drops fall into a cup, demonstrating the miracle I was talking about," Boron said. "It's so simple. . . ." And he began to smile.

"That's enough," Baudolino said, dejected. "Let's forget about the Grasal and go on."

"My friends," Rabbi Solomon said, with the detachment of a man who, being Jewish, was not greatly impressed by that sacred relic. "To have the Priest immediately make a gift of that significance seems exaggerated to me. And then, the reader of the letter could ask Frederick to display this wonder. All the same, we can't exclude the possibility that the stories heard by Kyot and by Boron are in circulation in many regions, and so a hint would be enough, and a word to the wise would suffice. Don't write Grasal, don't write cup; use a less precise term. The Torah never refers to the most sublime things in a literal sense, but in a secret sense, so the devout reader must gradually guess what the Almighty, always may his holy name be blessed, wanted to be understood at the end of time."

Baudolino suggested: "Let's say then that he is sending a casket, a coffer, an ark; let's say *accipe istam veram arcam,* accept this true ark..."

"Not bad," Rabbi Solomon said. "It conceals and reveals at the same time. And it opens the path to the vortex of interpretation."

They continued writing.

If you would deign to come to our dominions, we would consider you the greatest and the most worthy member of our court, and you could enjoy all our riches. With these, which are abundant among us, you shall be then heaped if you choose to return to your empire. Remember you must die, and you will never sin.

After this pious recommendation, the Priest went on to describe his power.

"No humility," Abdul urged. "The Priest stands so high that he can allow himself some haughtiness."

Indeed. Baudolino had no qualms, and he dictated. That *dominus dominatium* surpassed in power all the kings of the earth, and his wealth was infinite, seventy-two kings paid him tribute, seventy-two provinces obeyed him, even if not all were Christian—and so Rabbi Solomon was satisfied, as they placed in the kingdom also the lost tribes of Israel. His sovereignty extended over the three Indias, his territories reached the most remote deserts, as far as the tower of Babel. Every month, at the king's table, seven kings were served, sixty-two dukes, and three hundred and sixty-five counts, and every day at that same table were seated twelve archbishops, ten bishops, the Patriarch of Saint Thomas, the Protopapas of Samarkand, and the Archprotopapas of Susa."

"Isn't that too many?" Solomon asked.

"No, no," the Poet said, "we have to make the pope spit green, and the basileus of Byzantium, too. And add that the Priest has made a vow to visit the Holy Sepulcher with a great army to defeat the enemies of Christ. This will confirm what Otto said about him, and it will shut the pope's mouth if by any chance he points out that John never managed to cross the Ganges. John is ready to try again; for this reason it's worth going to find him and forming an alliance with him."

"Now give me some ideas about populating the kingdom," Baudolino said. "It has to have elephants, dromedaries, camels, hippopotamuses, panthers, onagers, white and red lions, mute cicadas, gryphons, tigers, llamas, hyenas, all the things we never see in our countries, and whose remains are precious for those who decide to go and hunt down there. And also men never seen, but spoken of in books on the nature of things and the universe...."

"Centaurs, horned men, fauns, satyrs, pygmies, cynocephali, giants forty cubits tall, one-eyed men," Kyot suggested.

"Good, good. Write, Abdul, write it down," Baudolino said.

For the rest, they had only to repeat what had been thought and said in previous years, with some embellishments. The land of Prester John dripped honey and was brimming with milk—and Rabbi Solomon was delighted to find echoes of Exodus, Leviticus, Deuteronomy—the land knew neither serpents nor scorpions, the river Physon flowed there, which emerges directly from the Earthly Paradise, and in the land were found ... stones and sand, Kyot suggested. No, Rabbi Solomon replied, that's the Sambatyon. Shouldn't we put the Sambatyon in here, too? Yes, but later. The Physon flows from the Earthly Paradise and therefore contains ... emeralds, topazes, carbuncles, sapphires, chrysolite, onyx, beryls, amethysts, Kyot contributed.

He had just arrived and didn't understand why his friends displayed signs of nausea. (If you give me one more topaz I'll swallow it, then shit it out the window, Baudolino cried.) By now, with the countless blest islands and paradises they had visited in the course of their research, they were all fed up with precious stones.

Abdul then proposed, since the kingdom was in the East, to name rare spices, and they chose pepper. Of which Boron said that it grows on trees infested with snakes, and when it is ripe you set fire to the trees and the snakes escape and hide in their lairs. Then you approach the tree, shake it, the pepper falls from the branches, and you cook it in some process that nobody knows.

"Now can we put the Sambatyon?" Solomon asked. "Oh, go ahead," the Poet said, "then it's clear that the ten lost tribes are on the other side of the river. Yes, let's mention them explicitly, so Frederick can also find the lost tribes and add another gem to his crown." Abdul observed that the Sambatyon was necessary because it was the insuperable obstacle that thwarts the will and heightens desire. In other words: jealousy. Someone proposed also mentioning an underground stream rich in precious stones, but he refused to pursue the idea, for fear of hearing someone say topaz again. On the testimony of Pliny and Isidore, they decided instead to place salamanders in those lands, snakes with four legs that live amid flames.

"It only has to be true and we'll include it," Baudolino said, "so long as we're not telling fairy tales."

The letter continued, insisting for a while on the virtue that reigned in those lands, where every pilgrim was welcomed with charity, no one was poor, there were no thieves, predators, misers, or flatterers. The Priest then declared that he believed there was no monarch in the world so rich or with so many subjects. To offer proof of these riches, which for that matter Sindbad had seen at Sarandib, there was then the great scene where the Priest described himself as he went to war against his enemies, preceded by thirteen crosses studded with jewels, each on a chariot, each chariot followed by ten thousand horsemen and a hundred thousand foot soldiers. When, on the contrary, the Priest rode out in peacetime, he was preceded by a wooden cross, recalling the passion of the Lord, and by a golden pot filled with earth, to remind everyone—and himself—that dust we are and unto dust we shall return. But so no one would forget that he who was passing was still the king of kings, here was another silver pot filled with gold. "If you put in any topazes, I'll smash this jug over your head," Baudolino warned. And Abdul, that time at least, omitted topazes.

"Write also that, down there, no adulterers exist, and no one can lie, and that anyone who lies dies that instant, or it's as if he died, because he is outlawed and no one pays any further heed to him."

"I've already written that there are no vices, no thieves. . . ."

"That's all right. Insist. The kingdom of Prester John must be a place where Christians succeed in keeping the divine commandments, while the pope has not managed to achieve anything similar with his children; indeed he himself lies, and worse than others. Anyway, insisting on the fact that nobody lies there, we make it self-evident that everything John says is true."

John continued, saying that every year he paid a visit, with a great army, to the tomb of the prophet Daniel in deserted Babylon, that in his country fish were caught whose blood was the source of purple, and that he exercised his sovereignty over the Amazons and the Brahmans. The Brahman idea seemed useful to Boron because the Brahmans had been seen by Alexander the Great when he reached the most extreme Orient imaginable. Hence their presence proved that in the kingdom of the Priest was incorporated the very empire of Alexander.

At this point nothing remained but to describe his palace and his magic mirror, and on this score the Poet had already said everything some evenings earlier. But he remembered it, whispering into Abdul's ear, so that Baudolino would hear no more talk of topazes, which clearly were required in this case.

"I believe that a future reader," Rabbi Solomon said, "will wonder why such a powerful king had himself called only Priest."

"True, and this allows us to arrive at the conclusion," Baudolino said. "Abdul, write":

Why, O most beloved Frederick, our sublimity does not grant us an appellative more worthy than that of Presbyter is a question that does honor to your wisdom. To be sure, at our court we have ministers on whom are conferred duties and names far more worthy, especially where the ecclesiastical hierarchy is concerned. Our dispenser is primate and king, king and archbishop our wine steward, king and archimandrite our blacksmith, king and abbot our chief cook. So then our own highness, unwilling to be designated with these same titles, or to receive the same orders in which our court abounds, in humility determined to be called by a less important name, of a lower rank. For the moment suffice it for you to know that our territory extends in one direction a distance of four months' march, whereas in the other direction no one knows how far it reaches. If you could number the stars of the sky and the sands of the sea, then you could measure our possessions and our power.

It was almost daybreak when our friends finished the letter. Those who had taken the honey were still in a state of smiling stupefaction; those who had drunk only wine were tipsy; the Poet, who had again tasted both substances, could hardly stand. They walked, singing, through the narrow streets and the squares, touching that parchment with reverence, now convinced that it had just arrived from the kingdom of Prester John.

"Did you send it at once to Rainald?" Niketas asked.

"No. After the Poet left, we reread it for months and polished it, scraping and rewriting many times. Every now and then someone would suggest a little addition."

"But Rainald was expecting the letter, I imagine...."

"The fact is that meantime Frederick had removed Rainald from the position of chancellor of the empire, which he gave then to Christian of Buch. To be sure, Rainald, as archbishop of Cologne, was also arch-chancellor of Italy, and he remained very powerful, so much so that it was still he who organized the canonization of Charlemagne; but that replacement, at least in my view, meant that Frederick had begun to feel Rainald was too aggressive. So how could we present to the emperor a letter that, after all, had been desired by Rainald? I was forgetting: in the same year as the canonization, Beatrice had a second son, and so the emperor had other things on his mind, also because, according to rumors I heard, the first child was always sickly. So, what with one thing and another, more than a year went by."

"Rainald didn't insist?"

"At first he also had other things on his mind. Then he died. While Frederick was in Rome to expel Alexander III and put his antipope on the throne, a pestilence broke out, and the plague takes the rich and the poor alike. So Rainald died. I was shaken, even though I had never really loved him. He was arrogant and rancorous, but he had been a bold man and had fought to the end for his master. Rest his soul. But at this point, without him, did the letter still make any sense? He was the only one sufficiently clever to know how to profit by it, having it circulate among the chancelleries of all the Christian world."

Baudolino paused. "Besides, there was the question of my city."

"What city? You were born in a swamp."

"That's true. I'm going too fast. We still have to build the city."

"At last you're telling me about a city that's not destroyed!"

"Yes," Baudolino said, "it was the first and only time in my life that I would see a city's birth, and not its death."

13

Baudolino sees the birth of a new city

Ten years had gone by since Baudolino came to Paris. He had read everything that could be read, had learned Greek from a Byzantine prostitute, had written poems and amorous letters that would be attributed to others, had practically constructed a kingdom that now no one knew better than he and his friends, but he had not completed his studies. He consoled himself with the thought that studying in Paris had in itself been a great feat, considering that he had been born among cows. Then he recalled that in all likelihood students would be penniless youths like him, and not lords' sons, who had to learn to make war and not to read and write. . . . In short, he didn't feel entirely satisfied.

One day, Baudolino realized that in a month or so he would be twenty-six, for he had left home at thirteen, and it was exactly thirteen years that he had been away. He sensed something that we would call homesickness for his native land, only he, who had never experienced it, did not know what it was. So he thought he was feeling a desire to see his adoptive father again, and he decided to join him in Basel, where he had stopped as he was once more returning to Italy.

Baudolino hadn't seen Frederick since the birth of the first son. While he was writing and rewriting the Priest's letter, the emperor had done all sorts of things, slipping like an eel from north to south, eating and sleeping on horseback like his barbarian forefathers, and his palace was simply the place where he happened to be at that moment. In those years he had returned to Italy another two times. The second time, along the way, he had suffered an insult at Susa, where the citizens rebelled against him, obliging him to flee in secret and in disguise, because they were holding Beatrice hostage. Then the Susani let her go, having done her no harm, but he had cut a sorry figure, and had sworn an oath against Susa. Nor did he rest when he came back across the Alps, because he had to make the German princes see reason.

When Baudolino finally saw the emperor, he found him with a very grave expression. Baudolino understood that, on the one hand, Frederick was more and more concerned about the health of his older son—also named Frederick—and, on the other, about the situation in Lombardy.

"Agreed," he admitted, "and I say this only to you: my governors and my viceroys and my tax collectors were not only demanding what was my due, but seven times that; for every hearth they exacted every year three solidi of old coinage, and twenty-four old dinaria for every mill that operated on navigable waters; from the fishermen they took away a third of the catch; and if someone died without children the inheritance was confiscated. I should have paid attention to the complaints that reached me, I know, but I had other things on my mind.... And now it seems that some months ago the Lombard communes formed a League, an anti-imperial League, you understand. And what was their first decision? To rebuild the walls of Milan!"

The Italian cities were turbulent and disloyal, yes; but a League was the formation of another *res publica*. Naturally, that League could not endure, given the way one city in Italy hated the next; it was not even to be thought, and yet it was still a *vulnus* for the empire's honor.

Who was joining the League? According to rumor, in an abbey

not far from Milan there had been a gathering of delegates from Cremona, Mantua, Bergamo, and perhaps also Piacenza and Parma, but that was unsure. The rumors did not stop there, however; they spoke of Venice, Verona, Padua, Vicenza, Treviso, Ferrara, and Bologna. "Bologna! Can you believe that?" Frederick cried, pacing up and down in front of Baudolino. "You remember, don't you? Thanks to me, their damned professors could make all the money they wanted with those double-damned students of theirs, without accounting to me or to the pope, and now they're joining up with that league? Could anything be more shameless? And Pavia! That's all we need!"

"And Lodi," Baudolino interjected, to say something outrageous.

"Lodi? Lodi!" Barbarossa yelled, his face red as his beard, as if he were about to have a stroke. "But according to the news I'm receiving, Lodi has already taken part in the meetings. I gave my heart's blood to protect them, that flock of sheep; without me the Milanese would have leveled them to the ground every new season, and now they're hand in glove with their own murderers and plotting against their benefactor!"

"But, dear Father," Baudolino asked, "why do you say 'it seems' and 'according to rumor'? Don't you receive reliable news?"

"Do you people who study in Paris lose all sense of how things proceed in this world? If there's a league, there's a conspiracy; if there's a conspiracy, those who used to be on your side have turned traitor, and they tell you the exact opposite of what they are doing down there, so the last to know what they're doing will be the emperor, like husbands who have an unfaithful wife that everyone in the town knows about except them!"

He could hardly have chosen a worse example, because at that very moment Beatrice entered, having learned of dear Baudolino's arrival. Baudolino knelt to kiss her hand, without looking at her face. Beatrice hesitated a moment. Perhaps it seemed to her that, by showing no sign of intimacy and affection, she would betray embarrassment; therefore she placed her other hand maternally on his head, mussing his hair—forgetting that a woman just over thirty could no longer act this way towards a man only a little younger than she. To Frederick it all seemed normal, he the father, she the mother, even if both adoptive. The one who felt out of place was Baudolino. That double contact, her nearness, which enabled him to catch the perfume of her dress as if it were that of her flesh, and the sound of her voice— luckily in that position he could not look into her eyes, for he would immediately have blanched and fallen senseless to the floor—filled him with unbearable joy, but it was poisoned by the sensation that with this simple act of homage he was once again betraying his father.

He would not have known how to take his leave if the emperor had not asked a favor of him, or given him an order, which was the same thing. To have a clearer view of the situation in Italy, trusting neither official messengers nor messenger officials, Frederick had decided to send down there a few trusted men, who knew the country, but were not immediately identifiable as imperials, so that they could sniff out the atmosphere and gather information not vitiated by treason.

Baudolino liked the idea of escaping the embarrassment he felt at court, but a moment later he felt something else. He felt extraordinarily moved by the idea of seeing his old places, and he realized finally that this was the reason he had undertaken his journey.

After moving through various cities, one day Baudolino, riding on and on—or, rather, bumping along on his mule, because he was passing himself off as a merchant, peacefully going from town to town—was attracted by those heights beyond which, after a good stretch of plain, he ought to be able to look at the Tanaro and reach, between stony fields and swamps, his native Frascheta.

Even though in those days, when you left home, you left without thinking of ever returning, Baudolino felt at this moment a tingling in his veins, as, all of a sudden, he was seized by an eagerness to know if his old parents were still alive.

Not only that. Suddenly faces of other boys of the neighborhood came into his mind: Masulu Panizza, with whom he used to set traps for hares; and Porcelli, known as Ghino (or was it Ghini, known as Porcello?), with whom, at first sight, they had thrown rocks at each other, Aleramo Scaccabarozzi, known as Bonehead, and Cuttica of Quargnento, from the days when they fished together in the Bormida. Good Lord, he said to himself, surely I'm not dying now, though they say that on the point of death you remember the things of your childhood so well....

It was the eve of Christmas, but Baudolino didn't know that, because in the course of his journey he had lost track of the days. He was trembling with cold, on his equally frozen mule, but the sky was clear in the sunset light, clean, with a smell of snow already in the air. He recognized these places as if he had passed by the day before. He remembered how he once went into these hills with his father, to deliver three mules, toiling up paths that could wear out the legs even of a boy, so you can imagine driving reluctant animals up them. But they enjoyed the return, looking at the plain from above and taking their time on the way down. Baudolino remembered that, not very far from the flowing river, the plain for a short stretch humped into a hillock, and from the top of that knoll one time he had seen, piercing a milky shroud, the spires of some towns: Bergoglio along the river, then Roboreto, and, farther on, Gamondio, Marengo, and the Palea, the area of marshes, of gravel and scrub, at whose edges perhaps there still stood the hut of the good Gagliaudo.

But when he was on the hillock, he saw a different view, as if all around, on the hills and in the valleys, the air was clear, and only the plain before him was murky with foggy vapors, those grayish, misty clumps that every now and then assail you on the road, enveloping you until you can see nothing, then they pass you, and off they go whence they came—so now Baudolino said to himself: Why, look at that, it could be August here, but over Frascheta the eternal fog rules, like the snow on the peaks of the Alps—nor did this displease him, because one who is born in fog always feels at home in it. Gradually, however, as he descended towards the river, he realized that those vapors were not fog, but clouds of smoke that allowed glimpses of the fires that fed them. From the smoke and fires, Baudolino now understood that, in the plain beyond the river, around what had once been Roboreto, the town had overflowed into the countryside, and everywhere there was a sprouting, mushroomlike, of new houses, some of stone, others of wood, many still only half-built, and to the west you could make out the beginning of a girdle of walls, such as there had never been in those parts. And on the fires, in the freezing cold, pots were boiling, heating water, for, farther on, men were pouring it into holes filled with lime or perhaps mortar. Baudolino had seen the beginning of the construction of the new cathedral in Paris, on the island in the middle of the river, and now he recognized the machines and the scaffoldings that master masons use: judging by what he knew of cities, he realized that over there people were about to bring one into existence from nothing, and it was a sight that—if you're lucky—you see once in a lifetime.

"Madness!" he said to himself. "You turn your back for a moment and they pull a trick like this on you," and he spurred his mule to reach the valley as quickly as possible. After crossing the river, on a big barge that transported stones of every kind and size, he stopped where some workers, on an unsteady scaffolding, were constructing a little wall, while others, from the ground, with a winch, were raising to those above some baskets of rubble. But it was a winch only after a manner of speaking, for a more crude contraption could hardly be imagined: made of withes instead of sturdy stakes, it swayed constantly, and the two men on the ground made it spin. They were less concerned with pulling the rope than with controlling that menacingly wide sway of the baskets. Baudolino promptly said to himself: There, it's obvious, the people from around here, when they do something, they do it either bad or worse. Just look; is this any way to work? If I were master here, I'd grab all of them by the seat of the pants and throw them in the Tanaro."

Then he saw, a bit farther on, another group, supposedly constructing a loggetta, with crudely hewn stones, beams clumsily finished, and capitals that seemed shaped by an animal. To hoist the construction material they had rigged up a kind of pulley, and Baudolino realized that, compared with this bunch, the men at the little wall were masters worthy of Como. He then stopped making comparisons as, proceding a little farther, he saw others building the way children do when they play with mud, and they were putting the finishing touches, the last licks, you might say, on a construction similar to three others near it, made of mud and shapeless stones, with roofs of straw carelessly packed: thus a sort of street was being born of hovels very ill-made, as if the workers were competing to see who could finish first before the holiday, with no regard for the rules of the art.

As he tried to find his bearings in that multitude of crafts, Baudolino discovered a multitude of dialects—which showed how one collection of huts was being made by peasants of Solero, a twisted tower was the work of Monferrato people, that mortar was being stirred by the Pavesi, those planks were being sawed by men who until then had cut down trees in the Palea. But when he heard someone giving orders, or saw a band working properly, he heard Genoese spoken.

Have I fallen into the midst of the construction of the tower of Babel? Baudolino asked himself. Or into the Hibernia of Abdul, where those seventy-two sages have reconstructed the speech of Adam, putting all languages together, just as you mix water and clay, pitch and bitumen? But here they no longer speak the language of Adam and, though altogether they speak seventy-two languages, men of such different breeds, who as a rule would be hitting one another, they are all mixing in loving harmony!

He had approached a group that was skillfully covering a construction of wooden beams, as if it were an abbatial church, using a windlass of great dimensions which was not moved by manpower but by the toil of a horse. Not oppressed by the collar still in use in some rural districts, that would constrict his throat, the animal pulled with great energy thanks to a comfortable harness. The workmen emitted sounds surely Genoese, and Baudolino addressed them at once in their vernacular—even if not in a manner sufficiently correct to hide the fact that he was not one of them.

"What are you up to?" he asked, to open the conversation. And one of them, giving him a nasty look, said they were building a machine to scratch their cock. Now, since all the others started laughing and it was clear they were laughing at him, Baudolino (already in a temper from having to act the unarmed merchant on a mule, while in his baggage he kept, carefully wrapped in a bolt of cloth, his courtier's sword) replied in the Frescheta dialect, which after all this time returned spontaneously to his lips, that he had no need of a machine because, as a rule, his prick, as respectable people called it, was regularly scratched by those sluts of their mothers. The Genoese didn't understand clearly the meaning of his words, but they guessed their intention. They abandoned their tasks, one grabbing a stone, another a pick, to form a semicircle around the mule. Fortunately, at that moment some other men were approaching, one of whom looked like a knight, and in a language half-Frank and half-Latin, half-Provençal and half God knows what, he told the Genoese that the traveler spoke like a man of these parts, and so they were not to treat him as someone who had no right to pass this way. He had asked questions like a spy, the Genoese explained, and the knight replied that if the emperor did send spies, so much the better, because it was time he knew that a city had risen here, just to spite him. And then he said to Baudolino: "I've never seen you before, but you look like someone returning home. Have you come to join us?"

"My lord," Baudolino replied with urbanity, "I was born in

Frascheta, but I left it many years ago, and I knew nothing of all that is happening here. My name is Baudolino, son of Gagliaudo Aulari...."

Before he could finish speaking, from the group of newcomers an old man with white hair and beard raised a stick and began shouting: "Wicked, heartless liar, may lightning strike you. How dare you use the name of my poor son Baudolino, son of Gagliaudo, here in person, and Aulari too, who left his home so many years ago with a grand Alaman lord, and after all maybe was one who made monkeys dance because I never heard another word about my poor boy and after all this time he has to be dead, so my sainted wife and I have suffered these thirty years, for the greatest sorrow of our life, that was already miserable enough, but to lose a son is a sorrow no one can know unless he's suffered it himself!"

At which Baudolino cried: "Dear Father! It's really you!" His voice broke and tears came to his eyes, but they could not conceal a great happiness. Then he added: "And it hasn't been thirty years of suffering, because I left only thirteen years ago, and you should be pleased because I've spent those years well, and now I'm somebody." The old man came over to the mule, looked carefully into Baudolino's face, and said: "Why, you're really you! Even if it was thirty years, that jackass look you've never lost, so you know what I have to say to you? Maybe you're now somebody, but you mustn't wrong your father, and if I said thirty years it's because to me it's seemed thirty, and in thirty years you could have sent news, you wretch. You're the ruin of our family. Get off that animal that you probably stole, and I'll break this stick over your head!" He seized Baudolino by the boots, trying to pull him down from the mule, but the man who seemed the leader stepped between them. "Come now, Gagliaudo, you find your son again after thirty years—"

"Thirteen," Baudolino said.

"You shut up! The two of us will talk later—you find him after thirty years and in this situation you embrace and thank God, for God's sake!" Baudolino had already dismounted and was about to fling himself into the arms of Gagliaudo, who was now crying, when the lord who seemed a leader again stepped in and seized Baudolino by the collar: "But if there's anyone here who has a score to settle it's me."

"And who might you be?" Baudolino asked.

"I'm Oberto del Foro, but you don't know that, and you probably don't remember anything. I was maybe ten years old and my father deigned to visit yours, to see some calves that were for sale. I was dressed the way a gentleman's son should be, and my father didn't want me to go into the stable with him for fear I would get dirty. I was wandering around outside the house, and you were right after me, so dirty and ugly you looked like you'd come out of a dunghill. You faced me, looked at me, and asked me if I wanted to play a game; I stupidly said yes, and you gave me a shove that sent me into the pigs' trough. When my father saw me in that state, he gave me a whipping because I had spoiled my new clothes."

"That may be," Baudolino said, "but it happened thirty years ago...."

"First of all, it was thirteen, and since then I've thought about it every day, because I've never been so humiliated in my life as I was that time, and, growing up, I kept telling myself that if I one day met the son of Gagliaudo, I'd kill him."

"And you want to kill me now?"

"Not now, no. On the contrary, because we're all here and we've almost finished constructing a city, to fight the emperor when he sets foot again in these parts, so obviously I don't have time to waste killing you. For thirty years..."

"Thirteen."

"For thirteen years I've had this rage in my heart, and now, at this very moment, strangely enough, it's gone."

"Like they say, sometimes..."

"Now don't try to be smart. Go and embrace your father. Then, if you apologize to me for that day, we can go to a place nearby where

154

they're celebrating the completion of a building, and in these situations we draw from the keg of the best and, as our old folks used to say, we drink the night away."

Baudolino found himself in a huge cellar. The city wasn't yet finished, and already the first tavern was open, in a cave that was all hogsheads and long wooden tables, full of fine mugs, and salami made with ass's meat, which (Baudolino explained to a horrified Niketas) arrived looking like swollen wineskins; you pierce them with a knife, drop them in some oil and garlic to fry, and they are a delicacy. And that's why all those present were in high spirits, stinking and tipsy. Oberto del Foro announced the return of the son of Gagliaudo Aulari, and immediately some of the men threw themselves on Baudolino, punching his shoulders, as he first widened his eyes, surprised, then responded, in a whirl of recognitions that threatened never to end. "Good Lord, why you're Scaccabarozzi, and you're Cuttica of Quargnento—and who are you? No, don't tell me, I want to guess. You must be Squarciafichi! And are you Ghini or Porcelli?"

"No, he's Porcelli, the one who always threw stones at you! I was Ghino Ghini, and to tell the truth I still am. The two of us used to go and slide on the ice, in winter."

"Good Lord Jesus, it's true: you're Ghini! Weren't you the one who could sell anything, even the dung of your goats, like that time when you passed some off on a pilgrim as the ashes of San Baudolino?"

"That's right, I did! In fact, now I'm a merchant. Talk about fate! Now look at him—try and say who he is. . . ."

"Why, it's Merlo! What was it I always used to say to you?"

"You used to say: 'Lucky Merlo, stupid as you are, you never take offense.' Now, look at me; instead of taking, I've lost . . ." and he held up his right arm, the hand missing. "At the siege of Milan, ten years ago."

"Yes, I was going to ask. As far as I know, the people of Gamondio, Bergoglio, and Marengo have always been for the emperor. So how is it you used to be for him and now you're building a city against him?"

They all started trying to explain, and the only thing Baudolino understood clearly was that around the old castle and the church of Santa Maria of Roboreto a city had risen, made up of people from the neighboring settlements, places like Gamondio, Bergoglio, and Marengo, but with whole families who had come from everywhere, from Rivalta Bormida, from Bassignana or Piovera, to build the houses they would then live in. So that since May three of them, Rodolfo Nebia, Aleramo of Marengo, and Oberto del Foro had brought to Lodi, to the communes assembled there, the support of the new city, even if it existed, at that moment, more in their intentions than on the banks of the Tanaro. But they had all worked like animals, all summer and autumn, and the city was nearly ready, ready to block the emperor's path, the day he came down again into Italy, as was his bad habit.

What did they think they were blocking? Baudolino asked, slightly skeptical. "He could simply skirt it. . . ."

"No, no," they answered, "you don't know the emperor [Imagine!]. A city that rises without his consent is an offense to be cleansed in blood; he'll be forced to lay siege to it [on this point they were right; they well knew Frederick's character]; that's why you need solid walls and streets designed specially for warfare, and that's why we needed the Genoese, who are sailors, true, but they go to distant lands and build many new cities, and they know how it's done."

"But the Genoese aren't the kind to do something for nothing," Baudolino said. "Who paid them?"

"They paid! They've already given us a loan of a thousand Genovese solidi, and they've promised another thousand for the coming year."

"And what do you mean by saying you make streets specially designed for warfare?"

156

"Have Emanuele Trotti explain that to you. It was his idea. You speak: you're the Poliorcete!"

"What's the Polior thing?"

This Trotti (who, like Oberto, had the air of a *miles,* a knight, in other words, a vassal of a certain dignity) said: "A city must resist the enemy, prevent him from scaling the walls, but if unfortunately he does scale them, the city must still be ready to stand up to him, and break his neck. If the enemy, inside the walls, immediately finds a tangle of alleyways where he can slip in, you'll never catch him again; some go here, some there, and after a while the defenders end up like a mouse. No, the enemy must find an open area under the walls, where he remains exposed long enough to be assailed by arrows and stones from around the corners and from the windows, and before he can move past that space, half of his forces will be done for."

(True, Niketas sadly interjected, on hearing the story, this is what they should have done in Constantinople; instead, at the base of the walls they allowed that tangle of alleyways to develop.... Yes, Baudolino would have liked to reply, but you'd also need men with balls like my countrymen, and not a bunch of namby-pambies like your weak-kneed imperial guard—but he remained silent so as not to hurt his interlocutor, and he said: "Be quiet, don't interrupt Trotti, let me continue.")

Trotti said: "If the enemy then gets past the open area and slips into the streets, they should not be straight, made with a plumb line, not even if you are inspired by the ancient Romans, who designed a city on a grid. Because with a straight street the enemy always knows what's awaiting him, but not if the streets are full of corners, or elbows, if you like. The defender waits around the corner, on the ground and on the rooftops, and he always knows what the enemy is doing, because on the next roof there's another defender, crouching on a corner, who glimpses the enemy and signals to those who haven't yet seen him. The enemy never knows what's in store for him, so he slows down his advance. Therefore a good city must have its houses badly arranged, like a crone's teeth, which seems ugly but is what's really beautiful. And, finally, you want the false tunnel!"

"You haven't told us about that yet," Boidi interjected.

"Naturally. I just heard about it myself from a Genoese who heard it from a Greek, and it was an idea of Belisarius, the general of the emperor Justinian. What does a besieger want? He wants to dig tunnels under the walls that will lead him to the heart of the city. So what is his dream? To find a tunnel already made. So we promptly dig a tunnel for him, which from outside leads inside the walls. On the outside, we conceal the mouth of the tunnel with rocks and bushes, but not cleverly enough to prevent the enemy from discovering it sooner or later. The end of the tunnel, the one that opens inside the city, must be a passage so narrow that only one man, or at most two, can go through at a time. It is closed with a metal grating, and the first one to reach it will see a square and perhaps the corner of a chapel, a sign that the passage leads right into the city. At the grating you set a guard, and when the enemy arrives, they have to emerge one by one, and as each comes out, the guard fells him. . . ."

"And the enemy are all stupid and they keep coming out, not noticing that those ahead of them are dropping like figs," Boidi snickered.

"Who says enemies are stupid? Calm down. Maybe the idea should be studied a bit more, but it isn't something to reject."

Baudolino stepped to one side with Ghini, who was a merchant and must therefore be a man of sense with his feet on the ground, not like those knights, vassals of vassals, who to achieve military fame fling themselves even into lost causes. "Listen to me a minute, Ghini, pass me that wine and tell me something. I'll go along with the idea that, when you make a city here, Barbarossa is forced to besiege it to save his reputation, and that gives time to those of the League to strike him from behind after he's worn himself out with the siege. But the losers in all this are the people of the city. You'd have me believe that our people will leave the places where, for better or worse, they were getting along, and come here to get themselves killed to please the people of Pavia? You're telling me that the Genoese, who wouldn't shell out a penny to ransom their mothers from the Saracen pirates, are giving you money and labor to build a city that, at best, serves the purposes of Milan?"

"Baudolino," Ghini said, "the story is much more complicated than that. Take a good look at where we are." He dipped a finger in the wine and began to make marks on the table. "Here's Genoa, right? And here are Terdona, then Pavia, then Milan. These are rich cities, and Genoa is a port. So Genoa must have free access for its trade with the Lombard cities, right? The passes go through the Lemme valley, then the Orba valley, the Bormida, and the Scrivia. We're talking about four rivers, aren't we? And they all intertwine more or less along the shore of the Tanaro. So if you have a bridge over the Tanaro, from there your way is open to trade with the lands of the marquess of Monferrato, and God knows where else. Is that clear? Now, while Genoa and Pavia were getting along nicely, it was fine for them if these valleys remained without a lord, or else, if the situation demanded, they formed alliances, for example, with Gavi or with Marengo, and things went smoothly.... But with the arrival of this emperor, Pavia on one side and Monferrato on the other, both allied with the empire, Genoa is cut off to the left and also to the right, and if it goes over to Frederick, it can kiss its trade with Milan good-bye. So they have to remain on good terms with Terdona and Novi, since one will allow them to control the valley of the Scrivia and the other, the Bormida. But you know what happened: the emperor razed Terdona, Pavia seized control of the Terdona region as far as the Appenines, and all our towns went over to the empire, and, by God, I ask you: puny as we were, could we have tried acting strong? What did the Genoese have to give us to persuade us to change sides? Something we'd never dreamed of having: namely, a city, with consuls and soldiers, and a bishop, and walls, a city that collects tolls on transients and goods. You realize, Baudolino, that just by controlling a bridge over the Tanaro you make piles of money, you sit there comfortably and you ask money of one man, a couple of hens from the next, a whole ox from the one after that, and they pay up right away. A city is a gold mine. Remember how rich the people of Terdona were compared to us in the Palea. And this city, which is good for us, is good also for the League, and good for Genoa, as I was telling you, because, weak as it might be, by the mere fact of being there, it disrupts the schemes of all the others and guarantees that in this area neither Pavia nor the emperor can be master, nor can the marquess of Monferrato...."

"Yes, but then Barbarossa comes along and squashes you like a bug."

"Just a moment. Who says so? The problem is that when he arrives, the city is already there. Then you know well what happens: a siege costs time and money, we make a fine show of submission, he's happy (because with such people it's honor above all) and he goes off somewhere else."

"But the League people and the Genoese have thrown their money away to build the city, and you tell them to go screw themselves?"

"It depends on when Barbarossa arrives. As you can see, in the space of three months these cities change their allegiance like it was nothing. We sit and wait. Maybe at that moment the League is allied with the emperor." ("Master Niketas," Baudolino said, "I swear by my own eyes, six years later, at the siege of the city, there were Genoese slingers. You understand? Genoese! The ones who had helped build it!")

"Otherwise," Ghini continued, "we face the siege. Dammit to Hell, in this world you get nothing for nothing. Enough of this talk, come and see."

He took Baudolino by the hand and led him out of the tavern. Evening had fallen, and it had turned colder. They came out into a little square, from which, it seemed, at least three streets should lead,

160

but only two corners were built, with low houses, a single story, the roofs of straw. The little square was illuminated by lights coming from the surrounding windows, and by a few braziers kept burning by vendors, who were crying: "Hey, you women! Hey! The holy night is beginning and you surely don't want your husband not to find something tasty on the table." Near what would become the third corner was a knife grinder, who made the knives squeak as he sprinkled the wheel. Farther on, at a stand, a woman was selling chickpea flour, dried figs, and carobs, and a shepherd wearing a fleece jacket held a little basket. "Right here, ladies! Good fresh cheese," he shouted. In an empty space between two houses, two men were discussing the sale of a pig. In the background, a pair of girls were lazily leaning against a door, their teeth chattering, their shawls allowing a glimpse of an ample low-cut bodice; one of them said to Baudolino: "What a pretty boy you are! Why don't you come spend Christmas with me, and I'll teach you how to make the beast with eight paws?"

They turned the corner and found a wool carder, crying in a loud voice that this was their last chance for mattresses and paillasses, to sleep warm, and not freeze like the Baby Jesus, and next to him a waterman was shouting, and as they continued along the streets, still roughly laid out, they could see doorways where a carpenter was working his plane, and over there a smith striking his anvil in a festival of sparks, and farther on another man taking loaves from an oven that glowed like the mouth of Hell; and merchants were arriving from afar to do business on this new frontier, also people who usually lived in the forest: charcoal burners, honey gatherers, peddlers of ashes for soap, collectors of bark for making cord or tanning leather, vendors of rabbit skins, jailbird faces who assembled in the new settlement thinking they would find profit there, and the blind and the halt and the maimed and the scrofulous, for whom begging in the streets of a town, and during the holy holidays, promised to be richer than wandering along the deserted roads of the countryside.

The first snowflakes were beginning to fall; they grew thicker, and for the first time there was a layer of white on those young roofs, though no one could know if they were capable of bearing the weight. At a certain point Baudolino, remembering his invention in conquered Milan, opened his eyes wide: three merchants entering on three asses through an arch in the wall seemed to him to be the Magi; they were followed by their servants, carrying pots and precious stuffs. Behind them, beyond the Tanaro, he thought he could make out some flocks descending the slopes of the silvered hill, the shepherds playing bagpipes, and caravans of Oriental camels with Moors wearing great varicolor-striped turbans. On the hill sparse fires were dying under the twinkling snow, more persistent now, but to Baudolino one of them seemed a great caudate star, which moved in the sky towards the city that was wailing in birth pangs.

"You see what a city is?" Ghini said to him. "And if it's like this before it's even finished, imagine what will happen afterwards: it's another life. Every day you see new people—for the merchants, just think, it's like having the Heavenly Jerusalem; for the knights, since the emperor forbade them to sell lands so as not to divide the fief, and they were bored to death in the countryside, now they command companies of bowmen, they ride out in parades, they give orders left and right. But things don't prosper just for the gentry and the merchants: it's a providence also for a man like your father, who doesn't have much land but has some livestock, and people arrive in the city and ask him for stock and pay cash; they're beginning to sell for ready money and not through barter. I don't know if you understand what that means: if you exchange two chickens for three rabbits sooner or later you have to eat them, otherwise they grow too old, whereas two coins you can hide under your mattress and they're good ten years from now, and if you're lucky they stay there even if enemies come into your house. Besides, it's happened in Milan and in Lodi and Pavia, and it will also happen here with us: it's not that the Ghinis or the Aularis have to keep their mouths shut and only the Guascos or the Trottis give the orders. We're all part of those who make the decisions; here you can become important even if you're not a noble, and this is the fine thing about a city, and it's specially fine for one who isn't noble, and is ready to get himself killed, if he really has to (but it's better not), because his sons can go around saying: My name is Ghini and even if your name is Trotti, you're still shit."

Obviously, at this point Niketas asked Baudolino what this city was called. What a talent that Baudolino had as a storyteller, having kept that revelation in suspense until this moment! The city didn't yet have a name, except a generic Civitas Nova, which was a *genus* name, not an *individuum*. The choice of name would depend on another question, and no small one: legitimation. How does a new city, without history and without nobility, gain the right to exist? Ideally by imperial investiture, just as the emperor can create a knight or a baron; but here we were dealing with a city born against the emperor's wishes. So? Baudolino and Ghini went back to the tavern, as all there were debating that very question.

"If this city is born outside the imperial law, it can only become legitimate through some other law, just as strong and ancient."

"And where will we find that?"

"Why, in the *Constitutum Constantini*, in the donation that the emperor Constantine made to the church, giving it the right to govern territories. We donate the city to the pope and, seeing that at this moment there are two popes around, we donate it to the one who is siding with the League, that is to say, Alexander III. As we said before at Lodi, months ago, the city will be called Alessandria, and it will be a papal fief."

"First of all, at Lodi you should have kept quiet, because we hadn't yet decided anything," Boidi said, "but that's not the point. As names go, it's a beautiful name, or at least it's no uglier than a lot of others. But what sticks in my craw is that here we bust our behinds to make a city and then we present it to the pope, who already has so many. And that way we'll have to pay him tribute, and any way you look at it, it's still money that we lose, so we might as well be paying the emperor."

"Boidi, don't be dumb, as usual," Cuttica said to him. "First, the emperor doesn't want the city, not even if they make him a present of it; and if he was ready to accept it, then it wasn't worth it. Second, it's one thing not to pay taxes to the emperor, who then comes and chops you to pieces, as he did with Milan; and it's another thing not to pay them to the pope, who's a thousand miles away and, with all the problems he has, he's not likely to send an army just to collect small change. Third..."

Baudolino spoke up: "If you'll allow me to express an opinion, I've studied in Paris and I have some experience of how you make letters and diplomas; there are all sorts of ways of making presents. You draw up a document that says Alessandria is being founded in honor of Alexander the pope and consecrated to Saint Peter, for example. As proof, you build a cathedral to Saint Peter on allodial land, which has no feudal obligations. And you build it with money contributed by all the people of the city. After which you make a gift of it to the pope, with all the formulas that your notaries find most suitable and most binding. You flavor it with expressions of filial devotion and all those things, you send the parchment to the pope, and you receive all his benedictions. Anybody who later scrutinizes that document will see that, in the final analysis, you've given him only the cathedral and not the rest of the city, and I can't see a pope coming here to take away his cathedral and carry it to Rome."

"It sounds magnificent to me," Oberto said, and all agreed. "We'll do what Baudolino says, as he seems to me very clever and I really hope he'll stay here to give us more good advice, since he's also a grand Paris scholar."

Here Baudolino had to resolve the most embarrassing part of that fine day: namely, reveal, without anyone being able to reproach him, since they too had been imperials until a short time past, that he was a ministerial of Frederick, to whom he was bound by filial affection—and then to tell the whole story of those thirteen wondrous years, while Gagliaudo did nothing but murmur: "If they would've told me, I'd never believe it" and "Just think: he looked like a worse fool than the others, and here he really is somebody."

"Not all ills come to harm," Boidi said then. "Alessandria isn't yet finished, and we already have one of us at the imperial court. Dear Baudolino, you mustn't betray your emperor, since you love him so much, and he loves you. But you will remain at his side and stand up for us whenever necessary. This is the land where you were born and nobody can blame you if you try to defend it, within the limits of loyalty, of course."

"Still, for tonight it would be best if you went to see that sainted woman your mother and slept at Frascheta," Oberto said delicately, "and tomorrow you leave, without staying here to see how the streets are made and how thick the walls are. We're sure that, out of love for your natural father, if you were to learn one day that we were in great danger, you would send us word. But if you have the heart to do this, who knows? Maybe for the same reason one day you would not warn your adoptive father of some machination of ours too painful for him. In any case, the less you know, the better."

"Yes, my son," Gagliaudo said then, "after all the troubles you've caused me, do at least this one good thing. I have to stay here, because, as you see, we're discussing serious matters, but don't leave your mother alone on this night, for if she sees you, in her great joy she won't see anything else, and she won't notice that I'm not there. Go, and I'll tell you something else: you even have my blessing, for God only knows when we'll see each other again."

"Very well," Baudolino said. "In a single day I find a city and I lose it. Oh, son of a bitch! Do you realize—if I want to see my father again, I'll have to come and lay siege to him?"

That, Baudolino explained to Niketas, was more or less what happened. On the other hand, there was no way of doing it differently, a sign that those were truly difficult times.

"And then?" Niketas asked.

"I set out to find my house. The snow on the ground came up to my knees, what fell from the sky was now a chaos that made your eyeballs spin and slashed your face, the fires of the Civitas Nova had disappeared, and between the white below and the white above I couldn't figure out what direction to take. I thought I could remember the old paths, but at this point there weren't any paths, and you couldn't tell what was solid ground and what was swamp. Obviously, to build the houses, they had cut down entire groves and I could no longer find even the shapes of those trees that once I had known by heart. I was lost, like Frederick the night he met me, only now it was snow and not fog, for if it had been fog, I'd still have found my way. Fine thing, Baudolino, I said to myself, you get lost on your own ground; my mamma was right to say that those who can read and write are stupider than those who can't, and now what do I do? Do I stop here and eat my mule, or tomorrow morning, after they dig and dig, will they find me looking like a rabbit's skin left out overnight in the hard of winter?"

If Baudolino was there to tell the story, it meant that he survived, but through a near-miracle. Because while he was proceeding, without direction, he glimpsed once again a star in the sky, very pale, but still visible, and he followed it, until he realized he was in a low valley and the star seemed high because he was low, but once he climbed the slope, the light grew ever brighter before him, until he realized that it came from one of those sheds where they keep the livestock when there isn't enough room in the house. In the shed was a cow, and a frightened ass braying, a woman with her hands between the legs of a sheep, and the sheep producing a lamb, bleating its heart out.

He stopped on the threshold to wait for the lamb to emerge, before he kicked the ass out of the way, and rushed to lay his head in the woman's lap, crying: "Dearest mother!" For a moment the woman was stunned, then she pulled up his head, turning it towards the fire, and she started to cry, stroking his hair and murmuring between her sighs, "O Lord, O Lord, two lambs in a single night, one being born and the other coming back from the devil's own land: it's like having Christmas and Easter together, but it's too much for my poor heart. Hold me, I'm about to faint. That's enough, Baudolino. I've heated water in the pot to wash this poor little creature. Can't you see you're getting blood all over you? But where did you get those clothes that look like a gentleman's? You haven't stolen them, have you, you rascal?"

For Baudolino it was as if he heard angels singing.

14

Baudolino saves Alessandria with his father's cow

"And so, to see your father again you had to besiege him?" Niketas said, towards evening, as he invited his guest to taste some sweets of yeast flour, shaped to look like flowers or plants or other objects.

"Not exactly: the siege was six years later. After witnessing the birth of the city, I went back to Frederick and told him what I had seen. Before I had even finished speaking, he was already in a roaring fury. He shouted that a city is born only with the emperor's consent, and if it's born without that consent it must be razed before they can finish building it, otherwise anyone can grant consent in place of the emperor, and that spelled the end of the *nomen imperii*. Then he calmed down, but I knew him well: he wouldn't forgive. Luckily, for about six years he was occupied with other matters. He entrusted me with various missions, including that of sounding out the intentions of the Alessandrians. So I went twice to Alessandria to see if my fellow citizens wanted to concede anything. In fact, they were ready to concede a great deal, but the truth is that Frederick wanted only one thing: the city had to disappear into the vacuum from which it had come. You can imagine the Alessandrians! I don't dare repeat to you what they told me to say to him. . . . I realized that those journeys were only a pretext to spend as little time as possible at court, because it was a source of constant suffering to meet the empress and to maintain my vow...."

"Which you did maintain?" Niketas asked, almost as an affirmation.

"Which I did maintain, and forever, Master Niketas. I may be a counterfeiter of parchments, but I know what honor is. She helped me. Motherhood had transformed her. Or at least that was the impression she wanted to give, and I never understood what she felt for me. I suffered, and yet I was grateful to her for the way she helped me behave with dignity."

Baudolino by now was over thirty, and tempted to consider the Prester John letter a youthful caprice, a fine exercise in epistolary rhetoric, a *jocus,* a *ludibrium.* He had found the Poet again, who, after the death of Rainald, had remained without a patron, and you know what happens at court in such cases: you're no longer worth anything, and there are those who start saying your poems were never all that great. Gnawed by bitterness and rancor, the Poet had spent some ill-considered years in Pavia, resuming the only activities in which he shone, namely, drinking and reciting the poems of Baudolino (especially one verse, prophetic, that went *quis Papie demorans castus habeatur,* can he who lives in Pavia be chaste?). Baudolino brought his friend back to court, and in his company the Poet appeared as one of Frederick's men. Further, the Poet's father had died meanwhile, he had come into his inheritance, and even the enemies of the deceased Rainald no longer saw him as a parasite, but as another *miles,* and no more dissipated than the others.

Together, they relived the days of the letter, each complimenting the other on that great achievement. Considering a game as a game does not mean ceasing to play it. Baudolino still felt a yearning for the kingdom he had never seen, and from time to time, alone, he would recite the letter to himself, aloud, continuing to perfect the style.

———

"The proof that I couldn't forget the letter is that I managed to convince Frederick to invite my Parisian friends to court, all of them together, telling him that in the chancellery of an emperor it was good to have people who were familiar with other countries, their languages and their customs. To be truthful, since Frederick was employing me more and more as a confidential messenger in various situations, I wanted to create my little personal court, the Poet, Abdul, Boron, Kyot, and Rabbi Solomon."

"You don't mean to tell me the emperor brought a Jew to his court?"

"Why not? He didn't have to appear in the great ceremonies, or go to Mass with him and his archbishops. If the princes of all Europe and the pope himself have Jewish physicians, why not keep at hand a Jew who knew the life of the Moors in Spain and many other things about the countries of the Orient? Besides, the Germanic princes have always been more clement towards the Hebrews, more than all the other Christian kings. As Otto told me, when Edessa was reconquered by the infidels and many Christian princes again took up the cross, following the preaching of Bernard de Clairvaux (and that was when Frederick himself took up the cross), a monk by the name of Radulph incited the pilgrims to slaughter all the Jews in the cities they passed through. And it was truly a massacre. But many Jews sought the emperor's protection, and he allowed them to take refuge and live in the city of Nuremberg."

In short, Baudolino was reunited with all his cronies. Not that, at court, they had much to do. Solomon, in every city through which Frederick passed, got in touch with his fellow-Jews, and they were to be found everywhere ("like weeds," the Poet taunted him). Abdul discovered that the Provençal of his songs was understood better in Italy than in Paris. Boron and Kyot wore themselves out in dialectical battles: Boron tried to convince Kyot that the nonexistence of the vacuum was crucial in establishing the uniqueness of the Grasal, Kyot obstinately believed that it was a stone fallen from the heavens, *lapis ex coelis,* and as far as he was concerned it could even have arrived from another universe, crossing totally empty spaces.

Apart from these weaknesses, they often discussed the letter of the Priest, and Baudolino's friends asked why he didn't press Frederick to make the journey they had worked so hard to prepare. One day, as Baudolino was trying to explain that, in those years, Frederick had too many problems still to be resolved, both in Lombardy and in Germany, the Poet said that perhaps it would be worthwhile for them to go off themselves in search of the kingdom, without awaiting the emperor's convenience. "The emperor could draw some dubious advantage from this enterprise. Suppose he reaches the land of John and does not come to an agreement with that monarch. He would return defeated, and we would have done him only harm. On the other hand, if we go on our own, however things turn out, we will surely return from such a rich and miraculous land with something extraordinary."

"That's the truth," Abdul said. "What are we waiting for? Let's set out; it is a long way...."

"Master Niketas, I felt sick at heart, as I saw them seized by the Poet's proposal, and I understood why. Both Boron and Kyot were hoping to find the kingdom of the Priest in order to take possession of the Grasal, which would have given them God knows what glory and power in those Northern lands where all were still searching for it. Rabbi Solomon would find the ten lost tribes, and would become the greatest and most honored, not only among the rabbis of Spain, but among all the sons of Israel. In the case of Abdul, there was little to say: he had by now identified the kingdom of Prester John as that of his princess, except that—growing in age and wisdom—distance satisfied him less and less, while the princess, may the god of lovers forgive him, was someone he wanted to be able to put his hands on. As for the Poet, who knows what he had been brooding over in Pavia?

Now, with a modest fortune of his own, he seemed to want John's kingdom for himself, not for the emperor. This explains why for some years, in my disappointment, I didn't speak to Frederick of the Priest's kingdom. If this was the game, it was better to leave that kingdom where it was, saving it from the desires of those who failed to understand its mystical greatness. The letter had thus become my personal dream, and I no longer wanted anyone else to enter it. I needed it to quell the sufferings of my unhappy love. One day, I told myself, I will forget all this because I will move towards the land of Prester John.... But now we should return to the affairs of Lombardy."

In the days of Alessandria's birth, Frederick had said that if Pavia were to go over to his enemies, that would be the last straw. And two years later Pavia did choose the anti-imperial League. It was a bitter blow for the emperor. He did not react at once, but in the course of the following years the situation in Italy became so murky that Frederick resolved to return, and it was clear to all that he was aiming precisely at Alessandria.

"Forgive me..." Niketas said, "so he was going back into Italy for the third time?"

"No, the fourth. Wait, let me remember.... It must have been the fifth, I think. Sometimes he stayed, maybe for four years, like that time of Crema and the destruction of Milan. Or had he gone back in the meantime? No, no, he spent more time in Italy than at his own home—but what was his home? Accustomed as he was to traveling, he felt at home, I had realized, only along the banks of a river: he was a good swimmer, the cold never frightened him, or deep water, or whirlpools. He flung himself into the water, swam, and he seemed to feel he was in his own element. In any case, the time I'm now talking about, he went down very angry, ready for a hard war. With him was the marquess of Monferrato, as well as the cities of Alba, Acqui, Pavia, and Como..."

"But you just said that Pavia had gone over to the League?"

"Did I? Oh, yes, before. But in the meantime it had come back to the emperor."

"Oh, Lord!" Niketas cried, "our emperors dig each other's eyes out, but at least, as long as they see, we know whose side they are on...."

"You people have no imagination. Anyway, in September of that year Frederick descended, through the Mont Cenis pass to Susa. The affront he had suffered seven years earlier was not forgotten, and he put the town to the sword and burned it. Asti surrendered at once, giving him free passage, and there he was encamped in Frascheta, along the Bormida, but he had deployed other men all around, even beyond the Tanaro. It was time to settle scores with Alessandria. I received letters from the Poet, who had followed the expedition, and it seems that Frederick was breathing flame and fire, and felt he was the very incarnation of divine justice."

"Why weren't you with him?"

"Because he was good, truly. He realized the anguish I could feel at witnessing the severe punishment he was going to inflict on the people of my land, and with some pretext he urged me to stay far away until Roboreto was nothing but a heap of ashes. You understand? He didn't call it Civitas Nova or Alessandria, because a new city, without his permission, couldn't exist. So he spoke of the old place, Roboreto, as if it had only expanded a little."

This was early November. But November, in that plain, meant deluge. It rained and rained, and even the cultivated fields became swamp. The marquess of Monferrato had assured Frederick that those walls were of earth, and behind them were some strays who would shit green at the very name of the emperor, but instead those vagabonds proved good defenders, and the walls turned out to be so solid that the cats, the imperial rams, broke their horns against them. The horses and the soldiers wallowed in the mud, and the besieged at

173

one point deviated the course of the Bormida, so the best of the Alaman cavalry was in mud up to its neck.

Finally, the Alessandrians sent out a machine like the ones seen at Crema: a scaffolding of wood that clung well to the ramparts, and projected a very long gangway, a slightly tilted bridge that permitted them to dominate the enemy beyond the walls. And along that gangway they rolled barrels filled with dry wood, impregnated with oil, lard, suet, and liquid pitch, to which they set fire. The barrels moved very fast, and they fell on the imperial machines, or else on the ground, where they resumed rolling like balls of fire, until they reached another machine and set fire to it.

At that point the besiegers' greatest task was transporting kegs of water to put out the fires. There was no lack of water, with the rivers, the swamp, and the water pouring down from heaven, but if all the soldiers were carrying water, who would kill the enemy?

The emperor had decided to devote the winter to reordering his army, because it is hard to attack walls when you're sliding on ice or sinking into the snow. Unfortunately that February was very severe, the army was disheartened, and the emperor even more so. Frederick, who had subjugated Terdona, Crema, and even Milan, ancient cities well-trained in the arts of war, was helpless against a mass of hovels that was a city only by miracle, and housed people that came from only God knew where. And only God knew why they were so attached to those walls, which, in any case, had never belonged to them.

Kept at a distance to prevent his seeing the destruction of his people, Baudolino decided to go to those places for fear that his people might harm the emperor.

So here he was, facing the plain where stood the city he had seen in its cradle, all bristling with banners sporting a great red cross on a white ground, as if the inhabitants wanted to muster their courage by displaying, newly born as they were, the quarterings of an ancient nobility. Facing the walls was a mushrooming field of cats, pulleys, catapults, and, among them, drawn by horses in front and pushed by men behind, three towers advanced, teeming with rowdy people, shaking their weapons at the walls as if to say: "Here we come!"

Accompanying the towers, he saw the Poet, riding along with the mien of one making sure that everything is being done properly. "Who are those madmen on the towers?" Baudolino asked. "Genoese crossbowmen," the Poet replied, "the most fearsome assault troops in a well-ordered siege."

"The Genoese?" Baudolino was dumbfounded. "But they helped found the city!" The Poet laughed and said that in the mere four or five months since he had arrived in these parts, he had seen more than one city change its allegiance. In October, Terdona had sided with the communes, then saw that Alessandria was holding out too well against the emperor, and the Dertonesi began to suspect that the city could become too strong, and a good number of them were now insisting that their city should go over to Frederick. Cremona, at the time of Milan's surrender, was with the empire, in recent years it had passed to the League, but now for some mysterious reason of its own, it was dealing with the imperials.

"And how is the siege going?"

"It's proceeding badly. Either those inside the walls are defending themselves well or else we don't know how to attack. If you ask me, the mercenaries Frederick has brought with him this time are worn out. You can't trust them; they run off at the first difficulty. Many deserted this winter, only because it was cold and yet they were Flemings, so they didn't come from *hic sunt leones*. Finally, in the camp they're dying like flies, of a thousand diseases, and inside the walls I don't believe they're any better off, because they must have run out of provisions."

Baudolino at last presented himself to the emperor. "I've come here, dear Father," he said, "because I know these places and I could be of use to you."

"Yes," Barbarossa replied, "but you also know the people, and you won't want any harm done to them."

175

"And you know me: if you don't trust my heart, you know you can trust my words. I will not harm my people but I will not lie to you."

"On the contrary. You will lie to me, but you won't do me any harm either. You will lie and I'll pretend to believe you because you always lie for good ends."

He was a rough man, Baudolino explained to Niketas, but capable of great subtlety. "Can you understand what I felt then? I didn't want to destroy that city, but I loved him, and I wanted his glory."

"You had only to convince yourself," Niketas said, "that his glory would have shone even more if he were to spare the city."

"God bless you, Master Niketas, it's as if you read my soul at that time. This was the idea in my head as I moved back and forth between the camps and the walls. I had made it clear to Frederick that obviously I would establish some contact with the natives, as if I were a kind of ambassador, but evidently it wasn't clear to all that I could move without arousing any suspicion. At court some people envied my familiarity with the emperor, the bishop of Speyer, for example, and a certain Count Ditpold, whom everyone called the Bishopess, perhaps because he had the blond hair and rosy cheeks of a maiden. Perhaps he didn't give himself to the bishop; in fact he always talked about his Tecla, whom he had left behind up there in the north. Who knows? . . . He was handsome, but, happily, he was also stupid. It was those two who set their spies, even there in the camp, to follow me and then went and told the emperor that the night before I had been seen riding towards the walls and talking with people of the city. Fortunately the emperor sent them to the devil, because he knew I went towards the walls in the daytime and not at night."

So Baudolino did go to the walls, and even inside the walls. The first time was not easy because as he trotted towards the gates, he heard the whistle of a stone—a sign that in the city they were beginning to save their arrows and were using slingshots, which since the time of David had proved effective and cheap. He had to shout in pure Frescheta dialect, making broad gestures with his weaponless arms, and fortunately he was recognized by Trotti.

"O Baudolino," Trotti shouted down at him, "are you coming to join us?"

"Don't play the fool, Trotti, you already know I'm on the other side. But I'm surely not here with bad intentions. Let me come in: I want to speak to my father. I swear on the Virgin that I won't say a word about what I may see."

"I trust you. Open the gates, down there! Did you hear me, or are all of you weak in the head? This is a friend. Or almost. I mean he's with them, but he's one of ours. He's one of us but he's one of theirs. Hey, just open the gates or I'll kick your teeth in!"

"All right, all right," those wide-eyed fighters said. "No telling here who's in and who's out; yesterday that man went out dressed like a Pavese."

"Shut your mouth, you animal," Trotti shouted. And "Ha ha" Baudolino laughed, as he entered. "You've sent spies to our camp.... Don't worry. I told you: I won't see anything or hear anything."

And now Baudolino is embracing Gagliaudo—still vigorous and as if strengthened by enforced fasting—near the well of the little square just inside the walls. Then he finds Ghini and Scaccabarozzi opposite the church; and when he asks where Squarciafichi is, they weep and tell him that Squarciafichi took a Genoese dart in the throat in the last attack, and Baudolino also weeps, for he has never liked war and now less than ever, and he fears for his old father. Here is Baudolino in the beautiful main square, bright in the pale March sunshine; he sees children carrying big baskets of stones to reinforce the defenses, and skins of water for the sentries, and he is proud of the indomitable spirit that has gripped the citizens; here is Baudolino wondering who all these people are crowding into Alessandria as if for a wedding feast, and his friends tell him that this is their great misfortune, that fear of the imperial army has brought here people fleeing all the surrounding villages, and, yes, the city has many hands, but also too many mouths to feed; here is Baudolino admiring the new cathedral, which may not be big but is well made, and he says: "Why, it even has a tympanum with a dwarf on the throne," and around him they say: "Oh yes," as if to say you see what we're able to do, but that isn't a dwarf, stupid, it's Our Lord, maybe not well done, but if Frederick had come a month later he would have found the whole Last Judgment with the oldsters of the Apocalypse; here is Baudolino asking for a glass of the good stuff, and they all look at him as if he came from the camp of the imperials, because it's clear that wine, bad or good, is not to be found, not even a drop; it's the first thing they give to the wounded to keep their spirits up, and to the families of the dead to keep their mind off their troubles; and here is Baudolino seeing around him wan faces and asking how long they can hold out, and they make superstitious gestures, raising their eyes as if to say these things are in the hands of the Lord; and finally here is Baudolino meeting Anselmo Medico, who commands five hundred foot soldiers from Piacenza, who have rushed to help the Civitas Nova, and Baudolino is pleased at this fine show of solidarity, and his friends Guasco, Trotti, Boidi, and Oberto del Foro say that this Anselmo is a man who knows how to fight, but the Piacenza men are the only ones; the League urged us to rebel but now they don't give a damn about us, the Italian communes are a fraud, if we come out of this siege alive, from now on we owe nothing to anyone, they can deal with the emperor on their own, and amen.

"But how is it that the Genoese are against you, when they helped you build the city, and gave you gold?"

"The Genoese know how to run their business, you can count on that, so now they're with the emperor because it's in their interest; everybody knows, and they know, that, once it's here, the city won't go away, not even if they knock it down, like Lodi or Milan. So they wait for the afterwards, and afterwards what remains of the city is still useful to them to control the trade routes, and maybe they'll pay to rebuild what they helped destroy, but meanwhile money keeps changing hands, and the Genoese are always there."

"Baudolino," Ghini said to him, "you've just arrived and you didn't see the attacks in October and the ones in the last weeks. They're fighters, not just the Genoese crossbowmen, but those Bohemians with the mustaches almost white, who if they manage to set a ladder in place it's a real job knocking it down. . . . It's true that, in my opinion, more of their men died than ours because, even if they have the rams and the cats, they've taken plenty of clods on the head. Anyway, it's hard, and we tighten our belts."

"We've received a message," Trotti said, "that the League's troops are on the move, and they want to surprise the emperor from behind. Do you know anything about that?"

"We've heard the same thing, and that's why Frederick wants to make you surrender first. You . . . you aren't thinking of giving up now, are you?"

"What an idea! Our head is harder than our cock."

And so, for some weeks, after every skirmish, Baudolino went home, to tally the dead more than for any other reason (Panizza, too? Yes, Panizza, too, and he was a good man), and then he returned to tell Frederick that those men . . . surrender? Not a chance. Frederick no longer cursed, but confined himself to saying: "What can I do about it?" It was clear that by now he repented having got himself into this mess: his army was falling apart, the peasants were hiding the grain and their stock in the woods or, worse, in the swamps, he couldn't press forward to north or east, or he would encounter some vanguard of the League—in short, it wasn't that these rustics were better than the people of Crema, but bad luck is bad luck. However, he couldn't just go away, because he would be humiliated forever.

As for saving face, Baudolino realized, from something the emperor said one day, referring to his boyhood feat—the time he had persuaded the Terdona people to surrender—that if Frederick could only exploit a sign from heaven, any sign, allowing him to announce *urbi et orbi* that heaven itself was suggesting they go back home, Frederick would seize the opportunity...

One day, while Baudolino was talking with the besieged, Gagliaudo said to him: "You're so intelligent and you've studied the books where everything is written—don't you have some idea that will make everybody leave, now that we've had to slaughter our cows, except for one, and your mother is going to die of suffocation, penned up in the city like this?"

And then Baudolino had a fine idea, and he immediately asked if they had actually invented that false tunnel Trotti had talked about a few years before, the tunnel the enemy was to believe led straight into the city, but really led the invader into a trap. "Of course," Trotti said, "come and see. Look. The tunnel opens over there, in that thicket two hundred feet from the walls, just below a kind of boundary stone that looks like it's been there for a thousand years but really we brought it from Villa del Foro. And anyone who enters there ends up here, beneath that grating, from which you can see the tavern and nothing else."

"And as one comes out, you do him in?"

"The fact is that, generally, with a tunnel that narrow, it would take days for all the besiegers to come through, so they send only one squad of men, who are supposed to reach the gates and open them. Now, apart from the fact that we don't know how to inform the enemy that there's a tunnel, after you've killed maybe twenty or, at most, thirty poor bastards, was it worth the effort to do all that work? It's nothing but a cheap trick."

"If it's only to hit them on the head. But listen to the scene I can almost see with these eyes of mine: the moment the men come in, a blast of trumpets sounds and, in the light of ten torches, from that corner appears a man with a long white beard and a white cloak, on a white horse with a great white cross in his hand, and he shouts: Citizens, citizens, wake up, the enemy is here. Before the invaders have made up their mind to move a step, our people appear at the windows and on the rooftops. And after the enemies are captured, our people sink to their knees and cry that the man in white is Saint Peter, who is protecting the city, and they push the imperials back into the tunnel, saying, Thank God that we're sparing your lives; go to the camp of your Barbarossa and tell them that the New City of Pope Alexander is protected by Saint Peter in person...."

"And will Barbarossa believe a tale like that?"

"No, because he's not stupid, but since he's not stupid, he will pretend to believe it because he's more anxious to end this than you people are."

"Let's suppose you're right. Who'll arrange to have the tunnel discovered?"

"Me."

"And where are you going to find the asshole who falls for it?"

"I've already found him, and he's such an asshole that he'll fall right into the trap on his shitty face, as he deserves, but anyway we agree that nobody gets killed."

Baudolino had in mind that fop Count Ditpold, and to spur Ditpold into action it was enough to make him believe he was harming Baudolino. So all they had to do was let Ditpold find out that there was a tunnel and that Baudolino didn't want it discovered. How? Nothing easier, since Ditpold had his spies following Baudolino.

After nightfall, returning to the camp, Baudolino first passed through a little clearing, then entered the wood, but once he was among the trees, he stopped and looked back just in time to see, in the moonlight, an agile shadow slipping, almost on all fours, through the open space. It was the man Ditpold had put on his heels. Baudolino waited among the trees until the spy was about to fall on him, pointed his sword at the man's chest and, while the other was stammering in fear, he said to him in Flemish: "I recognize you. You're one of the Brabantines. What were you doing outside the camp? Speak! I'm one of the emperor's ministerials!"

The man said something about a woman, and sounded almost convincing. "All right," Baudolino said. "In any case it's lucky you're here. I need someone to guard my back while I do something."

For the other man this was a blessing. Not only had he not been discovered, but he could continue his spying arm-in-arm with its object. Baudolino reached the thicket Trotti had mentioned. He didn't have to pretend, because he really did have to scratch around to find the stone, while he grumbled as if to himself about receiving word from one of his informers. He found the stone, which did look as if it had grown there with the bushes; he worked over it, scraping foliage away until he had uncovered a grating. He asked the Brabantine to help him lift it: there were three steps. "Now listen," he said to the Brabantine. "Go down these steps and move forward until you reach the end of the tunnel, where you may see some lights. Take a good look at what you see and don't forget any of it. Then come back and report. I'll stay here on guard."

To the soldier it seemed natural, however painful, that a gentleman should first ask him to stand guard and then should stand guard himself, while sending him into the unknown. Baudolino had brandished his sword, surely to cover his back, but with lords there was never any telling. The spy made the sign of the cross and set out. When he returned after about twenty minutes, gasping, he reported what Baudolino already knew: that at the end of the passage there was another grating, not very hard to lift, and beyond it was a solitary little square, and so this tunnel led right into the heart of the city.

Baudolino asked: "Were there some turns, or did you go straight forward?" "Straight," the man replied. And Baudolino, as if talking to himself, said: "So the exit is a few dozen meters from the gates. That traitor was right...." Then, to the Brabantine: "You realize what we've discovered. The first time there's an attack on the walls, a squad of brave men can enter the city, fight their way to the gates and open them; we just have to have more troops outside, ready to enter. My fortune is made. But you must tell no one what you have seen tonight, because I don't want anyone taking advantage of my discovery." With a munificent air he handed him a coin, and the price of silence was so ridiculous that, if not out of loyalty to Ditpold, at least for revenge, the spy would immediately run and tell him everything.

It requires little imagination to picture what was to happen. Thinking that Baudolino wanted to keep the news secret, so as not to harm his besieged friends, Ditpold hurried to tell the emperor that his beloved son had discovered an entrance into the city but was taking care not to reveal it. The emperor raised his eyes to heaven as if to say: the dear boy, him too, then he said to Ditpold: very well, I offer you the glory; towards sunset I'll deploy for you a good attack force just outside the gate, I'll have some onagers and some rams placed near the thicket. When you slip into the tunnel with your men it will be almost dark and nobody will notice you, you enter the city, open the gates from inside, and overnight you become a hero."

The bishop of Speyer immediately claimed the command of the forces outside the gate, because Ditpold, he said, was like his own son. Imagine!

And so, on the afternoon of Good Friday, when Trotti saw the imperials waiting outside the gate, as always when darkness was falling, he understood it was a display to distract the besieged, and behind it there was the hand of Baudolino. So, discussing it with Guasco, Boidi, and Oberto del Foro, he took care to provide a credible Saint Peter; one of the original consuls, Rodolfo Nebia, volunteered, and had the suitable physique. They wasted only a half hour debating whether the apparition should hold the cross or the usual keys, deciding on the cross, which would be more visible in the gloaming.

Baudolino was a short distance from the gates, certain that there would be no battle, because someone would first emerge from the tunnel bearing the news of the celestial assistance. And, in fact, in the time of three Paters, Aves, and Glorias, from inside the walls a great stir was heard, a voice that to all seemed superhuman shouted: "To arms, to arms, my faithful Alessandrians!" and a chorus of terrestrial voices cried: "It's Saint Peter! Oh, miracle! Miracle!"

But right at this point something went wrong. As they would later explain to Baudolino, Ditpold and his men had been promptly caught and everyone tried to convince them that Saint Peter had appeared. They would probably have fallen for it, the lot of them, except Ditpold, who knew very well from whom the revelation of the tunnel had come, and—stupid, but not that stupid—he realized that the idea had been conceived by Baudolino. He freed himself from his captors' grip, ran down a narrow street shouting in such a loud voice that nobody could understand what language he was talking, and in the twilight they believed he was one of them. But when he was on the wall, it was obvious that he was addressing the besiegers, to warn them of a trap—it wasn't clear what he was protecting them against, since those outside, if the gate wasn't opened, couldn't come in and therefore were hardly at risk. It made no difference that, precisely because of his stupidity, Ditpold had courage and was at the top of the wall waving his sword and challenging all the Alessandrians. They—as the rules of a siege demand—could not admit that an enemy had reached the wall, even if arriving from within. Above all, only a few were in on the plot, and the rest suddenly saw an Alaman in their midst as if nothing had happened. So someone decided to stick a pike into Ditpold's back, flinging him down from the bastion.

At the sight of his best-beloved comrade falling lifeless at the foot of the keep, the bishop of Speyer lost his head completely and ordered the attack. In a normal situation, the Alessandrians would have behaved as usual, firing on the attackers from the top of the fortifications, but as the enemy pressed at the gates, a rumor was spreading that Saint Peter had appeared, to save the city from danger, and he was preparing to lead a victorious sortie. Meanwhile, Trotti had thought to exploit this misunderstanding, and had sent his bogus Saint Peter to go out first, drawing all the others after him.

In short, Baudolino's trick, which should have clouded the minds of the assailants, clouded instead those of the assailed: the Alessandrians, gripped by mystic furor and by the most bellicose ecstasy, were flinging themselves like beasts against the imperials—and in such a disordered way, contrary to the rules of the art of war, that the bishop of Speyer and his knights, bewildered, fell back, imitated by those who were meant to push the crossbowmen's towers, leaving them at the very edge of the fatal thicket. For the Alessandrians it was an open invitation: immediately Anselmo Medico with his Piacentines slipped into the tunnel, which now was truly helpful, and emerged behind the Genoese, with a group of bold men carrying poles on which they had stuck balls of burning pitch. And so the Genoese towers caught fire like kindling. The crossbowmen jumped off, but as they hit the ground, the Alessandrians were there to strike their heads with clubs; one tower first tilted, then crumbled, spreading flames among the bishop's cavalry, the horses seemed crazed, upsetting the ranks of the imperials even more, and those not on horseback contributed to the disorder, because they ran through the ranks of the riders shouting that Saint Peter in person was arriving, and perhaps also Saint Paul, and some had even seen Saint Sebastian and Saint Tarcisius—the whole Christian Olympus, in other words, had joined that loathsome city.

At night, some men brought to the imperial camp, already in deep mourning, the corpse of the bishop of Speyer, struck in the back as he was fleeing. Frederick sent for Baudolino and asked what his part in this story was and what he knew of it, and Baudolino wanted to sink through the ground, because that evening many brave men had died, including Anselmo Medico of Piacenza, and valorous sergeants, and poor foot soldiers, and all for that fine plan of his—which should have resolved everything without a hair of anyone's head being touched. He threw himself at Frederick's feet, telling him the whole truth, how he had thought to offer him a credible pretext for raising the siege and instead things had gone as they had.

"I'm a wretch, dear Father," he said. "Blood revolts me, and I wanted to keep my hands clean, and spare many other deaths, and look at the slaughter I've wrought. All these deaths are on my conscience!"

"Curse you, or curse those who botched the plan," Frederick replied, apparently more saddened than angered, "because—don't tell this to anyone—that pretext would have indeed been a help to me. I have had fresh news: the League is on the move, perhaps as soon as tomorrow we'll have to fight on two fronts. Your Saint Peter would have convinced the soldiers, but now too many have died, and my barons are demanding revenge. They're going around saying that this is the right moment to teach the people of this city a lesson. It was enough to see those people when they came out: thinner than we are, and they were really making their final effort."

By then it was Holy Saturday. The air was tepid, the fields were decked with flowers, and the trees were joyously sprouting. The people were sad as at a funeral, the imperials because each said it was time to attack and nobody felt like doing it, the Alessandrians because, after the effort of the last sortie, their spirits were high, though their bellies were hanging between their legs. Thus it was that Baudolino's fertile mind set to work again.

He rode once more towards the walls, and found Trotti, Guasco, and the other leaders grave and frowning. They also knew about the arrival of the League, but they had heard from a reliable source that the various communes were deeply divided as to how to proceed, and very uncertain as to whether they should actually attack Frederick.

"Because it's one thing, Master Niketas—now mind you, this is a very fine point that maybe Byzantines aren't subtle enough to grasp—it's one thing to defend yourselves when the emperor is besieging you, and another thing to start a battle on your own initiative.

I mean: if your father hits you with his belt, you have the right to try to grab it and tear it from his hands—that's self-defense—but if you're the one who raises his hand to strike your father, then it's patricide. Once you have definitively shown disrespect to the holy and Roman emperor, what do you have left to keep the Italian communes together? You understand, Master Niketas, there they were, having just torn Frederick's troops to pieces, but they continued to recognize him as their sole lord. They didn't want him underfoot, but it would have been awful if he no longer existed: they would have massacred one another not even knowing if they were acting well or badly, because the criterion of right and wrong was, in the end, the emperor."

"So," Guasco said, "the best thing would be for the emperor to abandon immediately the siege of Alessandria, and I assure you the communes would allow him passage to reach Pavia." But how could he be permitted to save appearances? We had already tried the sign from heaven, and the Alessandrians had gained a great satisfaction, but they were again back where they started from. Saint Peter had been too ambitious, Baudolino then remarked, and a vision or an apparition, whatever you choose to call it, is something that's there and isn't there. Besides, the next day it's easy to deny it. Finally, why trouble the saints? Those mercenaries were people who didn't believe even in the Father Almighty; the only thing they believed in was a full belly and a hard cock...."

"Let's suppose..." Gagliaudo said then, with the wisdom that God—as all know—gives only to poor folk, "let's suppose that the imperials capture one of our cows, and they find her so stuffed with wheat that her belly's about to explode. Then Barbarossa and his men will think that we still have so much food that we can hold out in *sculasculorum,* and so it'll be those very same lords and soldiers who'll say let's clear out, otherwise we'll still be here for next Easter...."

"I've never heard such a stupid idea," Guasco said, and Trotti agreed with him, tapping his brow with one finger, as if to say the old man was by now weak in the head. "And if there was still a cow alive, we'd have already eaten her, even raw," Boidi added.

"Not because this man's my father, but the idea doesn't seem to me something to be disregarded," Baudolino said. "Maybe you've forgotten it, but there *is* one cow left, and it's Gagliaudo's very own Rosina. The only problem is whether, even if you scrape every corner of the city, you'll find enough wheat to make the animal burst."

"The problem is that you're a dumb animal yourself, you animal!" Gagliaudo leaped to his feet. "Because obviously to understand that she's full of wheat, the imperials have not only to find her, but also cut her open, and we haven't slaughtered my Rosina because for me and your mother she's like the daughter the Lord never granted us, so nobody's going to touch her: I'd sooner send you to the shambles, after you stay thirty years away from home, while she's stayed here with us, without any bees in her bonnet."

Guasco and the others, who until a moment before were thinking this idea worthy of a madman, once Gagliaudo opposed it became instantly convinced that it was the best conceivable plan, and they bent every effort to convince the old man that, when the fate of the city is involved, you sacrifice even your personal cow, and it was useless for him to say he'd rather give up Baudolino, because cutting open Baudolino wouldn't convince anyone, whereas cutting open the cow might make Barbarossa drop everything. As for the wheat, they didn't have any to squander, but by scratching around, a bit here and a bit there, they should collect enough to fatten Rosina, and without being over-fussy, because once it was in the stomach, it was hard for anyone to say if it was wheat or chaff, and without bothering to remove the weevils, or roaches, or whatever you call them, for in wartime you found them even in the bread.

"Come now, Baudolino," Niketas said, "you're not going to tell me that everyone was seriously considering such a piece of nonsense."

"Not only did we consider it seriously, but—as you'll see subsequently—the emperor took it seriously, too."

In fact, this is how the story went. Towards the third hour of that Holy Saturday all the consuls and the persons of greatest authority in Alessandria were under a shed where a cow was lying, and a more skinny and moribund cow it would be hard to imagine, the hide blotchy, the legs like sticks, the teats seemed ears, the ears seemed nipples, a stunned gaze, even her horns drooping, and the rest more carcass than body, not so much a cow as the ghost of a cow, a *Totentanz* cow, lovingly tended by Baudolino's mother, who stroked Rosina's head, saying that after all this may be for the best, her sufferings would end, and after a hearty meal, and hence she was better off than her master and mistress.

Nearby, sacks of wheat and seeds kept arriving, collected as best anyone could, and Gagliaudo put the food under the muzzle of the poor creature, urging her to eat. But the cow now looked upon the world with moaning detachment, and no longer even recalled what ruminating meant. So, finally, some hardy souls held her legs fast, others her head, and still others forced her mouth open, and as she was weakly mooing her refusal, they thrust the wheat down her throat, as is done with geese. Then, perhaps out of an instinct for self-preservation, or stirred by the memory of better days, the animal began moving with her tongue all that plenty, and a bit through her own will and a bit through the help of the bystanders, she started to swallow.

It was not a joyous meal, and more than once it seemed to all that Rosina was about to give up her animal soul to God, for she ate as if she were giving birth, between one moan and the next. But then the life force took the upper hand, the cow struggled to her four hoofs and went on eating by herself, sticking her muzzle directly into the sacks that were offered her. In the end what they were all seeing was a quite odd cow, very skinny and melancholy, with her spine protruding and marked as if the bones wanted to escape the hide imprisoning them, while the belly, on the contrary, was opulent, rotund, hydropsical, and taut as if she were heavy with ten calves.

"It won't work, it won't work." Boidi shook his head, in the face of this profoundly sad portent. "Even a fool can see that this animal isn't fat: she's just a cow hide that's been stuffed...."

"And even if they do believe she's fat," Guasco said, "how could they accept the idea that her master still takes her out to pasture, risking the loss of both his life and his precious animal?"

"My friends," Baudolino said, "don't forget that, whoever the men who find her are, they'll be so hungry that they won't stop to see if she's fat here and thin there."

Baudolino was right. Towards the ninth hour Gagliaudo had barely ventured out the gate, to a meadow half a league from the walls, when from the woods came a band of Bohemians, who were surely out hunting for birds, if there was still a bird alive in those parts. They saw the cow, unable to believe their ravenous eyes, they flung themselves on Gagliaudo. He promptly held up his hands, and they dragged him and the animal towards the camp. Soon a crowd had gathered around them, warriors with hollow cheeks and bulging eyes, and poor Rosina's throat was soon slashed by a Como man who seemed to know the art, because he did it with one stroke, and Rosina, in the time it takes to utter an amen, was alive one moment and dead the next. Gagliaudo really did cry, and so the scene appeared convincing to all.

When the animal's belly was cut open, what was to happen happened: all that food that had been so hastily forced into her now poured out on the ground as if it were still intact, and to all it seemed indubitable that it was wheat. The amazement was such that it prevailed over appetite, and in any case hunger had not robbed those armed men of an elementary ratiocination: if, in a besieged city, the cows could feast to this degree, it went against every rule, human and divine. A sergeant, among the bystanders, was able to repress his own instincts, and decided that his commanders should be informed of the wonder. Shortly the news reached the ear of the emperor, with whom Baudolino was lingering, with apparent indolence, while tense and nervously awaiting events.

The carcass of Rosina, a canvas sheet in which the overflowing grain had been gathered, and Gagliaudo in irons were brought before Frederick. Dead and split in two, the cow no longer seemed fat or thin, and the only thing that could be seen was all that stuff inside and outside her belly. A sign that Frederick did not underestimate, as he immediately asked the peasant: "Who are you? Where are you from? Whose cow is that?" And Gagliaudo, even without understanding a word, replied in the purest dialect, I don't know, I wasn't there, I have nothing to do with this, I was just passing by chance, and this is the first time I've ever seen this cow, and if you hadn't told me yourself, I wouldn't even have known it's a cow. Naturally Frederick did not understand, and he turned to Baudolino; "You know this bestial language, tell me what he's saying."

Scene between Baudolino and Gagliaudo (translation): "He says he knows nothing about the cow, that a rich peasant in the city gave her to him to take out to pasture, and that's all."

"Ask him how that happened."

"He says that all cows, after they've eaten and before they've digested, are full of what they've eaten."

"Tell him not to play dumb, or I'll tie his neck to that tree! In this town, in this city of bandits, do they always give wheat to their cows?"

Gagliaudo: "With lack of hay and lack of straw, we feed the stock on wheat . . . and *arbioni*."

Baudolino: "He says no, only now when there's a shortage of hay, because of the siege. And anyway it's not all grain, there are also some dry *arbioni*."

"*Arbioni*?"

"*Erbse, pisa,* peas."

"By the devil, I'll give him to my falcons to peck at, or my dogs to

191

tear limb from limb, what does he mean by saying there's a shortage of hay but none of wheat and peas?"

"He says that in the city they've collected all the cows of the area, and now they can eat beefsteaks till the end of the world, but the cows have eaten all the hay, and that people, if they can eat meat don't eat bread, or—even less—dried peas, so a part of the wheat they had stored up they are giving to the cows. He says it's not like it is here with us, who have everything; there they have to make do the best they can because they are poor citizens under siege. He says this is why they gave him the cow to take outside, so she could eat a bit of grass, because this stuff by itself is bad for her and she gets ringworm."

"Baudolino, do you believe what this clod is saying?"

"I'm only translating what he says. As far as I recall from my infancy, I'm not sure that cows like to eat wheat, but this one was surely full of the stuff, and the evidence of your eyes can't be denied."

Frederick stroked his beard, narrowed his eyes, and took a good look at Gagliaudo. "Baudolino," he said then, "I have the impression that I've seen this man before, only it must have been a long time ago. You don't know him?"

"Father, I know more or less everybody around here. But the problem now isn't to ask who this man is, but whether it's true that in the city they have all these cows and all this wheat. Because, if you want my sincere opinion, they could be trying to deceive you, by stuffing their last cow with the last of their wheat."

"Good thinking, Baudolino. That hadn't occurred to me."

"Most Holy Majesty," the marquess of Monferrato spoke up, "we must not credit these peasants with more intelligence than they possess. It seems to me we have a clear sign that the city is better supplied than we had supposed."

"Oh, yes, yes," all the other lords said with one voice, and Baudolino concluded that he had never seen so many people of bad faith, all together, each clearly recognizing the bad faith of the others. But it was a sign that this siege was by now intolerable for all.

"And so apparently it must seem to me," Frederick said diplomatically. "The enemy army is pressing us from behind. Taking Roboreto wouldn't save us from having to face the other army. Nor can we think of conquering the city and shutting ourselves up inside those walls, so ill-made they'd be an insult to our dignity. So, my lords, we have come to this decision: we'll abandon this wretched town to its wretched cow herders, and prepare ourselves for quite different conflict. Have the appropriate orders issued." And then, coming out of the royal tent, he said to Baudolino: "Send that old man home. He's surely a liar, but if I had to hang all liars, you would have left this world long since."

"Hurry home, Father. You've been lucky," Baudolino whispered, removing Gagliaudo's irons, "and tell Trotti that I'll be waiting for him this evening at the place he knows."

Frederick did it all in haste. There was no need to remove any tents, those tatters that now constituted the besiegers' camp. He lined the men up and ordered everything to be burned. At midnight the vanguard of the army was already marching towards the fields of Marengo. In the background, at the foot of the Tortona hills, some fires were glowing: in the distance the army of the League was waiting.

Asking leave of the emperor, Baudolino rode off in the direction of Sale, and at a crossroads he found Trotti waiting for him with two consuls of Cremona. They rode together for a mile, until they reached an advanced post of the League. There Trotti introduced Baudolino to the two leaders of the communal army, Ezzelino da Romano and Anselmo da Dovara. A brief council followed, sealed by a handshake. Having embraced Trotti (it's turned out fine, thanks to you; no, no, thanks to you), Baudolino went back as quickly as possible to Frederick, who was waiting at the edge of a clearing. "It's settled, Father. They won't attack. They have neither the desire nor the nerve. We will pass, and they will hail you as their lord."

"Until the next fight," Frederick murmured, "but the army's tired. The sooner we're quartered in Pavia, the better. Let's go."

It was the early hours of the feast of Easter. In the distance, if he had turned around, Frederick would have seen the walls of Alessandria shining with tall fires. Baudolino turned and saw them. He knew that many flames were those of the war machines and the imperial lodgings, but he preferred to imagine the Alessandrians dancing and singing to celebrate victory and peace.

After a mile they came upon a vanguard of the League. The squad of horsemen separated and formed two wings, between which the imperials passed. It was not clear if this movement was a greeting or if the troops were drawing aside as a precaution; you never can tell. Some of the League men raised their weapons and this gesture could have been interpreted as a salute. Or perhaps it was a show of impotence, a threat. The emperor, frowning, pretended not to see them.

"I don't know," he said. "I feel as if I were retreating, and these men are showing me the honor of arms. Baudolino, am I doing the right thing?"

"Yes, you are, Father. You are no more surrendering than they are. They don't want to attack you in the open field out of respect. And you must be grateful for this respect."

"It's my due," Barbarossa said stubbornly.

"If you think they owe it to you, then be happy that they are giving it to you. What are you complaining about?"

"Nothing, nothing. As usual, you are right."

Towards dawn they glimpsed in the distant plain and on the first hills the main body of the opposing army. It blended with a light mist, and once again it wasn't clear whether they were moving away from the imperial army out of prudence, or simply gathering around, or if they were pressing closely, and menacingly. In little groups the people of the communes were moving, sometimes accompanying the imperial process for a stretch, sometimes posting themselves on a hillock to watch the army pass. At other times they seemed to flee it.

The silence was profound, broken only by the sound of the horses' hoofs and the tread of the soldiers. From one peak to the next they occasionally glimpsed, in the very pale morning, slender threads of smoke rising, as if one group were sending signals to another, from the top of some tower concealed in the green, up there on the hills.

This time Frederick decided to interpret that perilous passage as occurring in his own honor: he had the standards raised and the oriflammes, and he marched past as if he were Caesar Augustus, who had put down the barbarians. However it was, he passed, father of all those unruly cities that could, that night, have annihilated him.

By now on the road to Pavia, he called Baudolino to his side. "You're the usual rogue," he said. "But after all I did have to find some excuse to leave that mud puddle. I forgive you."

"For what, dear Father?"

"I know what. But you mustn't think I've forgiven that nameless city."

"It has a name."

"It doesn't, because I haven't baptized it. Sooner or later I'll have to destroy it."

"Not immediately."

"No, not immediately. But before then, I imagine you'll have invented another of your tricks. I should have understood, that night, that I was taking a rascal home with me. By the way, I've remembered where I saw that man with the cow before!"

But Baudolino's horse seemed to rear up, and Baudolino, pulling on the reins, had been left behind. So Frederick could not tell him what he had remembered.

15

Baudolino at the battle of Legnano

With the siege over, Frederick, relieved at first, withdrew to Pavia, but he was not content. A bad year followed. His cousin Henry the Lion was giving him trouble in Germany, the Italian cities continued to be unruly and turned a deaf ear every time he demanded the destruction of Alessandria. By now he had few men, reinforcements failed to arrive, and when they did arrive, they were insufficient.

Baudolino felt somewhat guilty because of the cow trick. To be sure, he hadn't deceived the emperor, who had simply gone along with his game, but now both of them felt some awkwardness looking each other in the eye, like two children who have devised a prank and are then ashamed of it. Baudolino was touched by the almost childish embarrassment of Frederick, who was now beginning to go gray, and it was, in fact, his handsome copper beard that first lost its leonine glints.

Baudolino was more and more fond of that father, who continued to pursue his imperial dream, risking more and more the loss of his lands beyond the Alps, to keep control over an Italy that was eluding him on all sides. One day it occurred to Baudolino that, in Frederick's situation, the letter of Prester John would have allowed the emperor to extract himself from the Lombard swamps without seeming to renounce anything. In short, the Priest's letter was a bit like Gagliaudo's cow. He then tried to talk to Frederick about it, but the emperor was in a bad mood and told Baudolino he had far more serious things to concern himself with than the senile fancies of Uncle Otto, rest his soul. Then he gave the youth some other missions, sending him back and forth across the Alps for almost twelve months.

At the end of May of the year of Our Lord 1176 Baudolino learned that Frederick was installed in Como, and he decided to join him in that city. In the course of his journey he was told that the imperial army was now moving towards Pavia, so then he turned southwards, hoping to meet it halfway.

He met it along the Olona, not far from the fortress of Legnano, where a few hours earlier the imperial army and the army of the League had met, without any desire on either side to join battle, though both were forced into a conflict to save their honor.

As soon as he arrived at the edge of the field, Baudolino saw a foot soldier running towards him with a long pike. He spurred his horse, trying to run the man down, hoping to frighten him. The soldier was frightened, and fell on his back, letting go of the pike. Baudolino dismounted and seized the pike, while the man shouted threats to kill him, standing up and drawing a dagger from his belt. But he was shouting in the Lodi dialect. Baudolino had become accustomed to the idea that the people of Lodi were with the empire, and keeping the soldier at bay with the pike, because he seemed out of his mind, Baudolino shouted: "What are you doing, you fool, I'm with the empire too!" The man shouted back: "I know. That's why I'm going to kill you!" At that point Baudolino remembered that Lodi now was on the side of the League, and he asked himself: What shall I do? Kill him? The pike is longer than his knife. But I've never killed anybody!"

He jabbed the pike between the man's legs, sending him sprawling full length on the ground, then aimed the weapon at his throat.

"Don't kill me, *dominus,* because I have seven children, and if I die they'll die of hunger tomorrow," the Lodi man cried. "Let me go. I can't do your people much harm: you see how I give in like an idiot!"

"You're an idiot, all right—anyone can see that at the distance of a day's march. But if I let you go with something in your hand, you could still do some harm. Take off your breeches!"

"My breeches!"

"That's right. I'll spare your life, but I'm making you go around with your balls in the air. I want to see if you go back to fighting like that, or if you run straight home to your lousy children!"

The enemy took off his breeches, and began to run through the fields, leaping over the hedges, not so much from shame, but because he was afraid an enemy knight could see him from behind and, thinking he was displaying his buttocks in contempt, impale him, Turkish-style.

Baudolino was content that he had not had to kill anyone, but now a man on horseback was galloping towards him. The rider wore French dress, so was obviously not a Lombard. Baudolino decided to sell his life dearly and he drew his sword. The rider passed by him, shouting: "What are you doing, you lunatic? Can't you see that today we screwed you imperials! Go home; that's best for you!" And off he rode, not seeking any trouble.

Baudolino remounted and asked himself where he should go, because he understood absolutely nothing of this battle, and until now he had seen only sieges, in which case you clearly know who is on this side and who on the other.

He rode around a clump of trees, and in the midst of the plain saw something he had never seen before: a great open wagon, painted red and white, with a long pennon and banners at its center, and an altar surrounded by some soldiers with long trumpets like the ones angels hold, which perhaps served to urge the men into battle, whereupon he said—as they said around his part of the country: "Hey, that's enough!" For a moment he thought he had happened upon

198

Prester John, or was in Sarandib at the very least, where they went into battle on a wagon drawn by elephants, but the wagon he now saw was drawn by oxen, even if all decked out like gentlemen, and around the wagon there was no fighting. The men with trumpets let out a blast every so often, then stopped, unsure what to do next. Some of them pointed to a tangle of people on the shore of the river, who were still flinging themselves on one another, letting out cries to wake the dead; others were trying to make the oxen move, but restive as they generally are, they now seemed even more reluctant to get mixed up in the brawling.

What shall I do? Baudolino wondered. Shall I jump into the midst of those fanatics down there, not even knowing who the enemies are, unless they speak first? And maybe, while I'm waiting for them to speak, they'll kill me?

As he was pondering the question, another knight came towards him, and this was a ministerial whom he knew well. The man also recognized him and shouted: "Baudolino! We've lost the emperor!"

"What do you mean you've lost him, for Christ's sake?"

"Somebody saw him fighting like a lion in the midst of a horde of foot soldiers, pushing his horse towards that little wood, then they all disappeared among the trees. We went over there but couldn't find anybody left. He must have tried to escape in some direction, but he surely didn't return to the main body of our cavalry...."

"Where is the main body of our cavalry?"

"Actually, the problem isn't only that he didn't rejoin the main body of the cavalry, it's that the main body of the cavalry no longer exists. There was a slaughter, curse this day. In the beginning Frederick and his horsemen hurled themselves on the enemy, who seemed all on foot, all gathered around that catafalque. But those foot soldiers fought back, and suddenly the Lombard cavalry turned up, so our men were attacked on two sides."

"You mean to say you've lost the holy Roman emperor? And you tell me in this tone? God help us."

"You look like you just got here. You don't know what we've been through! Some say they actually saw the emperor fall, and then he was dragged off by the horse, his foot caught in the stirrup!"

"What are our men doing now?"

"They're running away. Look there. They're scattering among the trees, throwing themselves into the river. Now there's a rumor that the emperor's dead, and each man is trying to get to Pavia as best he can."

"The cowards! And nobody's looking for our lord any more?"

"Darkness is falling. Even the men who had kept on fighting are about to stop. How could you find anyone here, or God knows where?"

"Cowards!" Baudolino said again. Though he was not a man of war, he had a great heart. He spurred his horse and, with sword drawn, flung himself upon a great pile of corpses, as he called in a loud voice for his beloved adoptive father. Seeking a dead man on that plain, among so many other corpses, and shouting to him to give a sign, was a desperate enterprise, so much so that the last Lombard squads he encountered let him pass, taking him for some saint from Paradise who had come to lend them a hand, and greeting him with festive gestures.

Where the fighting had been most bloody, Baudolino began turning over the bodies that lay face down, still hoping and at the same time fearing to discover in the dim twilight the beloved features of his sovereign. He wept, and proceeded so blindly that, emerging from a grove, he bumped into that great ox-drawn wagon, which was slowly leaving the battlefield. "Have you seen the emperor?" he shouted, in tears, without reason or restraint. The men started laughing, and one said to him: "Yes. He was in those bushes over there, screwing your sister!" and one blew clumsily into his trumpet to produce an obscene blast.

They had spoken idly, but Baudolino went to look in those bushes. There was a little pile of corpses, three prone on top of a fourth, supine. He lifted the three, and underneath he saw a red beard, but red with blood: Frederick. He realized at once that he was alive, because a kind of faint rattle came from his parted lips. There was a wound on his upper lip, which was still bleeding, and a broad dent on his brow stretching to the left eye; both hands were still clenched, a dagger in each, like one who, on the verge of losing consciousness, had still been able to stab the three wretches who had attacked him.

Baudolino raised his father's head, cleansed his face, called him; Frederick opened his eyes and asked where he was. Baudolino touched him, to see if he had any other wounds. Frederick cried out when his foot was touched; perhaps it was true that his horse had dragged him, dislocating his ankle. Still talking to him, while he asked again where he was, Baudolino helped him sit up. Frederick recognized Baudolino and embraced him.

"My lord and father," Baudolino said, "now you will mount my horse, but you mustn't strain yourself. We must proceed cautiously, even if night has fallen, because all around us are the troops of the League, and our only hope is that they're in some village carousing, since, no offense, it seems they've won. But some could still be nearby looking for their dead. We'll have to go through woods and ditches, staying off the roads, to reach Pavia, where your troops have withdrawn. You can sleep on the horse: I'll take care you don't fall off."

"And who'll take care that you don't fall asleep while you're walking?" asked Frederick, with a taut smile. Then he said: "It hurts when I laugh."

"I see you're well, now," Baudolino said.

They proceeded through the night, stumbling in the dark, even the horse, over roots and low bushes. Only once did they see, in the distance, some fires, and they went out of their way to avoid them. As they advanced, to keep himself awake, Baudolino talked, and Frederick remained awake to keep him awake.

"This is the end," Frederick said. "I will never bear the shame of this defeat."

"It was only a skirmish, Father. Anyway, they all believe you are

201

dead. You'll reappear like Lazarus resurrected, and what was considered a defeat will be considered a miracle by everyone, and they'll sing a *Te Deum*."

In truth, Baudolino was only trying to console a wounded and humiliated old soldier. That day the prestige of the empire had been compromised, *rex et sacerdos* or not. Unless Frederick were to return on stage in a halo of new glory. And at this point Baudolino couldn't help recalling Otto's hopes for the letter of the Priest.

"The fact is, dear Father," he said, "that from what has happened you should finally learn one thing."

"And what would you like to teach me, master wise man?"

"You don't have to learn from me, God forbid, but from heaven. You must consider carefully what Bishop Otto used to say. In this Italy the farther you go the more you get stuck in the mud; you can't be emperor where there is also a pope; with these cities you will always lose, because you want to impose order, which is a work of artifice, whereas they, on the contrary, want to live in disorder, which is in accord with nature—or, rather, as the Parisian philosophers would say, is the condition of the *yle,* the primogenial chaos. You must turn east, beyond Byzantium, impose the banners of your empire in the Christian lands that extend beyond the kingdoms of the infidels, joining the one, true *rex et sacerdos,* who has ruled there since the time of the Magi. Only when you have sealed an alliance with him, or he has sworn submission to you, can you return to Rome and treat the pope like your scullion, and the kings of England and France like your stableboys. Only then will your victors of today again be afraid of you."

Frederick hardly remembered the prophecies of Otto, and Baudolino had to remind him of them. "That Priest again?" Frederick said. "Does he really exist? And where is he? And how can I move a whole army to go and look for him? I would become Frederick the Foolish, and so I would be remembered through the centuries."

"No, not if in all the chancelleries of all the Christian kingdoms, Byzantium included, there was a letter in circulation that this Prester

John has written to you, to you alone, recognizing you as his only equal, and inviting you to join your two kingdoms."

And Baudolino, who knew it almost by heart, began reciting in the darkness the letter of Prester John, also explaining what was the most precious relic in the world, which the Priest was sending him in a coffer.

"But where is this letter? Do you have a copy of it? Are you sure you didn't write it yourself?"

"I recomposed it in good Latin, I joined the *membra disiecta* of things that the wise already knew and said, though nobody listened to them. But everything in that letter is true as Gospel. We might say, if you like, that my hand simply placed the address on it, as if the letter were sent to you."

"And this Priest could give me the—what did you call it?—the Grasal in which the blood of Our Lord was collected? To be sure, that would be the ultimate, perfect unction..." Frederick murmured.

So that night, along with the fate of Baudolino, the fate of his emperor was also decided, even if neither of the two had yet grasped where they were heading.

As both still daydreamed of a distant realm, towards dawn, near a ditch, they found a horse that had fled the battle and was unable to find his way. With two horses, even though they took a thousand minor roads, the ride to Pavia went much faster. Along the way they encountered bands of retreating imperials, who recognized their lord and emitted shouts of joy. Since they had plundered the villages they passed through, they had sustenance, and rushed off to inform others who were farther ahead: so two days later Frederick arrived at the gates of Pavia preceded by the joyous news, to find the leaders of the city and his allies awaiting him with great pomp, still unable to believe their eyes.

There was also Beatrice, dressed in mourning, because by then they had told her that her husband was dead. She was holding her two children by the hand, little Frederick, who was already twelve but looked half that, frail as he had been since birth, and Henry, who on the contrary had inherited all his father's strength, but on this day was weeping in bewilderment, constantly asking what had happened. Beatrice discerned Frederick in the distance, and moved towards him, sobbing, and embraced him with passion. When he told her he was alive thanks to Baudolino, she noticed that the young man was also there, and she went deep red, then quite pale, then she wept, and finally extended her hand to touch his heart and begged heaven to reward the merit of what he had done, calling him son, friend, brother.

"At that precise moment, Master Niketas," Baudolino said, "I realized that, by saving the life of my lord, I had paid my debt. But for this very reason I was no longer free to love Beatrice. And thus I realized that I loved her no more. It was like a healed wound, the sight of her aroused welcome memories but no yearning, I felt that I could remain at her side without suffering, or leave her without feeling sorrow. Perhaps I had finally become a man, and all youthful ardor was spent. I felt no displeasure, only a slight melancholy. I felt like a dove that had billed and cooed without restraint, but now the season of love was over. It was time to move, to go beyond the sea."

"You were no longer a dove; you'd become a swallow."

"Or a crane."

16

Baudolino is deceived by Zosimos

On Saturday morning Pevere and Grillo came to announce that order was somehow returning in Constantinople. Not so much because the pilgrims' thirst for looting was sated, but because their leaders had realized that the looters had also seized many venerable relics. A chalice or a damask vestment might be winked at, but the relics should not be dispersed. So the doge Dandolo had ordered that all the precious objects so far stolen should be brought to Saint Sophia, for fair distribution. Which meant primarily division between pilgrims and Venetians, as the latter were still awaiting payment for having brought the others here on their vessels. Then they would proceed, calculating the value of every piece in silver marks, and the knights would have four parts, the cavalry sergeants two, and the infantry sergeants one. It was easy to imagine the reaction of the soldiery, who were not allowed to seize anything.

There were murmurs that Dandolo's men had already taken the four gilded bronze horses from the Hippodrome, to send them to Venice; and everyone was in a bad humor. Dandolo's only reply was to order the search of troops of every rank, and a further search of their quarters in Pera. One knight of the count of Saint-Pol had been found with a phial upon his person. He said it was a medicine, now

dried up, but when they shook it, the warmth of their hands produced the flow of a red liquid, which was obviously the blood that
had flowed from the ribs of Our Lord. The knight cried that he had
honestly bought that relic from a monk before the sack; but to set an
example, he was hanged on the spot, with his shield and its coat of
arms around his neck.

"Shit! He looked like a codfish," Grillo said.

Sadly, Niketas listened to the news, but Baudolino, immediately
embarrassed, as if he were guilty, changed the subject and promptly
asked if the time had come to leave the city.

"The confusion is still great," Pevere said, "and you have to be
careful. Where did you want to go, Master Niketas?"

"To Selymbria, where we have trusted friends who can take us in."

"Selymbria...not easy," Pevere said. "It's to the west, near the
Long Walls. Even if we had mules, it's three days on the road, and
maybe more, and with a pregnant woman." And imagine, too: crossing the city with a fine stable of mules, you look like someone important, and the pilgrims will fall on you like flies." So the mules had to be
prepared outside the city, and their party had to cross the city on foot.
They would have to pass the walls of Constantine and then avoid the
coast, where surely there were more people, skirt the church of Saint
Mocius, and leave by the Pégé gate in the walls of Theodosius.

"It's not likely to go so well that nobody will stop you," Pevere
said.

"Ah," Grillo commented, "to get it in the ass is a moment's work,
and all these women will make the pilgrims foam at the mouth."

It still took a full day, since the young women had to be prepared.
The leper scene couldn't be repeated because by now the pilgrims had
realized that lepers didn't roam about inside the city. Some dots, some
scabs had to be made on their faces, so they would appear to have
scabies, enough to make them unattractive. Then all this group, for
three days, would have to eat, because, as the saying goes, an empty
sack won't stand up. The Genoese would prepare some baskets with

an entire pan of *scripilita,* their bread made of chickpea flour, thin and crusty, which they would cut into strips, wrapped in broad leaves; with a little pepper on top it would be delicious enough to nourish a lion; and broad slices of flat cake. With oil, sage, cheese, and onions.

These barbarian dishes didn't appeal to Niketas, but, since they would have to wait another day, he decided he would devote it to savoring the final delicacies that Theophilus could still prepare and listen to the final adventures of Baudolino, because he didn't want to leave just as the story was reaching its peak, and not knowing how it ended.

"My story is still too long," Baudolino said. "In any case, I will go with you. Here in Constantinople I've nothing more to do, and every corner stirs nasty memories. You have become my parchment, Master Niketas, on which I write many things that I had forgotten, as if my hand proceeded on its own. I think that one who tells stories must always have another to whom he tells them, and only thus can he tell them to himself. You remember when I wrote letters to the empress, but she didn't see them? If I committed the foolishness of letting my friends read them, it was because otherwise my letters would have had no meaning. And later, there was that moment of the kiss with the empress—I could never tell anyone of that kiss, and I carried the memory of it inside me for years and years, sometimes savoring it as if it were your honeyed wine, and sometimes tasting a toxin in my mouth. It was only when I could tell it to you that I felt free."

"And why could you tell it to me?"

"Because, now, when I tell you, all those who were connected with my story are no more. Only I remain. Now you are as necessary to me as the air I breathe. I will come with you to Selymbria."

As soon as he had recovered from the wounds suffered at Legnano, Frederick called for Baudolino, along with the imperial chancellor, Christian of Buch. If the letter of Prester John was to be taken seriously, it was best to begin at once. Christian read the parchment that Baudolino showed him, and, clever chancellor that he was, he voiced some objections. The writing, to begin with, did not seem to him worthy of a chancellery. That letter was to circulate among the papal court, the courts of France and England, reach the basileus of Byzantium, and therefore it had to be formed as important documents are prepared throughout the Christian world. Then, he said, it would take time to make seals that really looked like seals. If a serious job was to be done, it had to be done scrupulously.

How was the letter to be purveyed to the other chancelleries? If it was sent by the chancellery of the empire, it would not be credible. What? Prester John writes you privately to enable you to find him in a land unknown to all, and you let it be known *lippis et tonsoribus,* so that someone else could arrive there before you? Rumors concerning the letter should certainly spread, not only to legitimize a future expedition, but above all to astound the whole Christian world—but all this had to happen a little bit at a time, as if a profound secret were being divulged.

Baudolino suggested using his friends. They would be agents above suspicion, scholars of the *studium* of Paris and not Frederick's men. Abdul could contraband the letter in the kingdoms of the Holy Land, Boron in England, Kyot in France, and Rabbi Solomon could see it reached the Jews living in the Byzantine empire.

So the following months were spent on these various tasks, and Baudolino found himself directing a *scriptorium* where all his old companions were at work. Frederick from time to time asked for news. He had ventured the suggestion that the offer of the Grasal be a bit more explicit. Baudolino explained the reasons why it was best left vague, but he realized that this symbol of royal and priestly power had fascinated the emperor.

As they were debating these matters, Frederick was again beset with new trials. He now had to resign himself to seeking an agreement with Pope Alexander III. Seeing that the rest of the world did not take very seriously the imperial antipopes, the emperor would agree to pay Alexander homage and acknowledge him as the sole and genuine Roman pontiff—and this was a big step—but in return the pope had to make up his mind to withdraw all support of the Lombard communes—and this was even bigger. Was it worthwhile— both Frederick and Christian asked themselves at this point—while extremely cautious plots were being woven, to provoke the pope with a renewed call for the union of *sacerdotium* and *imperium*? These delays made Baudolino champ at the bit, but he could not protest.

Indeed, Frederick removed him from his plans, sending him on a very delicate mission to Venice, in April of 1177. It was a matter of organizing with great care the various details of the meeting that, in July, would take place between pope and emperor. The reconciliation ceremony should be arranged in every detail and no untoward incident should disturb it.

"Christian was particularly afraid that your basileus might want to provoke some disturbance, to make the meeting fail. You must know that for some time Manuel Comnenius had been plotting with the pope, and certainly that agreement between Alexander and Frederick would foil his plans."

"It scotched them forever. For ten years Manuel had been proposing to the pope the reunification of the two churches: he would recognize the religious primacy of the pope and the pope would recognize the basileus of Byzantium as the sole, authentic Roman emperor, of both East and West. But with such a pact Alexander did not gain much power in Constantinople and he wouldn't get Frederick out of his way in Italy and would perhaps alarm the other European sovereigns. So he was choosing the alliance most advantageous for himself."

"But your basileus sent spies to Venice. They passed themselves off as monks. . . ."

"Probably they were monks. In our empire the men of the Church work for their basileus, and not against him. But as far as I can understand—and remember, at that time I was not yet at court—they did not send anyone to stir up trouble. Manuel was resigned to the inevitable. Perhaps he wanted only to be informed about what was happening."

"Master Niketas, surely you know, since you were logothete of countless secrets, that when spies from opposing sides meet on the same field of intrigue, the most natural thing is for them to maintain relations of cordial friendship, each confiding his own secrets to the others. Thus they run no risk of stealing them from one another, and they look very clever to those who have sent them. And so it happened between us and those monks: we immediately told one another why we were there, we to spy on them, and they to spy on us, and afterwards we spent some delightful days together."

"These are things an astute statesman foresees, but what else should he do? If he questioned the foreign spies directly—and, for that matter, he doesn't know them—they would tell him nothing. So he sends his own spies, with secrets of scant importance to reveal, and comes to know the things he should know, which usually are known already to everyone save himself," Niketas said.

"Among these monks there was a certain Zosimos of Chalcedon. I was struck by his haggard face, a pair of eyes like carbuncles constantly rolling, illuminating a great black beard, and by his very long hair. When he spoke, he seemed to be talking with a crucified man, bleeding two palms' length from his face."

"I know the type. Our monasteries are full of them. They die very young, of consumption."

"Not him. In my whole life I have never seen such a glutton. One evening I even took him to the house of two Venetian courtesans, who, as you probably know, are specially famous among the practitioners of that art as old as the world. By three in the morning I was drunk and I left, but he stayed on and, some time later, one of the girls told me she had never had to deal with such a demon."

"I know the type. Our monasteries are full of them. They die very young, of consumption."

Baudolino and Zosimos had become, if not friends, companions in debauchery. Their association began when, after a first and generous drinking bout together, Zosimos uttered a horrible blasphemy and said that he would have given, that night, all the victims of the massacre of the innocents for a maid of indulgent morality. Asked if that was what was taught in the monasteries of Byzantium, Zosimos replied: "As Saint Basil taught, there are two demons that can trouble the intellect, that of fornication and that of blasphemy. But the second operates briefly and the first, if it does not agitate our thought with passion, does not prevent the contemplation of God." They went immediately to demonstrate obedience, without passion, to the demon of fornication, and Baudolino realized that Zosimos had, for every situation in life, a maxim from some theologian or hermit that made him feel at peace with himself.

On another occasion they were again drinking together, and Zosimos was singing the praises of Constantinople. Baudolino was embarrassed, because he could tell him only about the back streets of Paris, full of the excrement people flung from the windows, or about the sullen waters of the Tanaro, which could hardly compare with the gilded sea of the Propontis. Nor could he tell him of the *mirabilia urbis Mediolani*, because Frederick had ordered all of them destroyed. He didn't know how to silence his companion. So, to amaze him, he showed him the letter of Prester John, as if to say that somewhere there was an empire that made Zosimos's look like a barren heath.

Zosimos had barely read the first line when he asked, suspiciously: "Presbyter Johannes? Who is he?"

"You don't know?"

"Happy is he who has attained that ignorance beyond which it is not licit to proceed."

"You may proceed. Read on!"

He read on, with eyes that became more and more fiery, then he put down the parchment and said, in a detached tone: "Ah yes, Prester John. In my monastery I read many accounts by those who had visited his kingdom."

"But before reading this, you didn't even know who he was."

"The cranes form letters in their flight without knowing the art of writing. This letter tells of a Priest named John and it lies, but it speaks of a real kingdom, which in the accounts I have read is that of the Lord of the Indias."

Baudolino was ready to bet that this rogue was guessing, but Zosimos didn't give him time to doubt sufficiently.

"The Lord asks three things of the man who is baptized: true faith of his soul, sincerity of his tongue, and continence of his body. This letter of yours cannot have been written by the Lord of the Indias because it contains too many errors. For example, it names many extraordinary creatures of those parts, but says nothing of—let me think—nothing, for example, of the methagallinarii, of the thinsiretae, and of the cametheterni."

"And what are they?"

"What are they? Why the first thing that happens to anyone who arrives in the region of Prester John is that he encounters a thinsireta and if he isn't prepared to confront it...scrunch...he's devoured in one mouthful. Eh, those are places when you can't just go as if you were going to Jerusalem, where at most you find a camel or two, a crocodile, a pair of elephants, and such. Furthermore, the letter seems suspicious to me because it's very odd it should be addressed to your emperor rather than to our basileus, since the kingdom of this John is closer to the empire of Byzantium than to that of the Latins."

"You speak as if you knew where it is."

"I don't know exactly where it is, but I'd know how to go there, because he who knows the destination knows also the way to it."

"Then why have none of your Romei ever gone?"

"Who told you no one ever tried to go there? I could say that if the basileus Manuel ventured into the lands of the sultan of Iconium, it was precisely to open the way towards the realm of the Lord of the Indias."

"You could say it, but you haven't."

"Because our glorious army was defeated in those very lands, at Myriocephalum, two years ago. And now, before our basileus can mount a new expedition, it will take some time. But if I had great funds at my disposal, and a band of well-armed men capable of facing a thousand difficulties, with an idea of which direction to take, I would have only to set out. Then, along the way, you inquire, you follow the advice of the natives . . . There would be many signs, and once you were on the right road you would begin to see trees that flourish only in those lands and to come upon animals that live only down there, like the methagallinarii, in fact."

"Three cheers for the methagallinarii," Baudolino said, raising his glass. Zosimos invited him to join in a toast to the kingdom of Prester John. Then he challenged him to drink the health of Manuel, and Baudolino agreed provided Zosimos drink the health of Frederick. Then they drank to the pope, to Venice, to the two courtesans they had met a few evenings before, and in the end Baudolino collapsed first, asleep, with his head on the table, while he could still hear Zosimos's laborious muttering: "This is the monk's life: never act with curiosity, never walk with the unjust, never snatch with your hands. . . ."

The next morning Baudolino said, his tongue still thick, "Zosimos, you're a rascal. You haven't the slightest idea where your Lord of the Indias is. You want to set out on instinct, and when somebody tells you he saw a methagallinarius over there, you go off in that direction and in no time you come to a palace all of precious stones, you see some character and you say good morning, Father John, how are you? You can tell this sort of thing to your basileus, not to me."

"But I happen to have a good map," Zosimos said, opening his eyes.

Baudolino objected that, even with a good map, everything would still remain vague and hard to decide, because everyone knows that maps are not precise, especially for places where, at most, Alexander the Great has been, and no one else after him. And he made a rough sketch of the map drawn by Abdul.

Zosimos burst out laughing. Of course, if Baudolino followed the most perverse and heretical idea that the earth is a sphere, he couldn't even begin the journey.

"Either you trust the Holy Scriptures, or else you're a pagan who still thinks the way they thought before Alexander—who, for that matter, was incapable of leaving us any map. The Scriptures say that not only the earth but the whole universe is made in the form of a tabernacle, or, rather, that Moses built his tabernacle as a faithful copy of the universe, from the earth to the firmament."

"But the ancient philosophers..."

"The ancient philosophers, not yet enlightened by the word of the Lord, invented the Antipodes, while in the Acts of the Apostles it says that God from one man devised our humankind to inhabit the entire face of the earth, its face—not the other side, which doesn't exist. And Luke's Gospel says that the Lord gave the apostles the power to walk on serpents and scorpions, and to walk means to walk above something, not below. Anyway, if the earth were a sphere and suspended in the vacuum, it would have neither an above nor a below, and so there would be no sense, no direction in the walking. Who thought the heavens were a sphere? The Chaldean sinners from the top of the tower of Babel, insofar as they were able to erect it, misled by the feeling of terror that the looming sky inspired in them! What Pythagoras or what Aristotle has been able to announce the resurrection of the dead? And would ignoramuses of that stripe have under-

214

stood the shape of the world? Would this world shaped like a sphere have served to predict the rising or setting of the sun, or the day on which Easter falls, whereas most humble people, who have studied neither philosophy nor astronomy, know very well when the sun sets and when it rises, according to the seasons, and in different countries they calculate Easter in the same way, without deceiving themselves? Is it necessary to know a geometry other than the one a good carpenter knows, or an astronomy different from what a peasant observes when he sows and when he reaps? And besides, what ancient philosophers are you talking to me about? Do you Latins know Xenophanes of Colophon, who, while asserting that the world was infinite, denied that it was spherical? The ignoramus can say that, considering the universe like a tabernacle, you can't explain eclipses or equinoxes. Well, in the empire of us Romans, centuries ago there lived a great sage, Cosmas Indicopleustes, who traveled to the very confines of the world, and in his *Christian Topography* demonstrated in irrefutable fashion that the earth truly is in the form of a tabernacle, and that only thus can we explain the most obscure phenomena. Could you say that the most Christian of kings—John, I mean—would not follow the most Christian of topographies, which is not only that of Cosmas, but also that of the Holy Scriptures?"

"What I say is that my Prester John knows nothing of the topography of your Cosmas."

"You told me yourself that the Priest is a Nestorian. Now the Nestorians had a dramatic argument with other heretics, the Monophysites. The Monophysites held that the earth was made like a sphere, the Nestorians like a tabernacle. Cosmas was also known to be a Nestorian, or in any case a follower of Nestor's teacher, Theodore of Mopsuestia, who all his life fought against the Monophysite heresy of John Philoponus of Alexandria, who followed pagan philosophers like Aristotle. Cosmas a Nestorian, Prester John a Nestorian: both cannot but believe firmly in the earth as a tabernacle."

"Just a moment. Both your Cosmas and my Priest are Nestorians:

no argument there. But since, as far as I know, the Nestorians were wrong about Jesus and his mother, they could also be wrong about the shape of the universe, couldn't they?"

"This is where my finest reasoning comes into play! I want to demonstrate to you that—if you want to find Prester John—you must in any case stick with Cosmas and not the pagan topographers. Let us suppose for a moment that Cosmas wrote things that are false. Even so, these things are thought and believed by all the nations of the Orient that Cosmas visited, otherwise he wouldn't have learned them, in those lands beyond which lies the kingdom of Prester John, and surely the inhabitants of that kingdom itself think that the universe is in the form of a tabernacle, and they measure distances, confines, the course of rivers, the extension of seas, coasts, and gulfs, not to mention mountains, according to the wondrous design of the tabernacle."

"Once again, it doesn't seem a valid argument to me," Baudolino said. "The fact that they believe they live in a tabernacle doesn't mean they really do live in one."

"Let me finish my demonstration. If you asked me how to arrive at Chalcedon, where I was born, I could explain it to you easily. Perhaps I measure the days of travel in a way different from you, or perhaps I call right what you call left—in any case I have been told that the Saracens draw maps where the south is above and the north is below, and therefore the sun rises to the left of the lands they depict. But if you accept my way of representing the course of the sun and the shape of the earth, following my directions you would surely arrive at the place where I want to send you, while you would never understand them if you refer to your maps. So . . ." Zosimos concluded triumphantly, "if you want to reach the land of Prester John you must use the map of the world that Prester John would use and not your own—mind you, even if your map is more correct than his."

Baudolino was won over by the cogency of the argument and asked Zosimos to explain how Cosmas and, consequently, Prester

John saw the universe. "Ah no," Zosimos said. "I know very well where to find the map, but why must I give it to you and to your emperor?"

"If he were to give you enough gold to set out with a band of well-armed men."

"Exactly."

From that moment on, Zosimos didn't allow one word to escape him on the subject of Cosmas's map, or, rather, he hinted at it every now and then, when he reached the peak of intoxication, but tracing vaguely with his finger some mysterious curves in the air, then falling silent, as if he had said too much. Baudolino would pour him more wine and ask him apparently bizarre questions. "But when we are close to India, and our horses are exhausted, will we have to ride elephants?"

"Perhaps," Zosimos said, "because in India there live all the animals mentioned in your letter, and others besides, except for horses. Still they do have some, because they bring them in from Tzinista."

"What country is that?"

"A country where travelers go in search of worms for silk."

"Worms for silk? What does that mean?"

"It means that in Tzinista there exist some tiny eggs that are placed in women's bosoms and, enlivened by the warmth, they produce little worms. These are set on mulberry leaves, which nourish them. When they are grown they spin silk from their bodies and wrap themselves in it, as in a tomb. Then they turn into marvelous, vari-colored butterflies and they break free of the cocoon. Before flying away, the males penetrate the females from behind and both live without food in the warmth of their embrace until they die and the female dies brooding over her eggs."

"There's no trusting a man who wants to make you believe silk comes from worms," Baudolino said to Niketas. "He was spying for his basileus, but he would have set out in search of the Lord of the

217

Indies even in Frederick's pay. Then, when he got there, we would never see him again. And yet his mention of the map of Cosmas excited me. That map appeared to me like the star of Bethlehem, except that it pointed in the opposite direction. It would tell me how to follow, backwards, the route of the Magi. And so, believing myself more clever than he, I prepared to lead him to excess in his intemperance, to make him duller and more talkative."

"And instead?"

"And instead he was more clever than I. The next day I couldn't find him anywhere, and some of his fellows told me he had returned to Constantinople. He left me a farewell message. It said: "As fish die if they remain out of water, so monks who linger outside the cell weaken the vigor of their union with God. These past days I have dried up in sin; let me find again the cool living water.""

"Maybe it was the truth."

"Not at all. He had found the way to milk gold from his basileus. And to my harm."

17

Baudolino discovers that Prester John
wrote to too many people

The following July, Frederick arrived in Venice by sea, accompanied from Ravenna to Chioggia by the doge's son, then he reached the church of San Niccolò al Lido, and on Sunday the 24th, in Saint Mark's Square, prostrated himself at the feet of Alexander. The pope raised him and embraced him with a show of affection, and all the witnesses sang the *Te Deum*. It was truly a triumph, even if it was not clear for which of the two. In any case it ended a war that had lasted eighteen years, and in those same days the emperor signed a six-year truce with the communes of the Lombard League. Frederick was so happy that he decided to stay on in Venice for another month.

It was August when, one morning, Christian of Buch summoned Baudolino and his friends and asked them to come with him to the emperor. Arriving in Frederick's presence, Christian handed him, with a dramatic gesture, a parchment heavy with seals: "Here is the letter of Prester John," he said, "as it has reached me, confidentially, from the court of Byzantium."

"The letter?" Frederick exclaimed. "Why, we haven't yet sent it."

"In fact, this is not ours: it's another letter. It's not addressed to you, but to the basileus Manuel. For the rest, it's the same as ours."

"So this Prester John first offers an alliance to me and then he offers it to the Romei?" Frederick was enraged.

Baudolino was dumbfounded, because the Priest's letter, as he well knew, existed in a single draft, and he had written it. If the Priest existed, he could also have written another letter, but surely not this one. He asked permission to examine the document, and after glancing at it in haste, he said: "No, it's not exactly the same. There are some little variants. If you will allow me, Father, I'd like to study it more closely."

He withdrew with his friends, and together they read and reread the letter several times. First of all, it, too, was in Latin. Curious, Rabbi Solomon observed, because the Priest is sending it to the Greek basileus. In fact, it began:

The Priest Johannes, by the grace of God and power of Our Lord Jesus Christ, king of kings, greets Manuel, governor of the Romei, wishing him health and perpetual enjoyment of divine benediction.

"A second oddity," Baudolino said, "he calls Manuel governor of the Romei, and not basileus. So it surely wasn't written by a Greek in the imperial train. It was written by someone who doesn't recognize Manuel's title."

"Therefore," the Poet concluded, "by the real Prester John, who considers himself the *dominus dominantium*."

"Let's proceed," Baudolino said, "and I'll show you some words and phrases that weren't in our letter."

Our majesty has learned that you held in high esteem our Excellency and that you had received word of our greatness. We have also learned from a secretary of ours that you desired to send us some things pleasing and interesting, for our delight. Being human, we gladly accept the gift, and through our apocrisiary, we are sending some token, desirous of knowing whether, like us, you follow the true faith and in every way be-

lieve in Our Lord Jesus Christ. For while we are well aware of our mor-
tality, your Greeklings believe that you are a god, even if we well know
that you are mortal and subject to human corruption. In the breadth of
our munificence, if you need something that may procure pleasure for
you, inform us, either by a word to our apocrisiary or by a testimony of
your affection.

"Here the oddities are too numerous," Rabbi Solomon said. "On the one hand he treats the basileus and his Greeklings with condescension and contempt approaching insult, on the other, for 'secretary' he uses the term *apocrisiarius,* which I believe is Greek."

"Its precise meaning is ambassador," Baudolino said, "but listen to this: where we said that at the Priest's table sit the metropolitan of Samarkand and the archpriest of Susa, here it's written that there are the *protopapas Samargantinum* and the *archiprotopapas de Susis.* And, further, among the wonders of the kingdom is mentioned an herb called *assidios,* which drives out evil spirits. Again, three Greek terms."

"So," the Poet said, "the letter is written by a Greek, but one who uses Greek very badly. I don't understand."

Abdul meanwhile had picked up the parchment. "There's something else: where we mentioned the pepper harvest, there are added details. And here it says that in John's kingdom there are few horses. And here where we merely named salamanders, it says they are a species of worm, which wrap themselves in a kind of film like the worms that produce silk, and the film is then washed by the palace women to make royal cloths and dress which are washed only in a violent fire."

"What? What?" Baudolino asked, alarmed.

"And finally," Abdul went on, "in the list of creatures that inhabit the kingdom, among the horned men, the fauns and satyrs, the pygmies, the cynocephali, there also appear methagallinarii, cametheterni, and thinsiretae—all creatures we didn't name."

"By the Virgin Mother of God!" Baudolino exclaimed. "That worm story was told me by Zosimos! And it was Zosimos who also told me that, according to Cosmas Indicopleustes, in India horses don't exist! And it was Zosimos who told me of methagallinarii and those other beasts! Son of a whore, pot of excrement, liar, thief, hypocrite, trimmer and counterfeiter, adulterer, glutton, coward, voluptuary, sodomite, usurer, simoniac, necromancer, sower of discord, cheat!"

"Why, what did he do to you?"

"Haven't you realized that yet? The evening that I showed him the letter, he got me drunk and made a copy of it! Then he went back to that shit of a basileus of his, told him that Frederick was about to reveal himself as friend and heir of Prester John, and they wrote another letter addressed to Manuel, sending it off before ours! That's why he appears so haughty towards the basileus, to ward off suspicions that the letter might have been produced in his chancellery! That's why it contains so many Greek terms, to show that this is the Latin translation of an original written by John in Greek. But it's in Latin because it's meant to convince not Manuel but the chancelleries of the Latin kings and the pope!"

"There's another detail that escaped us," Kyot said. "You remember the story of the Grasal, which the Priest was to send to the emperor? We wanted to remain reticent, speaking only of a *veram arcam.* . . . Did you say anything about this to Zosimos?"

"No," Baudolino said. "I kept quiet about that."

"Here, your Zosimos has written *yerarcam.* The Priest is sending the basileus a *yerarcam.*"

"And what's that?" the Poet wondered.

"Zosimos doesn't know that himself," Baudolino said. "Look at our original letter. At this point Abdul's writing isn't very legible. Zosimos didn't understand what it was, he assumed it was some strange and mysterious gift, which only we knew about, and so that word is explained. Oh, the wretch! All my fault: I trusted him. How shameful! What can I say to the emperor?"

It wasn't the first time they told lies. They explained to Christian and to Frederick the reasons why the letter had obviously been written by someone in Manuel's chancellery, precisely to prevent Frederick from circulating his, but they added that probably there was a traitor in the chancellery of the Holy Roman Empire, who had sent a copy of their letter to Constantinople. Frederick vowed that if the man was found he would have everything protruding from his body torn off.

Then Frederick asked if they shouldn't worry about some initiative from Manuel. What if the letter had been written to justify an expedition to the Indias? Christian wisely pointed out that just two years earlier Manuel had moved against the Seleucid sultan of Iconium, in Phrygia, and had suffered a dramatic defeat at Myriocephalum. Enough to keep him away from the Indias for the rest of his life. Indeed, when you thought about it, that letter was a specific if slightly puerile way to regain a bit of prestige just when he had lost a great deal.

Still, did it make sense, at this point, to circulate the letter to Frederick? Wasn't it perhaps necessary to alter it, so that nobody would believe it had been copied from the one sent to Manuel?

"Were you aware of this story, Master Niketas?" Baudolino asked.

Niketas smiled. "In those days I was not yet thirty, and I was collecting taxes in Paphlagonia. If I had been counsellor to the basileus, I would have advised him not to recur to such childish machinations. But Manuel lent an ear to too many courtiers, to those who shared his bed, *cuniculari,* and the eunuch attendants of his chambers, even to servants, and often he succumbed to the influence of some visionary monks."

"The thought of that worm gnawed at me. But also the fact that Pope Alexander was a worm worse than Zosimos, and worse than the salamanders was discovered in September, when the imperial chancellery received a document that probably had been communicated

223

also to the other Christian kings and to the Greek emperor. It was the copy of a letter that Alexander III had written to Prester John!"

Surely Alexander had received a copy of the letter to Manuel, perhaps he was aware of the old mission of Hugo of Jabala, perhaps he feared that Frederick would draw some advantage from the news of the existence of the king and priest, and here Alexander was the first, not to receive an appeal, but to send one directly, for his letter said he had immediately dispatched an envoy of his to confer with the Priest.

Alexander bishop servant of the servants of God, to the most beloved Johannes, son in Christ, illustrious and magnificent sovereign of the Indias, wishes him health and sends his apostolic blessing.

After which the pope recalled that only one apostolic seat (namely, Rome) had received from Peter the mandate to be *caput et magistra* of all believers. He said that the pope had been told of the faith and the piety of John by his personal physician Magister Philip, and that this wise man, circumspect and prudent, had heard from trustworthy people that John wished finally to convert to the true faith, Roman and Catholic. The pope regretted that for the moment he could not send him *dignitaries of high rank, also because they were ignorant of linguas barbaras et ignotas,* but he was sending Philip, a discreet and most cautious man, to educate John in the true faith. As soon as Philip reached him, John should send the pope a letter of his intentions and—Alexander advised him—the less he indulged in boasting about his power and wealth, the better it would be for him, if he wished to be received as a humble son of the Holy Roman Apostolic Church.

Baudolino was scandalized by the idea that such shameless counterfeiters could exist in the world. Frederick shouted, venomously: "Son of the devil! Nobody has ever written to him, and out of spite he is the first to reply! And he is careful to refrain from calling him Johannes *Presbyter,* denying him all priestly dignity..."

"He knows that John is a Nestorian," Baudolino added, "and he proposes, in so many words, that John renounce his heresy and make an act of submission to him...."

"It is surely a letter of supreme arrogance," the chancellor Christian remarked. "He calls him son, doesn't send him even a mere bishop, but only his personal physician. He treats him like a child to be disciplined."

"This Philip must be stopped," Frederick then said. "Christian, send messengers, assassins, whatever you like, to overtake him along the way, strangle him, tear out his tongue, drown him in a stream! He must not arrive there! Prester John belongs to me!"

"Rest assured, dear Father," Baudolino said. "In my opinion, this Philip has never set out and it may be that he doesn't even exist. First, Alexander knows very well, if you ask me, that the letter to Manuel is bogus. Second, he has no idea where this Johannes is. Third, he wrote the letter precisely to say that Johannes belongs to him rather than to you, and further he is inviting both you and Manuel to forget the matter of the priest king. Fourth, even if Philip existed and were traveling to the Priest and even if he arrived there truly, just think for a moment of what would happen if he returned empty-handed because Prester John wasn't converted. For Alexander it would be like receiving a handful of dung in the face. He can't take such a risk."

In any case, it was by now too late to make the letter to Frederick public, and Baudolino felt dispossessed. He had begun dreaming of the Priest's kingdom after the death of Otto, and since then almost twenty years had passed.... Twenty years gone for nothing.

Then he picked himself up: no, the Priest's letter fades into nothingness, or becomes lost in a host of other letters; at this point anyone who so wishes can invent an amorous correspondence with the Priest, we live in a world of certified liars, but this doesn't mean that we have to give up seeking his kingdom. After all, Cosmas's map still exists. It would suffice to find Zosimos again, tear it away from him, and travel towards the unknown.

But where had Zosimos ended up? Even if we were to learn that he was living, covered with prebends, in the imperial palace of his basileus, how to go and unmask him there, amid the entire Byzantine army? Baudolino began questioning travelers, envoys, merchants, seeking some news of that scoundrel monk. At the same time he never stopped reminding Frederick of the project: "Dear Father," he would say, "now it makes even more sense than before, because in the past you could think that the kingdom was only a fancy of mine, now you know that the basileus of the Greeks believes in it and so does the pope of the Romans, and in Paris they told me that if our mind is able to conceive of a thing that is greater than anything, surely that thing exists. I am on the trail of someone who can give me information about the correct route. Authorize me to spend some money." He succeeded in gaining enough gold to corrupt all the Greeklings who passed through Venice, he had been put in touch with reliable people in Constantinople, and he was awaiting news. When he received it, he would have only to induce Frederick to make a decision.

"More years of waiting, Master Niketas, and meanwhile your Manuel also died. Even if I had not yet visited your country, I knew enough about it to think that, with a new basileus, all the old advisers would be done away with. I prayed to the Blessed Virgin and all the saints that Zosimos had not been killed: even blinded, he would still suit me, he had only to give me the map so I could read it. And at the same time I felt the years flowing from me like blood."

Niketas urged Baudolino not to allow himself to be disheartened now by his former disappointment. He ordered his cook and servant to outdo themselves, and he wanted their last meal prepared under the sun of Constantinople to remind him of all the sweetness of his sea and his land. And so he wanted lobsters and porgies on the table, boiled prawns, fried crabs, lentils with oysters and clams, sea dates, accompanied by a puree of beans and rice with honey, girt with a crown of fish roe, and all served with Cretan wine. But this was only

226

the first course. Afterwards came a stew that wafted a delicious aroma, and in the pan were steaming four hearts of cabbage, hard and white as snow, a carp and about twenty little mackerel, fillets of salt fish, fourteen eggs, a bit of Wallachian sheep cheese, all bathed in a good quart of oil, sprinkled with pepper, and flavored with twelve heads of garlic. But with that second dish he asked for a wine of Ganos.

18

Baudolino and Colandrina

From the courtyard of the Genoese came the laments of Niketas's daughters, who were reluctant to have their faces smeared with dirt, accustomed as they were to the vermilion of their cosmetics. "Calm down," Grillo said to them, "beauty alone doesn't make a woman." And he explained that it wasn't even certain that these marks of ringworm and pox they were applying to their faces would suffice to disgust a lusty pilgrim—those men who were satisfying themselves on anyone they found, young or old, healthy or sick, Greeks or Saracens or Jews, because in these matters religion doesn't count. To arouse disgust, he added, they should be covered with bumps, like a grater. Niketas's wife lovingly collaborated in uglifying her daughters, adding a sore on the forehead or some chicken skin on the nose, to make it seem half eaten away.

Baudolino looked sadly at that sweet family group, and said abruptly: "And so, as I was casting about, not knowing what to do, I also took a wife."

He told the story of his marriage in a less merry tone, as if it were a painful memory.

"At that time I was moving back and forth between the court and Alessandria. Frederick still couldn't swallow the fact of that city's existence, and I was trying to patch things up between my fellow-citizens and the emperor. The situation was more favorable than in the past. Alexander III was dead, and Alessandria had lost its protector. The emperor was gradually coming to terms with the Italian cities, and Alessandria could no longer represent itself as the bulwark of the League. Genoa had by now come over to the side of the empire, and Alessandria had everything to gain by going with the Genoese, and nothing to gain by remaining the only city hostile to Frederick. A solution had to be found that would be honorable for all. So, while I was spending my days talking with my fellow-citizens, then returning to court to sound out the emperor's mood, I became aware of Colandrina. She was the daughter of Guasco, and she had grown up more or less before my eyes, though I hadn't realized she had become a woman. She was very sweet, and she moved with a somewhat awkward grace. After the story of the siege, my father and I were considered the saviors of the city, and she looked at me as if I were Saint George. When I spoke with Guasco, she would crouch near me, her eyes shining, as she drank in my words. I could have been her father, because she was barely fifteen and I was thirty-eight. I don't know if I had fallen in love with her, but I liked seeing her around me, and I began telling incredible stories to the others so that she would hear me. Guasco, too, had become aware of this. It's true that he was a *miles,* and therefore something bigger than a ministerial like me (a peasant's son into the bargain), but, as I told you, I was the city's pet, I wore a sword on my hip, I lived at court.... It would not have been a bad match, and it was Guasco himself who said to me: Why don't you marry Colandrina? She's become a burden here, she drops the pans, and when you're away she spends all her time at the window looking out to see if you're coming. It was a fine wedding, in the church of San Pietro, the cathedral we had given to the pope, rest his soul, though the new one didn't even know it existed. It was a strange marriage, because after the first night I had to go off and join Frederick, and so it went for a good year, with a wife I saw once in a blue moon, and it touched my heart to see her joy every time I came back."

"So you loved her?"

"I think I did, but it was the first time I'd taken a wife, and I didn't really know what to do with her, except those things that husbands do at night, but during the day I didn't know if I should pat her like a child, treat her as a lady, scold her for her clumsiness—because she still needed a father—or forgive her everything, and perhaps spoil her instead. But, at the end of the first year, she told me she was expecting a child, and then I began looking at her as if she were the Virgin Mary. When I came home, I would beg her forgiveness for having been away, I took her to Mass on Sunday to show everybody that Baudolino's fine wife was about to give him a son, and on the few evenings we spent together we told each other what we would do with that Baudolinetto Colandrinino she was carrying in her belly. She sometimes imagined that Frederick would give him a dukedom, and I was almost ready to believe it myself. I told her about the kingdom of Prester John, and she said she wouldn't let me go there alone for all the gold in the world, because there was no telling how many beautiful ladies there were down there, and she wanted to see if any place could be finer and bigger than Alessandria and Solero put together. Then I told her about the Grasal and her eyes widened: Just think, dear Baudolino, you go down there, you come back with the cup from which Our Lord drank, and you become the most famous knight of all Christendom, you build a shrine for this Grasal at Montecastello, and they come to see it all the way from Quargnento.... We daydreamed like children, and I said to myself: poor Abdul, you believe that love is a faraway princess, but mine is so close that I can tickle her behind the ear, and she laughs and tells me I give her goose bumps.... But it was short-lived."

"Why?"

"Because while she was pregnant, the Alessandrians made a pact with Genoa against the people of Silvano d'Orba. They were just a handful, but still they roamed the area and robbed the peasants. Colandrina that day went out beyond the city walls to gather some flowers because she had heard I was about to arrive. She stopped near a flock of sheep, to joke with the shepherd, who was one of her father's men, and a band of those bastards rushed over to seize the sheep. Perhaps they didn't mean to harm her, but they roughly pushed her about, flung her to the ground, the sheep ran off, trampling her underfoot.... The shepherd had already taken to his heels, and when her family found her, late in the evening, after realizing she hadn't come home, she had a fever. Guasco sent someone to find me, I came home at full speed, but meanwhile two days had gone by. I found her in bed, dying, and, on seeing me, she tried to apologize because, she said, the baby had come out ahead of time, and he was already dead, and she tormented herself because she hadn't even been able to give me a son. She looked like a little wax madonna, and you had to put your ear to her mouth to hear what she was saying. Don't look at me, Baudolino, she said, my face is all splotchy from weeping, and so you find not only a bad mother but also an ugly wife.... She died begging my forgiveness, while I was asking hers, for not having been at her side in her moment of danger. Then I asked to see the little corpse, but they didn't want to show it to me. It was...it was..."

Baudolino stopped. His held his face up, as if reluctant to let Niketas see his eyes. "It was a little monster," he said, after a moment, "like the ones we imagined in the land of Prester John. The face had tiny eyes, like two slits, a very thin chest, with little arms that looked like a polyp's tentacles. And from its belly to its feet it was covered with fine white hair, as if it were a sheep. I couldn't look at it for long. I ordered it buried, but I didn't know if a priest could be called. I left the city and wandered all night around the marsh, telling myself that until then I had spent my life imagining creatures of other worlds, and in my fancy they seemed wondrous portents, whose diversity bore witness to the infinite power of the Lord, but then, when the Lord asked me to do what all other men do, I had generated not

231

a portent but a horrible thing. My son was a lie of nature. Otto was right, but more than he had thought; I was a liar and I had lived the life of a liar to such a degree that even my seed had produced a lie. A dead lie. And then I understood...."

"You mean..." Niketas ventured, "you decided to change your life...."

"No, Master Niketas. I decided that if this was my fate, it was useless for me to try to become like other men. I was by now consecrated to falsehood. It is hard to explain what was going through my head. I said to myself: All the time that you were inventing, you invented things that were not true, but then became true. You made San Baudolino appear, you created a library at Saint Victoire, you sent the Magi wandering about the world, you saved your city by fattening a scrawny cow, if there are learned doctors in Bologna it is also your merit, in Rome you caused *mirabilia* to appear that the Romans themselves had never dreamed of, starting with the gabble of that Hugo of Jabala, you created a kingdom of supreme beauty, then you loved a ghost, and you made her write letters she had never written, and those who read them went into ecstasy, including the lady who had never written them, and she was an empress; but the one time you wanted to do something true, with the most sincere of women, you failed: you produced something no one can believe in or desire to exist. So it is best for you to withdraw into the world of your portents, for there at least you can decide yourself how portentous they are."

19

Baudolino changes the name of his city

"O poor Baudolino," Niketas said, as they continued the preparations for their departure, "robbed of a wife and a son, in the prime of life. And I, who could lose tomorrow the flesh of my flesh and my beloved wife at the hand of some of these barbarians. O Constantinople, queen of cities, tabernacle of the Lord most high, pride and glory of your ministers, delight of foreigners, empress of imperial cities, most rare spectacle of things rare to be seen, what will become of us who are about to abandon you, naked as when we came forth from our mothers? When shall we see you again, not as you now are, vale of tears, trampled by armies?"

"Silence, Master Niketas," Baudolino said to him, "and remember this may be the last time you will be able to taste these delights worthy of Apicius. What are these little balls of meat that have the aroma of our spice market?"

"Keftedes, and the aroma comes from cinnamon and a bit of mint," Niketas replied, already comforted. "And for this last day I have succeeded in having a little anise brought to us, which you must drink while it dissolves in water like a cloud."

"It's good, it doesn't dull the mind, it makes you feel as if you were dreaming," Baudolino said. "If only I could have drunk some after Colandrina's death perhaps I could have forgotten her, as you are already forgetting the misfortunes of your city as you lose all fear of what will happen tomorrow. But instead, I became heavy with the wine of our parts, which puts you suddenly to sleep, and when you wake you're worse off than before."

It took Baudolino a year to emerge from the melancholy madness that had gripped him, a year of which he remembered nothing except that he went on long rides through the woods and over the plains, then he would stop in some place and drink until he plunged into long and agitated sleep. In his dreams he saw the moment when he finally reached Zosimos and tore from him not only his beard, but also the map, in order to reach a kingdom where all newborn infants would be thinsiretae and methagallinarii. He did not return to Alessandria, fearing that his father or his mother, or Guasco and his family, would talk to him of Colandrina, and of the son never born. Often he took refuge with Frederick, paternally concerned and understanding, trying to distract him with talk of the great things Baudolino could do for the empire. Until one day, he said Baudolino should make up his mind and find a solution for Alessandria, for his wrath by now had evaporated, and to please Baudolino he wanted to heal that *vulnus* without being forced to destroy the city.

This mission gave Baudolino new life. Now Frederick was preparing to sign a definitive peace with the Lombard communes, and Baudolino told himself that in the end it was all a question of pride. Frederick could not tolerate the idea of a city they had made without his permission and one that, furthermore, bore the name of his enemy. Very well, if Frederick could found that city anew, even in the same place but with another name, as he had done at Lodi, in another place but with the same name, then he would not end up empty-handed. As for the Alessandrians—what did they want? To have a city and to conduct their business. It was pure chance that they had named it after Alexander III, who was dead, and therefore couldn't take offense if they now gave it a different name. Hence the idea: one fine morning Frederick would come with his knights to the walls of Alessandria, all the inhabitants would come forth, a cohort of bishops would enter the city, they would deconsecrate it, if it could be said ever to have been consecrated, or they would debaptize it and then rebaptize it with the name Caesarea, city of Caesar, the Alessandrians would pass slowly before the emperor, paying him homage, then they would go back inside, taking possession of their brand-new city, as if it were another, founded by the emperor, and they would live happily ever after.

Obviously, Baudolino was recovering from his despair, with another fine exploit of his fervid imagination.

Frederick did not dislike the idea, but in that period there were some difficulties in his returning to Italy, because he was settling some important matters with his Alaman vassals. Baudolino assumed responsibility for the negotiations. He hesitated before entering the city, but at the gate his parents came towards him, and all three of them dissolved in liberating tears. His old comrades acted as if Baudolino had never married, and before he could begin talking of his mission, they dragged him off to their old tavern, getting him good and drunk, but with a tart little white wine of Gavi, not enough to put him to sleep but enough to stimulate his genius. Then Baudolino told them his idea.

The first to react was Gagliaudo: "When I'm with this character, I become as foolish as he is. Now really: do we have to play out this farce, first coming out, then going back inside, and after you, no after you? All we need is a piper and we'll be dancing the trescone for the feast of San Baudolino. . . ."

"No, this is a good idea," Boidi said, "but afterwards, instead of being Alessandrians, we'll have to call ourselves Caesareans, and I'd be ashamed; I couldn't go and say it to the people of Asti."

"Enough of all this nonsense! No matter what, they'll still know us for who we are!" Oberto del Foro interjected. "For my part, they can go ahead and rename the city, but it's the passing in front of him and rendering homage that I can't stomach. After all, we're the ones who put one over on him, not him on us, so he shouldn't act too grand."

Cuttica of Quargnento said the rebaptizing was all right, and who cared if the city was called Caesaretta or Caesarona, for him even Caesira was fine, or Olivia or Sophronia or Eutropia. The problem is whether Frederick will want to send us his governor or will he be satisfied to give his legitimate investiture to the consuls we would elect.

"Go back and ask him what he plans to do," Guasco said. And Baudolino said, "Yes, of course. I keep going back and forth across the Alps until you come to an agreement. No sir. You delegate full powers to two of your people and they come with me to the emperor and they work out something that suits everybody. If Frederick sees another pair of Alessandrians he'll get a case of worms, and to get rid of the two, you'll see, he'll accept an agreement."

So two envoys from the city set out with Baudolino: Anselmo Conzani and Teobaldo, one of the Guascos. They met the emperor at Nuremberg, and the agreement was reached. Even the question of the consuls was resolved promptly; it was only a matter of saving appearances: the Alessandrians should go ahead and elect them; it would suffice if the emperor then appointed them. As for the homage, Baudolino took Frederick aside and said to him: Father, you can't come yourself; you must send a legate. So you send me. After all, I'm a ministerial, and as such, in your immense kindness, you've bestowed on me the sash of knighthood, and I'm a *Ritter*, as they say here."

"Yes, but you still belong to the nobility of service; you can have feudal estates but you can't confer them, and you are not entitled to have vassals, and..."

"What do you think that matters to my compatriots. For them, it's enough for a man to have a horse and issue orders. They pay homage to your representative, and hence to you, but your representative is me, and I'm one of them, and therefore they don't have the impression of paying homage to you. Then, if you like, the oaths and all those other things can be made to an imperial chamberlain of yours who is beside me, and they won't even know who's the more important. You also have to understand how people are made. If in this way we settle things finally, won't it be good for all?"

So in mid-March of 1183 the ceremony took place. Baudolino was in dress uniform, and he looked more important than the marquess of Monferrato; his parents devoured him with their eyes, as he, hand on the hilt of his sword, sat astride a white horse that wouldn't keep still. "He's decked out like a lord's dog," his mother said, dazzled. He was flanked by two ensigns bearing the imperial standards, the imperial chamberlain Rudolph, and many other nobles of the empire, and more bishops than you could count, though at that point nobody was noticing details. There were also representatives of the other Lombard cities, such as Lanfranco of Como, Siro Salimbene of Pavia, Filippo of Casale, Gerardo of Novara, Pattinerio of Ossona, and Malavisca of Brescia.

When Baudolino had taken his place before the gate of the city, all the Alessandrians filed out, with their little children in their arms and the old men leaning on them, and even the ill were carried out on carts, including the simple-minded and the lame, along with the heroes of the siege who had lost a leg or an arm, or even bare-assed on a plank with wheels, propelling themselves with their hands. Since they didn't know how long they would have to remain outside, many brought along provisions, some had bread and salami, others, roast chickens, and still others, baskets of fruit, and in the end it all looked like a grand picnic.

Truth to tell, it was very cold, and the fields were covered with frost, so sitting down was torture. Those citizens, now deprived of power, stood erect, stamped their feet, blew on their hands, and someone said: "Can we get this show over with quickly? We've left our pots on the stove."

The emperor's men entered the city and nobody saw what they did, not even Baudolino, who was outside, waiting for the return procession. At a certain point a bishop came out and announced that this was the city of Caesarea, by grace of the holy and Roman emperor. The imperials behind Baudolino raised their arms and their standards, cheering the great Frederick. Baudolino spurred his horse to a trot, approached the first line of citizens and, in his position as imperial envoy, announced that to this noble city including the seven towns of Gamondio, Marengo, Bergoglio, Roboreto, Solero, Foro, and Oviglio, the name of Caesarea had been given and he ceded it to the inhabitants of the afore-named places, here gathered, inviting them to take possession of this turreted gift.

The imperial chamberlain listed all the articles of the agreement, but everyone was cold, and they allowed the details of the donation to pass in haste: the *regalia,* the *curadia,* the tolls, and all those things that made a treaty valid. "Come, Rudolph," Baudolino said to the imperial chamberlain, "it's all a farce anyway and the sooner it's over the better."

The exiles took the return path, and they were all there except Oberto del Foro, who hadn't accepted the shame of this homage. He who had defeated Frederick had delegated in his stead, as *nuncii civitatis,* Anselmo Conzani and Teobaldo Guasco.

Passing before Baudolino, the *nuncii* of the new Caesarea swore their solemn oath, though speaking in Latin so horrible that if afterwards they said they had sworn the opposite nobody could have contradicted them. As for the others, they followed with lazy, grudging salutes, some saying *Salve,* Baudolino; how are things, Baudolino; hey there, Baudolino; long time no see; well, here we are again, eh? As Gagliaudo went by, he muttered that this thing wasn't serious, but he was sufficiently sensitive to raise his hat, and inasmuch as he raised it in front of that scapegrace son of his, as an homage it was more effective than if he had licked Frederick's feet.

When the ceremony was over, both the Lombards and the Teutonics went off as quickly as possible, as if they were ashamed of themselves. Baudolino, on the contrary, followed his fellow-citizens inside the walls and heard some saying:

"Look at this fine city!"

"You know something? It looks just like that other one—what was the name?—that was here before."

"These Alamans, they're really geniuses! In no time at all they've run up a city that's a true masterpiece!"

"Just look over there. That house looks exactly like mine! They've remade it exactly like it was."

"Now, boys," Baudolino shouted, "be thankful you've pulled it off without having to pay *iugaticum*!"

"As for you—don't put on too many airs! You'll end up believing what you say!"

It was a beautiful day. Baudolino laid aside all the signs of his power and went off to celebrate. In the cathedral square girls were dancing in a circle. Boidi took Baudolino to the tavern, and in that cave with its aroma of garlic they all went to draw the wine directly from the barrels, because on that day there were to be no more masters or servants, especially the tavern's serving wenches, some of whom had already been carried upstairs, but as everyone knows, men are born hunters.

"Blood of Jesus Christ!" Gagliaudo said, pouring a bit of wine on his sleeve, to show that the cloth wouldn't absorb it and the drop remained compact, with ruby glints, a sign that this was good stuff. "Now we'll go on calling it Caesarea for a few years, at least on the parchments with seals," Boidi whispered to Baudolino, "but then we'll start calling it what we called it before, and I want to see if anyone cares."

"Yes," Baudolino said, "then we'll call it by its old name, because that's what that angel Colandrina called it, and now that she's in

239

Paradise, there's a risk she might send her benedictions to the wrong address."

"Master Niketas, I felt almost reconciled to my misfortunes, because from me the son I never had and the wife I had had too briefly at least had received a city that nobody would afterwards oppress. Perhaps," Baudolino added, inspired by the anise, "one day Alessandria will become the new Constantinople, the third Rome, all towers and basilicas, a wonder of the universe."

"May God so will," Niketas wished, raising his cup.

20

Baudolino finds Zosimos again

In April, at Constance, the emperor and the League of the Lombard communes signed a final agreement. In June confused reports were arriving from Byzantium.

Manuel had been dead for three years. His son Alexius, hardly more than a child, had succeeded him. A naughty child, Niketas commented, who, still without any knowledge of joys and sorrows, devoted his days to the hunt and to his horses, playing with young boys, while at court various suitors aimed at winning his mother the dowager, covering themselves with perfume like idiots and bedecking themselves with necklaces as women do, others dedicating themselves to squandering public funds, each pursuing his own desires and combating the others—as if an erect supporting column had been removed and everything was tilting the wrong way.

"The omen that had appeared at Manuel's death was achieved," Niketas said. "A woman gave birth to a male child with stunted, badly articulated limbs, and an over-large head, and this was a presage of polyarchy, which is the mother of anarchy."

"What I learned immediately from our spies was that a cousin, Andronicus, was conspiring in the shadows," Baudolino said.

"He was the son of a brother of Manuel's father, and was therefore a kind of uncle to little Alexius. Until then he had been in exile, because Manuel considered him untrustworthy, a traitor. Now he slyly ingratiated himself with young Alexius, as if repentant of his past actions, desirous of offering him protection, and little by little he gained increasing power. Between plots and poisonings, he pursued his ascent to the imperial throne until, when he was by then old, steeped in envy and hatred, he spurred the citizens of Constantinople to revolt, having himself proclaimed basileus. As he received the sacred Host, he swore he was assuming power to protect his still-young nephew. But immediately afterwards, his evil genius, Stephen Agiochristoforites, strangled the boy Alexius with a bow string. When the wretched boy's corpse was brought to him, Andronicus ordered it to be cast into the depths of the sea, after severing the head, which was then hidden in a place called Katabates. I don't know why, since it is an old monastery long in ruins, just outside the Constantinian walls."

"I know why. My spies reported that, with Agiochristoforites, there was a very active monk whom Andronicus had wanted with him, after the death of Manuel, for he was an expert in necromancy. His name happened to be Zosimos, and reputedly he was able to raise the dead among the ruins of that monastery, where he had established an underground palace for himself....So then I had found Zosimos, or at least I knew where to catch him. This happened in November of 1184, when Beatrice of Burgundy suddenly died."

Another silence. Baudolino drank a long draft.

"I understood that death as a punishment. It was right that, after the second woman of my life, I should also lose the first. I was past forty. I had heard that in Terdona there was, or there had been, a church where those baptized lived to forty. I had passed the limit granted to the fortunate. I could die in peace. I couldn't bear the sight of Frederick: the death of Beatrice had prostrated him; he wanted to concern himself with his older son, who was now twenty but increasingly frail, and Frederick was slowly preparing the succession of his second son, Henry, having him crowned king of Italy. He was growing old, my poor father, now he was White-beard....I had returned once to Alessandria and found that my blood parents were still older. Pale, thin, delicate as those balls of white stuff that roll around the fields in spring, bent like saplings on a windy day, they spent their waking hours around the fire quarreling over a misplaced bowl or an egg that one or the other of them had dropped. And they scolded me, every time I went to see them, because I never came. I decided then to sell my life cheap, and go to Byzantium to look for Zosimos, even if that could mean ending up blinded, in a dungeon, for my remaining years."

Going to Constantinople could be dangerous because, a few years earlier, stirred up by Andronicus himself, even before he seized power, the inhabitants of the city had revolted against the Latins living there, killing no small number of them, looting their houses, and forcing many to take refuge in the Princes Islands. Now it seemed that Venetians, Genoese, and Pisans could again circulate in the city, because they were people indispensable to the welfare of the empire, but William II, king of Sicily, was moving against Byzantium, and for the Greeklings—Sicilian or Roman, Provençal or Alaman—all were Latins, and there was scant distinction. So they decided to sail from Venice and arrive by sea, like a caravan of merchants from Taprobane (this was Abdul's idea). Very few had any idea where Taprobane was, perhaps no one, nor in Byzantium would they know what language was spoken there.

So Baudolino dressed up as a Persian dignitary. Rabbi Solomon, who would have been singled out as a Jew even in Jerusalem, was the company's physician, with a fine dark cloak all spangled with signs of the zodiac; the Poet looked like a Turkish merchant wearing a pale-blue caftan; Kyot could have been one of those Lebanese who dress badly but have pockets full of gold pieces, Abdul shaved his head to eliminate his red hair, and in the end resembled a eunuch of high degree; and Boron passed as his servant.

As for their language, they decided to communicate among themselves in the thieves' argot they had learned in Paris, which they all spoke to perfection—and this says a great deal about their commitment to their studies in those blissful days. Incomprehensible even to Parisians, for the Byzantines it could well be the language of Taprobane.

After leaving Venice in early summer, they learned at a port of call in August that the Sicilians had conquered Thessalonia, and were perhaps swarming over the northern coast of the Propontis, so, having entered that arm of the sea in the heart of the night, the captain preferred to make a wide curve towards the opposite shore and head for Constantinople as if they were arriving from Chalcedon. To console them for that detour, he promised them an imperial arrival, because—he said—that is the way to discover Constantinople, arriving there with the first rays of the sun in your face.

When Baudolino and his friends went out on deck, towards dawn, they felt a moment's disappointment, because the shore was veiled in a thick haze, but the captain reassured them: this was the right approach to the city, slowly, in that haze, which, for that matter, already absorbing the first light of dawn, would little by little be dispelled.

After another hour's sail, the captain pointed to a white dot, and it was the top of a dome, which seemed to pierce the mist.... Soon, within the whiteness the columns of some palaces were outlined along the coast, and then the shapes and colors of some houses, spires turning pink, and, gradually, below, the walls and their towers. Abruptly, there was a great shadow, still covered by layers of vapor that rose from the top of a high plain, and strayed through the air, until you could see, harmonious and gleaming in the sun's first rays, the dome of Saint Sophia, as if it had miraculously risen out of nothingness.

From that moment on came a continuous revelation, with more

towers and more domes emerging in a sky that cleared little by little, amid a triumph of green spaces, golden columns, white peristyles, rosy marbles, and the entire glory of the imperial palace of the Bucoleon, with its cypresses in a pied labyrinth of hanging gardens. And then the entrance to the Golden Horn, with the great chain barring entry, and the white tower of Galata on the right.

As he told the story, Baudolino was moved, and Niketas repeated sadly how beautiful Constantinople had been, when it was beautiful.

"Ah, it was a city full of emotions," Baudolino said. "The moment we arrived we had an idea of what was happening there. We turned up at the Hippodrome just as they were preparing for the torture of an enemy of the basileus..."

"Andronicus was virtually insane. Your Latins from Sicily had put Thessalonia to the sword and fired it. Andronicus had had some fortifications constructed, then he seemed to lose interest in the danger. He gave himself over to a life of dissipation, saying their enemies were not to be feared; he put to torture those who could have helped him, he left the city in the company of prostitutes and concubines, buried himself in the valleys and forests as animals do, followed by his inamoratas like a cock by his hens, like Dionysus and his bacchantes; he had only to put on a stag's skin and a saffron-colored dress. He frequented only flautists and hetairai, as unrestrained as Sardanapalus, as lascivious as a polyp; he was unable to bear the weight of his own debaucheries and he ate an unclean animal of the Nile, like a crocodile, which was said to favor ejaculation.... But I wouldn't want you to consider him a bad ruler. He also did many good things; he limited taxes, issued edicts to prevent the wrecking of ships in our ports in order to sack them; he restored the ancient underground aqueduct, and also the church of the Holy Forty Martyrs..."

"A good man, in short..."

"Don't put words in my mouth. The fact is that a basileus can use his power to do good, but to hold on to his power he has to do evil.

You too have lived at the side of a man of power, and you too have admitted that he could be noble and wrathful, cruel and concerned with the common good. The only way not to sin is to seek isolation on the top of a column as the sainted fathers did in the past, but by now those columns have fallen in ruins."

"I won't argue with you about how this empire should be governed. It's yours, or at least it was. I'll go back to my story. We've come to live here, with these Genovese, because they were my trustworthy spies, as you must have sensed. And indeed Boiamondo discovered one day that, on that very evening, the basileus would go to the ancient crypt of Katabates to perform rites of divination and magic. If we were to find Zosimos, that was our chance."

When evening had fallen, they went towards the walls of Constantine to where there was a kind of little pavilion, not far from the church of the Most Holy Apostles. Boiamondo said that from there we would reach the crypt directly, without going through the monastery's church. He opened a door, had them descend some slippery little steps, and they found themselves in a corridor reeking of damp.

"Here we are," Boiamondo said. "Just keep going a bit and you'll be in the crypt."

"You're not coming?"

"I'm not coming anywhere where they do things with the dead. When it comes to doing things, I prefer the people to be alive, and female."

Going forward, they passed through a chamber with a low vaulted ceiling, where they could discern couches, rumpled beds, goblets lying on the floor, unwashed dishes with the remains of some debauch. Obviously that glutton Zosimos performed here not only his rituals with the deceased but also some ritual that wouldn't have displeased Boiamondo. But all that orgiastic equipment had been piled up in apparent haste in the darker corners, because that evening Zosimos had arranged to meet the basileus to make him speak with the dead and not with strumpets, because, as everyone knows, Baudolino said, people will believe anything provided it's the dead who speak.

Beyond the room, some lights could be seen, and in fact they entered a circular crypt illuminated by two tripods, already alight. The crypt was surrounded by a colonnade, and behind the columns they could glimpse openings of passages, or tunnels, leading God knows where.

In the center of the crypt was a basin filled with water, its edge forming a kind of channel filled with an oily substance, which ran in a circle around the surface. Next to the basin, on a little column, was a vague object, covered by a red cloth. Baudolino realized that Andronicus, after having entrusted himself to ventriloquists and astrologers, and having tried in vain to find in Byzantium someone who, like the ancient Greeks, could foretell the future through the flight of birds, and with no faith in the wretches who boasted that they could interpret dreams, had by now given himself over to hydromants, who, like Zosimos, could draw presages by immersing in water something that had belonged to a deceased person.

Passing behind the altar, they turned and saw an iconostasis, dominated by a Christ Pantocrator, who stared at them with widened, stern eyes.

Baudolino remarked that, if Boiamondo's information was correct, in a little while someone would surely arrive, so they had best hide themselves. They chose a part of the colonnade where the tripods cast no light, and they placed themselves there just in time, because the steps of someone arriving could be heard.

From the left side of the iconostasis they saw Zosimos enter, wrapped in a cloak that looked like Rabbi Solomon's. Baudolino had an instinctive reaction of anger and felt like going out into the open and laying hands on that traitor. Obsequiously the monk preceded a sumptuously dressed man, followed by two other figures. The respectful attitude of these two made it clear that the first man was the basileus Andronicus.

The monarch stopped short, struck by the scene. He blessed himself devoutly before the iconostasis, then asked Zosimos: "Why did you have me come here?"

"My lord," Zosimos answered, "I had you come here because true hydromancy can be performed only in consecrated places, establishing the proper contact with the realm of the dead."

"I am no coward," the basileus said, crossing himself again, "but you—aren't you afraid of calling up the dead?"

Zosimos laughed boldly. "My lord, I could raise these hands of mine and the sleepers of ten thousand graves in Constantinople would rush obediently to my feet. But I have no need to recall those bodies to life. I possess a portentous object that I will use to establish more rapid contact with the world of shadows."

He lighted a firebrand at one of the tripods and held it out to the channel at the rim of the basin. The oil began to burn, and a little crown of flame, running all around the surface of the water, illuminated it with dancing glints.

"I still see nothing," the basileus said, bending over the basin. "Ask this water of yours who is the man preparing to take my place. I sense unrest in the city, and I want to know whom I must destroy to dispel any fear."

Zosimos approached the object covered by the red cloth, lying on the little column. With a histrionic gesture he removed the veil, and handed the basileus a round object he had held between his hands. Our friends couldn't see what it was, but they saw the basileus draw back, trembling, as if trying to ward off an unbearable sight. "No, no," he said, "not this! You asked it of me for your rites, but I didn't know you would have it reappear before me!"

Zosimos raised this trophy of his and was presenting it to an imaginary congregation like a monstrance, turning it towards every

248

part of the cavern. It was the head of a dead child, its features still intact, as if it had just been severed from the trunk: eyes closed, the nostrils of the slender nose dilated, the little lips barely parted, revealing a full set of tiny teeth. The immobility and the alien illusion of life in that face were made more hieratic by the fact that it appeared to be of a uniform gilded hue, and seemed almost to sparkle in the light of the little flames that Zosimos was now approaching.

"I had to use the head of your nephew Alexius," Zosimos was saying to the basileus, "for the ritual to be achieved. Alexius was bound to you by blood ties, and his mediation will enable you to communicate with the realm of those who are no more." Then, slowly, he immersed in the water that horrid little object, until it reached the bottom of the basin, over which Andronicus bent, as closely as the crown of flames would allow. "The water is turning murky," he said in a whisper. "It has found in Alexius the terrestrial element it was awaiting, and it is questioning him," Zosimos murmured. "We will wait until this cloud is dispersed."

Our friends couldn't see what was happening in the water, but they realized that at a certain point it became clear again and revealed, on the bottom, the face of the boy basileus. "By Hell's power," Andronicus stammered, "it is finding again its former colors, and I can read some signs that have appeared on his brow.... Oh, miracle!... Iota, Sigma..."

You didn't have to be a hydromant to understand what had happened. Zosimos had taken the head of the boy emperor, had incised some letters on the brow, then had covered them with a gilded substance, soluble in water. Now, as that artificial patina dissolved, the wretched victim was giving to the man who had hired his killer the message that obviously Zosimos, or whoever had inspired him, wanted the basileus to receive.

In fact, Andronicus went on spelling it out: "Iota, Sigma, IS... IS..." He straightened up, twisted the hairs of his beard several times in his fingers, seemed to shoot fire from his eyes, bowing his head as if to reflect, then raising it like a fiery horse, barely held in check. "Isaac!" he cried. "The enemy is Isaac Comnenus! What is he plotting there on Cyprus? I will send out a fleet and destroy him before he can move, the wretch!"

One of the two attendants emerged from the shadows, and Baudolino noted that he had the face of a man prepared to roast his own mother if she failed to put meat on the table. "My Lord," the man said, "Cyprus is too far away, and your fleet would have to go beyond the Propontis, passing the area where now the army of the king of Sicily is spreading. But just as you cannot go to Isaac, so he cannot come to you. I would not think so much of Isaac Comnenus, but, rather of Isaac Angelus, who is here in the city, and you know how little love he has for you."

"Stephen!" Andronicus laughed, with contempt. "You'd have me worry about Isaac Angelus? How can you think that such a broken-winded, inept, impotent good-for-nothing could even think of threatening me? Zosimos, Zosimos," he said furiously to the necromancer, "this water and this head speak to me either of one who is too far away or of another who is too stupid! What good are your eyes if you can't read in this pot full of piss?" Zosimos realized that he was about to lose his eyes, but luckily for him, that Stephen who had spoken earlier now spoke up again. From the obvious pleasure with which the man was promising new crimes, Baudolino understood this was Stephen Agiochristoforites, the evil genius of Andronicus, the man who had strangled and decapitated the boy Alexius.

"My lord, do not scorn portents. You yourself have seen how on the boy's face signs have appeared that were surely not there when he was alive. Isaac Angelus may be a petty weakling, but he hates you. Others, smaller and weaker than he, have made attempts on the life of men great and courageous as you, if ever there have been such.... Give me your consent, and this very night I will go and capture Angelus and tear out his eyes with my own hands, then I will hang him from a column of his palace. The people will be told that you received

250

a message from heaven. Better to be rid at once of someone who does not yet threaten you, than leave him alive so that he may threaten you one day. Let us strike first."

"You are trying to use me to satisfy some grudge of your own," the basileus said, "but it may be that in doing evil you may also be favoring good. Get rid of Isaac for me. I only regret..." and he gave Zosimos such a look that he shivered with fear, "for, with Isaac dead, we will never know if he really wanted to harm me, or if this monk has told the truth. But in the end he has aroused in me a just suspicion, and if you think the worst, you are always right. Stephen, we are obliged to show him our gratitude. See that he has what he may ask." He made a gesture to the two attendants and went out, leaving Zosimos to recover slowly from the terror that had petrified him beside his basin.

"In fact, Agiochristoforites did hate Isaac Angelus, and obviously had arranged with Zosimos to make him fall out of favor," Niketas said. "But serving his own rancor did not do his master good, because as you must know, he hastened the basileus's ruin."

"I know," Baudolino said, "but actually, on that evening it mattered little to me that I understand what was going on. It was enough for me to know that now I had Zosimos in my grasp."

As soon as the sound of the royal visitors' footsteps had died away, Zosimos heaved a great sigh. The experiment, after all, had succeeded. He rubbed his hands, with a little smile of satisfaction, drew the boy's head from the water and laid it where it had been before. Then he turned, to examine the crypt, and began laughing hysterically, raising his arms and shouting: "I have the basileus in my power! Now I won't be afraid even of the dead!"

No sooner had he spoken than our friends slowly came out into the light. Those who perform magic, it so happens, finally are persuaded that, even if they don't believe in the devil, the devil surely believes in them. Seeing a band of lemurs arising as if it were Judgment Day, Zosimos, scoundrel though he was, at that moment behaved with exemplary spontaneity. Without trying to conceal his feelings, he fainted.

He came to as the Poet was sprinkling him with some divinatory water. He opened his eyes and found himself confronted by a Baudolino fearsome to see, more than if he were returning from the other world. At that moment Zosimos realized that, worse than the flames of an uncertain Hell, the certain vengeance of his former victim awaited him.

"I did it to serve my master," he hastened to say, "and to do you, too, a service: I've spread your letter more than you could ever have—"

Baudolino said: "Zosimos, I don't want to sound mean, but if I were to obey the inspiration I receive from Our Lord, I would smash your ass. But since that would be hard work, as you see, I am restraining myself." And he gave him a slap with the back of his hand that made his head spin around twice.

"I am a man of the basileus. If you touch a single hair of my beard, I swear—"

The Poet seized him by the hair, pulled his face to the flames that were still flickering around the basin, and Zosimos's beard began to smoke.

"You are all mad," Zosimos said, trying to elude the grip of Abdul and Kyot, who had grabbed him and were twisting his arms behind his back. And Baudolino, with a slap on the nape, pushed him headlong, to extinguish the beard's fire in the basin, preventing him from raising his head until the wretch, no longer fearing the fire, began to fear the water, and the more he feared it, the more he swallowed.

"From the bubbles you've made," Baudolino said serenely, pulling him up by the hair, "I can predict that tonight you will die not with your beard but with your feet toasted."

"Baudolino," Zosimos sobbed, vomiting water, "Baudolino, we

can still come to some agreement.... Let me cough, I beg you. I can't escape. What are you going to do, all of you against one lone man? Have you no pity? Listen, Baudolino, I know you don't want to take revenge for that moment of weakness on my part; you want to reach the land of that Prester John of yours, and I told you I have the very map to get you there. If you throw dust on the fire of the hearth it will go out."

"What does that mean, you bandit? Enough of your pronouncements!"

"It means that if you kill me, you'll never see the map. Often fish, playing in the water, leap out beyond the confines of their natural dwelling. I can enable you to go far. Let us make a pact, like two honest men. You let me go, and I will lead you to the place where the map of Cosmas the Indicopleustes is. My life for the kingdom of Prester John. Doesn't that seem a fair bargain to you?"

"I'd rather kill you," Baudolino said, "but I need you alive to get the map."

"And afterwards?"

"Afterwards we'll keep you well tied up and wrapped in a carpet until we find a reliable ship that will take us far from here, and only then will we unroll the carpet, because if we let you go at once you will immediately have every killer in the city on our heels."

"And you'll unroll it in the water..."

"Enough! We're not murderers. If I wanted to kill you later, I wouldn't be slapping you now. And—you see?—I do it for a good reason, personal satisfaction, since I don't plan to do anything worse." And he began calmly dealing out blows, first with one hand, then with the other, one blow swinging the head to the left, another swinging it to the right, twice with the palm hard, twice with tensed fingers, twice with the back of the hand, twice with the edge, twice with the fists, until Zosimos became purplish and Baudolino had almost dislocated his wrists. "Now it's beginning to hurt me," he said, "and I'll stop. Let's go see this map."

Kyot and Abdul dragged Zosimos by the armpits, for by now he could no longer stand on his own feet, and could barely point out the way with a trembling finger, as he murmured: "The monk who is despised and bears it is like a plant that is watered every day."

Baudolino said to the Poet: "Zosimos once taught me that anger more than any other passion upsets and troubles the soul, but sometimes helps it. When in fact we use it calmly against the wicked and sinners to save them or confound them, we give the soul sweetness, because we are proceeding directly towards the ends of justice." Rabbi Solomon commented: "As the Talmud says, there are punishments that cleanse all the iniquities of a man."

21

Baudolino and the sweets of Byzantium

The monastery of Katabates was in ruins, and everyone now considered it uninhabited, but at ground level some cells still existed, and the old library, now without books, had become a kind of refectory. Here Zosimos lived with two or three acolytes, and only God knew what their monastic rites were. When Baudolino and the others emerged from underground with their prisoner, the acolytes were sleeping, but, as was clear the following morning, they were sufficiently stupefied by their excesses that they did not represent a danger. The group decided it was best to sleep in the library. Zosimos had troubled dreams as he lay on the ground between Kyot and Abdul, who had now become his guardian angels.

In the morning all sat around a table, and Zosimos was invited to come to the point.

"The point is," Zosimos said, "that the map of Cosmas is in the Bucoleon palace, in a place known to me and where only I have access. We will go there late this evening."

"Zosimos," Baudolino said, "you are beating about the bush. First of all, explain to me clearly what this map says."

"Why, it's quite simple, isn't it?" Zosimos said, taking a parchment and a stylus. "I told you that every Christian who follows the true faith must agree to the fact that the world is made like the tabernacle of which the Scriptures speak. Now listen carefully to what I say: in the lower part of the tabernacle there was a table with twelve loaves of bread and twelve fruits, one for each month of the year; all around the table ran a plinth that depicted the Ocean, and around the plinth there was a frame one palm wide that depicted the land of the beyond, where to the east the Earthly Paradise is situated. The sky was represented by the vault, which rested entirely on the extremities of the earth, but between the vault and the base extended the veil of the firmament, beyond which lies the celestial world that only one day will we see face to face. In fact, as Isaiah said, God is he who is seated above the earth, whose inhabitants are as locusts. He who like a thin veil has unfurled the sky and spread it out like a tent. And the psalmist praises him who spreads out the sky like a pavilion. Then Moses placed, below the veil, south of the candelabrum that illuminated all the expanse of the earth, seven lamps to signify the seven days of the week and all the stars of the sky."

"But you are explaining to me how the tabernacle was made," Baudolino said, "not how the universe is made."

"But the universe is made like the tabernacle, and so if I explain to you what the tabernacle was like, I am explaining what the universe is like. Why can't you understand something so simple? Look..." And he made a drawing.

It showed the form of the universe, exactly like a temple, with its curving vault, whose upper part remained concealed from our eyes by the veil of the firmament. "Below the ecumen extends, that is, all the inhabited earth, which, however, is not flat, but rests on the Ocean, which surrounds it, and rises through an imperceptible and continuous slope towards the extreme north and towards the west, where a mountain stands, so high that its presence escapes our eye and its peak is lost in the clouds. The sun and the moon, moved by the angels—to whom we owe also rain, earthquake, and all other atmospheric phenomena—pass in the morning from east towards the

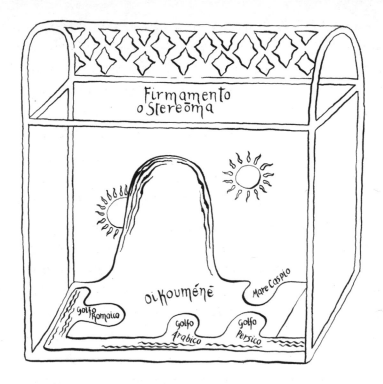

Firmamento o Stereōma

Oikouménē

Mare Caspio

Golfo Romaico

Golfo Arabico

Golfo Persico

south, in front of the mountain, and illuminate the world, and in the evening they reascend towards the west and disappear behind the mountain, giving us the impression of sunset. And so, while for us night is falling, on the other side of the mountain it is day, but that day is seen by no one, because the mountain on the other side is desert, and no one has ever been there."

"And with this drawing we're supposed to find the land of Prester John?" Baudolino asked. "See here, Zosimos, our agreement was your life for a good map, but if the map is no good, then the conditions change."

"Calm down. Considering that, to depict the tabernacle as it is, our art is incapable of showing everything that remains covered by its walls and by the mountain, Cosmas drew another map, which shows the earth as if we were looking down on it from above, flying in the firmament, as the angels see it. This map, which is kept in the Buca-leon, shows the position of the lands that we know, included within the frame of the Ocean, and beyond the Ocean, the lands inhabited by man before the Flood, where, after Noah, no one has ever set foot."

"Once again, Zosimos," Baudolino said, putting on a ferocious face, "if you think that by talking to us of things you won't let us see—"

"But I see these things, as if they were here before my eyes, and soon you will also see them."

With that haggard face, made all the more pathetic by the bruises, his eyes shining with things that only he could discern, Zosimos was convincing even to those who distrusted him. It was his strength, Baudolino explained to Niketas, and in this way he had hoodwinked him before, and was hoodwinking him now and would continue to do so for several more years. He was so convincing that he wanted even to clarify how it was possible, with the tabernacle of Cosmas, to explain eclipses also, but eclipses didn't interest Baudolino. What convinced him was that with the true map perhaps they could really set out in search of the Priest. "Very well," he said, "we'll wait till this evening."

Zosimos had one of his monks serve some cooked greens and fruit, and when the Poet asked if there was nothing else, he answered: "Frugal food, uniformly regulated, will quickly lead the monk to the harbor of his invulnerability." The Poet told him to go to the devil, then seeing that Zosimos ate with great gusto, he looked more closely into the dish of greens and discovered that the acolytes had concealed there, just for Zosimos, some nice chunks of fat lamb. Without a word, he exchanged plates.

So they were prepared to spend the day waiting when one of the acolytes entered with a stunned expression and reported what was happening. In the night, immediately after the ritual, Stephen Agiochristoforites, with a squad of armed men, went to the house of Isaac Angelus, near the Pribleptos monastery, the shrine of the Famous Virgin, and called for his enemy in a loud voice to come forth; or, rather, he shouted to his own men to break down the door, seize

258

Isaac by the beard, and carry him out head down. Isaac then—though according to report he was hesitant and fearful—decided to risk all or nothing: he seized a horse in the courtyard and, sword drawn, scantily clad, a bit ridiculous with his two-colored cloak that barely reached his loins, suddenly rode out, catching his enemy by surprise. The Agiochristoforites didn't have time to draw his own weapon when Isaac, with a single blow of his sword, split his enemy's head in two. Then he turned to the now bicephalic Stephen's henchmen, slicing the ear off one of them, as the others ran away in fear.

Killing the emperor's trusted aide was an extreme act, and demanded an extreme remedy. Isaac, revealing a great sense of how the populace should be dealt with, dashed to Saint Sophia, demanding the asylum that tradition granted homicides, and loudly implored forgiveness for his own misdeed. He tore off what little clothing he had on as well as the hairs of his beard; he displayed his still-bloody sword, and, while he was asking for mercy, suggested he had acted in self-defense, reminding all of the crimes of the slain man.

"I don't like this story," Zosimos said, distraught because of the sudden death of his grim, dire protector. Less likable still would be the news that arrived subsequently, hour by hour. Isaac had been overtaken at Saint Sophia by illustrious figures including Johannes Doukas; Isaac continued to harangue the constantly swelling crowd; towards evening a great number of citizens had gathered around Isaac in the church to protect him though some were beginning to murmur that it was time to put an end to the tyrant.

Whether Isaac, as Zosimos's necromancy asserted, had long been preparing his coup, or whether he happily exploited a misstep by his enemies, it was clear that the throne of Andronicus was now tottering. It was equally clear that, in this situation, it would be madness to enter the royal palace, which could at any moment become a public shambles. All agreed that it was necessary to await the outcome of events at Katabates.

The next morning half the citizenry was out in the streets calling

259

in loud voices for the imprisonment of Andronicus and the raising of Isaac to the imperial throne. The populace attacked the public prisons, liberating many innocent victims of the tyrant, men of illustrious name who immediately joined in the uprising. But by now it was not so much an uprising as a revolt, a revolution, a seizure of power. The citizens, in arms, ranged through the streets, some with sword and buckler, some with clubs or sticks. Some of them, including many imperial dignitaries, who had concluded that this was perhaps the right time to choose a new autocrat, lowered the crown of Constantine the Great, which hung over the main altar of the church, and crowned Isaac.

Swarming from the church in fighting mood, the crowd lay siege to the imperial palace; Andronicus put up a desperate resistance, firing arrows from the top of the highest tower, the so-called Kentenarion. But he had to give in to the now imperious fury of his subjects. It was said that he tore the crucifix from his chest, took off his purple sandals, stuck a pointed barbarian-style cap on his head, and proceeded, through the labyrinths of the Bucoleon to board his ship, taking with him his wife and the prostitute Maraptica, with whom he was madly in love. Isaac triumphantly entered the palace. The crowd overran the city, attacked the mint or, as it was called, the Golden Lavabos, entered the armories, and turned to sacking the palace churches, tearing ornaments from the holy images.

Now Zosimos, at every new rumor, trembled more and more, since it was already being said that, once an accomplice of Andronicus was identified, he was put to the sword. On the other hand, Baudolino and his friends also considered it unwise to venture at this time into the corridors of the Bucoleon. And so, unable to do anything but eat and drink, our friends spent a few more days at Katabates.

Until it was learned that Isaac had moved from the Bucoleon to the Blachernae palace, at the far northern tip of the city. This perhaps made the Bucoleon less protected and (since there was nothing left to sack), fairly deserted. On that same day, Andronicus was captured on the shore of the Euxine and was brought before Isaac. The courtiers had kicked and beaten him, torn out his beard, knocked out his teeth, shaved his head; now they cut off his right hand and flung him into prison.

When news arrived that in the city joyful dancing and festivities had sprung up at every corner, Baudolino decided that in the confusion they could head for the Bucoleon. Zosimos pointed out that he might be recognized, and the friends told him not to worry. Arming themselves with every instrument they had at their disposal, they shaved his head and beard, while he wept, considering himself dishonored by the loss of those insignia of monastic venerability. In fact, hairless as an egg, Zosimos appeared totally without chin, his upper lip protruding, his ears pointed like a dog's, and, Baudolino observed, he looked more like Cichinisio, an idiot who roamed the streets of Alessandria shouting obscenities at the girls, than like the accursed ascetic he had so far passed himself off as. To adjust this deplorable effect, they sprinkled him with cosmetics, and at the end he seemed a freak, a character that in Lombardy children would have followed with taunts and a shower of rotten fruit, but in Constantinople it was an everyday sight, Baudolino said, like going around Alessandria dressed as a vendor of *sirasso,* or ricotta as it is also called.

They crossed the city and witnessed the passage of Andronicus, more mangy-looking than the mangy camel on which he had been hoisted; he was almost naked, with a foul clump of bloody rags on the stump of his right wrist, and clotted blood on his gaunt cheeks, because they had just gouged out one of his eyes. Around him the most desperate of the city's inhabitants, whose lord and autocrat he had been for so long, sausage-makers, tanners, and the dregs of every tavern, collecting like swarms of flies in spring around a horse turd, struck his head with their clubs, stuffed ox excrement in his nostrils, squeezed sponges soaked in cow piss over his nose, thrust skewers into his legs; the milder threw stones at him, calling him rabid dog and son of a bitch in heat. From a brothel window, a prostitute emptied a pan of boiling water over him. Then the crowd's fury increased further; they pulled him down from the camel and hanged him by his feet from the two columns beside the statue of the she-wolf giving suck to Romulus and Remus.

Andronicus behaved better than his tormentors, not emitting a moan. He confined himself to murmuring "*Kyrie eleison. Kyrie eleison,*" and asked why they were breaking a chain already shattered. Once he was strung up, a man with a sword neatly cut off his genitals, another stuck a spear in his mouth, impaling him to his viscera, while still another impaled him through the anus. There were also some Latins present, who had scimitars and moved as if they were dancing around him, slashing away all his flesh, and perhaps they were the only ones entitled to vengeance, given what Andronicus had done to those of their race a few years before. Finally the wretch still had the strength to raise to his mouth his right stump, as if he wanted to drink his blood, to make up for the blood that he was losing in great spurts. Then he died.

Having fled that spectacle, our friends tried to reach the Bucoleon, but when they were near, they quickly realized that it was impossible to gain entry. Isaac, disgusted by all the looting, had now set his guards to protect it, and anyone attempting to pass that defense was executed on the spot.

"You can get by in any case, Zosimos," Baudolino said. "It's simple: you enter, get the map, and bring it to us."

"What if they cut my throat?"

"If you don't go, then we'll cut it."

"My sacrifice would make sense if the map were in the palace. But, to tell you the truth, the map isn't there."

Baudolino looked at him as if unable to comprehend such shameless behavior. "Ah," he roared, "and now at last you're telling the truth? Why have you continued to lie until now?"

"I was trying to gain time. Gaining time isn't a sin. For a monk, wasting time is a sin."

"We'll kill him here on the spot," the Poet said. "This is the right moment, in this massacre nobody will notice. Let's decide who strangles him, and it's over."

"One moment," Zosimos said. "The Lord teaches us how to abstain from the deed that is not profitable. I lied, true, but for good reason."

"What good?" Baudolino said, exasperated.

"My own," Zosimos answered. "I had every right to protect my life, since you meant to take it from me. Monks, like cherubim and seraphim, must be all covered with eyes, or—this is how I interpret the saying of so many of the desert fathers—they must exercise wit and cleverness in the face of the enemy."

"But the enemy those fathers of yours were talking about was the devil, not us!" Baudolino cried.

"The stratagems of devils are different: they appear in dreams, they create hallucinations, they conspire to deceive us, they transform themselves into angels of light and they spare us to make us feel a false security. What would you have done in my place?"

"And what will you do now, you filthy Greekling, to save your life once again?"

"I will tell you the truth, as is my habit. Cosmas's map does really exist, and I have seen it with these eyes. Where it is now, I don't know, but I swear that I have it in my head as if it were printed there...." And he tapped his brow, now free of hair. "I could tell you, day by day, the distances that separate us from the land of Prester John. Now, obviously, I cannot remain in this city, and you have no reason to stay here either, since you came for me and now you have me, and for the map, which you don't have. If you kill me, you'll have nothing. If you take me with you, I swear by all the holy apostles that I will be your slave and I will devote my days to tracing for you an itinerary that will lead you straight to the land of the Priest. Sparing my life costs you nothing, except a mouth to feed. Killing me, you lose everything. Yes? Or no?"

"This is the most shameless of all the shameless creatures I've met in my life," Boron said, and the others agreed. Zosimos waited, composed, in silence. Rabbi Solomon ventured to say: "The Holy One, be his name always blessed..." but Baudolino wouldn't let him finish: "No more proverbs; this rogue says enough of them. He's a rogue, but he's right. We have to take him along. Otherwise Frederick will see us return empty-handed and will think we've spent his money wallowing in Oriental orgies. We'll at least return with a prisoner. But you, Zosimos, swear: swear that you won't try some other trick on us...."

"I swear by all twelve of the holy apostles," Zosimos said.

"Eleven! Eleven, you wretch," Baudolino shouted at him, seizing his clothes, "If you say twelve, you're including Judas!"

"All right then, eleven."

"And so," Niketas said, "this was your first journey to Byzantium. I wouldn't be surprised, after what you saw, if you considered what's happening now a purification."

"You see, Master Niketas," Baudolino said, "purification, as you call it, has never appealed to me. Alessandria may be a miserable town, but where I come from, when someone in command arouses our dislike, we say good-bye to him and choose a new consul. And even Frederick, choleric as he may have been, when his cousins bothered him, he didn't castrate them, he gave them another duchy. But this isn't the story. I was aleady at the extreme confines of Christendom, I could have continued towards the east, or to the south, and I would have found the Indias. But by then we had spent all our money, and to be able to go to the Orient, I had to return to the Occident. By then I was forty-three. I have been on the trail of Prester John since I was sixteen, or even younger, and once again I was forced to postpone my journey."

22

Baudolino loses his father and finds the Grasal

The Genoese sent Boiamondo out with Theophilus to make a preliminary inspection of the city, to see if the situation was favorable. It was, more or less, they reported on their return, because a great number of the pilgrims were in the taverns, and the rest seemed to have gathered in Saint Sophia, to gaze with greedy eyes on the hoard of relics that had been accumulated there.

"It was enough to blind you!" Boiamondo said. But he added that the accumulation of loot had turned into a filthy game. Some pretended to deposit their prey, putting a bit of gimcrackery in the pile, while covertly they slipped a saint's bone into their tunic. Since nobody wanted to be caught with a relic on his person, immediately outside the church a kind of market had grown, with still-wealthy citizens and Armenian traders.

"And so," Boiamondo snickered, "the Greeks who saved a Byzantine coin, shoving it up a hole, have pulled it out to trade for a shinbone of Saint Somebody. Which maybe had been in the church next door all along. Maybe they then will sell it back to the church, because the Greeks are smart. It's all a big feeding trough, and then they say we Genoese are the ones who think only of cash."

"What are they bringing into the church?" Niketas asked.

Theophilus gave him a more precise account. He had seen the casket containing the purple cloak of Christ, a piece of reed used in the flagellation, the sponge held up to Our Lord on the cross, the crown of thorns, a case containing a piece of the bread consecrated at the Last Supper, the one Jesus offered to Judas. Then a glass box arrived with hairs from the beard of the Crucified, torn out by the Jews after the deposition from the cross, and the case was wrapped in the Lord's garments, which the soldiers had gambled over at the foot of the cross. And then the flagellation stake, intact.

"I also saw them bring in a piece of the Madonna's mantle," Boiamondo said.

"How sad!" Niketas sighed. "If you saw only a piece that means they have already divided it up. It existed whole, in the Blachernae palace. Long, long ago two men named Galbius and Candidus went on a pilgrimage to Palestine and in Capernaum they learned that the Virgin's *pallion* was preserved in the house of a Jew. They made friends with him, spent the night with him, secretly took the measurements of the wooden case that contained the garment, then in Jerusalem they had an identical case made, went back to Capernaum, switched the cases at night, and brought the cloak to Constantinople, where the church of Saints Peter and Mark was built to house it."

Boiamondo also reported a rumor that two Christian knights had taken, and not yet handed over, two heads of Saint John the Baptist, one each, and all were wondering which one was the good one. Niketas smiled, tolerantly: "I knew that two were being venerated here in the city. The first was brought by Theodosius the Great, and was placed in the church of the Precursor. Then Justininan found another at Emmaus. I believe he donated it to some cenobium; people said it had been brought here, but nobody knew any longer where it was."

"But how is it possible to forget a relic, considering what one is worth?" Baudolino asked.

"The piety of the populace is fickle. For years they are excited by a sacred memento, and then something even more miraculous arrives and they become enthusiastic about that, while the earlier one is forgotten."

"Which head is the right one?" Boiamondo asked.

"Holy things must not be spoken of in human terms. Whichever of the two relics was given me, I assure you that in bending to kiss it, I would sense the mystical perfume that it emanates, and I would know it was the true head."

At that moment Pevere also arrived from the city. Extraordinary things were happening. To prevent the soldiery, too, from stealing from the heap in Saint Sophia, the Doge had ordered a first rapid listing of the things collected, and they had also brought in some Greek monks to identify the various relics. Here it was discovered that, after the majority of the pilgrims had been forced to return what they had taken, now in the church there were not only two heads of the Baptist, which they already knew, but two sponges for the gall and wormwood and two crowns of thorns, not to mention other duplications. A miracle, said Pevere, laughing, with a glance at Baudolino: the most precious among Byzantium's relics had multiplied, like the loaves and fishes. Some of the pilgrims saw the event as a favorable sign from heaven, and they shouted that, if there was such a wealth of these valuable things, the Doge should allow each man to carry home what he had taken.

"No, it's a miracle favorable to us," Theophilus said, "because the Latins will never know which relics are genuine, and they'll be obliged to leave everything here."

"I'm not so sure," Baudolino said. "Each prince or marquess or vassal will be content to take home some holy relic, which will attract crowds of the devout, and donations. But then if there's a rumor that another, similar relic exists a thousand miles away, they'll say that one is fake."

Niketas turned pensive. "I don't believe in this miracle. The Lord doesn't confound our minds with the relics of his saints. . . . Baudolino,

267

in these past months, since your arrival in the city, you haven't in-vented some trick with relics, have you?"

"Master Niketas!" Baudolino tried to say in an offended tone. Then he held his hands out, as if to impose calm on his interlocutor. "All right, if I have to tell you everything, the moment will come when I'll have to tell you a story about relics. I'll tell it to you later. Anyway, you yourself said just now that holy things mustn't be spo-ken of in human terms. But it's late, and I think that in an hour, under cover of darkness, we can set out. We must be ready."

Wanting to set out well refreshed, Niketas had, a while ago, or-dered Theophilus to prepare a *monokythron*, which required some time to be cooked properly. It was a bronze pot full of beef and pork, bones not entirely stripped and Phrygian cabbage, saturated with fat. Since there was little time remaining for a lengthy supper, the logothete had abandoned his good habits and was dipping into the pan not with three fingers, but with open hands. It was as if he were consummat-ing his last night of love with the beloved city, virgin, prostitute, and martyr. Baudolino had no appetite and confined himself to sipping the resinous wine, for who knows what he would find in Selymbria.

Niketas asked him if Zosimos played a role in this story of relics, and Baudolino said that he preferred to proceed in order.

"After the horrible things we saw in the city we returned over-land, because there wasn't enough money to pay for the voyage by ship. The confusion of those days allowed Zosimos, with the help of one of those acolytes he was about to abandon, to lay hands on some mules, no telling how. During the journey, after hunting in some for-est and with the hospitality of some monasteries along the way, we fi-nally arrived in Venice, and then in the Lombard plain...."

"And Zosimos never tried to escape?"

"He couldn't. From that time on, even after our return, and al-ways at Frederick's court and on the journey to Jerusalem we made later, for more than four years he remained in chains. That is, when he was with us, he was free to move, but when we had to leave him alone, he was chained to his bed, to a stake, to a tree, according to where we were, and if we were on horseback, he was tied to the reins in such a way that if he tried to dismount the horse would rear up. Afraid that this would make him forget his obligations, every evening, before he went to sleep, I gave him a slap. By then he knew it was coming and awaited it, like a mother's kiss, before sleeping."

During their march the friends had, above all, never ceased prodding Zosimos to reconstruct the map, and he displayed willingness, every day recalling a detail, so that he had already succeeded in calculating the true distances.

"Roughly," he said, drawing in the dust with one finger, "from Tzinista, the land of silk, to Persia it is fifty days' march, crossing Persia takes a hundred and fifty days more, from the Persian border to Seleucia thirteen days, from Seleucia to Rome and then to the Iberian land, a hundred and fifty days. More or less, to go from one end of the world to the other, four hundred days' march, if you do thirty miles a day. Earth, moreover, is more long than wide—and you will recall that in Exodus it is said that in the tabernacle the table must be two cubits long and one cubit wide. So from north to south you can calculate fifty days from the northern regions to Constantinople, from Constantinople to Alexandria another fifty days, from Alexandria to Ethiopia on the Arabic Gulf, seventy days. In short, more or less two hundred days. Therefore, if you set out from Constantinople towards farthest Indias, calculating that you are proceeding obliquely and will have to stop often to find your way, and who knows how many times you will have to turn back, I reckon you would find Prester John after a year's journey."

Speaking of relics, Kyot asked Zosimos if he had heard the Grasal spoken of. He had heard it mentioned, to be sure, and by the Galatians, who lived around Constantinople, people who traditionally knew the stories of the very ancient priests of the extreme north. Kyot asked if he had heard of that Feirefiz who supposedly took the

Grasal to Prester John, and Zosimos said that certainly he had heard of him, but Baudolino remained skeptical. "What is this Grasal then?" he asked. "The cup, the cup in which Christ consecrated the bread and the wine; you've said that yourself." Bread in a cup? No, wine: the bread was on a plate, a *patena,* a little tray. But what was the Grasal then, the plate or the cup? Both, Zosimos attempted to equivocate. If you thought about it, the Poet suggested, with a fearsome expression, it was the spear with which Longinus had pierced the ribs. Yes, of course, that must be it. At this point Baudolino gave him a slap, even if it wasn't yet time to go to bed, but Zosimos defended himself: the stories were vague, yes, but the fact that they circulated also among the Galatians of Byzantium was the proof that this Grasal really existed. And so it went on: of the Grasal the knowledge was always the same, that there was very little knowledge.

"Of course," Baudolino said, "if we were the ones who bring Frederick the Grasal, and not a gallows-bird like you...."

"You can still take it to him," Zosimos suggested. "Just find the proper vessel...."

"Ah, so now it's also a vessel? I'll put you in that vessel! I'm not a counterfeiter like you!"

Zosimos shrugged and stroked his chin, testing the regrowth of his beard, but it was all the uglier now, for he looked like a catfish, whereas, before, the chin had been shiny and smooth like a ball.

"Furthermore," Baudolino muttered, "even if we know it's a chalice or a vase, how can we recognize it when we find it?"

"Oh, you can rest assured," Kyot spoke up, his eyes lost in the world of his legends, "you'll see the glow, you'll sense the perfume...."

"Let's hope so," Baudolino said. Rabbi Solomon shook his head: "It must be something you gentiles stole from the Temple in Jerusalem when you sacked it and scattered us through the world."

They arrived just in time for Henry's wedding. The second son of Frederick, crowned king of the Romans, was to marry Constance of

Altavilla. The emperor now placed all his hopes in this junior son. Not that he didn't cherish the older boy. He did. He had even named him king of Swabia, but it was obvious that Frederick loved him with sadness, as happens with children who are born ill. Baudolino saw him: pale, coughing, always blinking his left eyelid as if to chase away a gnat. Even during regal celebrations he often went off by himself, and Baudolino had seen him riding in the countryside, nervously slashing bushes with his crop, as if to calm something that was gnawing him inside.

"It's an effort for him to live," Frederick said to Baudolino one evening. He himself was aging, old White-beard; he moved as if he had a crick in his neck. He wouldn't give up hunting, and as soon as he saw a river, he would throw himself into the water, swimming as of old. But Baudolino was afraid that one of these days, caught in the clutch of cold water, he would have a stroke, and he told him to be careful.

To console Frederick, Baudolino told of the success of their mission, how they had captured that faithless monk and soon they would have a map that would lead them to the land of the Priest, and how the Grasal was not a fable and one of these days Baudolino would place it in his hands. Frederick nodded. "The Grasal, ah, the Grasal," he murmured, his eyes lost in some unknown place, "to be sure, with that I could..." Then he would be distracted by some important message, sigh again, and with effort prepare to fulfill his duty.

Every now and then he would take Baudolino aside and tell him how much he missed Beatrice. To console him, Baudolino would tell how much he missed Colandrina. "Eh, I know," Frederick would say. "You, who loved Colandrina, understand how much I loved Beatrice. But perhaps you don't realize how truly lovable Beatrice was." And, for Baudolino, the wound of his old remorse was reopened.

In the summer the emperor returned to Germany, but Baudolino could not follow him. Word came that his mother had died. He rushed to Alessandria, and along the way he kept thinking of that woman who had borne him, and to whom he had never shown any genuine tenderness, except on that Christmas evening so many years before, while the ewe was giving birth. (Damn! he said to himself, already more than fifteen winters have passed—my God, maybe even eighteen.) He arrived after his mother had been buried, and found that Gagliaudo had abandoned the city and gone back to his old house in the marsh.

He was lying down, with a wooden bowl full of wine at his side, lazily waving his hand to chase the flies from his face. "Baudolino," he said at once, "ten times every day I would be angry with that poor woman, begging heaven to strike her with lightning. And now that heaven has struck her I don't know what to do any more. In this house I can't find anything: she always put things in order. I can't even find the pitchfork for the muck, and in the stable the stock have more dung than hay. And so, what with one thing and another, I've decided to die, too. Maybe that's best."

The son's protests were of no avail. "Baudolino, you know that in our parts we have hard heads and when we get something into our head there's no way to make us change our mind. I'm not a good-for-nothing like you, here one day and there the next—a fine life you gentlemen have! People who think only about how to kill others, yet one day, if you tell them they have to die, they shit their pants. But I've lived well and never harmed a fly, beside a woman who was a saint, and now that I've decided to die, I'll die. Let me go off like I say, and I'll be satisfied, because the more I stay here the worse it gets."

Every now and then he drank a little wine, and fell asleep, then reopened his eyes and asked: "Am I dead?" "No, Father," Baudolino answered him, "luckily you're still alive." "Oh, poor me," he said, "another day. But I'll die tomorrow, don't worry." He wouldn't touch food on any account.

Baudolino stroked the old man's brow and brushed away the flies, and then, not knowing how to console his dying father but wishing to show him that his son wasn't the fool he had always thought, Baudolino told him about the holy quest he had been preparing for so long, and how he wanted to reach the kingdom of Prester John. "If you only knew..." he said, "I will go and discover marvelous places. In one of them there is a bird like nothing anyone's ever seen, the Phoenix, it lives and flies for five hundred years. When five hundred years have gone by, the priests prepare an altar, sprinkling spices and sulphur on it. Then the bird arrives and catches fire and turns to ashes. The next day among the ashes a worm appears, the second day a full-grown bird, and the third day this bird flies off. It is no bigger than an eagle, on its head it has a feathery crest like a peacock's, the neck is a golden color, the beak is indigo blue, and the wings purple, the tail striped with yellow, green, and red. So the Phoenix never dies."

"That's all bullshit," Gagliaudo said. "For me, it would be enough just to bring Rosina back to life, poor animal; you killed her stuffing her with all that spoiled wheat. To Hell with your Feliks."

"When I come back, I'll bring you some manna; it's found on the mountains in the country of Job. It's white and very sweet. It comes from the dew that falls from heaven on the grass, where it clots. It cleanses the blood, drives away melancholy."

"Cleanse my balls. That's stuff good for your court scum, who eat snipe and pastry."

"Don't you want a piece of bread, at least?"

"I don't have time. I have to die tomorrow morning."

The next morning Baudolino told him how he would give the emperor the Grasal, the cup from which Our Lord had drunk.

"Oh, yes? What's it like?"

"It's all gold, studded with lapis lazuli."

"You see what a fool you are? Our Lord was a carpenter's son and he lived with people who were even hungrier than he was. All his life he wore the same clothes; the priest in church told us they didn't have seams so as not to wear out before he was thirty-three, and you come

273

here to tell me he was roistering with a cup made of gold and lapissy-ouylee. Fine tales you tell. He was lucky if he had a bowl like this, that his father had carved out of a root, the way I did, something that lasts a lifetime and you can't break it, not even with a hammer. And now that I think of it: give me some more of this blood of Jesus Christ; it's the only thing that helps me die well."

By the devil! Baudolino said to himself. This old man is right. The Grasal should be a cup like this one. Simple, poor as the Lord himself was. And for this reason perhaps it is there, within everyone's grasp, and no one has ever recognized it because they have been searching all their lives for something gleaming.

But it's not that Baudolino, at that moment, was giving so much thought to the Grasal. He didn't want to see his father die, but he realized that, in allowing him to die, he was doing the old man's will. After a few days, old Gagliaudo was as wrinkled as a dried chestnut, and breathing with difficulty, now rejecting even wine.

"Father," Baudolino said to him, "if you really want to die, make your peace with the Lord and you will enter Paradise, which is like the palace of Prester John. The Lord God will be seated on a great throne at the top of a tower, and above the back of the throne there will be two golden apples, and in each of them two great carbuncles that shine all night long. The arms of the throne will be of emerald. The seven steps to the throne will be of onyx, crystal, jasper, amethyst, sardonyx, cornelian, and chrysolite. Columns of fine gold will be all around. And above the throne, flying angels will sing sweet songs...."

"And there will be some devils who will kick my behind out of there, because in a place like that a man stinking of cowshit is someone they don't want around them. Just shut up..."

Then, all of a sudden, he opened his eyes wide, tried to sit erect, as Baudolino held him. "Dear Lord, now I'm dying, because I can really see Paradise. Oh, how beautiful it is...."

"What do you see, Father?" Baudolino was now sobbing.

"It's just like our stable, only all cleaned up, and Rosina is there,

274

too. . . . And there's that sainted mother of yours, wicked bitch, now you'll tell me where you put the pitchfork for the muck. . . ."

Gagliaudo belched, dropped the bowl, and remained wide-eyed, staring at the celestial stable.

Baudolino gently ran a hand over his face, because, by now what the old man had to see he saw even with his eyes closed, and then Baudolino went to tell the people in Alessandria what had happened. The citizens wanted the great old man to be honored with solemn funeral ceremonies, because he was the man who had saved the city, and they decided they would place his statue over the portal of the cathedral.

Baudolino went back once more to his parents' house, to look for some memento, since he had decided never to return. On the ground he saw his father's bowl, and picked it up as a precious relic. He washed it carefully, so that it wouldn't stink of wine, because, he told himself, if one day it were said that this was the Grasal, after all the time that had gone by since the Last Supper, it should no longer smell of anything, if not perhaps of those aromas that, thinking this was the True Cup, all would surely perceive. He wrapped the bowl in his cloak and carried it off.

23

Baudolino on the Third Crusade

When darkness fell over Constantinople they set off. It was a sizeable party, but in those days various bands of citizenry moved like lost souls from one end of the city to another, to look for a porch where they could spend the night. Baudolino had taken off his crusader garb, because, if someone were to stop him and ask him the name of his lord, he would have difficulty replying. At their head went Pevere, Boiamondo, Grillo, and Taraburlo, with the air of four men accidentally taking the same path. But they looked around at every corner, clutching their just-sharpened knives under their clothing.

Shortly before they reached Saint Sophia a ruffian with blue eyes and long yellow mustache rushed towards the group, grabbed the hand of one of the girls, no matter how ugly and pocked she appeared, and tried to drag her off. Baudolino told himself the moment had come to give battle, and the Genoese were with him, but Niketas had a better idea. He saw a group of horsemen coming down the street and he flung himself on his knees before them, asking justice and mercy, appealing to their honor. They were probably the Doge's men, and they set to striking the barbarian with the flat of their swords, driving him off and restoring the girl to her family.

Beyond the Hippodrome the Genoese chose safer streets: narrow alleys, where the houses were all burned or bore obvious signs of scrupulous looting. The pilgrims, if they were still looking for something to steal, had gone elsewhere. Towards night they passed the walls of Theodosius. There the rest of the Genoese were waiting with the mules. They bade farewell to their protectors, with many embraces and good wishes, and went off along a country road, under a springtime sun, with the moon almost full on the horizon. A light wind was blowing off the sea. They had all rested during the day, and the journey did not seem to tire even the wife of Niketas. But he was extremely tired, gasping at every jolt of his steed, and every half hour he had to ask the others to let him rest for a while.

"You ate too much, Master Niketas," Baudolino said to him.

"Would you deny an exile the final delicacies of his homeland as it is dying?" Niketas replied. Then he looked for a boulder or a fallen tree trunk on which to sit: "But it's my eagerness to learn the rest of your adventure. Sit here, Baudolino, feel this peace, smell the good odors of the countryside. Let us rest a little, and go on with your story."

As later, in the three days following, they traveled by day and rested at night beneath the open sky, to avoid places inhabited by God knows whom. It was under the stars, in a silence broken only by the rustle of boughs and by sudden sounds of nocturnal animals, that Baudolino continued his account.

At that time—and we're in the year 1187—Saladin unleashed the last attack on Christian Jerusalem. He won. He behaved generously, allowing all those who could pay a tax to leave the city, unharmed, and he confined himself to beheading before the walls all the Knights Templar because, as all admitted, he was generous, yes, but no general worthy of the name could have spared the chosen troop of the invader enemy, and even the Templars knew that, in following their trade, they were accepting the rule that no prisoners were taken. But for all Saladin's demonstrated magnanimity, the whole Christian world was shaken by the end of that Frankish rule overseas that had resisted for almost a hundred years. The pope appealed to all the monarchs of Europe for a third expedition of crusaders again to liberate Jerusalem, now reconquered by the infidel.

For Baudolino, his emperor's participation in that enterprise was the occasion he had been awaiting. To descend on Palestine meant preparing to move to the East with an invincible army. Jerusalem would be retaken in a flash, and afterwards nothing would remain but to continue towards the Indias. However, it was on this occasion that he discovered how weary and uncertain Frederick felt. He had pacified Italy, but surely he feared that, leaving it, he would lose the advantages he had gained. Or perhaps he was troubled by the idea of a new expedition towards Palestine, remembering his crime during the previous expedition, when, driven by rage, he had destroyed that Bulgarian monastery. Who knows? He hesitated. He asked himself if it was his duty, and when you start asking this question (Baudolino said to himself) it's already a sign that there is no duty that is drawing you on.

"I was forty-five years old, Master Niketas, and I was risking the dream of my life, or my life itself, since my life had been built around that dream. And so, coldly, I decided to give my adoptive father a hope, a sign from heaven of his mission. After the fall of Jerusalem, the survivors of that ruin arrived in our Christian lands, and through the imperial court had passed seven knights of the Temple who, God knows how, had escaped the vengeance of Saladin. They were in bad shape, but perhaps you don't know what the Templars are like: drinkers and fornicators, and they'll sell you their sister if you give them yours to grope—or, better still, it is said, your little brother. In short, let's say I gave them refreshment, and everyone saw me going around the taverns with them. Hence it wasn't hard for me one day to tell Frederick those shameless simoniacs had stolen in Jerusalem the

Grasal itself. I said that, since the Templars were broke, I gave them all the money I had, and I bought it. Frederick naturally was dumbfounded at first. But wasn't the Grasal in the hands of Prester John, who wanted to give it to him? And weren't we planning to go look for John precisely to receive that most holy relic as a gift? So it was, my Father, I said to him, but obviously some treacherous minister robbed it from John, and sold it to some band of Templars, who had come raiding those parts, not realizing where they were. It wasn't important to know the how and the when. We were now proposing to the holy and Roman emperor another and more extraordinary opportunity: he could seek out Prester John with the aim of returning the Grasal to him. Not using that incomparable relic to gain power, but to fulfill a duty, which would win him the gratitude of the Priest and eternal fame throughout all Christendom. Between seizing the Grasal and returning it, between hoarding it and returning it to where it had been stolen, between possessing it (as all dreamed) and performing the supreme sacrifice of depriving himself of it—it was obvious on which side the true blessing lay, the glory of being the one and true *rex et sacerdos*. Frederick would become the new Joseph of Arimathea.

"You were lying to your father."

"I was acting for his good, and the good of the empire."

"You didn't ask yourself what would happen if Frederick really reached the Priest, handed him the Grasal, and the Priest widened his eyes, wondering what this bowl was that he had never seen before? Frederick would have become not the glory but the laughingstock of Christendom."

"Master Niketas, you know men better than I. Imagine: you are Prester John, a great emperor of the West kneels at your feet, and hands you such a relic, saying it is rightfully yours, and you start snickering and saying you've never seen that tavern bowl before? Come now! I'm not saying the Priest would have pretended to recognize it. I'm saying that, dazzled by the glory that would fall on him, its acknowledged custodian, he would have recognized it at once, believing he had always possessed it. And so I took to Frederick, as a most precious object, the bowl of my father Gagliaudo, and I swear to you that at that moment I felt like the celebrant of a sacred rite. I handed over the gift and the memory of my carnal father to my spiritual father, and my carnal father was right: that most humble thing, with which he had communicated all his life as a sinner, was truly, spiritually the cup used by poor Christ, who was heading for death, for the redemption of all sinners. In saying the Mass, doesn't the priest take the most common bread and the most common wine and make them become the body and blood of Our Lord?"

"But you weren't a priest."

"And, in fact, I didn't say that the object was the blood of Christ, I said only that it had contained that blood. I wasn't usurping any sacramental power. I was bearing witness."

"False witness."

"No. You told me that, believing a relic true, you catch its scent. We believe that we, only we, need God, but often God needs us. At that moment I believed it was necessary to help him. That cup must truly have existed, if Our Lord had used it. If it had been lost, it had been through the fault of some worthless man. I was restoring the Grasal to Christianity. God would not have contradicted me. The proof is that even my companions believed in it immediately. The sacred vessel was there, before their eyes, now in the hands of Frederick, who raised it to heaven as if he were in ecstasy, and Boron knelt, seeing for the first time the object over which he had long raved, Kyot said at once that he seemed to see a great light, Rabbi Solomon admitted that—even if Christ were not the true Messiah awaited by his people—surely this receptacle emanated a fragrance, as of incense, Zosimos widened his visionary eyes and blessed himself backwards several times, as you schismatics do, Abdul was trembling in every limb and murmured that possessing the sacred relic was equivalent to having conquered all the kingdoms beyond the sea—and it was clear that he would have liked to donate it as a token of love to his faraway princess. I had tears in my eyes, and was asking myself why heaven had chosen me as mediator of that portentous event. As for the Poet, frowning, he chewed his nails. I knew what he was thinking: that I had been a fool, that Frederick was old and would never be able to derive advantage from that treasure, and we might as well have kept it for ourselves, and if we had set off towards the lands of the north, they would have bestowed a kingdom on us. Confronted by the obvious weakness of the emperor, he was returning to his fantasies of power. But I was almost consoled because I understood that, reacting like this, he also considered the Grasal a genuine object."

Frederick devoutly enclosed the cup in a coffer, hanging the key around his neck, and Baudolino thought that he himself had acted well, because at that instant he had the impression that not only the Poet but all his other friends would have been ready to steal that object, to rush towards their own personal dreams.

Afterwards, the emperor affirmed that now, truly, it was necessary to set out. An expedition of conquest had to be prepared carefully. In the following year Frederick sent ambassadors to Saladin, and sought encounters with envoys of Stephen Nemanya, prince of the Serbs, to arrange passage through their territories.

While the kings of England and France were deciding to leave by sea, in May of 1189, Frederick had gone overland from Ratisbon with fifteen thousand horsemen and fifteen thousand squires; some were saying that in the plains of Hungary he passed in review sixty thousand horsemen and a hundred thousand foot soldiers. Others were even to speak of six hundred thousand pilgrims. Perhaps all were exaggerating, even Baudolino was in no position to say how many they really were; perhaps in all they came to twenty thousand men, but in any case it was a great army. Without anyone's going out and counting them one by one, from a distance they were a tented horde whose beginning you could see but not their end.

To avoid the massacres and lootings of the previous expeditions, the emperor would not have them followed by those swarms of outcasts who, a hundred years earlier, had shed so much blood in Jerusalem. This was something to be done properly, by men who knew how a war is waged, not by wretches who set off with the excuse of winning Paradise and came home with the spoils of some Jew whose throat they had cut along the way. Frederick accepted only those who could support themselves for two years, and the poor soldiers received three silver marks for food during the journey. If you want to liberate Jerusalem, you have to spend what it takes.

Many Italians had joined the venture. There were the Cremonese with Bishop Sicardo, the men of Brescia, of Verona with Cardinal Adelardo, and even some Alessandrians, including old friends of Baudolino like Boidi, Cuttica of Quargnento, Porcelli, Aleramo Scaccabarozzi known as Bonehead, Colandrino the brother of Colandrina, who was therefore a brother-in-law, and also one of the Trotti men, Pozzi, Ghilini, Lanzavecchia, Peri, Inviziati, Gambarini, and Cermelli, all at their own expense or supported by their city.

Theirs was a sumptuous departure along the Danube to Vienna; at Breslava, in June, they met the king of Hungary. Then they entered the Bulgarian forest. In July they met the prince of the Serbs, who sought an alliance against Byzantium.

"I believe that this meeting," Baudolino said, "worried your basileus Isaac. He feared that the army wanted to conquer Constantinople."

"He wasn't mistaken."

"He was mistaken by fifteen years. At that time, Frederick really did want to reach Jerusalem."

"But we were uneasy."

"I understand. An immense foreign army was about to cross your territory, and you were concerned. But you certainly made our life difficult. We arrived at Serdica and we didn't find the promised supplies. Around Philippopolis we were confronted by your troops, and

282

then they retreated in full flight, as happened in every conflict during those months."

"You know that, at that time, I was governor of Philippopolis. We received conflicting news from the court. At one point the basileus ordered us to construct a girdle of walls and to dig a moat, to oppose your arrival, then immediately after we had done that, an order came that we were to destroy everything, so the city wouldn't serve as a haven for your people."

"You blocked the mountain passes, having trees chopped down. You attacked our men singly if they went off to look for food."

"You were sacking our lands."

"Because you weren't providing the promised rations. Your people lowered food from the walls in baskets, but they mixed lime and other poisonous substances in the bread. During that journey the emperor received a letter from Sybille, former queen of Jerusalem, who informed him that Saladin, to halt the advance of the Christians, had sent to the emperor of Byzantium bushels of poisoned grain, and a pot of wine so heavily poisoned that a slave of Isaac's, forced to sniff it, died on the spot."

"Fairy tales."

"When Frederick sent ambassadors to Constantinople, your basileus made them remain standing, then imprisoned them."

"Afterwards they were sent back to Frederick."

"When we entered Philippopolis, we found it empty, because all had slipped away. You weren't there either."

"It was my duty to evade capture."

"That may be. But it was after our entry into Philippopolis that your emperor changed his tone. That is where we encountered the Armenian community."

"The Armenians considered you brothers. They are schismatics like you, they don't venerate the holy images, they use unleavened bread."

"They are good Christians. Some of them spoke at once in the name of their prince, Leo, guaranteeing passage and assistance through their country. But things weren't that simple, as we learned at Adrianopolis, when ambassadors arrived from the Seleucian sultan of Iconium, Kilidj Arslan, who proclaimed himself lord of the Turks and the Syrians, and also of the Armenians. Who was in command? And where?"

"Kilidj was trying to halt the supremacy of Saladin, and wanted to conquer the Christian kingdom of Armenia, so he was hoping that Frederick could help him. The Armenians were confident that Frederick could contain Kilidj's demands. Our Isaac, still smarting from the defeat suffered at the hands of the Seljuks at Miriokephalon, hoped that Frederick would clash with Kilidj, but he wouldn't have been displeased if there had also been conflict with the Armenians, who were causing our empire no little trouble. That's why, when he learned that both the Seljuks and the Armenians were guaranteeing Frederick passage through their lands, he realized he should not halt that march but encourage it, allowing him to cross the Propontis. He was sending him against our enemies and away from us."

"My poor father. I don't know if he suspected he was a weapon in the hands of a tangle of interwoven enemies. Or perhaps he did understand, but hoped he could defeat them all. What I do know is that, glimpsing the possibility of an alliance with a Christian kingdom, the Armenian, beyond Byzantium, Frederick was eagerly thinking of his final goal. He dreamed (and I, with him) that the Armenians would be able to open the road for him towards the kingdom of Prester John. . . . In any case, it's as you said: after the envoys from the Seljuks and the Armenians, your Isaac gave us the ships. And it was, in fact, at Gallipolis, which you people call Kallioupolis, that I saw you, when in the name of your basileus, you offered us the vessels."

"It was not an easy decision on our part," Niketas said. "The basileus risked turning Saladin against him. He had to send messengers to him to explain the reasons for our concessions. A great lord, Saladin, he understood at once, and bore us no ill will. I repeat, from the Turks we have nothing to fear: our problem is with your schismatics, always."

Niketas and Baudolino agreed that there was no point in exchanging recriminations or explanations of that bygone episode. Perhaps Isaac was right: every Christian pilgrim who passed through Byzantium was always tempted to stop there, where there were so many beautiful things to conquer, without going and risking too much before the walls of Jerusalem. But Frederick truly wanted to go on.

They arrived at Gallipolis and, while it wasn't Constantinople, the army was seduced by that festive place, the port full of galleys and dromons, ready to take on board horses, horsemen, and victuals. It was not the work of a day, and meanwhile our friends had time on their hands. From the beginning of the journey Baudolino had decided to employ Zosimos for something useful, and forced him to teach Greek to the group. "In the place where we are going," he said, "nobody knows Latin, to say nothing of German, Provençal, or my language. With Greek, there's always some hope of making yourself understood." And so, between visits to the bordello and the reading of some texts of the fathers of the Eastern church, the waiting was not burdensome.

In the port there was a vast market, and they decided to venture into it, conquered by the distant gleaming and the odor of spices. Zosimos, whom they had freed so that he could be their guide (but under the vigilant surveillance of Boron, who didn't take his eyes off him for a second), now warned them: "You Latin and Alaman barbarians are ignorant of the civilization of us Romans. You should know that in our markets, at first glance, you wouldn't want to buy anything because they ask too much, and if you immediately pay what they ask, it's not that they take you for fools, because they already know you are fools, but they are offended because the merchant's joy is bargaining. So offer two coins when they ask ten, they'll come down to seven, you offer three and they come down to five, you stick to three, until they give in, weeping and swearing they'll end up homeless with all their family. At that point, go ahead and buy, but you should know that the object was worth one coin."

"Then why should we buy?" the Poet asked.

"Because they also have a right to live, and three coins for what is worth one represents an honest trade. But I must give you another warning: not only do merchants have a right to live, but so do thieves, and since they can't rob one another, they'll try to rob you. If you prevent them, that's your right; but if they succeed, you mustn't complain. So I advise you to carry little money in your purse, just the amount you've decided to spend, and no more."

Instructed by a guide so wise in local ways, our friends ventured into a tide of people stinking of garlic, like all Greeklings. Baudolino bought himself two Arab daggers, well made, to keep at either side of his belt, to be extracted rapidly, as he crossed his arms. Abdul found a little transparent box that contained a lock of hair (God knows whose, but it was clear whom he had in mind). Solomon called the others in a loud voice when he discovered the tent of a Persian selling miraculous potions. The vendor of elixirs displayed a phial that, according to him, contained a very potent drug that, taken in small doses, stimulated the vital spirits, but if drained quickly could cause death. Then he held up a similar phial, which, however, contained the most powerful of antidotes, capable of canceling the action of any poison. Solomon, who dabbled also in the art of medicine, like all Jews, bought the antidote. Belonging to a race more clever than the Romei, he managed to pay one coin instead of the ten asked, and he was tormented by the fear of having paid at least double the value.

Leaving the apothecary's tent, Kyot found an elegant scarf, and Boron, after considering all the merchandise at length, shook his head, murmuring that, for one in the service of an emperor who possessed the Grasal, all the treasures of the world were filth, and these things worst of all.

They came upon Boidi, the Alessandrian, who by now had become one of their group. He was enchanted by a ring, perhaps of gold (the vendor wept at selling it because it had belonged to his mother), which contained in its mount a wondrous cordial, a single sip of which could heal a wounded man and, in certain cases, resuscitate a dead one. He bought it, he said, because if they really had to risk their necks before the walls of Jerusalem, it was best to take some precaution.

Zosimos was ecstatically contemplating a seal bearing the initial Z, his own, which was being sold with a little stick of sealing wax. The Z was so worn that perhaps it would leave no mark on the wax, but this fact testified to the distinct antiquity of the object. Naturally, as a prisoner, he had no money, but Solomon, touched, bought the seal for him.

At a certain point, driven by the crowd, they realized they had lost the Poet, but they found him again as he was pulling down the price of a sword that, according to the merchant, dated back to the conquest of Jerusalem. But when he reached for his purse, he realized that Zosimos was right: with his pale-blue pensive Alaman eyes, he attracted thieves like flies. Baudolino was moved and made him a present of the sword.

The next day a richly dressed man turned up at the encampment, with exaggerated obsequious manners, accompanied by two servants. He asked to see Zosimos. The monk conferred with him for a while, then came to tell Baudolino that this was Makhitar Ardzrouni, a noble Armenian dignitary, who had been charged with a secret mission by Prince Leo.

"Ardzrouni?" Niketas said. "I know about him. He came several times to Constantinople, in the days of Andronicus and afterwards. I understand why he sought out Zosimos, because he had the reputation of an amateur of magical sciences. One of my friends in Selymbria—but God knows if we will find him still there—was also a guest in his castle at Dadjig. . . ."

"So were we, as I will tell you, and for our misfortune. The fact that he was Zosimos's friend was for me a very unfortunate sign, but I informed Frederick, who wanted to see him. This Ardzrouni was very reticent about his credentials. He had been sent, or not sent, by Leo, or he had been sent but he wasn't to say so. He was there to guide the imperial army through the territory of the Turks into Armenia. Ardzrouni expressed himself with the emperor in acceptable Latin, but when he wanted to remain vague he pretended he was unable to find the right word. Frederick said he was treacherous, like all Armenians, but a man familiar with the locality was convenient and he decided to add him to the army, asking me merely to keep an eye on him. I must say that during the journey, he behaved impeccably, always giving information that proved correct."

24

Baudolino in the castle of Ardzrouni

In March 1190 the army entered Asia and reached Laodicea, then headed for the territories of the Seljuk Turks. The old sultan of Iconium called himself an ally of Frederick, but his sons deposed him and attacked the Christian army. Or perhaps Kilidj had also changed his mind: we never really found out. Clashes, skirmishes, outright battles: Frederick advanced as victor, but his army had been decimated by the cold, by hunger, and by the attacks of the Turkomans, who arrived suddenly, struck the flanks of his army and fled, knowing well the passes and the hiding places.

Struggling through sun-baked desert territories, the soldiers had been forced to drink their own urine, or the blood of the horses. When they arrived at Iconium, the pilgrims' army was reduced to no more than a thousand horsemen.

And yet it was a fine siege, and young Frederick of Swabia, sickly though he was, fought well, taking the city himself.

"You speak coldly of young Frederick."

"He didn't love me. He mistrusted everyone; he was jealous of his younger brother, who was stealing the imperial crown from him, and surely he was jealous of me, who was not of his blood, jealous of his father's affection for me. Perhaps as a child he had been troubled by the way I looked at his mother, or she looked at me. He was jealous of the authority I had gained by giving the Grasal to his father, and on this matter he always displayed some skepticism. When there was talk of an expedition to the Indias, I heard him murmur that it could be discussed at the proper time. He felt dethroned by all. That's why at Iconium he behaved with valor, even though he had a fever that day. Only when his father praised him for that fine achievement, and in front of all his barons, did I see a light of joy gleam in his eyes. The one time in his life, I believe. I went to pay him homage, and I was truly happy for him, but he thanked me absently."

"Like me, Baudolino. I too wrote and am writing the chronicles of my empire, emphasizing more the petty jealousies, the hatred, the envy that jeopardized both poweful families and great public under-takings. Even emperors are human beings, and history is also the story of their weaknesses. But do go on."

"Once Iconium was conquered, Frederick immediately sent am-bassadors to Leo of Armenia, asking his help in proceeding across his territories. A pact existed; they had been the ones to promise this. And yet Leo hadn't yet sent anyone to receive us. Perhaps he was seized by the fear of meeting the same end as the sultan of Iconium. So we went ahead, not knowing if we would receive aid; and Ardzrouni guided us, saying that surely the ambassadors of his prince would arrive. One June day, turning southwards, having passed Laranda, we ventured into the Taurus Mountains, and finally we saw some cemeteries with crosses. We were in Cilicia, in Christian coun-try. We were immediately received by the Armenian lord of Sibilia, and, farther on, near a cursed river whose name I have chosen to for-get, we encountered a deputation that arrived in Leo's name. The moment it was sighted, Ardzrouni warned us that it was best for him to keep out of sight, and he vanished. We met two dignitaries, Con-stant and Baudouin de Camardeis, and I have never seen ambassa-dors of more uncertain intentions. One announced as imminent the arrival in great pomp of Leo and Gregory the Catholicos; the other hemmed and hawed, pointing out that, while most eager to help the emperor, the Armenian prince couldn't show Saladin that he was opening the way to his enemies, and therefore he had to act with great prudence."

When the delegation had left, Ardzrouni reappeared and took Zosimos aside, who then went to Baudolino and, with him, to Frederick.

"Ardzrouni says that, far be it from him to have any wish to betray his lord, but he suspects that for Leo it would be a stroke of luck if you went no farther."

"In what sense?" Frederick asked. "Does he want to offer me wine and maidens so I'll forget I must go on to Jerusalem?"

"Wine perhaps. Poisoned wine. He says you should remember the letter of Queen Sybille," Zosimos said.

"How does he know about that letter?"

"Rumors spread. If Leo were to arrest your march, he would do something very pleasing to Saladin, and Saladin could help him achieve his dream of becoming sultan of Iconium, since Kilidj and his sons have been shamefully defeated."

"And why is Ardzrouni so concerned about my life—even to the point of betraying his master?"

"Only Our Lord gave his life for love of humanity. The seed of men, born in sin, is like the seed of animals: even the cow gives you milk only if you give her hay. What does this holy maxim teach us? That Ardzrouni would not object one day to taking the place of Leo. Ardzrouni is respected by many of the Armenians; Leo isn't. And so, winning the gratitude of the holy and Roman emperor, he could one day rely on the most powerful of friends. So for this reason he suggests proceeding to his castle at Dadjig, on the banks of this same river, to encamp your men in the vicinity. While waiting till we can understand what Leo is really guaranteeing, you could stay with him, safe from any trap. And he urges you, above all, to be careful, especially about the food and the drink that any compatriot of his might offer you."

"By the devil!" Frederick shouted. "For a year I've been going from one nest of vipers to another! My fine German princes were lambs by comparison and—you know something?—even those treacherous Milanese who caused me so much suffering, at least they faced me in the open field, without trying to stab me in my sleep! What shall we do?"

His son Frederick suggested accepting the invitation. Better to watch out for a single, known enemy than many unknown ones. "He's right, Father," Baudolino said. "You stay in that castle, and my friends and I will represent a barrier around you, so that no one can approach you without passing over our bodies, day or night. We will taste first every substance presented to you. Don't say anything: I'm not a martyr. Everyone will know that we will eat and drink before you, and nobody will consider it wise to poison one of us because then your wrath would be unleashed on every inhabitant of that castle. Your men need rest, Cilicia is inhabited by Christian peoples, the sultan of Iconium no longer has troops to pass the mountains and attack you again, Saladin is still too far off, this region is made up of peaks and crevasses that are excellent natural defenses, it seems to be the ideal land for restoring everyone's strength."

After a day's march in the direction of Seleucia, they entered a gorge that left them barely enough space to follow the course of the river. All of a sudden the gorge opened out, allowing the river to run over a vast flat stretch, before accelerating its course and descending, engulfed by another gorge. Not very far from the shore, sprouting from the plain like a mushroom, rose a tower of irregular lines, standing out, pale blue, before the eyes of those coming from the east, while the sun was setting behind it, so that, at first sight, it was impossible to tell whether the tower was the work of man or of Nature. Only as you neared it could you understand that it was a sort of rocky mass on which a castle was built, from which obviously one could dominate both the plain and the girdle of surrounding mountains.

"There," Ardzrouni said then. "My lord, you may encamp your army in the plain, and I advise you to deploy it over there, below the river, where there is space for the tents, and water for men and animals. My castle is not large, and I suggest you climb up to it only with a group of trusted men."

Frederick instructed his son to deal with the encampment, and to remain with the army. He decided to take with him only about ten men, along with Baudolino and his friends. His son tried to protest, saying he wanted to be near his father, and not a mile away. Once again he looked at Baudolino and his men with scant trust, but the emperor could not be swayed. "I will sleep in that castle," he said. "Tomorrow morning I will bathe in the river, and for that I have no need of you. I will swim to your camp to wish you good day." The son said that his will was law, but reluctantly.

Frederick separated himself from the main body of the army, with his ten armed men, Baudolino, the Poet, Boron, Abdul, Solomon, and Boidi, who was dragging Zosimos on his chain. All were curious to learn how they would climb up to that refuge, but, going around the massif, they discovered finally that to the west the drop was less severe, only a little, but enough to dig into it and carve a stepped path, on which no more than two flanked horses could pass at once. Anyone wishing to ascend with hostile intentions had to climb the broad steps slowly, so just a pair of lone archers, from the battlements of the castle, could wipe out the invaders, two by two.

At the end of the climb a portal opened into a courtyard. From the exterior of that gate the path continued, grazing the walls, and, even narrower, the brink of the cliff, to another, smaller gate, on the north side, then it ended, over the void.

They entered the courtyard, which gave access to the actual castle, its walls bristling with slits, but defended in their turn by the walls that separated the courtyard from the abyss. Frederick deployed his guards on the outer ramparts, so they could survey the path from above. It did not seem that Ardzrouni had men of his own, beyond a few attendants who guarded the various doors and passages. "I don't need an army here," Ardzrouni said, smiling with pride. "I cannot be attacked. And besides, as you, Holy Emperor, will see, this is not a place of war, it is the refuge where I pursue my studies of air, fire, earth, and water. Come, I will show you where you can be lodged in a worthy fashion."

They climbed a great staircase, and at the second turn they entered a spacious *salle d'armes*, furnished with some benches and with panoplies on the walls. Ardzrouni opened a solid wood door with metal studs, and led Frederick into a sumptuously furnished chamber. There was a bed, with a canopy, with cups and candelabra of gold, surmounted by an ark of somber wood, perhaps a coffer or a tabernacle, and there was a broad fireplace ready to be lighted, with logs and pieces of a substance similar to coal, but covered by some oily matter, which probably was to feed the flame, all neatly laid out on a bed of fresh boughs, and covered with sprigs of aromatic berries.

"It's the best room at my disposal," Ardzrouni said, "and for me it is an honor to offer it to you. I do not advise you to open that window. It's an eastern exposure and tomorrow morning the sun might bother you. These colored panes—a wonder of Venetian art—will delicately filter the light."

"No one can enter through that window?" the Poet asked.

Ardzrouni laboriously opened the window, which was, in fact, shut with various bolts. "You see?" he said. "It's very high. And beyond the court are the ramparts, where the emperor's men are already on guard." In fact, the ramparts of the outer walls could be seen, the gallery on which, at intervals, the guards passed, and, just an arrow's shot from the window, two great circles or plates of shiny metal, deeply concave, set on a support between the battlements. Frederick asked what this was.

"They are mirrors of Archimedes," Ardzrouni said, "with which that sage of ancient times destroyed the Roman vessels that were besieging Syracuse. Each mirror captures and refracts the rays of light that fall parallel to its surface, and for that matter it reflects objects. But if the mirror is not flat and is curved in the proper way, as geometry, that supreme science, teaches us, the rays are not reflected parallel, but are all concentrated in a specific point in front of the mirror, according to its curve. Now, if you so orient the mirror that it captures the sun's rays at its moment of maximum radiance and bring them to strike, all together, a single distant point, such a concentration of solar rays on that precise point creates combustion, and you can set fire to a tree, the planking of a ship, a war machine, or the dry brush around your enemies. There are two mirrors because one is curved so that it strikes at a distance, the other sets fire at a closer range. So with these two very simple machines I can defend this castle of mine better than if I had a thousand bowmen."

Frederick said that Ardzrouni should teach him that secret, because then the walls of Jerusalem would fall better than those of Jericho, not through the sound of trumpets but through the rays of the sun. Ardzrouni said he was there to serve the emperor. Then he closed the window and said: "Air doesn't enter here, but through other fissures. Despite the season, since the walls are thick, you might feel cold tonight. Rather than light the fire, which smokes annoyingly, I advise you to cover yourself with these furs you see on the bed. I apologize for my vulgarity, but the Lord created us with a body: behind this little door there is a cubbyhole, with a less than royal seat, but anything your body wants to expel will fall into a cistern undergound, without infecting this space. This room can be entered only by the door we have just passed through; beyond that, once you have fastened it from inside with the latch, your courtiers will be sleeping on those benches, perhaps not comfortably, but they will guarantee your serenity."

They noticed on the breast of the fireplace a circular relief. It was a Medusa head, the hair twisted like snakes, eyes closed, and an open fleshy mouth, which displayed a dark cavity whose bottom could not be seen ("like the one I saw with you in the cistern, Master Niketas"). Frederick became curious and asked what it was.

Ardzrouni said that it was a Dionysius ear: "It is one of my magic devices. In Constantinople there are still old stones of this sort; it was enough simply to carve the mouth better. There is a room, below, where as a rule my little garrison stays, but as long as you, Emperor, are here it will be left empty. Everything that is said down there comes forth from this mouth, as if the speaker were just behind the sculpture. So if I choose, I can hear what my men are talking about."

"If only I could know what my cousins are talking about," Frederick said. "Ardzrouni, you are invaluable. We will talk further also of this. Now let us make our plans for tomorrow. In the morning I want to bathe in the river."

"You can reach it easily, by horse or on foot," Ardzrouni said, "and without even passing through the courtyard where you entered. In fact, beyond the door of the *salle d'armes* there is a little stairway that leads to a second court. From there you can find the main path again."

"Baudolino," Frederick said, "have some horses ready in that court for tomorrow morning."

"Dear Father," Baudolino said, "I know very well how much you like to face the most turbulent waters. But now you are tired from your journey and from all the trials you have undergone. You are unfamiliar with the waters of this river, which seems to me full of whirlpools. Why do you want to risk this?"

"Because I am not so old as you think, my son, and because, if it weren't late, I would go to the river at once; I feel filthy with dust. An emperor must not stink, unless it be with the oil of holy unctions. Arrange for the horses."

"As Ecclesiastes tells us," Rabbi Solomon said timidly, "thou shalt not swim against the river's current."

"And who says I will swim against it?" Frederick laughed. "I'll follow it."

"It is not good to wash oneself too often," Ardzrouni said, "unless under the guidance of an expert physician, but here you are master. Now it is still early; for me it would be an undeserved honor to show you around my castle."

He led them back down the grand staircase. On the lower floor they crossed a hall reserved for the evening banquet, already alight with many candelabra. Then they passed through a saloon full of stools, on some of which was carved a great overturned snail, a spiral structure that closed into a funnel, with a central hole. "This is the guards' room I told you about," he said, and those who speak with their mouths to this aperture can be heard in your chamber."

"I would like to hear how it works," Frederick said. Baudolino, in jest, said that during the night he would come here to greet him as he was sleeping. Frederick laughed and said no, because that night he wanted to rest peacefully. "Unless," he added, "you have to warn me that the sultan of Iconium is entering through the fireplace flue."

Ardzrouni led them along a corridor, and they entered a hall with vast vaults, which glowed and was smoky with swirls of steam. There were some cauldrons in which a molten matter was boiling, retorts and alembics, and other curious receptacles. Frederick asked if Ardzrouni produced gold. Ardzrouni smiled, saying that such were the tall tales of alchemists. But he knew how to gild metals and produce elixirs that, if they did not grant long life, at least extended the very brief life that is our lot. Frederick said he didn't want to taste them: "God has set the length of our life, and we must resign ourselves to his will. Perhaps I'll die tomorrow, perhaps I'll live to be a hundred. It's all in the hands of the Lord." Rabbi Solomon observed that his words were very wise, and the two conversed a while on the matter of divine decrees, and it was the first time that Baudolino heard Frederick speak of these things.

While the two were talking, out of the corner of his eye Baudolino saw Zosimos, stepping through a little door into an adjoining room, with Ardzrouni, looking concerned, immediately after him. Fearing that Zosimos knew some passage that would allow him to escape, Baudolino followed the two and found himself in a little room where there was only a kneading trough, and, on top of it, seven gilded heads. All of them portrayed the same bearded countenance, and were set on pedestals. They were obviously reliquaries, because it was clear that the heads could be opened like containers, but the edges of the lids, on which the face was drawn, were fixed to the rear part by a seal of dark wax.

"What are you looking for?" Ardzrouni was asking Zosimos, not noticing Baudolino.

Zosimos replied: "I have heard that you make relics, and for them you use your diabolical skill in gilding metals. They're heads of the Baptist, aren't they? I have seen others, and now I know for sure where they come from."

Baudolino delicately cleared his throat. Ardzrouni wheeled around and put his hands to his mouth, his eyes rolling with fear. "I beseech you, Baudolino, say nothing to the emperor, or he'll have me hanged," he said in a low voice. "Well, yes, these are reliquaries with the true head of Saint John the Baptist. Each of them contains a skull, treated with fumigations so that it shrinks and seems very ancient. I live in this land without any resources of nature, without fields to sow, and without livestock, and my wealth is limited. I fabricate relics, true, and they are much in demand both in Asia and in Europe. I have only to sell one of these heads at a great distance from the other: for instance, one in Antioch and the other in Italy, and nobody realizes that there are two of them." He smiled with oily humility, as if asking indulgence for a sin that was, after all, venial.

"I never took you for a virtuous man, Ardzrouni," Baudolino said, laughing. "Keep your heads, but let's leave here at once; else we'll arouse the suspicions of the others, including the emperor." As they went out, Frederick was concluding his exchange of religious reflections with Solomon.

The emperor asked what other prodigious things their host had to show them, and Ardzrouni, anxious to get them out of that room, led them back into the corridor. From there they came to a closed double door, beside which was an altar of the kind pagans used for their sacrifices, altars of which Baudolino had seen many remains in Constantinople. On this one there were faggots and twigs. Ardzrouni poured over them a thick, dark liquid, took one of the torches illuminating the corridor, and set the pile afire. Immediately the altar flared up, and in the space of a few minutes they began to hear a faint subterranean churning, a slow creak, while Ardzrouni, with arms upraised, uttered formulas in a barbaric language, but looking now and then at his guests, as if to let them know he was imitating a hierophant or necromancer. Finally, to the amazement of all, the two leaves of the door opened without anyone's having touched them.

"Wonders of the hydraulic art"—Ardzrouni smiled with pride—"which I cultivate, following the learned mechanics of Alexandria, of many centuries ago. It's quite simple: beneath the altar there is a metal vessel that contains water, which is heated by the fire on the altar. The water is transformed into steam and, through a syphon, which is merely a bent pipe that serves to decant the water from one place to another, this steam goes to fill a bucket where, as the steam cools, it is transformed back into water; the weight of the water makes the bucket fall lower; descending, the bucket, through a little pulley from which it hangs, moves two wooden cylinders, which act directly on the hinges of the door. And the door opens. Simple, isn't it?"

"Simple?" Frederick said. "Amazing! But did the Greeks really know such wonders?"

"These and others, and they were known also to the Egyptian priests, who used this device to command, by speaking, the opening of the doors of a temple, while the faithul cried miracle," Ardzrouni said. Then he invited the emperor to cross the threshold. They entered a room in whose center rose another extraordinary instrument. It was a leather sphere fixed to a circular surface by what seemed to be handles bent at right angles, and the surface held a kind of metallic basin beneath which there was another pile of wood. From the sphere, above and below, ran two little pipes, which ended with two taps facing in opposite directions. On closer observation, you could see that the two handles holding the sphere to the round level were also pipes, which below were fixed to the basin, and above penetrated the interior of the sphere.

"The basin is filled with water. Now we'll heat this water," Ardzrouni said, and again he started a great fire. They had to wait a few minutes before the water came to a boil, then a hissing was heard, faint at first, then louder, and the sphere began to revolve around its supports, while from the taps came puffs of steam. The sphere turned for a little while, then its impetus seemed to weaken, and Ardzrouni hastened to seal the little faucets with a kind of soft clay. He said: "Here again the principle is simple. The water boiling in the basin is transformed into steam. The steam rises in the sphere, but, emerging violently from opposite directions, it imposes on it a rotary motion."

"And what miracle does it pretend to be?" Baudolino asked.

"It doesn't pretend anything, but it demonstrates a great truth: namely, it allows us to see the existence of the vacuum."

Just imagine Boron then. Hearing the vacuum mentioned, he became suspicious at once and asked how this hydraulic toy proved that the vacuum exists. "It's simple," Ardzrouni said. "The water in the basin becomes steam and fills the sphere, the steam escapes the sphere making it rotate; when the sphere looks as if it will stop, it's a sign that it has no more steam, so you close the taps. And then what remains in the basin and in the sphere? Nothing: that is to say, the vacuum."

"I'd really like to see it," Boron said.

"To see it, you'd have to open the sphere, and then air would immediately enter. However, there is a place where you can stand and sense the presence of the vacuum. But you are aware of it only briefly, because, for lack of air, you will die of suffocation."

"And where is this place?"

"It's a room above us. Now I'll show you how I can create a vacuum in that room." He held up the torch and showed us another machine that till then had remained in the shadows. It was far more complex than the two previous ones, because it had, so to speak, its viscera exposed. There was an enormous alabaster cylinder, which showed in its interior the dark shadow of another cylindrical body that occupied half of it, while half protruded, its upper part bolted to a kind of enormous handle that could be operated by a man's two hands, as if it were a lever. Ardzrouni operated that lever, and the inner cylinder was seen to move first up, then down, until it completely occupied the exterior cylinder. To the upper part of the alabaster cylinder a great tube was attached, made of pieces of animal bladders, carefully sewn together. This tube was finally swallowed by the ceiling. On the lower part, at the base of the cylinder, a hole opened.

"Now then," Ardzrouni explained, "here we have no water. Only air. When the inner cylinder is lowered, it compresses the air contained in the alabaster cylinder, expelling it through the hole at the base. When the lever raises it, the cylinder operates a lid that blocks the hole on the inside, so that air that has left the alabaster cylinder cannot reenter. When the inner cylinder is raised completely, it operates another lid that allows air to enter through the tube you can see; it comes from the room I have told you about. When the inner cylinder is lowered again, it expels that air also. Little by little the machine draws all the air from that room and expels it here, so in that room the vacuum is created."

"And no air enters that room from anywhere else?" Baudolino asked.

"No. As soon as the machine is set in motion, through the ropes

301

to which the lever is attached, every hole or fissure that might allow air in the room is sealed."

"But with this machine you could kill a man if he were in that room," Frederick said.

"I could, but I have never done so. I did put a chicken there. After the experiment I went up to the room and the chicken was dead."

Boron shook his head and murmured into Baudolino's ear: "Don't trust him. He's lying. If the chicken was dead, it would mean that the vacuum exists. But since it does not exist, the chicken is still alive and kicking. Or if it's dead, it died of overwork." Then he said, raising his voice, to Ardzrouni: "Have you ever heard of animals dying also at the bottom of a well, where candles go out? Some have drawn the conclusion that there is no air down there; there is no air and hence there is a vacuum. On the contrary, at the bottom of wells fine air is lacking but the thick and mephitic air remains, and it suffocates both men and a candle's flame. You breathe the fine air, but the thick remains, which doesn't allow us to inhale it, and that's enough to kill your chicken."

"Enough," Frederick said. "All these devices are charming, but, except for the mirrors up above, none could be used in a siege or in a battle. So what use are they then? Let's go, I'm hungry. Ardzrouni, you promised me a good supper. It seems to me the time for it has come."

Ardzrouni bowed and led Frederick and his men into the banquet hall, which, truth to tell, seemed splendid, at least to people who for weeks had eaten the scant provender of the camp. Ardzrouni offered the best of Armenian and Turkish cuisine, including some very sweet cakes that gave his guests the sensation of drowning in honey. As all had agreed, Baudolino and his friends tasted every dish before it was offered to the emperor. Contrary to court protocol (but in war protocol always suffers numerous exceptions) they all sat at the same table, and Frederick drank and ate merrily, as if he were one of them, listening with curiosity to a debate that had begun between Boron and Ardzrouni.

Boron was saying: "You insist on talking about the vacuum, as if it were a space lacking any other body, even aerial. But a space lacking all bodies cannot exist, because space is a relation among bodies. Further, the vacuum cannot exist because Nature holds it in horror, as all the great philosophers tell us. If you suck air through a reed immersed in water, the water rises because it cannot leave a space empty of air. Furthermore, listen: objects fall towards the earth, and an iron statue falls more rapidly than a piece of cloth. Birds fly because by moving their wings they stir up much air, which supports them in spite of their weight. They are supported by the air just as fish are supported by the water. If the air weren't there, the birds would fall, but—mind you—at the same speed as any other body. Hence, if in the sky there were the vacuum, the stars would have an infinite velocity, because they would not be restrained in their fall, or in their circling, by the air, which resists their immense weight."

Ardzrouni rebutted: "Who ever told you that the speed of a body is in proportion to its weight? As John Philoponus said, it depends on the movement that is impressed on it. And anyway, tell me this: if there were no vacuum, how would things move? They would bump against the air, which wouldn't allow them to pass."

"Oh no! When a body moves, the air from the space the body then occupies shifts and fills the space that the body has left! Like two people going in opposite directions along a narrow street: they suck in their bellies, each pressing against the wall, as one gradually slips in one direction, the other slips in the opposite, and finally one man has taken the other's place."

"Yes, because each of the two, thanks to his own will, impresses a movement on his own body. But it isn't the same with air, which has no will. It moves because of the impetus imposed on it by the body bumping into it. But the impetus generates a movement in time. At the moment when the object moves and imposes an impetus on the air opposite it, the air has not yet moved, and therefore is not yet in the place that the object has just left to press against it. And what is in that place, if only for an instant? The vacuum!"

Baudolino until then had been amused, following the altercation, but now he had had his fill of it. "Enough!" he said. "Tomorrow perhaps you can try putting another chicken in the upper room. Now, speaking of chickens, let me eat this one, and I hope it was slaughtered in the usual fashion."

25

Baudolino sees Frederick die twice

The supper went on until late, and the emperor asked to retire. Baudolino and his friends followed him to his chamber, which they inspected again with attention, by the light of two torches set in the walls. The Poet chose also to take a look at the flue of the fireplace, but it narrowed almost immediately, allowing no room for the passage of a human being. "You're lucky if the smoke can pass through here," he said. They also peered into the little defecation cubbyhole, but nobody could have climbed up from the bottom of the pit.

By the bed, along with a lamp already lighted, there was a jug of water, and Baudolino insisted on tasting it. The Poet remarked that they could have put a poisonous substance on the pillow where Frederick's mouth would rest while he was sleeping. It would be a good thing, he pointed out, if Frederick were to have an antidote always within reach. You never know....

Frederick told them not to exaggerate their fear, but Rabbi Solomon humbly asked permission to speak. "My lord," Solomon said, "you know that, even though I am a Jew, I have devoted myself loyally to the mission that will crown your glory. Your life is as dear to me as my very own. Hear me. In Gallipolis I bought a wondrous antidote. Take it," he added, removing the phial from his coat, "it is my gift to you, because in my poor life I will have few occasions to be deceived by powerful enemies. If by chance, one of these nights you were to feel ill, swallow this promptly. If something harmful were served you, it would save you at once."

"I thank you, Rabbi Solomon," Frederick said, moved, "and we Teutonics were right to protect those of your race, and so we shall continue to do for the coming centuries: I swear this in the name of my people. I accept your beneficent draft, and this is what I will do with it." He drew from his traveling sack the coffer with the Grasal, which now he always carried jealously with him. "Here, you see," he said, "I pour the liquid that you, a Jew, have given me, in the cup that contained the blood of the Lord."

Solomon bowed, but murmured, perplexed, to Baudolino: "The potion of a Jew becomes the blood of the false Messiah. . . . May the Holy One, blessed be he always, forgive me. But, after all, this story of the Messiah is something you gentiles invented, not Yeoshoua of Nazareth, who was a just man, and our rabbis tell us that he studied the Talmud with Rabbi Yeoshoua ben Pera'hia. And besides, I like your emperor. I believe one must obey the impulses of the heart."

Frederick had picked up the Grasal and was about to replace it in its ark when Kyot interrupted him. That evening all of them felt authorized to address the emperor without being asked: an atmosphere of familiarity had been established between those loyal few and their lord, pent up in a place that they could not yet deem hospitable or hostile. Kyot then said: "Sire, you mustn't think I doubt Rabbi Solomon, but he too could have been deceived. Allow me to taste this liquid."

"Sire, I beg you, let Kyot do so," Rabbi Solomon said.

Frederick nodded. Kyot raised the cup, with a celebrant's movement, then held it barely to his mouth, as if in Communion. At that moment it seemed to Baudolino that an intense light spread through the room, but perhaps it was one of the torches that had flared up, at a point where the resin was thicker. For a few moments Kyot remained bowed over the cup, moving his mouth as if to absorb thoroughly the scant amount of liquid he had imbibed. Then he turned, holding the cup to his chest, and put it, delicately, in the ark. He closed that tabernacle slowly, so as not to make the slightest sound.

"I smell the perfume," Boron was murmuring.

"You see this glow?" Abdul was saying.

"All the angels of heaven are descending around us," Zosimos said, convinced, blessing himself backwards.

"Son of a strumpet," the Poet whispered into Baudolino's ear, "with this pretext he's celebrated his holy Mass with the Grasal, and when he goes home he'll brag from Champagne to Brittany." Baudolino whispered back, telling him not to be malicious, because Kyot had acted truly like one rapt in the highest heavens.

"Now no one can deflect us," Frederick said, gripped by strong and mystical emotion. "Jerusalem will soon be liberated. And then, we will all go and return this most holy relic to Prester John. Baudolino, I thank you for what you have given me. I am truly king and priest."

He smiled, yet he was also trembling. That brief ceremony seemed to have overwhelmed him. "I'm tired," he said. "Baudolino, now I will shut myself in that room with the latch. Keep good watch, and thank you also for your devotion. Don't waken me until the sun is high in the sky. Then I will go and swim." And he repeated: "I am terribly tired; I'd like not to wake again for centuries and centuries."

"A long peaceful night will restore you, dear Father," Baudolino said affectionately. "You don't have to set off at dawn. If the sun is high, the water will not be so cold. Sleep well."

They went out. Frederick drew the leaves of the door closed, and they heard the click of the latch. They stretched out on the surrounding benches.

"We don't have an imperial cubbyhole at our disposal," Baudolino said. "Let's go quickly and perform our corporal functions in the courtyard. One at a time, so we won't ever leave this room unmanned. This Ardzrouni may be good, but we can trust only ourselves." After a few minutes, all of them had returned. Baudolino put out the lamp, bade all a good night, and tried to sleep.

"But I was uneasy, Master Niketas, for no good reason. I fell into an anxious sleep, and I kept waking up after brief, intense dreams, as if interrupting a nightmare. In my drowsiness I saw my poor Colandrina, drinking from a grasal of black stone, then falling dead to the ground. An hour later I heard a sound. The *salle d'armes* also had a window, from which came a very pale nocturnal light; I believe the moon was in the fourth quarter. I realized it was the Poet, who was going out. Perhaps he hadn't sufficiently emptied his body. Later—I don't know how much later, because I would fall back asleep and then wake again, and each time it seemed to me that only a few minutes had passed, but perhaps this was not true—Boron went out. Then I heard him come back, and I heard Kyot murmur to him that he too was nervous and wanted a breath of air. But after all, my duty was to keep an eye on anyone trying to enter, not on those who left, and I knew that all of us were tense. Then I don't remember, I wasn't aware of when the Poet reentered, but, long before dawn, all were deep in sleep, and so I saw them still, when, at the sun's first rays, I woke for good."

The *salle d'armes* was now illuminated by a triumphant morning. Some servants brought wine and bread and local fruits. Though Baudolino warned them not to make a sound, so as not to disturb the emperor, all were in noisy good humor. After an hour had gone by, it seemed to Baudolino that, although Frederick had asked not to be wakened, it was late enough. He knocked at the door, without receiving a reply. He knocked again.

"He's sleeping heavily." The Poet laughed.

"I hope he's not unwell," Baudolino ventured.

They knocked again, louder and louder. Frederick didn't respond.

308

"Yesterday he seemed really exhausted," Baudolino said. "He may have had some kind of seizure. Let's break the door open."

"Keep calm, everybody," the Poet said, "violating the door that protects the emperor's sleep is almost a sacrilege."

"We'll commit the sacrilege," Baudolino said. "I don't like this."

In disorder, they hurled themselves against the door, which was sturdy, and the bolt barring it must have been solid.

"Once more, all together! When I say go," the Poet said, now aware that if an emperor doesn't wake up while they're breaking down his door, his sleep is obviously suspect. The door again resisted. The Poet went and liberated Zosimos, who was sleeping in his chains, and he arranged the group into two lines, so that together they could push forcefully against both leaves. At their fourth attempt the door gave way.

Then they saw Frederick, lying in the middle of the room, lifeless, almost naked, as he had gone to bed. Beside him was the Grasal, which had rolled on the ground, empty. The fireplace held only some charred remains, as if the fire had been lighted and had finally gone out. The window was shut. The room was dominated by a smell of burnt wood and charcoal. Boron, coughing, went to open the panes and allow some air to come in.

Thinking that someone had entered, and was still in the room, the Poet and Boron rushed, swords drawn, to examine every corner, while Baudolino, kneeling beside Frederick's body, raised his father's head and gently slapped him. Boidi remembered the cordial he had bought in Gallipolis, opened the mount of his ring, forced the emperor's lips apart, and poured the liquid into his mouth. Frederick remained lifeless. His face was ashen. Rabbi Solomon bent over him, tried to open his eyes, touched his brow, his neck, his wrist, then said, trembling: "This man is dead, may the Holy One, forever blessed be he, have mercy on his soul."

"Jesus Christ the Lord! That can't be!" Baudolino shouted. Though he had no knowledge of medicine, he realized that Frederick, holy and Roman emperor, guardian of the most Holy Grasal, hope of Christendom, last and legitimate descendant of Caesar Augustus and Charlemagne, was no more. Immediately he wept, covered that wan face with kisses, called himself his beloved son, hoping to be heard, then realized that all was in vain.

He rose, shouted to his friends to search again everywhere, even under the bed; they looked for secret passages, they sounded every wall, but it was obvious that not only was no one hiding, but no one had ever hidden in that place. Frederick Barbarossa had died in a room hermetically sealed from inside, and protected on the outside by his most devoted son.

"Call Ardzrouni; he's an expert in the medical art," Baudolino shouted.

"I'm an expert in the medical art," Rabbi Solomon groaned. "Believe me: your father is dead."

"My God, my God," Baudolino was beside himself, "my father is dead! Tell the guards, call his son. We must look for his murderers!"

"Just a moment," the Poet said. "Why are you talking of murder? The room was locked. He's dead. At his feet you see the Grasal, which contained the antidote. Perhaps he felt ill, feared he had been poisoned, and drank. On the other hand, there was a burning fire. Who but he could have lighted it? I know of people who feel a strong pain in the chest, become covered with cold sweat, and try to warm themselves, their teeth chattering. And they die shortly afterwards. Maybe the smoke of the fire worsened his condition."

"But what was in the Grasal?" Zosimos cried, rolling his eyes and seizing Rabbi Solomon.

"Stop this, you villain," Baudolino said to him. "You saw yourself that Kyot tasted the liquid."

"Not enough, not enough," Zosimos repeated, shaking Solomon. "A sip won't make you drunk! You fools, trusting a Jew!"

"We were fools, but to trust a Greekling like you," the Poet shouted, giving Zosimos a shove and separating him from the poor Rabbi, whose teeth were chattering in fear.

Meanwhile Kyot had picked up the Grasal and religiously replaced it in its ark.

"So," Baudolino asked the Poet, "you mean to say he wasn't murdered, and he died by the Lord's will?"

"It's easier to think that than to think of a creature made of air who passed through the door that we were guarding so well."

"We must call his son, and the guards," Kyot said.

"No," the Poet said. "Friends, our heads are at stake here. Frederick is dead, and we know that no one could have entered that locked room. But his son, and the others, don't know that. They'll think we're the guilty ones."

"What a vile idea!" Baudolino said, still weeping.

The Poet said: "Baudolino, listen. Frederick's son doesn't love you, doesn't love us, and has always distrusted us. We were on guard, the emperor is dead, and so we are responsible. Before we can say a word, the son will have us hanged from some tree, and if there are no trees in this damned valley, he'll have us hanged from the walls. As you know, Baudolino, the son has always considered this Grasal story a plot to drag his father where he should never have gone. He'll kill us, and with one blow he's freed himself of the whole lot of us. And what about his barons? Word that the emperor has been killed will drive them to accuse one another: it will mean massacre. We are the scapegoat for the general good. Who will believe the testimony of a little bastard like you, forgive the expression, of a drunk like me, of a Jew and a schismatic, of three wandering clerks, and of Boidi, who, as an Alessandrian, more than anyone else had every reason to hate Frederick? We're already dead, Baudolino, just like your adoptive father."

"And so?" Baudolino asked.

"So," the Poet said, "the only solution is to make everyone believe

Frederick died somewhere away from here, where it wasn't our job to protect him."

"How?"

"Didn't he say he wanted to go to the river? We'll put some clothes on him and wrap him in his cloak. We'll go down to the small court, where there's nobody around, but where the horses have been waiting since yesterday evening. We'll tie him to his saddle, go to the river, and there the waters will carry him away. A glorious death for this emperor who, old as he is, confronts the forces of Nature. The son will decide whether to go on to Jerusalem or return home. And we can say that we are continuing on to the Indias, to carry out Frederick's last wish. The son, apparently, doesn't believe in the Grasal. We'll take it, we'll go and do what the emperor would have liked to do."

"But we'll have to stage a mock death," Baudolino said, his eyes dazed.

"Is he dead? He's dead. It grieves us all, but he's dead. We're not saying he's dead when he's still alive, are we? He's dead, may God receive him among the saints. We will simply say that he drowned in the river, in the open air, and not in this room that we were to defend. Are we lying? Only a little. If he's dead, what does it matter whether he died in here or out there? Did we kill him? Everyone knows that's not so. We will have him die where even the people most hostile towards us can't slander us. Baudolino, it's the only way. There's no other, if you hold your life dear and want to reach Prester John and celebrate in his presence the extreme glory of Frederick."

The Poet, though Baudolino cursed his coldness, was right; and they all agreed with him. They dressed Frederick, carried him to the second court, bound him to his saddle, thrusting a support behind his back, as the Poet had done once with the three Magi, so that he seemed erect on his horse.

"Only Baudolino and Abdul will carry him to the river," the Poet said, "because a large escort would attract the attention of the sentinels, who might think they should join the group. The rest of us will stay and guard the room, so Ardzrouni or others cannot think of entering, and we will tidy it up. Indeed, I'll go to the walls and chat with the men on guard, to distract them while the two of you ride out."

It seemed that the Poet was the only one in a condition to make sensible decisions. All obeyed. Baudolino and Abdul rode out of the court, slowly, with Frederick's horse between them. They took the side path until they reached the main one, descended the broad steps, then trotted over the plain, towards the river. From the ramparts the armigers saluted the emperor. That brief journey seemed to last an eternity, but finally they reached the shore.

They hid behind a clump of trees. "Here no one can see us," Baudolino said. "The current is strong, and the body will be swept away immediately. We'll ride into the water to attempt rescue but the bed is treacherous, and will not allow us to reach him. Then we will follow the body from the bank, calling for help.... The current goes towards the camps."

They untied Frederick's corpse, stripped it, leaving only what scant clothing the swimming emperor would have required to cover his shame. As soon as they pushed him into the middle of the river, the current seized the body, and it was pulled downstream. They entered the river, tugging on the bit so that the horses seemed to be shying in fear; they climbed out again and galloped after that poor relic, battered by water and rocks, as they waved their arms in alarm and shouted to the men in the camp to save the emperor.

Farther on some men noticed their signaling, but failed to understand what was going on. Frederick's body was caught in eddies, whirling in circles; it would vanish into the water, then rise briefly to the surface. From a distance it was hard to understand that a man was drowning. In the end some did understand; three horsemen entered the water, but when the body reached them, it slammed against the hoofs of the frightened horses and was dragged on. Farther ahead, some soldiers went into the water with pikes, and, finally succeeding in harpooning the corpse, pulled it ashore.

When Baudolino and Abdul arrived, Frederick lay there, bruised by the rocks, and no one could now imagine that he was still alive. Loud cries rose, the son was informed, and he also arrived, pale and even more feverish, lamenting that his father had wanted once again to challenge the river's waters. He raged against Baudolino and Abdul, but they reminded him that they didn't know how to swim, like almost all land creatures; and that the son knew very well, when the emperor wanted to dive into the water, no one could restrain him.

To all, Frederick's body seemed bloated with water, and yet—if he had been dead for hours—he surely hadn't swallowed any. But so it goes: if you pull a dead body from the river, he looks drowned and so you think he's drowned.

While Frederick of Swabia and the other barons laid out the remains of the emperor, debating in their anguish what steps were to be taken, and while Ardzrouni came down into the valley, informed of the terrible event, Baudolino and Abdul returned to the castle, to make sure that by now all was in order.

"Imagine what had happened in the meantime, Master Niketas," Baudolino said.

"It's not necessary to be a wizard." Niketas smiled. "The sacred cup, the Grasal, had disappeared."

"So it had. Nobody could then say whether it had disappeared while we were in the small court tying Frederick to his horse, or afterwards, when everyone was trying to tidy up the room. All were in an emotional state, buzzing around like bees; the Poet had gone to distract the guards and wasn't there to coordinate, with his usual common sense, the actions of each of the others. At a certain point, when they were about to leave the room, where by now it did not seem anything dramatic had happened, Kyot glanced at the ark, and realized the Grasal was no longer there. When I arrived with Abdul, each was accusing the other, whether of theft or of negligence, saying that perhaps, while we were putting Frederick on his horse, Ardzrouni

314

had entered the room. No, no, Kyot said, I helped carry the emperor down, but I came back up at once, precisely to make sure nobody entered; in that brief time Ardzrouni wouldn't have been able to come up. Then you seized him, Boron growled, grabbing him by the neck. No, if anything, you did, Kyot rebutted, pushing him away, while I was at the window throwing out the ashes collected in the fireplace. Calm down, calm down, the Poet shouted, and where was Zosimos while we were down in the court? I was with you, and I came back up with you, Zosimos swore, and Rabbi Solomon confirmed this. One thing was certain: somebody had taken the Grasal, and from there it was a short step to the conclusion that the thief was the same person who had somehow killed Frederick. It was all very well for the Poet to say that Frederick could have died naturally on his own, and then one of us had exploited the situation to take the Grasal, but nobody believed this. My friends, Rabbi Solomon said to calm us, human folly has imagined horrific crimes, from Cain on, but no human mind has ever been so twisted as to imagine a crime in a locked room. My friends, Boron said, when we came in the Grasal was here, and now it isn't. So one of us has it. Naturally, each then insisted that his bags be searched, but the Poet started laughing. If someone has taken the Grasal, he has put it in a secret place in this castle, where he can go and recover it afterwards. The solution? If Frederick of Swabia put up no opposition, all of us would set off together for the kingdom of Prester John, and nobody would remain behind to come and recover the Grasal. I said it was a horrible thing: we would undertake a journey full of dangers, each having to rely on the support of the others, and each (minus one) would suspect all the others of being Frederick's assassin. The Poet said it was that or nothing, and he was right, damn him. We would have to embark on one of the greatest adventures good Christians had ever faced, and all of us would distrust all the others."

"And did you set out?" Niketas asked.

"Not right away: it would have looked like flight. The entire court

315

met constantly to decide the fate of the expedition. The army was dissolving, many wanted to go home by sea, others wanted to sail for Antioch, still others for Tripoli. Young Frederick had chosen to proceed by land. Then the argument began over what to do with Frederick's body, some proposing to extract at once the viscera, the most corruptible part, and bury them as quickly as possible; others wanted to await our arrival at Tarsus, the homeland of the apostle Paul. But the rest of the body could not be preserved for long, and sooner or later it would have to be boiled in a mixture of water and wine, until all the flesh had separated from the bones, and could be buried at once, while the rest could be placed in a sepulcher in Jerusalem, once the city was reconquered. But I knew that before having the body boiled, it would have to be dismembered. I didn't want to witness that horror."

"I have heard that no one knows what became of those bones."

"I have heard the same. My poor father! On reaching Palestine young Frederick also died, consumed with grief, and with the hardships of the journey. For the rest, not even Richard the Lionheart or Philip Augustus ever arrived at Jerusalem. It was truly an unfortunate venture for all. But I learned these things only this year, after I returned to Constantinople. In those days in Cilicia I succeeded in convincing Frederick of Swabia that, to fulfill his father's wishes, we should set out for the Indias. The son seemed to me relieved by this proposal of mine. He wanted only to know how many horses I needed and what provisions. Go with God, Baudolino, he said to me, I believe we will never see each other again. Perhaps he thought I would be lost in distant lands, and it was he who was lost, poor unhappy youth. He was not bad, though he was consumed by humiliation and envy."

Each suspecting the others, our friends had to decide who would take part in the journey. The Poet pointed out that there should be twelve in the party. If they wanted to be treated respectfully along their way to the land of Prester John, it would be advisable for people to believe they were the twelve Magi Kings, on their return journey. But since it wasn't certain that the Magi really numbered twelve, or three, none of them should ever come out and say they were the Magi; on the contrary, if anyone asked, they should answer no, like someone forbidden to reveal a deep secret. Thus, denying it to all, each would believe what he chose to believe. The faith of others would make the group's reticence become truth.

Now there were Baudolino, the Poet, Boron, Kyot, Abdul, Solomon, and Boidi. Zosimos was indispensable, because he continued to swear that he knew the map of Cosmas by heart, even though the rest of them were a bit disgusted that this crook would pass as one of the Magi; but they couldn't be too particular. Four people were missing. At this point Baudolino trusted only the Alessandrians, and had let some in on the plan: Cuttica of Quargnento, Colandrina's brother Colandrino Guasco, Porcelli, and Aleramo Scaccabarozzi, known as Bonehead, but a sturdy, trustworthy man, who asked few questions. They had accepted because, by now, it seemed also to them that nobody would reach Jerusalem. Young Frederick provided twelve horses and seven mules, with food for a week. Afterwards, he said, Divine Providence would take care of them.

While they were making their preparations for the expedition, they were approached by Ardzrouni, who addressed them with the same reticent politeness he had earlier reserved for the emperor.

"My dear, dear friends," he said, "I know you are setting out for a distant kingdom...."

"How do you know that, lord Ardzrouni?" the Poet asked suspiciously.

"There are rumors.... I heard also some talk about a cup...."

"Which you've never seen, have you?" Baudolino said to him, moving so close to him that Ardzrouni had to draw back.

"Never seen it. But I've heard it mentioned."

"Since you know so many things," the Poet asked, "do you by any

317

chance know if someone entered this room while the emperor was dying in the river?"

"Did he really die in the river?" Ardzrouni asked. "That's what his son thinks, for the present."

"My friends," the Poet said, "it's obvious that this man is threatening us. With the confusion that exists these days between the camp and the castle, it would be a simple matter to stab him in the back, and fling him somewhere or other. But first I'd like to know what he wants from us. Then perhaps I'll cut his throat afterwards."

"My lord and friend," Ardzrouni said, "I do not desire your ruin; I want to avoid my own. The emperor died in my land, after eating my food and drinking my wine. From the imperials I can expect no favor, or protection. I'll have to thank them if they leave me unharmed. Here, however, I am in danger. Once I received Frederick as my guest, Prince Leo realized that I wanted to draw the emperor to my side, against him. As long as Frederick was alive, Leo could do nothing to me—and this is an indication of how that man's death has been for me the greatest of misfortunes. Now Leo will say that, through my fault, he, prince of the Armenians, was unable to assure the life of his most illustrious ally. An excellent opportunity to put me to death. I have no escape. I must disappear for a long time, and return with something that will restore my prestige and authority. You are leaving to discover the land of Prester John, and if you succeed it will be a glorious enterprise. I want to come with you. Doing so, above all, I will show you that I didn't take the cup you speak of, because if that were the case I would remain here and use it to negotiate with someone. I know well the lands to the east, and I could be useful to you. I know that the duke has given you no money, and I would bring with me what little gold I possess. Finally—and Baudolino knows this—I have seven precious relics, seven heads of Saint John the Baptist, and in the course of the journey we could sell them, one here and one there."

"And if we were to refuse," Baudolino said, "you would go and whisper into the ear of Frederick of Swabia that we were responsible for his father's death."

"I didn't say that."

"Listen, Ardzrouni, you're not a person I'd take with me anywhere, but at this point in this damned adventure each risks becoming the enemy of the other. One more enemy will make little difference."

"The truth is that this man would be a burden for us," the Poet said. "There are already twelve of us, and a thirteenth brings bad luck."

While they were arguing, Baudolino was thinking about the heads of the Baptist. He wasn't convinced that those heads could really be taken seriously; but if they could, undeniably they were worth a fortune. He had gone down into the room where he had seen them, and had picked them up one by one to examine them carefully. They were well made, the carved face of the saint, his great eyes wide and without pupils, inspired holy thoughts. To be sure, seeing all seven of them in a row emphasized their falsity, but displayed one by one, they would be convincing. He had replaced the heads on the kneading trough, and gone back upstairs.

Three of the group agreed to taking Ardzrouni along; the others were hesitating. Boron said that, after all, Ardzrouni did have the appearance of a man of rank; and Zosimos, partly for reasons of respect for those twelve venerable persons, said he could be passed off as a squire. The Poet objected that the Magi either had twelve servants or else they traveled on their own in great secrecy; a single squire would create a bad impression. As for the heads, the party could take them without having to take Ardzrouni. By now Ardzrouni was weeping and saying that truly they wanted him dead. In the end they postponed any decision to the next day.

It was, in fact, the next day, when the sun was already high in the sky, as they had almost completed their preparations, that suddenly someone realized that, for all that morning, Zosimos had not been seen. In the frenzy of the final two days, nobody had kept watch over him; he had also helped prepare the horses and load the mules, and had not been kept on his chain. Kyot noticed that one of the mules was missing, and Baudolino had a sudden inspiration: "The heads!" he cried. "The heads! Zosimos is the only one, besides me and Ardzrouni, who knows where they are!" He dragged everyone into the little room with the heads, and there they saw that the heads now numbered only six.

Ardzrouni dug under the trough, to see if by chance one head had fallen, and he discovered three things: a human skull, small and blackened, a seal with a "Z," and some burned residue of sealing wax. All was now, alas, clear. Zosimos, in the confusion of the fatal morning, had taken the Grasal from the ark where Kyot had replaced it, and in a flash had gone down to the little room, opened a head, taken out the skull, and hidden the Grasal in its place; with his seal from Gallipolis he had closed the lid, put the head back where it had been before, and gone upstairs innocent as an angel, to await the opportune moment. When he realized that the travelers would share out the heads, he knew he could wait no longer.

"It must be said, Master Niketas, that in spite of my rage at being tricked, I felt a certain relief, and I believe that all the others felt the same. We had found the guilty party, a rascal of most credible rascality, and we were no longer tempted to suspect one another. Zosimos's villainy made us livid with anger, but it restored our reciprocal trust. There was no evidence that Zosimos, having stolen the Grasal, had had anything to do with Frederick's death, because that night he had been tied to his own bed; but this brought us back to the Poet's hypothesis: Frederick hadn't been murdered."

They gathered and held council. First of all, Zosimos—if he had fled at nightfall—by now had a twelve-hour lead on them. Porcelli pointed out that they were on horseback and he on a mule, but Baudolino reminded them that there were mountains all around them, stretching God knew how far, and on mountain trails horses move more slowly than mules. It was impossible to pursue him at top speed. He had given himself a half-day's start, and that would remain. The only thing was to find out where he was heading, and then take the same direction.

The Poet said: "First of all, he can't have set out for Constantinople. There, with Isaac Angelus on the throne, the air isn't safe for him; further, he would have to cross the lands of the Seljuks, which we have just left after so many hardships, and he knows that sooner or later they would have his hide. The most sensible hypothesis, since he's the one who knows the map, is that he wants to do what we wanted to do: reach the Priest's kingdom, proclaim himself the envoy of Frederick, or whoever, return the Grasal, and be covered with honors. So to find Zosimos we have to journey towards the kingdom of the Priest, and overtake him along the way. We'll set out, we'll ask questions as we proceed, we'll look for the trail of a Greekling monk, since you can tell his race a mile off, then you will allow me finally the satisfaction of strangling him, and we'll recover the Grasal."

"Very good," Boron said, "but what direction do we take, since he's the only one who knows the map?"

"Friends," Baudolino said, "here Ardzrouni should prove useful. He knows the places and, further, there are now only eleven of us, and we need at all costs a twelfth King."

And so, to his great relief, Ardzrouni was solemnly allowed to become a part of that group of fearless men. As to the right road, he made sensible proposals: if the kingdom of the Priest lay to the east, near the Earthly Paradise, then we should head for the place where the sun rises. But in proceeding so directly, we risked having to cross lands of infidels, whereas he knew the way to advance, at least for a while, through territories inhabited by Christian peoples—also because we had to remember the Baptist heads, which couldn't be sold to Turks. He assured us that Zosimos would have reasoned in the same way, and he mentioned lands and cities our friends had never heard of. With his mechanic's skill, he had constructed a kind of puppet that, in the end, resembled Zosimos, with a long, wispy beard, hair made from charred millet, and two black stones to serve as eyes. The portrait seemed possessed, like the man it portrayed: "We will have to cross lands where they speak unknown languages," Ardzrouni said, "and to ask if they have seen Zosimos we can only show this image." Baudolino guaranteed that the unknown languages would create no problems, because when he had spoken with barbarians for a little while, he learned to speak as they did; but the portrait would still come in handy, because in some places there wouldn't be time to stop and learn the language.

Before departing, they all went downstairs and each took one of the Baptist's heads. They were twelve, and the heads now were six. Baudolino decided that Ardzrouni should refrain, Solomon surely wouldn't want to travel with a Christian relic, Cuttica, Bonehead, Porcelli, and Colandrino were late-comers; so the heads would go to himself, the Poet, Abdul, Kyot, Boron, and Boidi. The Poet was about to grab the first immediately, and Baudolino pointed out, laughing, that they were all the same, since the only good one had been chosen by Zosimos. The Poet blushed and let Abdul choose, with a broad and polite wave of his hand. Baudolino was satisfied with the last one, and each of them put his in his knapsack.

"That's the whole story," Baudolino said to Niketas. "Towards the end of the month of June in the year of Our Lord 1190, we set out, twelve of us, like the Magi, even if less virtuous than they, to reach finally the land of Prester John."

322

26

Baudolino and the journey of the Magi

From that moment on, Baudolino narrated his story to Niketas almost continuously, not only during their stops at night, but also in the daytime, as the women complained of the heat, the children had to stop to make water, the mules every now and then refused to go on. So it was a story broken up, as their journey was, where Niketas guessed at the gaps, the unfinished spaces, and the very long duration. And it was comprehensible because, as Baudolino continued narrating, the journey of the twelve lasted almost four years, between moments of bewilderment, bored delays, and painful vicissitudes.

Perhaps, traveling like that under blazing suns, eyes sometimes assailed by sandy gusts, listening to new tongues, the travelers spent moments in which they lived as if burned by fever, others of somnolent waiting. Countless days were devoted to survival, pursuing animals inclined to flight, bargaining with savage tribes for a loaf of bread or a piece of lamb, digging, exhausted, for springs in lands where it rained once a year. Besides, Niketas told himself, traveling under a sun beating down on your head, through deserts, as travelers tell, you are deceived by mirages, you hear voices echoing at night among the dunes, and when you find some bush you risk tasting berries that, rather than nourishing the belly, prompt visions.

This was not to say, as Niketas knew very well, that Baudolino wasn't sincere by nature; and if it's difficult to believe a liar when he tells you, for instance, that he has been to Iconium, how and when can you believe him when he tells you he has seen creatures that the most lively imagination would be hard pressed to conceive, and he himself is not sure of having seen?

Niketas had determined to believe in a single thing, because the passion with which Baudolino spoke of it bore witness to its truth: that, on their journey our twelve Magi were drawn by the desire to reach a goal, which became increasingly personal for each of them. Boron and Kyot wanted only to recover the Grasal, even if it hadn't ended up in the Priest's kingdom; Baudolino wanted that kingdom with increasingly irrepressible passion, and with him, also Solomon, because there he would find his lost tribes; the Poet, Grasal or not, sought any kingdom; Ardzrouni was interested only in escaping the place where he had come from; and Abdul, as we know, thought that, the farther he went, the closer he was coming to the object of his chaste desires.

The Alessandrians were the only ones who seemed to advance with their feet solidly on the ground; they had made a pact with Baudolino and they followed him out of solidarity, or perhaps greed, because if a Prester John has to be found then he has to be found, otherwise, as Aleramo Scaccabarozzi, also known as Bonehead, insisted, people wouldn't take you seriously any more. But perhaps they went on also because Boidi had got it into his head that, reaching the goal, they would stock up on wondrous relics (and not fakes like the Baptist's heads) and take them back to their native Alessandria, transforming that city, still without history, into the most celebrated shrine in Christendom.

Ardzrouni, to evade the Turks of Iconium, had immediately led them over certain passes where the horses risked breaking a leg, then for six days he guided them along a stony waste sown with corpses of huge lizards a palm long, dead from sunstroke. Thank God, we have provisions with us and don't have to eat those disgusting animals, Boidi said, with great relief, but he was mistaken, because a year later they would catch lizards even more repellent and, skewering them on twigs, they would roast them, as their mouths watered, waiting for them to be done.

Then they passed through some villages, and in each they displayed the effigy of Zosimos. Yes, one man said a monk just like that came this way, stayed for a month, then ran off because he'd got my daughter pregnant. But how could he have stayed a month when we'd been traveling only two weeks? When did it happen? Eh, maybe seven Easters ago: you see that boy, the one with scrofula over there, he's the fruit of the sin. Then that wasn't the man; all these pigs, these monks, look the same. Or else they said: yes, he looks right, with a beard just like this, maybe three days ago, a likable little hunchback... But if he was a hunchback, then it isn't our man. Baudolino, could it be that you don't understand the language and are just translating what comes into your head? Or they said: yes, yes, we've seen him, it was him—and they would point to Rabbi Solomon, perhaps because of the black beard. What was this? Were they maybe questioning the village idiots?

Farther on, they encountered some people who lived in circular tents, who greeted them, crying: "*La ellec olla Sila, Machimet rores alla.*" They replied with equal politeness in Alaman, since one language was worth as much as another. When they displayed the Zosimos puppet, the people burst out laughing, all talking at once, but from their gestures it could be deduced that they did recall Zosimos: he had passed through here, had offered the head of a Christian saint, and they had threatened to stick something up his behind. When our friends realized they had happened on a band of Turkish impalers, they went off with great gestures of farewell and smiles, baring all their teeth, while the Poet dragged Ardzrouni by the hair, pulled his head back, saying: Good, good for you, who know the road; you were

325

leading us right into the jaws of the Antichrists. And Ardzrouni gasped that he hadn't got the road wrong; these men were nomads, and you never know where nomads are.

"But farther ahead," he assured them, "we'll find only Christians, though they may be Nestorians."

"Good," Baudolino said, "if they're Nestorians, they're at least of the Priest's race, but from now on, before we say anything, we must take care, when we enter a village, to see if there are crosses and spires."

Spires, indeed! What they found were clumps of mud huts, and even if they included a church, you couldn't recognize it. These were people who were content with very little in order to praise the Lord.

"But are you sure Zosimos went this way?" Baudolino asked. And Ardzrouni told him to rest assured. One evening Baudolino saw him as he was observing the setting sun, and he seemed to be taking measurements in the sky with his arms outstretched and the fingers of his two hands entwined, as if to form some little triangular windows through which he peered at the clouds. Baudolino asked him why, and he said he was trying to discern the location of the big mountain beneath which the sun vanished every evening, under the great arch of the tabernacle.

"Madonna santissima!" Baudolino shouted. "Don't tell me you also believe in the story of the tabernacle like Zosimos and Cosmas Indicopleustes?"

"Of course, I do," Ardzrouni said, as if they were asking him if water was wet. "Otherwise how could I be so sure that we're following the same road Zosimos must have taken?"

"Then you know the map of Cosmas that Zosimos kept promising us?"

"I don't know what Zosimos promised you, but I have the map of Cosmas." He drew a parchment from his sack and showed it to the friends.

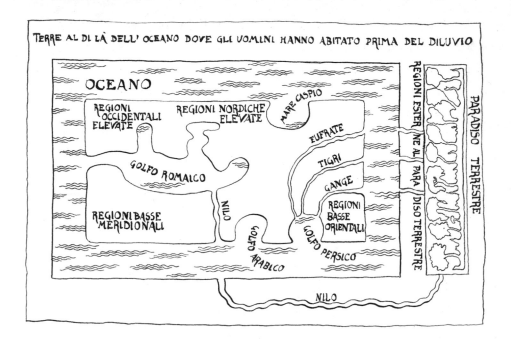

"There! You see? This is the frame of the Ocean. Beyond, there are lands where Noah lived before the Flood. Towards the eastern extreme of those lands, separated by the Ocean from regions inhabited by monstrous beings—and these are the lands through which we will have to pass—there is the Earthly Paradise. It's easy to see how, setting out from this blessed land, the Tigris, the Euphrates, and the Ganges pass beneath the Ocean to cross the regions towards which we are traveling, and then they empty into the Persian Gulf, whereas the Nile follows a more tortuous path through the antediluvian lands, enters the Ocean, resumes its course in the lower southern regions, and more precisely in the land of Egypt, emptying into the Romaic Gulf, which would be what the Latins first call Mediterranean and then Hellespont. Here, we must follow the route to the east, to encounter first the Euphrates, then the Tigris, then the Ganges, and turn towards the lower eastern regions."

"But," the Poet interjected, "if the kingdom of Prester John is very close to the Earthly Paradise, must we cross the Ocean to reach it?"

327

"It's close to the Earthly Paradise, but this side of the Ocean," Ardzrouni said. "But we will have to cross the Sambatyon...."

"The Sambatyon, the river of stone," Solomon said, clasping his hands. "So Eldad did not lie, and this is the road towards finding the lost tribes!"

"We mentioned the Sambatyon also in the Priest's letter," Baudolino said sharply, "and so obviously it must exist somewhere. Very well, the Lord has come to our aid, he has caused us to lose Zosimos, but he has allowed us to find Ardzrouni, who apparently knows more."

One day they saw, at a distance, a sumptuous temple, with columns and a decorated tympanum. But, nearing it, they saw that the temple was only a façade; the rest was a cliff, and, in fact, that entrance was up high, set into the mountain, and it was necessary to climb, God knows how, up to where the birds fly, in order to reach it. On more careful study, they saw that, along the circle of surrounding mountains, other façades stood out on high against steep walls of lava, and at times they had to narrow their eyes to distinguish the carved stone from the stone shaped by Nature, and they could also make out sculpted capitals, fornices and arches, and superb colonnades. The inhabitants, down below, spoke a language very similar to Greek, and said that their city was named Bacanor, but what they saw were churches of a thousand years past, when the place was under the dominion of Aleksandros, a great king of the Greeks, who honored a prophet who had died on a cross. By now they had forgotten how to climb to the temple, nor did they know what was still inside it, and they preferred to honor the gods (they actually said gods and not the Lord God) in the open, in an enclosed space, in the center of which stood the gilded head of a buffalo on a wooden stake.

That very day the entire city was celebrating the funeral of a young man whom all had loved. On the flat area at the foot of the mountain a banquet had been laid out, and in the center of the circle of tables already laden there was an altar with the body of the deceased on it. Up above, in broad curves, lower and lower, flew eagles, kites, ravens, and other birds of prey, as if they had been bidden to this feast. All dressed in white, the father approached the corpse, cut off its head with an axe, and placed it on a golden plate. Then some smiths, also dressed in white, cut the body into little pieces, and the guests were invited each to take one of those pieces and throw it to a bird, which caught it in midair, then vanished into the distance. Someone explained to Baudolino that the birds carried the dead man into Paradise, and for them their rite was far superior to those of other peoples, who allowed the body of the dead to rot in the earth. Then all sat down at the tables and each tasted the flesh of the head until, with only the skull remaining, clean and shiny as if it were metal, they made it into a cup from which all drank in joy, praising the departed.

Another time, they were crossing, for a week, an ocean of sand, which rose like the great waves of the sea, and it seemed that everything moved beneath their feet and beneath the horses' hoofs. Solomon, who had already suffered seasickness after embarking at Gallipolis, spent those days in continuous bouts of vomiting, but he could vomit very little because the party had been able to swallow very little, and it was lucky they had provided themselves with an ample supply of water before facing this predicament. Abdul began then to suffer fever and chills, which continued to torment him for the rest of the journey, preventing him from singing his songs, as the friends invited him to do when they stopped in the moonlight.

Sometimes they proceeded rapidly, over grassy meadows, and, not having to combat hostile elements, Boron and Ardzrouni conducted endless debates on the question that obsessed them, namely, the vacuum.

Boron employed his familiar arguments: that if there were a vacuum in the universe, nothing would prevent the existence, beyond our worlds, in the vacuum, of other worlds, et cetera, et cetera. But Ardzrouni pointed out that he was confusing the universal vacuum, which could be debated, with the vacuum created in the interstices between one corpuscle and another. And when Boron asked him what these corpuscles were, his opponent reminded him that, according to certain ancient Greek philosophers, and other wise Arab theologians, the followers of Kalam, namely, the Motokallimun, one should not think that bodies are solid substances. The whole universe, everything that is in it, and we ourselves are composed of indivisible corpuscles, which are called atoms, whose incessant movement is the origin of life. The movement of these corpuscles is the very condition of all generation and corruption. And between one atom and another, precisely in order for them to be able to move freely, is the vacuum. Without the vacuum between the corpuscles that compose every body, nothing could be cut, broken, or shattered, nor could it absorb water, or be invaded by heat or cold. How does nourishment spread in our body, if not by traveling through the empty spaces between the corpuscles that compose us? Stick a needle, Ardzrouni said, into a swollen bladder, before it begins to deflate only because the needle, moving, widens the hole it has made. How is it that for an instant the needle remains in the bladder that is still full of air? Because it is insinuated into the interstitial vacuum between the corpuscles of air.

"Your corpuscles are a heresy, and nobody has ever seen them except your Arabs, those Kallemotemum, or whatever you call them," Boron replied. "While the needle is entering, a bit of air is already escaping, leaving space for the needle."

"Then take an empty flask, immerse it in water with the neck down. The water won't enter, because there's air. Suck the air from the flask, close it with one finger so more air won't enter, immerse it in the water, remove your finger, and water will enter where you have created the vacuum."

"Water rises because Nature acts in such a way that the vacuum is not created. The vacuum is against Nature, and being against Nature it cannot exist in Nature."

"But while the water rises, and it doesn't rise abruptly, what is there in the part of the flask that is not yet filled, since you have removed the air?"

"When you suck out the air you eliminate only the cold air, which moves slowly, but you leave an amount of hot air, which moves rapidly. The water enters and immediately causes the hot air to escape."

"Now you again pick up that flask full of air, but heated, so that inside there is only hot air. Then you immerge it, neck down. Although it contains only hot air, water still won't enter. So the heat of the air is irrelevant."

"Oh, is it? Take the flask again, and on the bottom, towards the belly of the flask, make a little hole. Immerge it in the water, hole first. The water won't enter because there is air inside. Then put your lips to the neck, which has remained out of the water, and suck out all the air. Gradually, as you suck out the air, the water rises through the lower hole. Then pull the flask out of the water, keeping the upper hole closed, so the air won't press to enter. So you see that the water remains in the flask and doesn't escape by the lower hole, thanks to the disgust that Nature would feel if it left a vacuum."

"The water doesn't descend the second time because it rose the first, and a body cannot make a movement opposed to the first if it doesn't receive a new stimulus. Now listen to this. Stick a needle into a swollen bladder, allow all the air to escape, wffff, immediately close the hole made by the needle. Then, put your fingers on both sides of the bladder, as you might pull the skin here on your hand. And you see that the bladder opens. What is there in that bladder whose walls you have widened? The vacuum."

"Who told you the walls of the bladder will part?"

"Try it!"

"No, not I. I'm not a mechanic, I'm a philosopher, and I reach my conclusions on the basis of thought. Anyway, if the bladder opens, it's because it has pores, and after it is deflated, a bit of air has entered through the pores."

"Oh, really? First of all, what are pores if not empty spaces? And how can the air enter on its own if you have not imposed a movement on it? And why—once you have taken the air from the bladder—doesn't it swell up again spontaneously? If there are pores, then, when the bladder is swollen and well closed and you press it, imposing a movement on the air, why doesn't the bladder deflate? Because the pores are, true enough, empty spaces, but smaller than the corpuscles of air. Keep pressing harder and harder, and you'll see. Then leave the swollen bladder for a few hours in the sun, and you'll see that, little by little, it deflates on its own, because the heat transforms the cold air into hot air, which escapes more rapidly."

"Then take a flask..."

"With a hole on the bottom or without?"

"Without. Immerge it completely, tilted, into the water. You will see that, as the water gradually enters, the air emerges and goes plop plop, thus manifesting its presence. Now pull out the flask, empty it, suck out all the air, close its mouth with your thumb, put it tilted into the water, remove your thumb. The water enters but without your hearing or seeing any plop plop. Because inside there was the vacuum."

At this point the Poet yet again interrupted them to remind them that Ardzrouni should not be distracted, because with all that plop plop and those flasks everybody was growing thirsty, their bladders were now empty, and it would be wise to head for a river or some other place more damp than where they were.

Every now and then they heard something of Zosimos. This man had seen him, another had heard of a man with a black beard who was asking about the kingdom of Prester John. At which our friends would ask eagerly: "And what did you tell him?" The answer was almost always that they had told him what everyone in those lands knew, that Prester John was to the east, but it took years to arrive there.

Foaming with anger, the Poet said that in the manuscripts of the Saint Victoire library you could read that those who had traveled in those places did nothing but come upon splendid cities, with temples whose roofs were covered with emeralds, and palaces with golden ceilings, columns with ebony capitals, statues that seemed alive, golden altars with seventy steps, walls of pure sapphire, stones so luminous that they cast more light than torches, mountains of crystal, rivers of diamonds, gardens with trees emanating scented balms that permit the inhabitants to live by simply breathing in their odor, monasteries where only highly colored peacocks are bred, whose flesh does not undergo corruption, and, taken on a journey, that flesh lasts for thirty days or more even under a blazing sun, never causing a bad smell, and then glittering fountains whose water shines like the light of a thunderbolt and, if you put in it a salted fish, the fish would return to life and dart off, a sign that this is the fountain of eternal youth. But they so far had seen desert, scrub, massifs where you couldn't even rest on the stones because they would cook your buttocks, the only cities they had encountered were made of wretched hovels inhabited by repugnant rabble, like Colondiophontas, where they had seen the Artabants, men who walk prone like sheep, or like Iambut, where they had hoped to rest after having crossed seared plains, and the women, if not beautiful, weren't too ugly, but they discovered that, faithful to their husbands, they kept poisonous snakes in their vagina to defend their chastity—and if they had at least mentioned it beforehand, but no: one woman pretended to give herself to the Poet, who came close to having to accept perpetual chastity, and he was lucky because he heard the hiss and sprang back. Near the Catardese swamps they encountered men with testicles down to their knees, and at Necuveran, people naked as wild animals, who mated in the street like dogs, the father coupled with the daughter and the son with the mother. At Tana they met anthropophagi, who fortunately would not eat foreigners, whom they found revolting, but only their own children. By the river Arlon they came upon a village where the inhabitants danced around an idol and with sharpened knives inflicted wounds on themselves, in every limb, then the idol was placed on a wagon and borne through the streets, and many of the people joyfully flung themselves under the wagon's wheels, breaking their bones to the point of death. At Salibut they crossed a wood infested with fleas as big as frogs, at Cariamaria they met hairy men who barked, and not even Baudolino could understand their language, and women with boar's teeth, hair to their feet, and a cow's tail.

These and other most horrendous things had they seen, but the wonders of the East never, as if all those who had written about them were great bastards.

Ardzrouni urged patience, because he had also said that before the Earthly Paradise there was a very savage land, but the Poet replied that the savage land was inhabited by ferocious animals, which luckily they hadn't yet seen, and therefore it was still to come, and if the lands they had in fact seen were the not savage ones, they could imagine the rest. Abdul, more and more feverish, said that it was impossible that his princess would live in such Godforsaken places, and perhaps they had taken the wrong road. "But I certainly don't have the strength to turn back, my friends," he said faintly, "and therefore I believe I will die on the road to happiness."

"Oh, be quiet. You don't even know what you're saying," the Poet shouted at him. "You made us waste a thousand nights listening to you sing the beauty of your impossible love, and now that you see it really couldn't be more impossible, you should be happy, in seventh heaven!" Baudolino pulled at his sleeve and whispered to him that Abdul was delirious by now and it was wrong to make him suffer even more.

After a time that seemed endless, they came to Salopatana, a fairly wretched city, where they were received with amazement, the people moving their fingers as if to count the arrivals. Clearly, the fact that they were twelve made an impression: everyone knelt down, except for one man, who ran off to spread the word among the other inhabitants. A sort of archimandrite came towards them, chanting in Greek and bearing a wooden cross (a far cry from silver crosses encrusted with rubies, the Poet grumbled); he told Baudolino that here they had long awaited the return of the most holy Magi, who for thousands of years had experienced a thousand adventures, after they worshiped the Child in Bethlehem. And this archimandrite was in fact asking if they were returning to the land of Prester John, from whence they surely came, to relieve him of his long labor and resume the power they had once had over those blessed lands.

Baudolino was exultant. They asked many questions about what lay in store for them, but they realized that these people also did not know where the Priest's kingdom was, except that they firmly believed that it lay somewhere towards the east. Indeed, since the Magi actually came from down there, the local people were amazed that they themselves did not have accurate information.

"Most holy masters," the good archimandrite said, "you are surely not like that Byzantine monk who passed through here some time ago, seeking to return to the Priest some relic or other that had been stolen from him. That man had a suspect look, and was undoubtedly a heretic, like all the Greeks of the lands along the sea, because he constantly invoked the Most Holy Virgin Mother of God, and Nestorius, our father and light of truth, has taught us that Mary was the mother only of Christ the man. How would it be possible to think of a God in swaddling clothes, a God two months old, a God on the cross? Only pagans give a mother to their gods!"

"That monk is truly suspect," the Poet blurted, "and I must tell you that he stole that relic from us."

"May the Lord punish him. We allowed him to go on his way, not telling him anything of the dangers he would come upon, and therefore he knew nothing of the Abcasia, may God punish him and

335

plunge him into that darkness. And he will surely come upon the manticore and the black rocks of the Bubuctor."

"My friends," the Poet murmured, "these people could tell us many valuable things, but they would tell us only because we are the Magi; however, since we are the Magi, they don't think it's necessary to tell us anything. If you'll heed my advice, we'll leave here at once; because if we talk with them a little longer we'll end up making some slip and they'll understand that we don't know what the Magi should know. Nor can we offer them a Baptist's head, because I just can't see the Magi practicing simony. Let's clear out fast, because for all that they may be good Christians, nobody can assure us they're tender with anyone who tries to outsmart them."

Whereupon the friends took their leave, receiving many provisions as gifts, and wondering about that Abcasia whose darkness can so easily engulf you.

They soon learned what the black rocks of the Bubuctor were. They lay for miles and miles on the bed of that river, and some nomads they met shortly before had explained that whoever touched the rocks became as black as they were. Ardzrouni said, on the contrary, that they must be very precious stones, which the nomads sold at God knows what distant market, and they told this fairy tale to prevent others from collecting them. He had rushed to garner a good supply, and showed the friends how shiny they were and how perfectly shaped by the water. But, as he was speaking, his face, his neck, his hands quickly became as black as ebony; he opened his shirt and his chest was now totally black, he bared his legs and feet, and they also seemed made of coal.

Ardzrouni flung himself naked into the river, rolled around in the water, scraped his skin with gravel from the riverbed. . . . Nothing could be done. Ardzrouni had become black as night, and you could see only the whites of his eyes and his red lips beneath his beard, also black.

At first, the others laughed themselves sick, while Ardzrouni cursed their mothers; then they tried to console him: "We want to be taken for the Magi, don't we?" Baudolino said. "Well, at least one of them was black; I swear that one of the three lying in Cologne is black. And now our group becomes even more credible." Solomon, more considerate, remembered having heard of stones that change the color of the skin, but there are remedies, and Ardzrouni would be even whiter than before. "Yes, in a week of Fridays," Bonehead sniggered, and the hapless Armenian had to be restrained, because he wanted to tear the man's ear off with one bite.

One fine day they entered a forest thick with leafy trees, bearing fruit of every description, through which a river ran, its water white as milk. In the forest were green clearings, with palms and vines laden with splendid bunches of grapes the size of citrons. In one of these clearings there was a village of simple, sturdy huts, of clean straw, from which men emerged naked from head to foot, and some of the males chanced to have long and flowing beards that covered their pudenda. The women felt no shame in displaying their breasts and womb, but they gave the impression of doing so in a very chaste way: they looked the newcomers boldly in the eyes, but without prompting unsuitable thoughts.

These people spoke Greek and, politely welcoming the guests, they said they were gymnosophists—that is to say, creatures who, in innocent nudity, cultivated learning and practiced benevolence. Our travelers were invited to move freely in their sylvan village, and at evening they were bidden to a supper consisting only of foods produced spontaneously by the earth. Baudolino asked some questions of the oldest of their number, whom all treated with special reverence. He asked what they possessed, and the man replied: "We possess the earth, the trees, the sun, the moon, and the stars. When we are hungry we eat the fruits of the trees, which they produce by themselves, following the sun and the moon. When we are thirsty we go to

337

the river and drink. We have one woman each and, following the lunar cycle, each man fertilizes his companion until she has produced two sons, then we give one to the father and one to the mother."

Baudolino was surprised not to have seen a temple or a cemetery, and the old man said: "This place where we are is also our grave, and here we die, lying down in the sleep of death. The earth begets us, the earth nourishes us, beneath the earth we sleep the eternal sleep. As for the temple, we know that temples are erected in other places, to honor what they call the Creator of all things. But we believe that things are born through *charis,* thanks only to themselves, just as they maintain themselves on their own, and the butterfly pollinates the flower that, growing, then nourishes it."

"But, if I understand correctly, you practice love and reciprocal respect, you do not kill animals, and, still less, your similars. By what commandment do you act?"

"We do this to make up for the absence of any commandment. Only by practicing and teaching good can we console our similars for the lack of a Father."

"No one can do without a Father," the Poet murmured to Baudolino. "Look at the state to which our beautiful army has been reduced by the death of Frederick. These people wave their cocks in the air, but they don't really know how life works...."

Boron, on the contrary, was impressed by this wisdom, and he began asking the old man a series of questions.

"Which number is greater, that of the living or of the dead?"

"The dead are greater, but they can no longer be counted. So those you can see are more than those you cannot see."

"Which is stronger, death or life?"

"Life, because when it rises, the sun has luminous and splendid rays, and when it sets, it seems weaker."

"Which is more, earth or sea?"

"Earth, because the sea rests on the bed of earth."

"Which came first, night or day?"

"Night. Everything that is born is formed in the darkness of the womb and is only later brought into the light."

"Which is the better side, left or right?"

"Right. Indeed, the sun rises on the right and follows its orbit in the heavens to the left, and a woman suckles her babe first with the right breast."

"Which is the most fierce of animals?" the Poet asked then.

"Man."

"Why?"

"Ask yourself. You, too, are a wild beast, you have with you other beasts, and in your lust for power you want to deprive all other beasts of life."

Then the Poet said: "But if all were like you, the sea would never be sailed, the earth would never be tilled, the great kingdoms would not be born to carry order and greatness into the base disorder of earthly things."

The old man replied: "Each of these things is surely fortunate, but it is built on the misfortune of others, and that we do not desire."

Abdul asked if they knew where the most beautiful and most distant of all princesses lived. "Are you seeking her?' the old man asked, and Abdul answered yes. "Have you ever seen her?" Abdul answered no. "Do you want her?" Abdul answered that he did not know. Then the old man entered his hut and came out with a metal dish, so polished and gleaming that it mirrored everything surrounding it like a surface of clean water. He said: "We received this mirror once as a gift, and we could not refuse it out of courtesy towards the giver. But none of us would want to look into it, because that could lead to vanity of our body, or to horror at some flaw of ours, and thus we would live in fear of the others' scorn. In this mirror, perhaps one day you will see what you are seeking."

As they were about to fall asleep, Boidi said, his eyes moist: "Let's stay here."

"A fine figure you'd cut, naked as a worm," the Poet replied.

"Maybe we want too much," Rabbi Solomon said, "but at this point we can't help wanting it."

They set off again the next morning.

27

Baudolino in the darkness of Abcasia

After leaving the gymnosophists, they wandered at length, always asking themselves which was the path that led to the Sambatyon without passing through those horrible places that had been mentioned. But to no avail. They crossed plains, they forded streams, they struggled up steep cliffs, as Ardzrouni from time to time made calculations based on the map of Cosmas and declared that the Tigris or the Euphrates or the Ganges should not be far off. The Poet told him to shut up, nasty black creature! Solomon repeated to him that sooner or later he would be white again; and the days and the months went by, each like the last.

Once they camped beside a pond. The water was not very clear, but it would suffice, and the horses specially benefited by it. All were preparing for sleep when the moon rose and, in the light of its first rays, they saw in the shadows a sinister teeming: an infinite number of scorpions, all with the tips of their tails erect, in search of water, and they were followed by a band of snakes of a great variety of colors: some had red scales, others black and white, still others gleamed like gold. The whole zone was a single hissing, and an immense terror gripped the men. They formed a circle, their swords pointed outwards, trying to kill those malignant plagues before they could approach their barrier. But the snakes and the scorpions were more attracted by the water than by them, and when they had drunk their fill they gradually withdrew to their lairs in cracks in the earth.

At midnight, as the men were thinking they might get some sleep, crested serpents arrived, each with two or three heads. With their scales they swept the ground and they kept their jaws wide open, within which three tongues darted. Their stink was perceptible at a mile's distance, and all had the impression that their eyes, which sparkled in the lunar light, spread poison, as, for that matter, the basilisk does. . . . The men fought them for an hour, because these animals were more aggressive than the others, and perhaps were seeking meat. They killed some and other snakes attacked the corpses, feasting and forgetting the humans. The friends were by now convinced they had overcome this danger, when, after the snakes, the crabs arrived, more than a hundred, covered with crocodile scales, and their armor repelled the swords' blows. But then Colandrino had an idea inspired by desperation: he approached one of them, gave him a violent kick just below the belly, and the animal rolled on its back, wildly waving its claws. So they could surround them, scatter branches over them, and set them afire. Then they realized that, once stripped of their armor, they were good to eat, and so for two days they had a supply of sweet and chewy meat, actually quite good and nutritious.

Another time they really did encounter the basilisk, and it was, just as certain oft-told tales had narrated, undoubtedly true. It emerged from a cliff, splitting the rock, as Pliny had said. It had a cock's head and talons, and in the place of a crest it had a red excrescence, in the shape of a crown, yellow protruding eyes like a toad's, and a snake's body. It was emerald green, with silver glints, and at first sight it seemed almost beautiful, but everyone knew that its breath could poison an animal or a human being, and already at a distance you could catch its horrible smell.

"Keep away," Solomon cried, "and above all, don't look into its eyes, because they also give off a poisonous power!" The basilisk crawled towards them, the odor became more and more intolerable, until Baudolino realized there was a way to kill it. "The mirror! The mirror!" he shouted to Abdul. Abdul handed him the metal mirror he had received from the gymnosophists. Baudolino took it, and with his right hand he held it in front of himself like a shield, turned towards the monster, while with his left hand he covered his eyes to protect himself against that sight, and he measured his steps according to what he saw on the ground. He stopped before the beast, held the mirror out farther. Drawn by those glints, the basilisk raised his head and fixed his lizard eyes directly on this shining surface, exhaling his horrendous breath. But immediately his whole body trembled, he blinked his purple eyelids, let out a terrible cry, and sank down dead. All of them then remembered that the mirror reflects to the basilisk the power of his own gaze as well as the flow of breath he emits, and of these two wonders he himself remains the victim.

"We are already in a land of monsters," the Poet said, quite happily. "The kingdom is coming closer and closer." Baudolino no longer knew whether, in saying "kingdom," he was still thinking of the Priest's realm, or of his own, future, kingdom.

And so, encountering anthropophage hippopotami one day, and bats bigger than pigeons the next, they came to a village amid the mountains. At its foot stretched a plain with scarce trees, which at close range seemed immersed in a light mist, but then the mist grew more and more dense, gradually becoming a dark and impenetrable cloud, tranformed at the horizon into a single very black strip that contrasted with the red stripes of the sunset.

The inhabitants were cordial, but to learn their language, made up entirely of guttural sounds, Baudolino needed several days, in the course of which they were housed and fed on the flesh of certain mountain hare, abundant among those cliffs. When the people could be understood, they said that at the foot of the mountain began the vast province of Abcasia, which had four characteristics: it was a sole, immense forest where the deepest darkness always reigned, but not as if it were night, where at least you have the glow of the starry sky, but truly a solid darkness, as if you were at the bottom of a cave with your eyes closed. This province without light was inhabited by the Abcasians, who lived there comfortably, as do the blind in the places where they have grown up since infancy. It seems they oriented themselves through hearing and smell, but no one knew what they were like, because no one had ever dared venture into the region.

The friends asked if there were other ways to continue eastwards, and the people said yes, it sufficed to skirt Abcasia and its forest, but this, as the ancient tales narrated, would require more than ten years of travel, because the dark forest extended for one hundred and twelve *salamoc,* not that it was possible to understand how long a *salamoc* was for them, but certainly more than a mile, a stadium, or a parasang.

They were about to give up, when Porcelli, who had always been the most silent member of the party, reminded Baudolino that they, who came from Frascheta, were accustomed to proceed through fogs you could cut with a knife, which were worse than thick darkness, because in that grayness you could see, through tricks of your weary eyes, forms arise that didn't exist in the real world, and therefore even where you could have proceeded you had to stop, and if you succumbed to the mirage you changed path and fell over a cliff. "And in our fog at home, what do you do?" he said. "Why, you go ahead on your own judgment, instinct, guesswork, like bats, who are blind to everything, and you can't even follow your sense of smell, because the fog gets into your nostrils and the only thing you smell is the smell of fog. So," he concluded, "if you're used to fog, solid darkness is like walking in daylight."

The other Alessandrians agreed, and so it was Baudolino and his five neighbors who led the group, while each of the others tied himself to his horse and followed, hoping for the best.

At the beginning they advanced easily, because it really did seem they were in the fog of their home country, but after a few hours it was pitch black. The guides pricked up their ears to hear a sound of boughs, and when they could hear it no longer they surmised they had entered a clearing. The villagers had said that in those lands a strong wind blew always from south towards north, and so every now and then Baudolino moistened a finger, held it in the air, and felt the direction of the wind, then turned east.

They became aware of night falling because the air grew colder, and they would then stop to rest—a useless decision, the Poet said, because in such a place you could just as well rest in the daytime. But Ardzrouni pointed out that, when it was cold, you no longer heard animal noises, and you began hearing them again, especially the birds' song, when the first warmth arrived. A sign that all living things, in Abcasia, measured the day according to the alternation of cold and warmth, as if they were the appearance of the moon or the sun.

For many long days they sensed no human presences. When their supplies were exhausted, they stretched out their hands to touch the branches of the trees; and, groping branch after branch, sometimes for hours, they would find a fruit—which they ate, trusting that it was not poisonous. Often it was the acrid aroma of some vegetal wonder that gave Baudolino (whose sense of smell was the most re-fined) a clue to deciding whether to continue straight ahead, or to turn right or left. As the days passed all became more alert. Aleramo Scaccabarozzi known as Bonehead had a bow, and he kept it taut until he heard in front of him the flapping of some bird less swift and perhaps less airborne than our hens at home. He would shoot the arrow, and, most times, guided by a cry or a frenzied fluttering of dying wings, they could seize the prey, pluck the feathers, and cook it over a fire of twigs. The most amazing thing was that, rubbing some stones together, they could kindle the wood: the flame rose, suitably red, but illuminating nothing, not even the men gathered around it, and then it would break off at the point where, skewered on a bough, they set the animal to be roasted.

It was not hard to find water, because fairly often they heard the gurgle of some spring or rill. They advanced very slowly, and one time they realized that, after two days' journey, they were back at the place from which they had set out, because, near a little stream, as they groped around, they came upon the traces of their previous encampment.

Finally they sensed the presence of the Abcasians. First they heard voices, like whispering, all around them, excited voices, though still faint, as if the forest's inhabitants were pointing out to one another these unexpected visitors they had never seen, or, rather, never heard. The Poet let out a very loud cry, and the voices fell silent, while a stirring of grass and boughs suggested the Abcasians were fleeing in fear. But they came back, and resumed their whispering, more and more amazed by this invasion.

At a certain moment the Poet felt a hand graze him, or a hairy limb; he gripped something and heard a scream of terror. The Poet let go, and the voices of the natives moved off a bit, as if they had widened their circle, to remain at a safe distance.

Nothing happened for several days. The journey continued and the Abcasians accompanied them, though perhaps they were not the same ones as the first time, but others who had been told of their passage. In fact, one night (was it night?) they heard in the distance something like a roll of drums, or a sound as if someone were beating a hollow tree trunk. It was a soft noise, but it spread through the space around them, for miles perhaps, and they understood that with this system the Abcasians kept one another informed, at a distance, about what was happening in their forest.

At length they became accustomed to that invisible company. And they were growing more and more accustomed to the darkness, so much so that Abdul, who had particularly suffered from the sun's rays, said he felt better, his fever almost gone, and went back to his songs.

One evening (was it evening?) while he was warming himself at the fire, he took his instrument from his saddle and resumed singing:

> Happy and sad, at the end of my road,
> I hope to see my distant love,
> Will I see her? I don't know, where'er I go
> I will be too far from her.
> Hard is the pass and harsh my way,
> Nor shall I ever know my destiny,
> May the Lord's will be done.
>
> But to me it will seem great joy, as I implore,
> Through love of God, the distant refuge.
> If she please, I will find refreshment there,
> Near her, far though she be.
> And this song of mine, faint and fine
> If I have the joy to be near her,
> This song will bring sweetness to my heart.

They became aware that the Abcasians, who till then had murmured around them without cease, had fallen silent. They listened in silence to Abdul's song, then tried to reply: a hundred lips (were they lips?) were heard whistling, piping charmingly like tame blackbirds, repeating the melody Abdul had played. Thus they found a wordless accord with their hosts, and in the nights that followed each group awaited the other, one singing and the other apparently playing flutes. Once the Poet roughly bawled one of those tavern songs that in Paris made even the serving wenches blush, and Baudolino joined in. The Abcasians did not respond, but after a long silence one or two of them resumed imitating Abdul's melodies, as if to say those were good and acceptable, not the others. In this they displayed, Abdul observed, a tenderness of feeling and an ability to tell good music from bad.

As the only one authorized to "speak" with the Abcasians, Abdul felt reborn. We are in the reign of tenderness, he said, and therefore close to my goal. Let's move on. No, Boidi replied, fascinated, why don't we stay here? Is there perhaps any place more beautiful in the world than this, where, even if something ugly exists, you don't see it?

Baudolino also thought that, after he had seen so many things in the vast world, those long days spent in darkness had reconciled him to himself. In the darkness he returned to his memories, he thought of his boyhood, of his father, his mother, of Colandrina so sweet and unhappy. One evening (was it evening? Yes, because the Abcasians were silent, sleeping), unable to get to sleep, he moved, touching the tree's fronds with his hands, as if he were seeking something. Suddenly he found a fruit, soft to the touch and very aromatic. He picked it and bit into it, and he felt invaded by a sudden languor; he no longer knew if he was dreaming or awake.

All at once he saw, or felt close to him as if he saw her, Colandrina. "Baudolino, Baudolino," she called him with an adolescent voice, "don't stop, even if here everything seems beautiful. You must reach the kingdom of that Priest you told me about and give him that cup; otherwise who will make a duke of our Baudolinetto Colandrinuccio? Make me happy. Things are not bad here, but I miss you so."

"Colandrina, Colandrina," Baudolino cried, or thought he cried, "be quiet: You are a ghost, a trick, the fruit of that fruit! The dead do not return!"

"Generally not," Colandrina replied, "but I kept insisting. I said: You gave me only one season with my man, only a taste. Do me this holy favor, if you have a heart. I'm fine here, and I see the Blessed Virgin and all the saints, but I miss the caresses of my Baudolino that gave me goose bumps. They've granted me very little time, just to give you a kiss. Baudolino, don't stop along the way with the women of those places, who maybe have nasty diseases that I don't even know of. Put your foot in the road and go towards the sun."

She disappeared, as Baudolino felt a soft touch on his cheek. He stirred from his doze, had peaceful dreams. The next day he told his companions that they had to go on.

After many more days they perceived a glimmer, a milky glow. Again the darkness was being transformed into the gray of a thick and uniform brume. They realized that the Abcasians, who were accompanying them, had stopped, and were bidding them farewell with their piping. They heard them standing at the edge of a clearing, at the confines of that light that the Abcasians surely feared, as if they were waving their hands, and from the softness of their sounds it was clear they were smiling.

They passed through the fog and saw once more the light of the sun. They were dazzled, and Abdul was again shaken by feverish trembling. They thought that after the test of Abcasia they would enter the desired lands, but they had to revise that idea.

Immediately, above their heads, birds with human faces were darting and shouting: "On what soil are you treading? Go back! You cannot violate the land of the Blest! Go back and tread the land that was given you!" The Poet said this was witchcraft, perhaps one of the ways the land of the Priest was protected, and he convinced them to go on.

After a few days' march over a field of stones without a blade of grass, they saw three animals coming towards them. One was surely a cat, with an arched back, bristling fur, and eyes like two firebrands. Another had a lion's head, roaring, a goat's body, and the behind of a dragon, but from the goatlike back a second head rose, horned and bleating. The tail was a hissing serpent, thrust forward to threaten the travelers. The third had a lion's body, a scorpion's tail, and an almost human head, with shapely nose and yawning mouth, in which they could discern, above and below, a triple row of teeth, sharp as blades.

The animal that most worried them was the cat, notoriously the messenger of Satan and the domestic ally of necromancers. You can defend yourself against any monster, but not against this one, who, before you can draw your sword, springs on your face and scratches your eyes. Solomon muttered that nothing good could be expected of an animal that the Book of Books had never mentioned. Boron said that the second animal was surely a chimera, the only one that, if the vacuum existed, could fly buzzing inside it and suck out the thoughts of living beings. The third animal left no room for doubt, and Baudolino recognized it as a manticore, not unlike the leucrotta, an animal about which some time ago (how long was it now?) he had written to Beatrice.

The three monsters advanced towards them: the cat with agile feline steps, the other two with equal determination, but a bit slower, thanks to the difficulty that a triform animal has in adapting to the movement of its various composition.

The first to take the initiative was Aleramo Scaccabarozzi known as Bonehead, who now was never separated from his bow. He fired an arrow right in the center of the cat's head, and the animal sprawled lifeless. At this sight, the chimera made a leap forward. Bravely, Cuttica of Quargnento, shouting that at home he had been able to reduce enamored bulls to mild behavior, stepped forward to stab the monster, but it made a leap, fell upon him, and was tearing him with its leonine maw when the Poet, Baudolino, and Colandrino rushed to subdue the beast with slashes of their swords until it let go and sank to the ground.

Meanwhile the manticore attacked. It was confronted by Boron, Kyot, Boidi, and Porcelli, while Solomon hurled stones at it, muttering curses in his holy language. Ardzrouni retreated, black also with terror, and Abdul lay curled up, seized by more intense tremors. The beast seemed to consider the situation with a canniness both human and bestial. Surprisingly agile, it ducked those facing it and, before they could inflict a wound, it flung itself on Abdul, unable to defend

350

himself. With its tripled teeth it bit his shoulder, nor did it let go when the others rushed to free their comrade. It howled beneath the blows of their swords, but firmly clenched Abdul's body, which spurted blood from a spreading wound. Finally the monster could no longer survive the blows inflicted by the four enraged adversaries, and with a horrible rattle it died. But it was hard work opening its jaws and freeing Abdul from their grip.

At the end of that battle, Cuttica had a wounded arm, but Solomon was treating him with an unguent of his, saying the wound would not be serious. Abdul, on the contrary, was moaning faintly, losing much blood. "Bandage him," Baudolino said. "Weak as he was already, he mustn't go on bleeding!" They all tried to stanch the flow, using their clothes to stop the wound, but the manticore had bitten deep into his limbs, reaching the heart.

Abdul was delirious. He murmured that his princess must be very near and he couldn't die right at this very moment. He asked them to stand him on his feet, and they had to restrain him because it was clear that the monster had injected some unknown poison into his flesh.

Believing in his own deceit, Ardzrouni had taken from Abdul's sack the Baptist head, broken the seal, removed the skull from the reliquary, and placed it in Abdul's hands. "Pray," he said, "pray for your salvation."

"Imbecile," the Poet said to him scornfully. "First of all, he can't hear you, and, second, that head was God knows whose, and you stole it from some infidel graveyard."

"Any relic can revive the spirit of a dying man," Ardzrouni said.

In the late afternoon Abdul could no longer see, and he asked if they were again in the forest of Abcasia. Realizing that the supreme moment was coming, Baudolino made up his mind and—as usual out of good-heartedness—told another lie.

"Abdul," he said, "now you are at the peak of your desires. You have arrived at the place you yearned for, you had only to pass the test

351

of the manticore. Here, you see, your lady is before you. As she learned of your ill-starred love, from the farthest reaches of the earth where she lives, she has hastened to you, thrilled and moved by your devotion."

"No," Abdul gasped, "it's not possible. She comes to me, and I do not go to her? How can I survive such bounty? Tell her to wait. Raise me, please, that I may go and pay her homage. . . ."

"Be calm, my friend; if she has so decided, you must bow to her will. Here, open your eyes; she is bending over you." And, as Abdul raised his eyelids, Baudolino held out to his gaze, now clouded, the mirror of the gymnosophists, in which the dying man glimpsed, perhaps, the shadow of a countenance that was not unknown to him.

"I see you, my lady," he said in a faint voice, "for the first and last time. I never believed I could merit this joy. But I fear that you love me . . . and this could sate my passion. . . . Oh no, princess . . . now this is too much. Why do you bend to kiss me?" And he put his trembling lips to the mirror. "What do I feel now? Sadness at the end of my search or pleasure for the undeserved conquest?"

"I love you, Abdul, let that suffice," Baudolino had the courage to whisper into the ear of his friend, who was dying, and the friend smiled. "Yes, you love me, and that suffices. Isn't it what I have always wished, even if I dispelled the thought for fear it would happen? Or what I did not wish, for fear that it would not be as I had hoped? But now I could desire nothing more. How beautiful you are, my princess, and how red are your lips. . . ." He let the false skull of the Baptist roll on the ground, grasped with trembling hand the mirror, and moved his lips, in vain, to graze the mirror's surface, clouded by his breath. "Today we celebrate a joyous death, that of my sorrow. Oh, sweet lady, you have been my sun and my light, where you passed it was spring, and in May you were the moon that enchanted my nights." He came to, for a moment, and said, trembling: "But is it perhaps a dream?"

"Abdul," Baudolino whispered to him, remembering some verses he had one day sung, "what is life if not the shadow of a fleeting dream?"

"Thank you, my love," Abdul said. He made a final effort, as Baudolino supported his head, and he kissed the mirror three times. Then he bowed his now bloodless, waxen face, illuminated by the light of the sun that was setting over the fields of stones.

The Alessandrians dug a grave. Baudolino, the Poet, Boron, and Kyot, who were weeping for a friend with whom they had shared everything from the years of their youth, lowered the poor remains into the earth, on his chest they set that instrument which would never more sing the praises of the distant princess, and they covered his face with the gymnosophists' mirror.

Baudolino collected the skull and the gilded case, then went to fetch his friend's sack, where he found a roll of parchment with his songs. He was about to place the Baptist's skull, which he had put back in the reliquary, also in the bag, then he said to himself: "If he goes to Paradise, as I hope, he won't need it, because he will meet the Baptist, the real one, head and all the rest. And in any case, in those parts it's best for him not to be found with a relic that couldn't be more fake. I'll keep this myself, and if one day I sell it, I'll use the money to have made for him, if not a tomb, at least a fine plaque in a Christian church." He closed the reliquary, replacing the seal as best he could, and put it, along with his own, in his sack. For a moment he had the feeling he was robbing a dead man, but he decided after all he was borrowing something he would repay in another form. In any case he said nothing to the others. He collected everything else in Abdul's sack and went to lay it in the grave.

They filled the grave and set there, like a cross, their friend's sword. Baudolino, the Poet, Boron, and Kyot knelt in prayer, while at a slight distance Solomon murmured the litanies that the Jews habitually recite. The others remained a bit behind. Boidi wanted to begin a sermon, but then limited himself to saying: "Hmph!"

"When you think that just a few minutes ago he was here with us," Porcelli said.

"We're here today and gone tomorrow," said Aleramo Scaccabarozzi known as Bonehead.

"Why him, I wonder," Cuttica said.

"Fate," concluded Colandrino, who, though still young, was very wise.

28

Baudolino crosses the Sambatyon

"Halleluia!" Niketas cried after three days' marching. "There! Over there is Selymbria, decked in trophies." And with trophies it was truly decked, that little city of low houses and deserted streets, because—as they learned later—they were celebrating the day after the feast of some saint or archangel. The inhabitants had festooned a tall white column that stood in a field at the edge of the settlement, and Niketas explained to Baudolino that on the top of that column, centuries and centuries ago, a hermit had lived, who had not come down from it until after his death, and from up there he had performed numerous miracles. But nowadays men of that stamp no longer existed, and this, too, was perhaps one of the reasons for the misfortunes of the empire.

They headed at once for the house of the friend on whom Niketas was relying, and this Theophilactus, an elderly man, hospitable and jovial, welcomed them with genuinely fraternal affection. He inquired about their mishaps, wept with them over destroyed Constantinople, showed them his house with many rooms for the whole brigade of guests, refreshed them immediately with young wine and a plentiful salad with olives and cheese. These were not the delicacies to which Niketas was accustomed, but this rustic lunch was more than enough to make them forget the discomforts of the journey and their distant home.

"Remain in the house for a few days without wandering about," Theophilactus advised them. "Many refugees from Constantinople have arrived here, and these people of ours have never got along with the people of the capital. Now you are here to ask alms, you who gave yourselves such airs, is what they are saying. And for a crust of bread they demand its weight in gold. But if only that were all. Some time ago pilgrims also arrived here. First they acted the bully; you can imagine how they are now, when they have learned that Constantinople is theirs and one of their leaders will become the basileus. They strut around dressed in festive clothes they have stolen from our dignitaries, they put the miters stolen from the churches on the heads of their horses, and they sing our hymns in a Greek they've invented, mixing in who knows what obscene words from their own language, they cook their food in our sacred vessels, and they parade the streets with their whores dressed like great ladies. Sooner or later, this too will pass, but for the present stay quietly here with me."

Baudolino and Niketas asked for nothing better. In the days that followed, Baudolino continued his story beneath the olive trees. They had cool wine and olives, olives, and more olives to savor, whetting their thirst. Niketas was anxious to know if they finally arrived at the kingdom of Prester John.

Yes and no, Baudolino said. In any case, before telling where they arrived, it was necessary to cross the Sambatyon. And this was the adventure he began at once to recount. As he had been tender and pastoral in telling of Abdul's death, so now he was epic and majestic in reporting the fording of that river. A sign, Niketas thought once again, that Baudolino was like that strange animal of which he— Niketas—had only heard rumors, though perhaps Baudolino had even seen it: the so-called chameleon, similar to a tiny goat, which changes color according to the place where it is, and can vary from black to pale green; white, the color of innocence, is the only color it cannot assume.

Saddened after the death of their comrade, the travelers resumed their march and again found themselves at the beginning of a mountainous region. As they advanced they heard first a distant sound, then a crackling, a noise that became increasingly audible and distinct, as if someone were throwing a great number of boulders and pebbles from the peaks, and the avalanche were dragging with it earth and rubble, rumbling downwards. Then they made out a cloud of dust, like a mist or brume; but, unlike a great mass of humidity, which would have darkened the rays of the sun, this gave off myriad glints, as if the sun's rays were striking against a fluttering of mineral atoms.

At a certain point Rabbi Solomon was the first to understand. "It's the Sambatyon," he shouted, "so we are close to our goal!"

It was indeed the river of stone, as they realized when they arrived at its banks, dazed by the great din that almost prevented them from hearing one another's words. It was a majestic course of rocks and clods, flowing ceaselessly, and in that current of great shapeless masses could be discerned irregular slabs, sharp as blades, broad as tombstones, and between them, gravel, fossils, peaks, and crags.

Moving at the same speed, as if driven by an impetuous wind, fragments of travertine rolled over and over, great faults sliding above, then, their impetus lessening, they bounced off streams of spall, while little chips now round, smoothed as if by water in their sliding between boulder and boulder, leaped up, falling back with sharp sounds, to be caught in those same eddies they themselves had created, crashing and grinding. Amid and above this overlapping of mineral, puffs of sand were formed, gusts of chalk, clouds of lapilli, foam of pumice, rills of mire.

Here and there sprays of shards, volleys of coals, fell on the bank, and the travelers had to cover their faces so as not to be scarred.

"What day is today?" Baudolino shouted to his companions. Solomon, who kept the tally of every Saturday, remembered that the week had just begun, and for the river to halt its flow they would have to wait at least six days. "And then, when it stops, we won't be able to cross it, in violation of the Sabbath laws," he cried, distraught. "Why did the Holy One, may his name be forever blessed, in his wisdom not cause this river to stop on Sunday, since you gentiles are all un-believers anyway and you trample the festive repose under your feet?"

"Don't worry about Saturday," Baudolino cried. "For if the river were to stop, I would know very well how to make you cross it with-out causing you to sin. I would just prop you on a mule while you're asleep. The problem is what you yourself told us: when the river stops flowing, along the banks a barrier of flames springs up, so we're back at the beginning. . . . It's useless then to wait here for six days. Let's go towards the source, and perhaps there is a crossing place before the river is born."

"What? What?" his companions cried, not understanding any of it; but then, seeing him move, they followed, thinking that perhaps he had had a good idea. On the contrary, it was a very bad one, because they rode for six days, seeing that the river's bed did, indeed, narrow, becoming first a stream and then a creek, but they arrived at the source only towards the fifth day. By then, for two days they had seen above the horizon an impervious chain of high mountains, which loomed over the travelers, almost blocking their view of the sky, crammed as they were in an ever narrower passage, with no exit, from which, way, way above, could now be seen only a great cloud barely luminescent, that gnawed the top of those peaks.

Here, from a fissure, like a wound between two mountains, they saw the Sambatyon springing up: a roiling of sandstone, a gurgling of tuff, a dripping of muck, a ticking of shards, a grumbling of clotted earth, an overflowing of clods, a rain of clay, all gradually trans-formed into a steady flow, which began its journey towards some boundless ocean of sand.

Our friends spent a day trying to skirt the mountains and discover a pass above the source, but in vain. They were in fact threatened by sudden moraines that came and shattered at the hoofs of their horses; they had to take a more tortuous path, night caught them in a place where every now and then blocks of living sulphur rolled from the peak; farther on, the heat became unbearable, and they realized that, if they continued, even if they found a way to cross the mountains, when the water of their flasks was finished in that dead nature, they would find no form of humidity, so they decided to turn back. But they discovered they had become lost in those meanders, and it took them another day to find the source again.

They arrived when, according to Solomon's calculations, Saturday had already passed and, even if the river had stopped, it had now already resumed its course, and they would have to wait another six days. Uttering exclamations that certainly did not assure them the benevolence of heaven, they decided to follow the river, in the hope that it would open into a mouth, or delta, or estuary as might be, transforming itself into a more restful wasteland.

So they traveled for some dawns and some sunsets, moving away from the banks to find more welcoming zones, and heaven must have forgotten their abuses, because they came upon a little oasis with some greenery and a very meager pool of water, still sufficient to give them relief and a supply for a few more days. Then they went on, always accompanied by the flow of the river, under glowing skies occasionally striped with black clouds, fine and flat as the stones of Bubuctor.

Until, after almost five days' travel, and nights as sultry as the days, they realized that the continuous churn of that tide was changing. The river had assumed a greater speed, in its flow something like currents were visible, rapids that dragged along shreds of basalt like straws, a distant thunder was heard. . . . Then, more and more impetuous, the Sambatyon subdivided into myriad streamlets, which penetrated among mountainous slopes like the fingers of a hand in a clump of mud; at times a wave was swallowed by a grotto, then, from a sort of rocky passage that seemed impassable, it emerged with a roar and flung itself angrily towards the valley. Abruptly, after a vast curve they were forced to make because the banks had become impervious, lashed by granite whirlwinds, the friends reached the top of a plateau, and saw the Sambatyon below them, annihilated in a sort of maw of Hell.

There were cataracts that plunged down from dozens of rocky eaves arranged like an amphitheater, into a boundless final vortex, an incessant retching of granite, an eddy of bitumen, a sole undertow of alum, a churning of schist, a clash of orpiment against the banks. And on the matter that the vortex erupted towards the sky, but low with respect to the eyes of those who looked down as if from the top of a tower, the sun's rays formed on those silicious droplets an immense rainbow that, as every body reflected the rays with varying splendor according to its own nature, had many more colors than those usually formed in the sky after a storm, and, unlike them, seemed destined to shine eternally, never dissolving.

It was a reddening of haematrites and cinnabars, a glow of blackness as if it were steel, a flight of crumbs of aureopigment from yellow to bright orange, a blueness of armenium, a whiteness of calcinated shells, a greening of malachite, a fading of liothargirium into saffrons ever paler, a blare of risigallam, a belching of greenish earth that faded into dust of crisocolla and then transmigrated into nuances of indigo and violet, a triumph of aurum musivum, a purpling of burnt white lead, a flaring of sandracca, a couch of silvered clay, a single transparence of alabaster.

No human voice could make itself heard in that clangor, nor did the travelers have any desire to speak. They witnessed the death agony of the Sambatyon enraged at having to vanish into the bowels of the earth, trying to take with it all that surrounded it, clenching its stones to express all its impotence.

Neither Baudolino nor his friends realized how long they admired the wraths of the precipice where the river was unwillingly buried, but they must have lingered there at length, and the sunset of Friday had arrived, hence the beginning of Saturday; because all of a sudden, as if at a command, the river stiffened in cadaveric rigidity, and the vortex at the bottom of the abyss was changed into a scaly, inert valley where, sudden and terrifying, an enormous silence reigned.

They waited, expecting, as foretold by the story they had heard, a barrier of flames to rise along the banks. But nothing happened. The river was silent, the whirling particles above it slowly settled into its bed, the night sky became serene, displaying a glitter of stars till then hidden.

"So you see you mustn't always believe what they tell you," Baudolino concluded. "We live in a world where people invent the most incredible stories. Solomon, this is a tale you Jews put into circulation to prevent Christians from coming to these parts."

Solomon did not answer, because he was a man of quick intelligence, and at that moment he understood that Baudolino was pondering how to make him cross the river. "I will not fall asleep," he said at once.

"Don't think about it," Baudolino replied. "Rest, while we look for a ford."

Solomon would have liked to flee, but on Saturday he couldn't ride, still less travel over mountainous heights. So he remained seated all night, striking his head with his fists and cursing his fate and, with it, the accursed gentiles.

The following morning, when the others picked out a place where they could cross without risk, Baudolino went back to Solomon, smiled at him with affectionate understanding, and struck him with a club just behind the ear.

And so it was that Rabbi Solomon, alone among the sons of Israel, crossed the Sambatyon on the Sabbath, in his sleep.

29

Baudolino arrives at Pndapetzim

Crossing the Sambatyon did not mean they had arrived in the kingdom of Prester John. It meant simply that they had abandoned known lands where only the boldest travelers had gone. In fact, the friends had to proceed for many more days still, and through lands at least as rough as the banks of that river of stone. Then they reached a plain that was endless. On the far horizon they could make out a mountainous presence, fairly low, but jagged with peaks slender as fingers, which reminded Baudolino of the Alps when he had crossed them as a boy on the eastern slope, to travel from Italy into Germany—but those were far higher and more imposing.

The rise was, however, at the extreme horizon, and in that plain the horses advanced toilsomely because a hardy vegetation grew everywhere, like an endless field of ripe wheat, except that this was a species of green and yellow fern, taller than a man, and that sort of very fertile steppe stretched as far as the eye could see, like an ocean stirred by a constant breeze.

As they crossed a clearing, like an island in that ocean, they saw in the distance and in a single place that the surface no longer moved in uniform waves, but was agitated irregularly, as if some animal, an enormous hare, moved in sinuous curves and not in a straight line, at

362

a speed superior to that of any hare. Since these adventurers had already encountered animals, and of a sort that inspired no confidence, they tugged on their reins, and prepared for a new battle.

The serpentine line was coming towards them, and they could hear a rustle of disturbed ferns. At the edge of the clearing the grasses finally parted, and a creature appeared, thrusting the ferns aside with its hands, as if they were a curtain.

Hands they certainly were, and arms, those of the being coming towards them. For the rest it had a leg, but only one. Not that the other had been amputated; on the contrary, the single leg was attached naturally to the body, as if there had never been a place for another, and with the single foot of that single leg the creature could run with great ease, as if accustomed to moving in that way since birth. Indeed, as he came swiftly towards them, they couldn't tell if he moved in hops or managed, built as he was, to make steps, and his one leg went forwards and backwards, as we move with two, and every step bore him ahead. The speed with which he advanced was such that it was impossible to distinguish one movement from another, as with horses, of whom no one has ever been able to say if there is a moment when all four hoofs are raised from the ground, or if two at least are always firmly planted.

When the creature stopped before them, they saw that his sole foot was at least twice the size of a human foot, but well shaped, with square nails, and five toes that seemed all thumbs, squat and sturdy.

For the rest, he was the height of a child of ten or twelve years; that is he came up to a human waist, and had a shapely head, with short, bristling yellow hair on top, a pair of round affectionate eyes like those of an ox, a small snub nose, a broad mouth that stretched almost ear to ear and revealed, in what was undoubtedly a smile, a fine and strong set of teeth. Baudolino and his friends recognized him at once, for they had read about the creature and heard him spoken of many times: he was a skiapod, and they had even put skiapods in the Priest's letter.

The skiapod smiled again, raised both hands, clasping them above his head in a greeting and, erect as a statue on his single foot, he said, more or less: "*Aleichem sabi', Iani kala' bensor.*"

"This is a language I've never heard," Baudolino said. Then, in Greek, he said: "What language are you speaking?"

The skiapod replied in a Greek all his own: "I not know what language spoke. I believe you foreigners and spoke a language made up like foreigners. But you speak language of Presbyter Johannes and his deacon. I greet you. I is Gavagai, at your service."

Seeing that Gavagai was harmless, indeed benevolent, Baudolino and the others dismounted and sat on the ground, inviting him to do the same and offering him what little food they still had. "No," he said, "I thank, but I have ate very much this morning." Then he did something that, according to the best tradition, was to be expected from a skiapod: he first stretched out full length on the ground, then raised his leg so as to provide himself with shade from his foot, put his hands behind his head and again smiled blissfully, as if he were lying under an umbrella. "Some cool is good today, after much running. But you, who is? Too bad, if you was twelve, then you was the most holy Magi returning, even with one black. Too bad only eleven."

"Too bad indeed," Baudolino said, "but we are eleven. Eleven Magi don't interest you, I suppose."

"Eleven Magi no interest anybody. Every morning in church we pray return of the twelve. If eleven come we prayed wrong."

"Here they really are awaiting the Magi," the Poet murmured to Baudolino. "We have to find a way to persuade them that number twelve is around somewhere."

"But without ever using the word Magi," Baudolino insisted. "We are twelve, and they'll think the rest on their own. Otherwise Prester John will discover who we are and will have us eaten by his white lions or something like."

Then he addressed Gavagai again: "You said you are a servant of the Presbyter. Have we then come to the kingdom of Prester John?"

"You wait. You cannot say: here I am in kingdom of Prester John, after you have come a little way. Then everybody come. You are in great province of Deacon Johannes, son of Johannes, and rules all this land that you, if you want the Presbyter's kingdom, have to pass through. All visitors coming must first wait in Pndapetzim, great capital of deacon."

"How many visitors have already arrived here?"

"None. You people first."

"Really. Before us, a man with a black beard didn't arrive?"

"I never seen," Gavagai said. "You men first."

"So we must stay in this province to wait for Zosimos," the Poet grumbled, "and God knows if he will arrive. Maybe he's still in Abcasia, groping around in the dark."

"It would have been worse if he had already arrived and had given the Grasal to these people," Kyot said. "But without the Grasal, how will we present ourselves?"

"Stay calm; even haste demands some time," Boidi wisely observed. "Now we'll see what we find here, then we'll think up something."

Baudolino told Gavagai that they would gladly stay in Pndapetzim, waiting for their twelfth companion, who had been lost in a desert sand storm many days' march from where they were now. He asked Gavagai where the deacon lived.

"Down there, in his palace. I take you. No, first I tell my friends you arrive, and when you arrive there is feast. Guest is the Lord's gift."

"Are there other skiapods around here in the grass?"

"I don't believe. But just now I saw blemmy that I know. By chance, because skiapods not friends of blemmyae." He put his fingers to his mouth and emitted a long and very well-modulated whistle. After a few instants the ferns parted and another creature appeared. He was very different from the skiapod, and, for that matter, having heard a blemmy mentioned, the friends were expecting to see what they saw. The creature, with very broad shoulders, was hence very squat, but with slim waist, two legs, short and hairy, and no head, or even a neck. On his chest, where men have nipples, there were two almond-shaped eyes, darting, and, beneath a slight swelling with two nostrils, a kind of circular hole, very ductile, so that when he spoke he made it assume various shapes, according to the sounds it was emitting. Gavagai went to confer with him, pointing out the visitors; the other creature visibly nodded, by bending his shoulders as if he were leaning over.

He approached the visitors and said something like: "*Ouiii, ouioioioi, aueua*!" As a sign of friendship, the visitors offered him a cup of water. From a sack he was carrying the blemmy took something like a straw, stuck it in the hole beneath his nose, and began to suck the water. Then Baudolino offered him a large piece of cheese. The blemmy put it to his mouth, which suddenly became the same size as the cheese, which vanished into that hole. The blemmy said: "*Euaoi oea!*" Then he put a hand on his chest, or, rather, on his forehead, like someone making a promise, waved both arms, and went off through the grass.

"He arrive before us," Gavagai said. "Blemmyae not run like skiapods, but always better than slow animals you go upon. What is they?"

"Horses," Baudolino said, remembering that horses did not live in the Priest's kingdom.

"How is horses?" the curious skiapod asked.

"Like these," the Poet replied, "exactly like them."

"I thank. You men powerful, and go with animals like horses."

"But listen a moment. Just now I heard you say that skiapods are not friends of blemmyae. Do they not belong to the same kingdom or province?"

"Oh, no, they servants of the Presbyter like us, and like them also ponces, pygmies, giants, panotians, tongueless, nubians, eunuchs, and the satyrs-that-are-never-seen. All good Christians and faithful servants of Deacon and Presbyter."

"You are not friends because you are different?"

"What you say? Different?"

"Well, in the sense that you are different from us and—"

"Why I different you?"

"Oh, for God's sake," the Poet said. "To begin with, you have only one leg! We and the blemmyae have two!"

"Also you and blemmyae if you raise one leg, you have only one."

"But you don't have another one to lower!"

"Why should I lower leg I don't has? Do you lower third leg you don't has?"

Boidi intervened, conciliatory: "Listen, Gavagai, you must agree that the blemmy has no head."

"What? Has no head? Has eyes, nose, mouth, speaks, eats. How possible if has no head?"

"But haven't you noticed that he has no neck, and above the neck that round thing that you also have on your neck and he doesn't?"

"What means noticed?"

"Seen. Realized that. You know that."

"Maybe you say he not entirely same as me; my mother couldn't mistake him for me. But you too not the same as this friend because he has mark on cheek and you no. And your friend different from that other one black like one Magi, and him different from that other with black beard like a rabbi."

"How do you know I have a rabbi's beard?" Solomon asked hopefully, obviously thinking of the lost tribes, and deducing from those words a clear sign that they had passed through here or were living in this kingdom. "Have you ever seen other rabbis?"

"Me no, but all say rabbi's beard down in Pndapetzim."

Boron said: "Let's get to the point. This skiapod can't see the difference between himself and a blemmy, any more than we can see any between Porcelli and Baudolino. If you think about it, this happens when you meet strangers. Between two Moors, can you see a real difference?"

"Yes," Baudolino said, "but a blemmy and a skiapod aren't like us and Moors, since we see them only when we go to their country. They all live in the same province, and he can distinguish between one blemmy and another, if he says that the one we just saw is his friend, and the others not. Now listen to me carefully, Gavagai: you said that in the province live some panotians. I know what the panotians are, they are people almost like us, except they have two ears so huge that they come down to their knees, and when it's cold they wrap them around their body like a cloak. Is this how panotians are?"

"Yes, like us. I have ears, too."

"But not down to your knees, by God!"

"You have ears much bigger than your friend next you."

"But not like the panotians, dammit!"

"Each has the ears his mother made for him."

"Then why do you say that there is bad blood between the skiapods and the blemmyae?"

"Blemmyae think wrong."

"Wrong how?"

"They Christians who make mistake. They *phantasistoi*. They say right, like us, that Son not the same nature as Father, because Father exists since before time began, but Son is created by Father, not for need but for wish. So Son is adoptive son of God, no? Blemmyae say: Yes, Son has not same nature as Father, but this Verbum even if only adoptive son cannot make himself flesh. So Jesus never became flesh; what apostles saw was only ... how to say? ... *phantasma*. ..."

"Pure appearance."

"There. They say only *phantasma* of Son died on cross, not born in Bethlehem, not born of Maria, one day on river Jordan before John the Baptist he appear and all say Oh. But if Son not flesh, how he says this bread my body? And so they not make communion with bread and *burq*."

"Maybe because they would have to suck the wine, or whatever you call it, with that straw," the Poet said.

"And the panotians?" Baudolino asked.

"Oh, they don't care what Son does when he comes down to earth. They think only of Holy Spirit. I tell you: they say Christians in west think Holy Spirit proceeds from Father and from Son. They protest and say this from Son was put afterwards and in the Credo of Constantinople it doesn't say. Holy Spirit for them proceeds only from Father. They think contrary to pygmies. Pygmies says Holy Spirit proceeds only from Son and not from Father. Panotians hate most of all pygmies."

"Friends," Baudolino said, turning to his companions, "it seems obvious to me that the various races existing in this province give no importance to bodily differences, to color or shape, as we do, when even if we see a dwarf we consider him a horror of nature. But instead, like many of our learned men, for that matter, they attach great importance to the difference of ideas about Christ, or the Most Holy Trinity, of which we have heard so much talk in Paris. It is their way of thinking. We must try to understand this; otherwise we'll be forever lost in endless arguments. Very well, we'll pretend the blemmyae are like the skiapods, and what they think about the nature of Our Lord doesn't concern us after all."

"From what I understand, the skiapods share the terrible Arian heresy," Boron said, who, as always, was the one among them who had read the most books.

"So?" the Poet said. "It seems to me a question for Greeklings. We in the north were more concerned about which pope was the real one, and which the antipope, insisting that it all depended on a whim of our late Lord Rainald. Everyone has his own defects. Baudolino's right: let's act as if it were nothing and ask him to take us to his deacon, who won't amount to much but at least his name is John."

They then asked Gavagai to take them to Pndapetzim, and he set off, hopping moderately, to allow the horses to keep up with him. After two hours they reached the end of the sea of fern and entered a cultivated area of olive and fruit groves: below the trees were seated, looking at them with curiosity, some beings of almost human features, who greeted them with their hands while emitting only howls. They were, Gavagai explained, the tongueless, who lived outside the city because they were Messalians, believing you could go to heaven only thanks to silent and continuous prayer, without taking the sacraments, without performing works of mercy or other mortifications, without ritual practices. Therefore they never went to the churches of Pndapetzim. They were shunned by all because they believed that work was also an act of mercy and therefore useless. They lived in great poverty, feeding on the fruits of these trees, which, however, belonged to the whole community, and which they exploited without any restraint.

"Otherwise they are just like you, aren't they?" the Poet teased him.

"They are like us when we are silent."

The mountains were coming closer all the time, and the closer they came, the more the friends grew aware of their nature. At the end of the rocky area, some soft, yellowish little mounds rose gradually, as if, Colandrino suggested, they were made of whipped cream; no, of piles of spun sugar; wrong, heaps of sand placed one next to the other, as if they were forest. Behind rose what had seemed in the distance fingers, rocky peaks, which at their top were capped with darker rock, sometimes in the form of a hood, others like an almost flat lid, protruding before and behind. Seen more closely, the rises were less pointed, but each seemed riddled with holes like a wasp's nest, until it was clear that these were habitations, or hostels, of stone, caves that had been dug from the rock, and each of them was reached by a single wooden ladder, the various ladders bound to one another from level to level and all together forming, for each of those spurs, an aerial maze that the inhabitants, who from the distance still seemed ants, climbed with agility, up and down.

In the center of the city were seen actual houses or buildings, but they were also set into the rock, from which a few feet of façade jut-

ted, and all up high. Farther on, a more important massif was outlined, irregular in form, it, too, a hive of grottos, but of more geometric shape, like so many windows or doors, and in some instances
from those fornices terraces extended, loggias, little balconies. Some
of those entrances were covered by a colored curtain, others by mats
of woven straw. In other words, the friends were in the center of a
cloister of quite wild mountains, and at the same time in the center
of a populous and active city, even if surely not as magnificent as they
would have expected.

They could tell that the city was active and populous from the
crowd that animated what were not the streets and squares but,
rather, the spaces between peak and spur, between massif and natural
tower. It was a multicolored crowd, in which dogs and asses mingled,
and many camels, which the travelers had seen at the beginning of
their journey, but never so many and so different as in this place,
some with one hump, others with two, and still others even with
three. They saw also a fire-eater, performing before a cluster of inhabitants while holding a panther on a leash. The animals that most
surprised them were some very agile quadrupeds, trained to draw
carts: they had the body of a foal, quite long legs with bovine hoofs,
they were yellow with great brown spots, and, above all, they had a
very long neck surmounted by a camel's head with two little horns at
the top. Gavagai said they were cameleopards, difficult to capture because they fled very swiftly, and only the skiapods could pursue them
and rope them.

In effect, though without streets and without squares, that city
was all one immense market, and in every free space a tent had been
set up, a pavilion erected, a carpet spread out on the ground, a plank
laid horizontally on two stones. And they could see displays of fruit,
cuts of meat (especially prized, that of the cameleopard), carpets
woven with all the colors of the rainbow, clothing, knives of black
obsidian, stone hatchets, clay cups, necklaces of bones and of little

371

red and yellow gems, hats of the oddest form, shawls, blankets, boxes of inlaid wood, tools for working the land, balls and rag dolls for the children, and amphoras full of liquids, blue, amber, pink, and lemon, and bowls of pepper.

The only thing not to be seen in that fair was anything made of metal, and, when asked to explain why, Gavagai didn't understand the meaning of the words iron, metal, bronze, or copper, in whatever language Baudolino tried to name them.

In that crowd some very active skiapods were circulating, hopping and skipping with brimming baskets on their heads, and blemmyae, almost always in isolated groups, or behind counters where coconuts were sold, panotians with their ears flapping, except the females, who modestly folded their ears over their breasts, pressing them with one hand, like a shawl, and other people who seemed to have stepped from one of those books of wonders whose miniatures had so excited Baudolino when he was seeking inspiration for his letters to Beatrice.

They noticed some men who must have been pygmies, with very dark skin, a loincloth of straw, and, slung over one shoulder, that bow with which, as their nature required, they were at perennial war with cranes—a war that must have granted them no small number of victories, since many of them were offering passersby their prey, hung on a long stick, which it took four of them to carry, two at each end. Since the pygmies were shorter than the cranes, the hanging animals swept the ground, and for this reason they had hung them by the neck, so that it was the feet that left a long wake in the dust.

Then came the ponces and, even if our friends had read of them, they could not stop studying curiously these creatures with erect legs and no knee joints, walking stiffly, pressing their equine hoofs on the earth. But what made them remarkable was, for the men, their phallus, which hung from the chest, and for the women, in the same position, the vagina, though it could not be seen because they covered it with a shawl knotted behind their back. Tradition demanded that

372

they tend goats with six horns, and it was some of these animals that they were selling in the market.

"Just as was written in the books," Boron kept murmuring in wonderment. Then, in a louder voice, so that Ardzrouni could hear him: "And in the books it was also written that the vacuum does not exist." Ardzrouni shrugged, concerned with discovering if, in some phial, a liquid was being sold that would lighten the skin.

To temper the restlessness of all these people, now and then some very black men came by, of tall stature, naked to the waist, with Moorish trousers and white turban, armed only with enormous gnarled clubs that could have felled an ox with a single blow. Since the inhabitants of Pndapetzim were forming clusters as the foreigners passed, especially pointing out the horses, which obviously they had never seen before, the black men intervened to discipline the crowd, and they had only to swing their clubs to create immediately a vacuum around themselves.

It had not escaped Baudolino that, when the gathering grew thicker, it was always Gavagai who gave the alarm signal to the black men. From the gestures of many bystanders it was clear that they were eager to act as guide for the illustrious guests, but Gavagai was determined to keep them for himself, and indeed he swaggered, as if to say: "These are my property; hands off!"

As for the black men, they were, as Gavagai said, the deacon's nubian guards, whose ancestors had come from the depths of Africa, but they were no longer foreigners because, for countless generations, they had lived in the vicinity of Pndapetzim, and they were sworn to the deacon till death.

Finally they saw—much taller than the nubians, jutting many spans above the heads of the others—the giants, who besides being giants were also one-eyed. They were disheveled, ill-dressed, and, Gavagai said, their occupation was constructing dwellings on those rocks, or else they grazed sheep and oxen, and in this they were excellent, because they could bend a bull to the ground, grasping it by the horns, and if a ram strayed from the flock, they needed no dog, but seized the ram by its fleece and put it back in the place it had left.

"And are your people their enemies also?" Baudolino asked.

"Here nobody enemy of nobody," Gavagai answered. "You see them all together sell and buy like good Christians. Afterwards all go home, each of them, not stay together to eat or sleep. Each thinks what he wants, even if he thinks wrong."

"And the giants think wrong..."

"Uuh! Worse of all! They is Artotyrites, believe Jesus at Last Supper consecrates bread and cheese, because they say that normal food of ancient patriarchs. So they make communion, blaspheming, with bread and cheese and consider heretics all who make it with *burq*. But here people who think wrong is almost all, except the skiapods."

"You told me that in this city there are eunuchs? Do they also think wrong?"

"Better I not speak of eunuchs. Too powerful. They not mix with common people. But think different from me."

"And, apart from thinking, they are same as you, I imagine..."

"Why? What do I have different from them?"

"Well, you damn big-foot"—the Poet was worked up—"do you go with females?"

"With skiapod females, yes, because they do not think wrong."

"And with your skiapod females you put that thing inside, dammit, but where do you have it?"

"Here, behind leg, like everybody."

"Apart from the fact that I don't have it behind my leg, and we've just seen come characters who have it above their belly button, at least you know that eunuchs don't have that thing at all and don't go with females?"

"Maybe because eunuchs not like females. Maybe because in Pndapetzim never seen female eunuchs. Poor eunuchs, maybe they like females but don't find eunuch females and can't go with females of blemmyae or panotians, who think wrong."

"But you noticed that the giants have only one eye?"

"Me, too. You see? I close this eye, and only other one left."

"Hold me, or I'll kill him," the Poet said, his face flushed.

"Now then," Baudolino said, "the blemmyae think wrong, the giants think wrong, all think wrong, except the skiapods. And how does this deacon of yours think?"

"Deacon not think. He command."

As they were talking, one of the nubians had rushed in front of Colandrino's horse, knelt down, and, extending his arms and bowing his head, muttered some words in an unknown language, but in a tone that indicated it was a heartfelt prayer.

"What does he want?" Colandrino asked. Gavagai replied that the nubian was asking in the name of God to have his head cut off with that fine sword that Colandrino wore on his hip.

"He wants me to kill him? Why?"

Gavagai seemed embarrassed. "nubians strange people. You know: they Circoncellions. Good warriors because want to be marrtyrs. No war now, but they want to be martyrs right away. Nubian is like child, wants right away what he likes." He said something to the nubian, who went off, hanging his head. Asking to explain further these Circoncellians, Gavagai said that the Circoncellians were the nubians. Then he pointed out that sunset was approaching, the market was breaking up, and they had to go to the tower.

In fact the crowd was thinning, the vendors were collecting their goods in great baskets; from the various fornices that blinked in the rock walls some ropes were descending and some of the people, according to their habitations, were raising their merchandise. It was all an industrious up and down, and in a short time the city was deserted. It seemed now an immense cemetery with countless tombs, but, one after the other, those doors or windows in the rock began to come alight, a sign that the inhabitants of Pndapetzim were kindling fires and lamps to prepare for the evening. Thanks to who knows what invisible holes, the smoke of those fires came from all the peaks and spurs, and the now-pale sky was streaked with blackish plumes that rose and dissolved among the clouds.

They walked through what little remained of Pndapetzim, and reached an open area, beyond which the mountains left no further passage visible. Half-set into the mountain, the sole artificial construction of the entire city could be seen. It was a tower, or the anterior part of a stepped tower, vast at the base, and increasingly narrow as it rose, but not like a stack of pancakes, one smaller than the other superimposed to make many levels, because a spiral passageway proceeded without interruption from one plane to the next and apparently it also penetrated the rock, encircling the construction from base to summit. The tower was entirely punctuated by great arched doorways, one next to the other, with no free space between them except the frame that separated door from door, and the construction looked like a monster with a thousand eyes. Solomon said that this must be like the tower erected at Babel by the cruel Nembroth, to defy the Holy One, blessed always be his name.

"And this," Gavagai said in a proud tone, "this is the palace of Deacon Johannes. Now you stand still and wait, because they know you arrive and have prepared solemn welcome. I now go."

"Where are you going?"

"I cannot enter tower. After you is received and seen Deacon, then I come back to you. I your guide in Pndapetzim, I never leave you. Watch out with eunuchs; he is young man"—and he pointed to Colandrino—"they like young. *Ave, evcharistò, salam.*" Erect on his single foot, he saluted, in a vaguely military fashion, turned, and a moment later was already far away.

30

Baudolino meets the Deacon Johannes

When they were about fifty paces from the tower, they saw a procession emerging from it. First a squad of nubians, but more elaborately clothed than those in the market: from the waist down they were enfolded in white cloths wound tightly around their legs, covered by a little skirt that fell halfway down the thigh; they were barechested, but wore red capes, and at the neck a leather collar in which colored stones were set, not gems but pebbles from a riverbed, arranged like a bright mosaic. On their heads they wore white hoods with many bows. On their arms, wrists, and fingers they had rings and bracelets of woven string. Those in the first row were playing pipes and drums, those in the second held their enormous clubs against their shoulders, those in the third had only bows slung around their necks.

Then there followed a formation of what were surely the eunuchs, in ample and soft robes, made up like women and with turbans that seemed cathedrals. The one in the center carried a tray laden with cakes. Finally, escorted at either side by two nubians waving fans of peacock feathers over his head, came the man who was surely the highest dignitary of this company: his head was covered with a turban as high as two cathedrals, a plait of silken bands of different colors;

from his ears hung pendants of colored stone; his arms were decked with bracelets of gaudy feathers. He also wore a garment that reached his feet, and was bound at the waist by a sash of blue silk, a span wide, and on his chest hung a cross of painted wood. He was a man of some age, and the rouge on his lips and the bister on his eyes contradicted his skin, now yellowing and flaccid, calling even more attention to a double chin that quivered at every step he took. His hands were pudgy, with long nails as sharp as blades, painted red.

The procession stopped in front of the visitors, the nubians lined up in double file, while the eunuchs of lesser rank knelt as the one carrying the tray bowed and proffered the food. Baudolino and his men, at first uncertain how to act, dismounted and accepted pieces of cake, which they chewed dutifully, bowing. At their greeting the chief eunuch finally came forward and prostrated himself on the ground, then stood and addressed them in Greek:

"Since the birth of Our Lord Christ Jesus we have waited for your return, and if you are surely those whom we believe you to be, it pains me to know that the twelfth among you, but like you first among all Christians, was driven from his path by inclement Nature. While I will give orders to our guards to study the horizon ceaselessly in expectation of his arrival, I wish you a happy sojourn in Pndapetzim," he said in a white voice. "I say this to you in the name of Deacon John, I, Praxeas, supreme chief of the court eunuchs, protonotary of the province, sole vicar of the deacon to the Priest, supreme custodian and logothete of the secret path." He said this as if even the Magi should be impressed by such high rank.

"Give me a break," murmured Aleramo Scaccabarozzi known as Bonehead. "Just listen at him!"

Baudolino had thought many times about how he would introduce himself to the Priest, but never about how you should present yourself to a chief eunuch in the service of the Priest's deacon. He decided to follow the line they had established: "Sir," he said, "I express to you our joy in having reached this noble, rich, and wondrous city of Pndapetzim, the most beautiful and flourishing we have seen in all our journey. We come from afar, bearing for Prester John the greatest relic of Christianity, the cup from which Jesus drank at the Last Supper. Unfortunately, the devil, in his envy, has unleashed against us the forces of Nature, causing us to lose one of our brothers along the way, the very one who was bearing the gift, along with other tokens of our esteem for Priest Johannes. . . ."

"By which we mean," the Poet added, "one hundred ingots of solid gold, two hundred great apes, a crown of one thousand pounds of gold with emeralds, ten strands of inestimable pearls, eighty chests of ivory, five elephants, three tamed leopards, thirty anthropophage dogs and thirty fighting bulls, three hundred elephant tusks, a thousand panther skins, and three thousand ebony staves."

"We had heard of these riches and substances unknown to us which abound in the land where the sun sets," Praxeas said, his eyes gleaming, "and praise heaven if before leaving this vale of tears I may see them!"

"Can't you keep your shitty mouth shut?" Boidi hissed behind the Poet, punching him in the back. "What if Zosimos arrives now, and they see he's in even worse shape than us?"

"Shut up yourself," the Poet snarled, his mouth twisted. "We've already said the devil's at work here, and the devil will have eaten it all up. Except for the Grasal."

"But we still need a gift, at least one gift, to show that we're not beggars," Boidi went on murmuring.

"What about the Baptist's head?" Baudolino suggested in a whisper.

"We have only five left," the Poet said, still not moving his lips, "but it doesn't matter; as long as we stay in the kingdom we certainly can't pull out the other four."

Baudolino was the only one who knew that, counting the one he had taken from Abdul, there were still six heads. He took one from his sack and held it out to Praxeas, saying that for the moment—while they awaited the ebony, the leopards, and all those other fine things—they wanted him to deliver to the deacon the only memento left on earth of him who had baptized Our Lord.

Praxeas, deeply moved, accepted that gift, beyond price in his eyes because of the sparkling case, which he assumed was made of that precious yellow substance he had heard so much talk about. Impatient to venerate that sacred relic, and with the air of one who considers his own property any gift made to the deacon, opened it without effort (so it was Abdul's head, the seal already broken, Baudolino said to himself), took in his hand the brownish, dried-up skull, product of Ardzrouni's skill, exclaiming in a choked voice that never in his life had he contemplated a more precious relic.

Then the eunuch asked by what names he should address his venerable guests, because tradition had assigned them so many and no one now knew which ones were right. With great caution, Baudolino replied that at least until they were in the presence of the Priest, they wished to be called the names by which they were known in the distant West, and he gave the real names of each of them. Praxeas admired the evocative sound of names like Ardzrouni and Boidi, he found a loftiness in Baudolino, Colandrino, and Scaccabarozzi, and he dreamed of exotic lands hearing Porcelli and Cuttica named. He said that he respected their reserve, and concluded: "Now enter. The hour is late, and the deacon will be able to receive you only tomorrow. This evening you will be my guests, and I assure you that never will a banquet be more rich and sumptuous, and you will savor such delicacies that you will think with contempt of those that have been offered you in the lands where the sun sets."

"Why, they're dressed in rags the like of which would make our women torment their husbands to have something better," the Poet muttered. "We set out and we've undergone what we've undergone in order to see cascades of emeralds; when we wrote the Priest's letter, you, Baudolino, were disgusted with topazes, and there they are with a dozen pebbles and a few strings and they think they're the richest in the world!"

"Shut up. We'll wait and see," Baudolino murmured.

Praxeas led them inside the tower, and showed them into a hall without windows, illuminated by burning tripods, with a central carpet full of cups and trays of clay, and a series of cushions along the sides, on which the banqueters crouched with crossed legs. They were served by youths, surely also eunuchs, half-naked and sprinkled with fragrant oils. They offered the guests some pots with aromatic mixtures, in which the eunuchs dipped their fingers, then touched their nostrils and their earlobes. After sprinkling themselves, the eunuchs languidly caressed the youths and invited them to proffer the perfumes to the guests, who bowed to the customs of these people, though the Poet snarled that if one of that crew dared touch him he would knock out all his teeth with one finger.

The supper proceeded in this fashion: great dishes of bread, or, rather, those cakes of theirs; an enormous quantity of boiled greens, among which cabbages abounded, but did not smell because they were treated with various spices; cups of a very hot black sauce, which they called *sorq*, in which all dipped the cakes, and Porcelli, who was the first to try it, began to cough as if flames were darting from his nose, so then the rest of the band confined themselves to moderate tasting (and then they passed the night burning with an unslakable thirst); a freshwater fish, dry and skinny, that they called *thinsireta* (Think of that! the friends murmured), breaded with a kind of semolina and literally drowned in a boiling oil that must have been already employed for many meals; a linseed soup, which they called *marac* and which, according to the Poet, smacked of shit, wherein some shreds of fowl were floating, but so badly cooked that they seemed leather, and Praxeas said with pride that it was *methagallinarios* (Well, well, said the friends, with more nudging); a relish they called *cenfelec*, made of candied fruit but with more pepper than fruit. At each new course the eunuchs helped themselves greedily, and as they chewed they made noises with their lips, to express their pleasure, and they motioned to the guests, as if to say: "You like it? Isn't it a gift from heaven?" They ate, taking the food with their hands, even the soup, sipping it from their cupped palms, mixing different things in one handful and stuffing it all into their mouths with one shove. But only with the right hand, because the left was placed on the shoulder of the youth who was alert always to provide more food. They removed it only to drink, seizing some jugs which they held high above their heads, pouring the water into their mouths like a fountain.

Only at the end of this princely meal did Praxeas give a sign, and some nubians arrived to pour a white liquid into some minuscule goblets. The Poet drained his with one gulp and immediately turned red, emitted a kind of roar, and fell as if dead, until one of the youths sprinkled some water on his face. Praxeas explained that in their land the wine tree did not grow, and the only alcoholic beverage they could produce came from the fermentation of the *burq,* a berry very common in those parts. But the strength of that drink was such that it could be tasted only in tiny sips or by barely inserting the tongue into the goblet. A real pity that they did not have here that wine so often mentioned in the Gospels, because the priests of Pndapetzim, every time they said Mass, plunged into the most unsuitable drunkenness and had trouble reaching the *Ite missa est.*

"When it comes to that, what else were we to expect from these monsters?" Praxeas said with a sigh, moving off to a corner with Baudolino, while, with titters of curiosity, the other eunuchs examined the iron weapons of the travelers.

"Monsters?" Baudolino asked, with feigned ingenuousness. "I had the impression that here no one noticed the amazing deformities of the others."

"You must have been listening to one of those," Praxeas said with a scornful smile. "They have lived here together for centuries, they have grown accustomed to one another, and refusing to see the monstrosity of their neighbors, they ignore their own. Monsters, yes, more like animals than men, and capable of reproducing faster than rabbits. This is the people that we must govern, and mercilessly, to prevent them from exterminating one another reciprocally, each race beclouded by its own heresy. This is why, centuries ago, the Priest had them live here, at the confine of the kingdom, so their odious sight would not trouble his subjects, who are—as I assure you, Lord Baudolino—men of great beauty. But it is natural for nature also to generate monsters, and it is indeed inexplicable why the entire human race has not become monstrous, since it committed the most horrendous crime of all, crucifying God the Father."

Baudolino was coming to realize that even the eunuchs thought wrong, and he asked his host some questions. "Some of these monsters," Praxeas said, "believe that the Son was only adopted by the Father, others wearily debate who precedes whom, and each, monster that he is, is drawn into his monstrous error, multiplying the hypostases of the divinity, believing that the Supreme Good is three different substances or even four. What pagans! There is a single divine substance that is manifested in the course of human vicissitudes through various means or persons. The only divine substance in that it generates is the Father, in that it is generated it is the Son, in that it sanctifies it is the Spirit, but it is always the same divine nature: the rest is like a mask behind which God hides. One substance and one triple person and not, as some heretics affirm, three persons in one substance. But if this is so, and if God, all entire, mind you, and not delegating some adoptive offspring, was made flesh, then it is the Father Himself who suffered on the cross. Crucify the Father! Do you understand? Only an accursed race could arrive at such an outrage, and the duty of the faithful believer is to avenge the Father. No mercy for the accursed breed of Adam."

Since the beginning of the story of the journey, Niketas had listened in silence without interrupting Baudolino further. But now he did, because he realized that his interlocutor was uncertain how to interpret what he himself was saying. "Do you think," he asked, "that the eunuchs hated the human race because it had made the Father suffer, or that they had embraced that heresy because they hated the human race?"

"That's what I asked myself, that evening and afterwards, never finding an answer."

"I know how eunuchs think. I encountered many at the imperial palace. They try to amass power to escape their fury towards all those capable of reproducing. But often, in my long experience, I sensed that also many who are not eunuchs use their power to express what they would otherwise be unable to do. Perhaps commanding is a more overwhelming passion than making love."

"There were other things that left me puzzled. Listen: the eunuchs of Pndapetzim constituted a caste that reproduced itself by election, inasmuch as their nature did not allow other ways. Praxeas said that generation after generation the elders chose comely youths and reduced them to their own state, first making them servants and then heirs. Where did they find those youths, so lissome and well-made, when the entire province of Pndapetzim was inhabited only by freaks of nature?"

"Surely the eunuchs came from a foreign country. It happens in many armies and public administrations: those who hold power must not belong to the community they govern, so as not to feel tenderness or complicity towards the subjects. Perhaps this is what the Priest wanted, to maintain in subjection that deformed and unruly people."

"To be able to send them to die without remorse. Because from the words of Praxeas I sensed two other things: Pndapetzim was the last outpost before the beginning of the Priest's kingdom. After it, there was only a chasm between the mountains that led to another territory, and on the cliffs that dominated the pass the nubian guards were stationed, ready to provoke landslides of boulders on any who ventured into that narrow gorge. At the other end of the pass a swamp began, endless, a swamp so insidious that whoever tried to cross it was sucked under the muddy terrain or sand in perpetual movement, and after he sank up to his calves, he could no longer extricate himself, and then he vanished completely like someone drowned in the sea. In the swamp there was only one safe path, which permitted crossing, but it was known only to the eunuchs, who had been trained to recognize it by certain signs. Thus Pndapetzim was the gate, the defense, the access that had to be breached if one were to enter the kingdom."

"Since you were their first visitors in God knows how many centuries, that defense didn't represent a heavy task."

"On the contrary. Praxeas was very vague about this question, as if the very name of those who threatened them was covered by some veto, but once, in an aside, he decided to tell me that the whole province lived under the threat of a warrior people, the White Huns, who could at any moment attempt an invasion. If they were to arrive at the gates of Pndapetzim, the eunuchs would send skiapods, blemmyae, and all the other monsters to be slaughtered to arrest the conquest for a bit, then they would have to lead the deacon to the pass, send down from the peaks enough boulders to block every passage, and withdraw into the kingdom. If they failed and were captured, and because the White Huns might force one of them, under torture, to reveal the only true path to the land of the Priest, they had all been trained so that, before falling prisoner, they would kill themselves with a poison each kept in a little bag hanging around his neck, under his tunic. The horrible thing is that Praxeas was sure that they would be saved in any case, because at the last moment they would have the nubians as a shield. It is fortunate, Praxeas said, to have some Circoncellions as bodyguards."

"I have heard mention of them, but referring to a time many centuries ago on the coasts of Africa. There were heretics down there then known as Donatists, who believed that the church should be a society of saints, but that sadly all its ministers were by now corrupt. Therefore, according to them, no priest could administer the sacraments, and they were constantly at war with all the other Christians. The most determined of the Donatists were, in fact, the Circoncellions, a barbarian people of the Moorish race, who roamed through fields and valleys in search of martyrdom, flung themselves down from cliffs on wayfarers with shouts of "*Deo laudes,*" threatening them with their clubs, ordering them to kill them, so that they could experience the glory of sacrifice. And as the others took fright and refused to do it, the Circoncellions first robbed them of all their possessions, then bashed their heads in. But I thought those fanatics were extinct."

"Obviously the nubians of Pndapetzim were the descendants of those people. They would be, Praxeas told me with his usual contempt for his subjects, invaluable in warfare, because they would gladly allow themselves to be killed by the enemy, and during the time it would take to fell them all, the eunuchs would be able to block the pass. But for too many centuries the Circoncellians had been awaiting this event; no one had arrived to invade the province, and they were champing at the bit, unprepared for living in peace. Because they couldn't attack and rob the monsters they were ordered to protect, they vented their impatience by hunting and fighting barehanded the wild animals; sometimes they ventured beyond the Sambatyon, in the rocky wastes where chimeras and manticores were waiting, and some of the nubians had had the joy of meeting the same end as Abdul. But that didn't suffice. On occasion the more convinced among them went mad. Praxeas had already learned that one of them, that afternoon, had begged us to decaptitate him; others, while they were on guard at the pass, flung themselves from the peaks, and, in short, it was hard to restrain them. Only the eunuchs could keep them in a state of vigil, warning them daily of imminent danger, persuading them that the White Huns were really at the gates, and so the nubians often roamed the plains, narrowing their eyes, leaping with joy at every cloud of dust they could glimpse in the distance. They awaited the arrival of the invaders, in a hope that had been consuming them for centuries, generation after generation.

Meanwhile, since not all were truly prepared for the sacrifice, but announced in loud voices their yearning for martyrdom in order to be well-fed and well-clad, they had to be kept content with delicacies and quantities of *burq*. I understood how the resentment of the eunuchs increased from day to day, forced to govern monsters they hate, and having to entrust their lives to fanatical gluttons perennially drunk."

It was late, and Praxeas had had the nubian guard accompany them to their quarters, opposite the tower, in a stone hive of modest size, though its interior provided space for them all. They climbed those airy ladders and, exhausted by that singular day, they slept until morning.

They were wakened by Gavagai, prepared to serve them. He had been informed by the nubians that the deacon was ready to receive his guests.

They returned to the tower, and Praxeas personally led them up the broad outside steps, to the last floor. There they stepped through a door and found themselves in a circular corridor from which many other doors opened, one beside the other, like a set of teeth.

"I realized only later how that floor had been conceived, Master Niketas. It is hard for me to describe it, but I will try. Imagine that this circular corridor is the perimeter of a circle in whose center there is a hall, also circular. Every door that opens into the corridor leads into a passage, and each passage should be a radius of the circle, leading to the central room. But if the corridors were straight, anyone from the outer circular corridor could see what happens in the central hall and anyone in the central hall could see someone arriving along a passage. On the contrary, however, each passage began in a straight line, but at the end it bent, making a curve, and then led into the central hall. So no one from the outer corridor could glimpse the hall, guaranteeing the privacy of the one inhabiting it...."

"But the inhabitant of the hall could not see anyone arriving, either, except at the last moment."

"True, and this detail struck me immediately. You understand: the deacon, master of the province, was shielded from any intruder, but at the same time he could be surprised without advance warning by a visit of his eunuchs. He was a prisoner who could not be spied upon by his guardians, but could not spy upon them either."

"Those eunuchs of yours were more clever than ours. But now, tell me about the deacon."

They entered. The great circular hall was empty, except for some cupboards around the throne. The throne was in the center, it was of dark wood, surmounted by a baldachin. On the throne sat a human form, wrapped in a dark garment, his head covered by a turban, with a veil that fell over his face. His feet were shod in dark slippers, and dark also were the gloves that covered his hands, so nothing could be seen of the seated figure's features.

At either side of the throne, crouching next to the deacon, were two other veiled forms. One of them from time to time handed the deacon a vase in which perfumes were burning, so that he could inhale the fumes. The deacon tried to reject this, but Praxeas made a sign to him, imploring, commanding him to accept, and hence it must have been some kind of medicine.

"Stop at five paces from the throne, bow, and before offering your greeting, wait for his invitation," Praxeas whispered.

"Why is he veiled?" Baudolino asked.

"That is not asked. It is thus because it pleases him thus."

They did as they had been told. The deacon raised a hand and said, in Greek: "From my boyhood I have been prepared for the day of your coming. My logothete has already told me everything, and I will be happy to assist you and to have you as my guests while you await your august companion. I have also received your incompa-

388

rable gift. It is not merited, all the more so in that it comes to me from donors themselves so worthy of veneration."

His voice was unsteady, that of someone in pain, but the sound was youthful. Baudolino was profuse in greetings so reverent that no one could later have accused him of having boasted of the dignity that was being attributed to him. But the deacon observed that such humility was the obvious sign of their holiness, and so there was nothing to be done.

Then he invited them to be seated on a circle of eleven cushions that he had had prepared at five paces from the throne; he had them served with *burq* along with some sweet cakes that had a stale taste, and he said he was eager to learn from them, who had visited the fabled West, if truly there existed in that land all the wonders of which he had read in so many books that had passed through his hands. He asked if there were truly a country known as Enotria, where the tree grew which drips the beverage that Jesus had transformed into his own blood. If in that land the bread was not pressed flat, half-a-finger thick, but swelled miraculously every morning at the cock's crow, in the form of a fruit, soft and light beneath a golden crust. If it was true that churches there were to be seen built free of the cliffs, if the palace of the great priest of Rome had ceilings and beams of perfumed wood from the legendary island of Cyprus. If this palace had doors of blue stone mixed with the horns of the cerastes, which prevented anyone entering from bringing poison inside, and windows of a stone that allowed the passing of light. If in that same city there was a great circular construction where now Christians ate lions, and on its vault appeared two perfect imitations of the sun and the moon, as large as they really are, which followed their celestial arc, amid birds made by human hands that sang the sweetest of melodies. If beneath the floor, also of transparent stone, porphyry fish swam freely. If it was true that this construction was reached by a stairway where, at the base of a certain step, there was an aperture from which one

389

could watch all the things that took place in the universe as they were occurring, all the monsters of the depths of the sea, dawn and evening, the multitudes that live in Ultima Thule, a cobweb of mooncolored threads at the center of a black pyramid, flakes of a substance white and cold that fall from the sky on Africa Perusta in the month of August, all the deserts of this universe, every letter of every page of every book, sunsets the rose color above the Sambatyon, the tabernacle of the world set between two shining slabs that reproduce it to infinity, expanses of water, like lakes without shores, tempests, all the ants that exist on earth, a sphere that reproduces the movement of the stars, the secret throb of one's own heart and viscera, and the face of each of us when we will be transfigured by death...

"Who's been telling these people such whoppers?" the Poet, shocked, asked himself. While Baudolino was trying to reply prudently, saying that the wonders of the distant Occident were certainly numerous, even if surely their fame, which passes valleys and mountains enlarging them, loves to amplify and surely he could bear witness that he had never seen, there where the sun sets, Christians who ate lions. The Poet snickered, whispering: "At least, not on fast days..."

They realized that their mere presence had kindled the imagination of that young prince perennially shut up in his circular prison and that, if you live there where the sun rises, you cannot help but dream of the marvels of the sunset country (especially, the Poet went on murmuring—luckily in Teutonic—if you live in a shit-ass place like Pndapetzim).

Then the deacon understood that his guests also wanted to know some things and he remarked that perhaps, after so many years of absence, they did not remember how to return to the kingdom from which, according to tradition, they came, also because over the centuries a series of earthquakes, and other transformations of that land of theirs had profoundly altered mountains and plains. He explained how difficult it was to proceed through the pass and cross the swamp, he warned them that the rainy season was beginning, and it was not wise to set off on their journey at once. "Furthermore, my eunuchs," he said, "will have to send messengers to my father, to tell him of your visit, and they must then return with his consent to your journey. The road is long, and all this will take a year or even more. In the meantime, you must await the arrival of your brother. I may tell you that here you will be given lodging worthy of your rank." He said this in an almost mechanical voice, as if he were reciting a lesson just learned.

The guests asked him what was the function and the fate of a deacon John, and he explained that, perhaps in their day things did not yet proceed thus, for the laws of the kingdom had been in fact modified after the departure of the Magi. It should not be thought that the priest was a single person who had continued to reign for millennia; it was a high position. At the death of each priest, his deacon ascended the throne. Then, immediately, dignitaries of the kingdom went out to visit all the families, and they identified, by certain miraculous signs, a boy-child not yet three months of age, who became the future heir and putative son of the priest. The child was joyfully given up by his family and was immediately sent to Pndapetzim, where he spent his childhood and youth being prepared to succeed his adoptive father, to fear him, honor him, and love him. The young man spoke with a sad voice because, he said, it is fated that a deacon cannot remember his carnal father, nor see his putative one, not even on his catafalque, because from the moment of his death to the moment when the heir reached the capital of the kingdom, as he had said, a year went by, at least.

"I will see only—and I hope this occurs as late as possible—the effigy," he said, "imprinted on his winding sheet, in which he will be wrapped before the funeral, the body having been covered with oils and other miraculous substances that print the forms on the linen." Then he said: "You must stay here for a long time, and I ask that you come and visit me every now and then. I love hearing tales of the wonders of the Occident. Even stories of the thousand battles and sieges that, it is said, make life there worthy of being lived. I see weapons at your sides far more beautiful and powerful than those used here, and I imagine that you have led armies in battle, as befits a king, while in our country we have been preparing for war since time immemorial, but I have never had the pleasure of commanding an army in the open field." He was not inviting, he was almost beseeching, and in the tone of a young man whose mind has been fired by books of wondrous adventures.

"Provided you do not fatigue yourself excessively, sire," said Praxeas with great reverence. "Now it is late and you are tired; it would be best to dismiss your visitors." The deacon nodded, but from the gesture of resignation that accompanied his farewell, Baudolino and his friends realized who really commanded in this place.

31

Baudolino waits to leave
for the kingdom of Prester John

Baudolino had been talking too long, and Niketas was hungry. Theophilactus made him sit down to supper, offering him caviar of various fish, followed by a soup with onions and olive oil, served on a plate full of bread crumbs, then a sauce of minced shellfish, seasoned with wine, oil, garlic, cinnamon, oregano, and mustard. Not much, considering his tastes, but Niketas did himself proud. While the women, who had eaten by themselves, prepared to sleep, Niketas resumed questioning Baudolino, eager to learn if he had finally arrived at the kingdom of the Priest.

"You want to rush me, Master Niketas, but at Pndapetzim we remained two long years, and at first time passed slowly, unchanging. No news of Zosimos, and Praxeas reminded us that if the twelfth of our group did not arrive, without the announced gift for the Priest, it was pointless for us to set out on our journey. Besides, every week brought us further, disheartening news: the rainy season had lasted longer than predicted and the swamp had become more than ever impassable, there was no word of the envoys sent to the Priest, perhaps they were unable to find again the only path.... Then the good season came and there was talk that the White Huns were arriving, a nubian had sighted them to the north, and no men could be spared to accompany us on such a difficult journey, and so on and on. Not knowing what to do, we learned, little by little, to express ourselves in the various languages of that country; by now we knew that if a pygmy cried *ü Hekinah degul,* he meant that he was happy, and the greeting to exchange with him was *Lumus kelmin pesso desmar lon emposo,* which means that you pledged not to make war against him and his people; and that if a giant replied to a question with *Bodh-koom* it meant that he didn't know, that the nubians called a horse *nek* perhaps in imitation of *nekbrafpfar,* which was camel, while the blemmyae for horse said *houyhmhmm,* and this was the only time we heard sounds uttered that were not vowels, a sign that they were inventing a never-used term for an animal they had never seen; the skiapods prayed saying *Hai coba,* which for them meant Pater Noster, and they called fire *deba,* rainbow *deta,* and dog *zita.* The eunuchs, during their Mass, praised God singing: *Khondinbas Ospamerostas, kamedumas karpanemphas, kapsinumas Kamerostas perisimbasrostam-prostamas.* We were becoming inhabitants of Pndapetzim, so much so that the blemmyae or the panotians didn't seem all that different from us. We had been transformed into a band of idlers, Boron and Ardzrouni spent their days debating the vacuum, and in fact Ardzrouni had persuaded Gavagai to put him in touch with a ponce carpenter, and was contriving with him to see if it was possible to construct only from wood, without any metal, one of his miraculous pumps. When Ardzrouni was devoting himself to his mad venture, Boron went off with Kyot, riding into the plains and daydreaming of the Grasal as they kept their eyes alert to see if the ghost of Zosimos might appear on the horizon. Perhaps, Boidi suggested, he had taken a different route, had encountered the White Huns, God knows what he had told them, those probable idolaters, and he was convincing them to attack the kingdom.... Porcelli, Cuttica, and Aleramo Scaccabarozzi known as Bonehead, who had taken part in the founding of Alessandria and thus gained some knowledge of construction, had got it into their heads to convince the inhabitants of the province that four well-built walls were better than their pigeon roosts, and they had found some giants whose trade was scooping out those holes in the cliff, but were willing to learn how to mix concrete mortar or shape bricks of clay and put them in the sun to dry. At the edges of the city five or six hovels had risen, but one fine morning the friends saw them occupied by the men without tongues, vagabonds by vocation, and professional spongers. The locals tried to oust them by throwing rocks, but they were tough. Boidi, every evening, looked towards the pass, to see if good weather had returned. In other words, each of us had invented his own way of killing time, we had become accustomed to that disgusting food, and, worst of all, we could no longer do without *burq*. We were consoled by the fact that the kingdom was only a stone's throw away, that is, a year's march if all went well, but we no longer were obliged to discover anything, nor to find any road; we had only to wait until the eunuchs led us along the right one. We were, so to speak, blissfully enervated, and happily bored. Each of us, except for Colandrino, was by now along in years: I was past fifty; at that age people die if they haven't already died years before. We thanked the Lord, and obviously that air was good for us, because we all seemed rejuvenated; apparently I looked ten years younger than when I had arrived. Our bodies were vigorous and our spirits were lax, if I may put it that way. We had become so identified with the people of Pndapetzim that we had even begun to participate passionately in their theological debates."

"Whose side were you on?"

"Actually, it all began because the Poet's blood was hot. He couldn't go on without a woman, though even poor Colandrino could remain chaste, but then he was an angel from heaven, like his poor sister. Our eyes had really become accustomed to that place, I realized, when the Poet began to rave about a panotian beauty. He was attracted by those flapping ears, he was aroused by the whiteness of her skin, he found her supple, with well-shaped lips. He had seen two panotians coupling in a field and had sensed that the experience must have been delightful: each enfolded the other with the ears and they copulated as if they were inside a shell, or as if they were the minced meat wrapped in vine leaves that we had savored in Armenia. It must be splendid, he said. Then, receiving a shy reaction from the panotian he had tried to approach, he took a fancy to a blemmy female. He found that, apart from the lack of a head, she had a slender waist, an inviting vagina, and furthermore it would be great to kiss a woman on the mouth as if he were kissing her womb. So he tried to associate with those people. One evening he took us to a meeting of theirs. The blemmyae, like all the monsters of the province, would never have admitted any of the other races to their discussions of sacred matters, but we were different; they didn't think that we thought wrong; indeed each race was convinced that we thought the same as they did. The only one who would have liked to show his dismay at this familiarity of ours with the blemmyae was Gavagai, but by now this faithful skiapod adored us, and whatever we did could only be right. A bit out of naiveté and a bit out of love, he had convinced himself that we went to the blemmyae rites to teach them that Jesus was the adoptive son of God."

The blemmyae church was at ground level, a single façade with two columns and a tympanum, and the rest went deep into the cliff. Their priest summoned the faithful by striking a hammer against a slab of stone enveloped in ropes, which gave off the sound of a cracked bell. Inside, only the altar could be seen, illuminated by lamps that, judging from the smell, burned not oil but butter, perhaps made from goat's milk. There were no crucifixes, or any other images, because, as the blemmy acting as guide explained, they (the only ones who thought right) considered that the Word had not been made flesh, so they could not worship the image of an image. Nor, for the same reasons, could they take seriously the Eucharist, and therefore theirs was a Mass without any kind of consecration. They couldn't even read the Gospel, because it was a tale of deceit.

Baudolino asked at this point what sort of Mass they could celebrate, and the guide said that, in fact, they gathered to pray, then they discussed together the great mystery of the false incarnation, which they had not yet managed to comprehend fully. And, indeed, after the blemmyae had knelt down and devoted half an hour to their strange vocalizing, the priest began what he called the sacred conversation.

One of the faithful rose, to remind all that perhaps the Jesus of the Passion was not an outright ghost, in which case he would have been teasing the apostles, but rather a superior power emanated by the Father, an Eon who had entered the body of an ordinary, existing carpenter of Galilee. Another pointed out that perhaps, as others had suggested, Mary had actually given birth to a human being, but the Son, who could not be made flesh, had passed through her like water through a pipe, or perhaps had entered her through an ear. Then a chorus of protests arose, with many shouting "Paulician! Bogomil!," meaning that the speaker had uttered a heretical doctrine—and indeed he was driven from the temple. A third ventured to say that he who had suffered on the cross was the Cyrenian, who had replaced Jesus at the last moment, but the others indicated that, in order to replace someone, that particular someone had truly to be there. No, the first worshiper rebutted, the someone who was replaced was in fact Jesus as ghost, who as ghost could not have suffered, and without the Passion there would be no redemption. Another chorus of protests, because he was thus declaring that mankind had been redeemed by that wretched Cyrenian. A fourth reminded them that the Word had descended into the body of Christ in the form of a dove at the moment of the baptism in the Jordan, but surely in such a way that the Word was confused with the Holy Spirit, and that possessed body was not a ghost—so why would the blemmyae be, and rightly, fantasists?

Caught up in the debate, the Poet asked: "But if the Son, not incarnated, was only a ghost, then why in the Garden of Olives does he utter words of desperation and moan on the cross? What would a divine ghost care if they drove nails into a body that is pure apparition?

Was he only putting on an act, like a mummer?" He said this, thinking to seduce—displaying acumen and desire for knowledge—the
blemmy female he had his eye on, but he achieved the opposite effect.
The whole assembly started shouting: "Anathema! Anathema!" and
our friends realized this was the moment to leave that Sanhedrin.
And so it was that the Poet, through an excess of theological refinement, was unable to satisfy his coarse carnal passion.

While Baudolino and the other Christians devoted themselves
to these experiences, Solomon was questioning the inhabitants of
Pndapetzim one by one, to learn something about the lost tribes.
Gavagai's mention of rabbis, the first day, told him he was on the
right track. But, whether because the monsters of the various races
really knew nothing or because the subject was taboo, Solomon got
nowhere. Finally one of the eunuchs told him that, true, tradition
had it that through the kingdom of Prester John some communities
of Jews had passed, and this many centuries ago, and they had then
decided to resume their traveling, perhaps fearing the threatened invasion of the White Huns would oblige them to face a new diaspora,
and God only knows where they had gone. Solomon decided that the
eunuch was lying, and he continued to await the moment when he
and his friends would enter the kingdom, where he would surely find
his coreligionists.

Sometimes Gavagai tried to convert them to right thinking. The
Father is the most perfect and the most distant from us that can exist
in the universe, no? And therefore how could he have generated a Son?
Men generate sons in order to prolong themselves through offspring
and to live in them also in the time they themselves will never see because they will have been gathered by death. But a God who has to
generate a son would not be perfect from the beginning of centuries.
And if the Son had existed from the beginning together with the Father, being of his same divine substance or nature, whatever you may
call it (here Gavagai became confused, using Greek terms like *ousia*,

hyposthasis, physis, and *hyposopon,* which not even Baudolino managed to decipher), we would have the incredible case of a God, by definition not generated, who has been generated from the beginning of time. Therefore the Word, which the Father generates because he must concern himself with the redemption of the human race, is not of the same substance as the Father, is generated later, surely before the world, and is superior to every other creature, but just as surely inferior to the Father. Christ is not the power of God, Gavagai insisted, and is certainly not a commonplace power like the locust; he is, rather, a great power, but is the primogenitory and not the ingenitory.

"So, for you," Baudolino asked him, "the Son was only adopted by God and is not then God?"

"No, but is very holy all the same, as deacon is very holy and is adoptive son of Priest. If it functions with Priest, why not with God? I knows that Poet asking blemmyae why, if Jesus is ghost, he afraid in Garden of Olives and weeps on cross. Blemmyae, who think wrong, can't answer. Jesus not ghost. Jesus adoptive Son, and adoptive Son not know everything like his Father. You understand? Son not *homoousios,* same substance as Father, but instead *homoiousios,* similar but not same substance. We not heretics like Anomoeans; they believe Word not even similar to Father, all different. But luckily in Pndapetzim no Anomoeans. They think most wrong of all."

Since Baudolino, in repeating this story, also said that they continued to ask what difference there was between *homoousios* and *homoiousios,* and if the Lord God could be reduced to two little words, Niketas smiled and said: "There's a difference, yes, a difference. Perhaps in the Occident you people have forgotten these diatribes, but in the Roman empire they raged for a long time, and there were people who were excommunicated, banished, or even killed, for such nuances. What amazes me is that these arguments, which in our land were repressed long ago, survive still in that land you are telling me about."

And then he thought: I always suspect this Baudolino is telling me tall tales, but a semibarbarian like him, having lived among Alamans and Milanese, who can barely distinguish the Most Holy from Charlemagne, could not know these things if he hadn't heard them down there. Or did he perhaps hear them elsewhere?

From time to time our friends were invited to the disgusting suppers of Praxeas. Towards the end of one of those banquets, under the influence of *burq,* they must have said things highly unsuitable for Magi; and, for that matter, Praxeas by now had become confidential. So one night, when he was drunk and they were too, he said: "Gentlemen, most welcome guests, I have reflected at length on every word you have said since your arrival here, and I realize that you have never declared that you are the Magi we have been awaiting. I continue to believe that you are, but if by chance—and I say by chance—you are not, it would not be your fault that everyone believes you are. In any event, allow me to speak to you as a brother. You have seen what a sink of heresies Pndapetzim is, and how difficult it is to keep this monstrous rabble under control, with terror of the White Huns on the one hand, and on the other by making ourselves the interpreters of the will and the word of that Prester John whom they have never seen. You will have realized the purpose of our young deacon on your own. If we eunuchs can count on the support and the authority of the Magi, our power increases. It is increased and fortified here, but it can extend also ... elsewhere."

"Into the kingdom of the Priest?" the Poet asked.

"If you were to arrive there you should be recognized as legitimate lords. To arrive there you need us; we need you here. We are a strange breed, not like the monsters here who reproduce according to the wretched laws of the flesh. We become a eunuch because the other eunuchs have chosen us and made us so. In what many consider a misfortune, we all feel united in a sole family, I say we, including all the eunuchs who govern elsewhere, and we know that there are some

400

who are very powerful also in the remote Occident, not to mention many other kingdoms in India and Africa. It would suffice if, from a very powerful center, we could be bound in a secret alliance with our brethren all over the earth, and we would have established the most vast of all empires. An empire that no one could conquer or destroy, because it would not be made of armies and territories, but of a network of reciprocal understanding. You would be the symbol and the guaranty of our power."

Seeing Baudolino the next day, Praxeas confided that he had the impression that, the previous night, he had said bad and absurd things, things he had never thought. He apologized, begging Baudolino to forget those words. He left him, saying, "Please, remember to forget them."

"Priest or no priest," the Poet remarked that same day, "Praxeas is offering us a kingdom."

"You're crazy," Baudolino replied, "we have a mission, and we swore an oath before Frederick."

"Frederick is dead," the Poet replied sharply.

With the eunuchs' permission, Baudolino went often to visit the deacon. They had become friends. Baudolino told him of the destruction of Milan, the foundation of Alessandria, of how walls are scaled or what is needed to set fire to the besieger's mangonels and rams. At these tales Baudolino would have said that the young deacon's eyes were shining, even though his face remained veiled.

Then Baudolino asked the deacon about the theological controversies rampant in his province, and it seemed that, in answering him, the deacon had a melancholy smile. "The kingdom of the Priest," he said, "is very ancient, and it has been the refuge over the centuries for all the sects excluded from the Christian world of the Occident," and it was clear that for him even Byzantium, of which he knew little, was Extreme Occident. "The Priest was unwilling to take from any of these exiles their own faith, and the preaching of many of them has seduced the various races that inhabit the kingdom. But then, what does it matter to know what the Most Holy Trinity really is? It is enough that these people follow the precepts of the Gospel, and they will not go to Hell just because they think that the Spirit proceeds only from the Father. These are good people, as you will have realized, and it pains me to know that one day perhaps they must all perish, defending us against the White Huns. You see, as long as my father lives, I will govern a kingdom of the moribund. But perhaps I will die first myself."

"What are you saying, my lord? From your voice, and from your position itself as hereditary priest, I know you are not old." The deacon shook his head. Baudolino then, to cheer him, tried to make him laugh by telling him his own and his friends' feats as students in Paris, but he realized that he was stirring in that man's heart furious desires, and rage at not being able to satisfy them. In so doing, Baudolino revealed himself for what he was and had been, forgetting that he was one of the Magi. But the deacon, too, no longer paid any attention to this, and made it clear that he had never believed in those eleven Magi, and had only recited the lesson prompted by the eunuchs.

One day Baudolino, confronted by his obvious dejection in feeling himself excluded from the joys that youth grants all, tried to tell the deacon that one may also have a heart filled with love even for an unattainable beloved, and he told about his passion for a most noble lady and the letters he wrote her. The deacon questioned him in an excited voice, then burst into a moan like that of a wounded animal: "Everything is forbidden me, Baudolino, even a love only dreamed of. If you only knew how I would like to ride at the head of an army, smelling the wind and the blood. A thousand times better to die in battle murmuring the name of one's beloved than to stay in this cave awaiting . . . what? Perhaps nothing . . ."

"But you, my lord," Baudolino said to him, "you are destined to become the chief of a great empire, you—may God long preserve your father—will one day leave this cave, and Pndapetzim will be only the last and most remote of your provinces."

"One day I will do, one day I will be..." the deacon murmured. "Who can assure me of that? You see, Baudolino, my deep torment—God forgive me this gnawing suspicion—is that the kingdom may not exist. Who has told me of it? The eunuchs, ever since I was a child. To whom do the messengers return that they—they, mind you—send to my father? To them, to the eunuchs. Did these messengers really go forth? Did they really return? Have they ever really existed? All I know comes only from the eunuchs. And what if everything, this province, were the whole universe, if it were the fruit of a plot of the eunuchs, who make sport of me as if I were the lowest nubian or skiapod? What if not even the White Huns exist? Of all men a profound faith is required, if they are to believe in the creator of heaven and earth and in the most unfathomable mysteries of our holy religion, even when they revolt our intellect. But the necessity to believe in this incomprehensible God is infinitely less demanding than what is asked of me, to believe only in the eunuchs."

"No, my lord, my friend," Baudolino consoled him, "the kingdom of your father exists, because I have heard it spoken of not by the eunuchs but by people who believe in it. Faith makes things become true; my compatriots believed in a new city, one to inspire fear in a great emperor, and the city rose because they wanted to believe in it. The kingdom of the Priest is real because I and my companions have devoted two-thirds of our life to seeking it."

"Who knows?" the deacon said. "But even if it does exist, I will not see it."

"Now that's enough," Baudolino said to him one day. "You fear that the kingdom does not exist, and in waiting to see it, you decline in an endless boredom that will kill you. After all, you owe nothing to the eunuchs or to the Priest. They chose you, you were an infant and could not choose them. Do you want a life of adventure and glory?

403

Leave, mount one of our horses, go to the lands of Palestine, where valiant Christians are fighting the Moors. Become the hero you would like to be, the castles of the Holy Land are full of princesses who would give their life for one smile from you."

"Have you ever seen my smile?" the deacon then asked. With one movement he tore the veil from his face, and to Baudolino there appeared a spectral mask: eroded lips revealing rotten gums and foul teeth. The skin of the face was wrinkled, and patches of it had contracted baring the flesh, a repulsive pink. The eyes shone beneath bleary and gnawed lids. The brow was a single sore. He had long hair, and a wispy, forked beard covered what remained of his chin. The deacon removed his gloves, and scrawny hands appeared, marked by dark knots.

"This is leprosy, Baudolino. Leprosy, which spares neither kings nor the other powers of the earth. From the age of twenty I have borne this secret, of which my people are ignorant. I asked the eunuchs to send messages to my father, so he will know I will not live to succeed him, and so he may hasten to rear another heir—let them even say I am dead, I would go to hide in some colony of my similars and no one would hear of me again. But the eunuchs say that my father wants me to remain. And I don't believe it. For the eunuchs a frail deacon is convenient; perhaps I will die and they will go on keeping my embalmed body in this cavern, governing in the name of my corpse. Perhaps at the Priest's death one of them will take my place, and no one will be able to say that it is not I, because no one has ever seen my face, and in the kingdom they saw me only when I was still sucking my mother's milk. This, Baudolino, is why I accept death by starvation, I who am steeped to my bones in death. I will never be a knight, I will never be a lover. Even you now, unaware, have stepped back three paces. And as you may have noticed, Praxeas is always at a distance of at least five paces when he speaks to me. You see, the only ones who dare stand beside me are these two veiled eunuchs, young like me, stricken with the same disease, who can touch the objects I have touched, having nothing to lose. Let me cover myself again. Perhaps you will not consider me unworthy of your compassion, if not of your friendship."

"I sought words of consolation, Master Niketas, but I was unable to find any. Then I said to him that perhaps, more than all the knights who rode to attack a city, he was the true hero, who lived out his fate in silence and dignity. He thanked me, and, for that day, he asked me to leave. But by now I had grown fond of that unhappy man. I began seeing him daily, I told him of my past reading, the discussions heard at court. I described the places I had seen, from Ratisbon to Paris, from Venice to Byzantium, and then Iconium and Armenia, and the peoples we had encountered on our journey. He was fated to die without having seen anything but the caves of Pndapetzim, so I tried to make him live through my tales. And I may also have invented: I spoke to him of cities I had never visited, of battles I had never fought, of princesses I had never possessed. I told him of the wonders of the lands where the sun dies. I made him enjoy the sunsets on the Propontis, the emerald glints on the Venetian lagoon, the valley in Hibernia where seven white churches lie on the shores of a silent lake; I told him how the Alps are covered with a soft white substance that in summer dissolves into majestic cataracts and is dispersed in rivers and streams along slopes rich in chestnut trees; I told him of the salt deserts that extend along the coasts of Apulia; I made him shiver as I described seas I had never sailed, where fish leap as big as calves, so tame that men can ride them; I reported the voyages of Saint Brendan to the Isles of the Blest, and how one day, believing he had reached a land in the midst of the sea, he descended on the back of a whale, which is a fish the size of a mountain, capable of swallowing a whole ship, but I had to explain to him what ships were, fish made of wood that cleave the waves, while moving white wings; I listed for him the wondrous animals of my country, the stag, who has two great horns in the form of a cross, the stork, who flies from one land to another, and takes care of its own parents when they are old, bearing them on its back through the skies, and the ladybug, which is like a small mushroom, red and dotted with milk-colored spots, the lizard, which is like a crocodile, but so small it can pass beneath a door, the cuckoo, who lays her eggs in the nests of other birds, the owl, whose round eyes in the night seem two lamps and who lives eating the oil of lamps in churches; the hedgehog, its back covered with sharp quills who sucks the milk of cows, the oyster, a living jewel box that sometimes produces a dead beauty but of inestimable value, the nightingale that keeps vigil singing and lives worshiping the rose, the lobster, a loricate monster of a flame-red color, who flees backwards to escape the hunters who dote on its flesh, the eel, frightful aquatic serpent with a fatty, exquisite flavor, the seagull, that flies over the waters as if it were an angel of the Lord, but emits shrill cries like a devil, the blackbird, with yellow beak, that talks like a human, a sycophant repeating the confidences of its master, the swan, that regally parts the water of a lake and sings at the moment of its death a very sweet melody, the weasel, sinuous as a maiden, the falcon that dives on its prey and carries it back to the knight who has trained it. I imagined the splendor of gems that he had never seen—nor had I—the purplish and milky patches of murrhine, the flushed and white veins of certain Egyptian stones, the whiteness of orichalc, transparent crystal, brilliant diamond; and then I sang the praises of the splendor of gold, a soft metal that can be transformed into the finest leaf, the hiss of the red-hot slivers when they are plunged into water to be tempered, and the unimaginable reliquaries to be seen in the treasures of the great abbeys, the high and pointed spires of our churches, the high and straight columns of the Hippodrome of Constantinople, the books the Jews read, scattered with signs that seem insects, and the sounds they produce when they read them, and how a great Christian king had received from a caliph an iron cock that sang alone at every sunrise, then what a sphere is that turns belching steam, and how the mirrors of Archimedes burn, how frightening it is to see a windmill at night, and I told him also of the Grasal, of the knights still searching for it in Brittany, about ourselves and how we would give it to his father as soon as we found the unspeakable Zosimos. Seeing that these splendors fascinated him, but their inaccessibility saddened him, I thought it was good to convince him that his suffering was not the worst, to tell him of the torment of Andronicus with such details that they far surpassed what had been done to him, of the massacres of Crema, of prisoners with a hand, an ear, the nose cut off, I brought before his eyes images of indescribable maladies compared to which leprosy was the lesser evil, I told him how horrendously horrible were scrofula, erysipelas, St. Vitus' dance, shingles, the bite of the tarantula, scabies, which makes you scratch your skin, scale by scale, and the pestiferous action of the asp, the torture of Saint Agatha, whose breasts were torn away, and that of Saint Lucy, whose eyes were gouged out, and of Saint Sebastian, pierced by arrows, of Saint Stephen, his skull shattered by stones, of Saint Lawrence, roasted on a grill over a slow fire, and I invented other saints and other atrocities, such as Saint Ursicinus, impaled from the anus to the mouth, Saint Sarapion, flayed, Saint Mopsuestius, his four limbs bound to four horses, crazed and then quartered, Saint Dracontius, forced to swallow boiling pitch . . . It seemed to me these horrors brought him some relief, but then I feared I had gone too far and I began describing the world's other beauties, often a solace of prisoner's thoughts: the grace of Parisian girls, the lazy opulence of the Venetian prostitutes, the incomparable complexion of an empress, the childish laugh of Colandrina, the eyes of a far-off princess. He became excited, asked me to tell him more, wanted to know what the hair was like of Melisenda, countess of Tripoli, the lips of those abundant beauties who had enchanted the knights of Broceliande more than the Holy Grasal itself. He became excited; God forgive me, I believe that once or twice he had an erection and felt the pleasure of casting his seed. And more, I tried to make him understand how the universe was rich in spices with languid scents, and, since I had none with me, I tried to recall the names of both the spices I had known and those I had only heard of, words that would intoxicate him like perfumes, and for him I listed malabaster, incense, nard, lycium, sandal, saffron, ginger, cardamom, senna, zedoaria, laurel, marjoram, coriander, dill, thyme, clove, sesame, poppy, nutmeg, citronella, curcuma, and cumin. The deacon listened, on the threshold of delirium, touched his face as if his poor nose could not bear all those fragrances; he asked, weeping, what they had given him to eat till now, those accursed eunuchs, on the pretext that he was ill, goat's milk and bread soaked in *burq,* which they said was good for leprosy, and he spent his days stunned, almost always sleeping and with the same taste in his mouth, day after day."

"You were hastening his death, carrying him to the extreme frenzy, the consumption of all the senses. And you were satisfying your own taste for fairy tales; you were proud of your inventions."

"Perhaps. But for the short while he still lived, I made him happy. And then, I am telling you of these conversations of ours as if they all took place in one day, but in me too a new flame had been kindled, and I lived in a state of constant exaltation, which I tried to transmit to him, giving him, in disguise, some of my own happiness. I had met Hypatia."

32

Baudolino sees a lady with a unicorn

"Before that, there was the story of the army of monsters, Master Niketas. The terror of the White Huns had grown, and was more obsessive than ever, because a skiapod who had ventured to the extreme boundaries of the province (those creatures at times liked to run, infinitely, as if their will were dominated by that one tireless foot) came back and reported having seen them: they had yellow faces, with very long mustaches, and were short of stature. Mounted on horses, small as they were, but very swift, they seemed to form a single body. They traveled through deserts and steppes, carrying only, besides their weapons, a leather flask for milk and a little earthen pan for cooking the food that they found along the way, but they could ride for days and days without eating or drinking. They had attacked the caravan of a caliph, with slaves, odalisques, camels; they encamped in sumptuous tents. The caliph's warriors moved towards the Huns, and they were handsome and awful to see, gigantic men who dashed forward on their camels, armed with terrible curved swords. Under that rush, the Huns pretended to retreat, drawing their pursuers after them, then they formed a circle, swooping around them, and letting out fierce cries, as they massacred them. They invaded the camp and cut the throats of all the survivors—women, servants, all, even the children—leaving alive only one witness of the slaughter. They fired the tents and resumed their ride without even indulging in pillage, a sign that they destroyed only to spread everywhere the word that where they passed grass no longer grew, and at the next conflict their victims would already be paralyzed with terror. It may be that the skiapod spoke after he had refreshed himself with *burq*, but who could verify whether he was reporting things seen or was raving? Fear began to spread in Pndapetzim; you could sense it in the air, in the low voices of the people as they spread news from mouth to mouth, as if the invaders could already hear them. At this point the Poet decided to take seriously the offers of Praxeas, even if they had been disguised as a drunkard's ravings. He said the White Huns could arrive any moment, and what could he oppose them with? The nubians, of course, fighters prepared for sacrifice, but then? Except for the pygmies, who could handle a bow against the cranes, would the skiapods fight bare-handed, would the ponces attack with member shouldered, would the tongueless be sent out as advance scouts to report what they had seen? Yet from that collection of monsters, exploiting the possibilities of each, a fearsome army could be assembled. And if there was anyone who knew how to do it, it was the Poet."

"One can aspire to the imperial crown after having been a victorious general. At least so it has happened several times with us in Byzantium."

"To be sure, this was the intention of my friend. The eunuchs agreed at once. In my opinion, as long as they remained at peace, the Poet and his army did not represent a danger, and if there was to be a war, they might at least delay the entry of those wild men into the city, causing them to spend more time crossing the mountains. And besides, the building of an army kept the subjects in a state of obedient wakefulness, and this is surely what they had always wanted."

Baudolino, who did not like war, asked to be left out. Not the others. The Poet decided the five Alessandrians would be good captains, because he had experienced the siege of their city, and on the other side, the side of the defeated. He trusted also Ardzrouni, who perhaps could teach the monsters how to build some war machines. He did not overlook Solomon: an army, he said, must include a man expert in medicine, because you don't make an omelet without breaking eggs. In the end, he decided that even Boron and Kyot, whom he considered dreamers, could have a function in his plan, because as men of letters they could keep the army's books, tend to the stores, provide for the feeding of the warriors.

He carefully pondered the nature and the virtues of the various races. The nubians and the pygmies were ideal: he had only to decide where to deploy them in a future battle. The skiapods, swift as they were, could be used as assault squads: they could approach the enemy, slipping rapidly among ferns and grasses, popping up suddenly before those yellow faces with the big mustaches could be aware of them. They had only to be trained in the use of the blowpipe, or the fistula, as Ardzrouni suggested, easy to construct, since the area abounded in canebrakes. Perhaps Solomon, among all those herbs in the market, could find a poison in which arrows could be dipped, and he shouldn't go all squeamish because war is war. Solomon replied that his people, in the days of Masada, had given the Romans a hard time, because the Jews weren't people who suffered a slap without speaking up, as the gentiles might believe.

The giants could be employed well, not at a distance, because of that single eye of theirs, but for close fighting, perhaps jumping out of the grass right after the attack of the skiapods. With their height, they would completely overshadow the tiny horses of the White Huns, able to stop them with a punch on the nose, grabbing their mane with their bare hands, shaking them until the rider fell from his saddle, then finishing him off with a kick, since their feet were twice as big as a skiapod's.

The employment of the blemmyae, the ponces, and the panotians remained more complicated. Ardzrouni suggested that these last,

411

with those ears, could be used to glide down from above. If birds keep themselves in the air by flapping their wings, why couldn't the panotians do it with their ears. Boron agreed, and luckily they don't flap them in a vacuum. So the panotians were to be kept for the unhappy moment when the White Huns, having overcome the first defenses, entered the city. The panotians would await them in their high cliffside refuges, then would fall on their heads to slit their throats, if they were well trained in the use of the knife, even one made of obsidian. The blemmyae could not be used as lookouts, because in order to see they would have to expose their chests, and in combat this would be suicide. However, cleverly deployed, as an assault force they wouldn't be bad, because the White Hun has been (it was presumed) accustomed to aim at the head and, confronted by an enemy without a head, there would be at least a moment of bewilderment. This moment was what the blemmyae could exploit, falling on the horses with stone axes.

The ponces were the weak element in the Poet's military science, for how can you send people into the field with their penis on their belly? They would take the first impact on their balls, knocked flat on the ground, crying for their mother. They could, however, be used as sentries, because the friends had discovered that for the ponces that penis was like the antennae of certain insects, which at the slightest shift in the wind or change of temperature, stiffen, and start vibrating. And so they could act as scouts, sent ahead, and then if they all ended up being the first killed, the Poet said, war is war and leaves no room for Christian pity.

As for the tongueless, the first thought was that they could be left to stew in their own juice because they were so undisciplined; for a general they could create more problems than the enemy. Then it was decided that, after duly scourging them, they could work in the rear lines, helping the younger eunuchs, who, with Solomon, would tend the wounded, while keeping the women and children of every race calm, careful not to stick their head out of their holes.

Gavagai, at their first encounter, had mentioned the satyrs-that-are-never-seen, and the Poet presumed they could strike with their horns, and leap goatlike on their forked hoofs, but every question concerning this race received only evasive answers. They lived on the mountain, beyond the lake (which one?) and naturally no one had ever seen them. Formally subjects of the Priest, they lived to them-selves, never dealing with the others, and so it was as if they did not exist. Oh, well, the Poet said, they might even have curved horns, with the tips turned in or out, and to strike they'd have to lie on their backs or move on all fours; let's be serious about this: you can't con-duct a war with goats.

"Yes, you can conduct a war with goats," Ardzrouni said. He told of a great general who had tied torches to the horns of goats and then sent thousands of them at night into the plains from which the ene-mies were arriving, making them believe that the defenders had an immense army at their command. Since they had goats with six horns available, the effect would be powerful. Imposing. "That's if the enemy arrives at night," the Poet remarked, skeptically. In any case, Ardzrouni should prepare many goats and many torches. You never know.

On the basis of these principles, unknown to Vegetius and Fron-tinus, the training program began. The plain was populated with skia-pods, who practiced blowing into their brand-new fistulas, while Porcelli cursed every time they missed the target, and thank God he confined himself to cursing Christ, and for those heretics taking the name in vain of one who was only an adoptive son was not a sin. Colandrino took charge of teaching the panotians to fly, something they had never done, but it seemed as if the Almighty had created them for that very purpose. It was hard to move about the streets of Pndapetzim because, when you least expected it, a panotian would fall on your head. But all had accepted the idea that they were making ready for a war, and nobody complained. Happiest of all were the panotians, so amazed at discovering their incredible talents that by now even the women and children wanted to take part in the enter-prise, and the Poet gladly consented.

Scaccabarozzi trained the giants in the capture of horses, but the only horses around were those of the Magi, and after two or three sessions the animals risked giving up the ghost, so Bonehead turned to the asses. They were even better, because the asses kicked and brayed, and it was harder to catch them by the collar than a galloping horse, and the giants now became masters of this skill. However, they also had to learn how to run, bent over, through the ferns, so as not to be seen immediately by the enemies, and many of them com-plained because after every drill they had aching backs.

Boidi trained the pygmies, because a White Hun is not a crane and you had to aim between the eyes. The Poet himself indoctrinated the nubians, who were waiting for nothing better than to die in battle. Solomon looked for venomous potions and kept trying to dip some sharp point into them, but he managed only to put a rabbit to sleep for a few minutes, and another time he inspired a hen to fly. No mat-ter, the Poet said, a White Hun who falls asleep for the duration of a Benedicite or who starts flapping his arms is already a dead Hun. Keep at it.

Cuttica wore himself out with the blemmyae, teaching them to crawl under a horse and slice his belly with an axe blow, but trying this with an ass was not easy. As for the ponces, since they were part of the quartermaster corps, they were under the care of Boron and Kyot.

Baudolino informed the deacon of what was happening, and the young man seemed reborn. With the eunuchs' permission, he had himself led out onto the steps and from above he observed the drilling troops. He said he wanted to learn how to mount a horse, to lead his subjects, but immediately he felt faint, perhaps from excess emotion, and the eunuchs conducted him back to the throne, to lan-guish again.

It was during those days that, partly from curiosity and partly from boredom, Baudolino asked himself where the satyrs-that-are-never-seen might live. He asked everybody, even questioning one of the ponces, though he had never managed to decipher their language. The reply was: "*Prug frest frinss sorgdmand strochdt drhds pag brlelang gravot chavygny rusth pkalhdrcg,*" which wasn't much. Even Gavagai remained vague. Over there, he said, and he pointed to a series of bluish hills to the west, beyond which the distant mountains stood out, but over there was a place no one had ever gone, because the satyrs don't like intruders. "How do the satyrs think?" Baudolino asked, and Gavagai answered that they thought most wrong of all, because they held that there had never been original sin. Men had not become mortal as a result of that sin; they would be so even if Adam had never eaten the apple. So there is no need of redemption, and each can save himself through his own good will. The whole Jesus story served only to offer us an example of a virtuous life and nothing else. "Almost like the heretics of Mahumeth, who believes Jesus is only a prophet."

Asked why no one ever went to the satyrs' country, Gavagai answered that at the foot of the satyrs' hill there was a wood with a lake, and all were forbidden to go there, because it was inhabited by a race of bad women, all pagans. The eunuchs said that a good Christian does not go there, because he could encounter witchcraft, and no one went. But Gavagai, slyly, described so well the path to that place that it could be thought that he, or some other skiapod, in their dashing all over, had taken a peek there.

This was enough to stir Baudolino's curiosity. He waited until nobody was paying any attention to him, mounted his horse, and in less than two hours he crossed a vast expanse of brush and reached the edge of the wood. He tied his horse to a tree and entered that green expanse, cool and scented. Stumbling over the roots that surfaced at every step, grazing enormous mushrooms of every color, he finally arrived at the shore of a lake beyond which rose the slopes of the satyrs' hills. It was the sunset hour, the waters of the lake, very clear, were darkening, reflecting the long shadow of the many cypresses that lined it. A deep silence reigned everywhere, not broken even by birds' song.

While Baudolino was meditating on the shores of that mirror of water, he saw emerge from the wood an animal he had never come upon in his life, but he recognized it immediately. It looked like a horse, a foal, it was all white and its movements were delicate and supple. On its well-shaped muzzle, just above the brow, it had a horn, also white, spiral in form, ending in a sharp point. It was the leocorn or, as Baudolino used to say when he was little, the leoncorn, or unicorn, the monoceros of his childish imaginings. He admired it, holding his breath, when behind it, from the woods, a female form appeared.

Tall, enfolded in a long garment that gracefully outlined two erect little breasts, the creature walked with the step of a languid cameleopard, and her garment swept the grass that enhanced the lake shore, as if she were gliding over the earth. She had long soft blond hair, which fell to her hips, and a very pure profile, as if she had been modeled after an ivory brooch. Her complexion was a faint pink, and that angelic face was turned towards the lake in an attitude of mute prayer. The unicorn meekly pawed at the ground around her, sometimes raising its face with its little nostrils quivering, to receive a caress.

Baudolino watched, rapt.

"You, Master Niketas, must bear in mind that since the beginning of my journey I had not seen a woman worthy of that name. Don't misunderstand me: it was not desire that had overcome me, but a feeling of serene adoration, not just of her but also of the animal, the calm lake, the mountains, the light of that declining day. I felt as if I were in a temple."

Baudolino was trying, with his words, to describe his vision—something that is surely impossible.

"You see, there are moments when perfection itself appears in a hand or in a face, in some nuance on the flank of a hill or on the sea's surface, moments when your heart is paralyzed before the miracle of beauty.... That creature seemed to me at that moment a superb aquatic bird, a heron, or a swan. I said her hair was blond, but no: as the head slowly moved, the hair at times had bluish glints, at other times it seemed to have a light fire running through it. I could see the outline of her bosom, soft and delicate as the breast of a dove. I had become nothing but pure gaze. I saw something ancient, because I knew I was not seeing something beautiful, but beauty itself, like the holy thought of God. I was discovering that perfection, even glimpsing it once, and once only, was something light and lovely. I looked at that form from the distance, but I felt that I had no hold on that image, as happens when you are on in years and you seem to glimpse clear signs on a parchment, but you know that the moment you move closer they will blur, and you will never be able to read the secret that the page was promising you—or, as in dreams, when something you desire appears to you, you reach out, move your fingers in the void, and grasp nothing."

"I envy you that enchantment."

"Rather than shatter it, I transformed myself into a statue."

33

Baudolino meets Hypatia

But the enchantment was finished. A creature of the woods, the maiden sensed the presence of Baudolino, and turned towards him. She had not an instant of fear, only a bewildered gaze.

She said in Greek: "Who are you?" When he did not answer, she boldly approached him, examining, studying him closely, without shame and without coyness; and her eyes were like her hair, of shifting color. The unicorn had come to her side, his head lowered, as if to extend his beautiful weapon in the defense of his mistress.

"You are not from Pndapetzim," she then said. "You are neither a eunuch nor a monster. You are ... a man!" She showed that she recognized a man, as he had recognized the unicorn, from having heard man mentioned many times, but never having seen one. "You are beautiful, a man is beautiful. May I touch you?" She reached out and, with her slender fingers, she stroked his beard and grazed the scar on his face, as Beatrice had done that day. "This was a wound. Are you one of those men who make war? And what is that?"

"A sword," Baudolino answered, "but I use it in my defense against wild beasts; I am not a man who makes war. My name is Baudolino, and I come from the lands where the sun sets, over there," and he made a vague gesture. He noticed that his hand was trembling. "Who are you?"

"I'm a hypatia," she said, with the tone of someone amused to hear such a naive question, and she laughed, becoming still more beautiful. Then, remembering that she was speaking with a foreigner: "In this wood, beyond those trees, only we hypatias live. You're not afraid of me, like those of Pndapetzim are?" This time it was Baudolino who smiled: it was she who feared he was afraid. "Do you come here to the lake often?" he asked. "Not always," the hypatia answered. "Our mother does not wish us to come out of the wood alone. But the lake is so beautiful, and Acacios protects me." She pointed to the unicorn. Then she added, with a worried look, "It is late. I must not stay away so long. I should not meet the people of Pndapetzim either, if they come this far. But you are not one of them, you are a man, and no one has ever told me to keep away from men."

"I'll come back tomorrow," Baudolino dared to say, "but when the sun is high in the sky. Will you be here?"

"I don't know," the hypatia said, troubled, "perhaps." And she vanished lightly among the trees.

That night Baudolino couldn't sleep; in any case—he said—he had already dreamed, enough to remember that dream for all his life. However, the next day, just at noon, he took his horse and returned to the lake.

He waited till evening, not seeing anyone. Dejected, he turned towards home, and at the edge of the city he ran into a group of skiapods who were practicing with their fistulas. He saw Gavagai, who said to him: "You, look!" He aimed the reed up high, fired the dart, and killed a bird, which fell nearby. "I great fighter," Gavagai said, "if White Hun arrive I pass through him!" Baudolino congratulated him, and went off at once to sleep. That night he dreamed of the previous day's encounter and in the morning he told himself that one dream is not enough for a whole life.

He went back to the lake again. He remained seated by the water, listening to the song of the birds, who were celebrating morning, then the cicadas, at the hour when the noonday devil rages. But it was not hot, the trees spread a delightful coolness, and it cost him no pain to wait there for a few hours. Then she reappeared.

She sat down beside him and told him she had come back because she wanted to learn more about men. Baudolino didn't know where to begin, and he started describing the place where he was born, the events of Frederick's court, what empires are and kingdoms, how you hunt with a falcon, what a city is and how you build one, the same things he had told the deacon, avoiding grim or lewd stories, and realizing, as he spoke, that men could even be portrayed with affection. She listened to him, her glistening eyes changing color according to her emotion.

"How well you talk. Do all men tell beautiful stories like you?" No, Baudolino admitted, perhaps he told more and better ones than the others of his race, but among them there were also the poets, who could speak better still. And he began singing one of Abdul's songs. She didn't understand the Provençal words but, like the Abcasia, she was bewitched by the melody. Now her eyes were veiled with dew.

"Tell me," she asked, blushing slightly, "do men also have their... their females?" She asked this as if she had understood that what Baudolino sang was addressed to a woman. Yes, indeed, Baudolino answered, just as male skiapods mate with female skiapods, so men mate with women; otherwise they cannot make children, and that's how it is, he added, in the whole universe.

"That's not true," the hypatia said, laughing, "hypatias are simply hypatias, and there are no—how can I say it?—no hypatios!" And she laughed again, amused at the very idea. Baudolino wondered what it would take to hear her laugh again, because her laughter was the sweetest sound he had ever heard. He was tempted to ask her how

420

hypatias are born, but was afraid of marring her innocence. At this point, however, he did feel encouraged to ask her who the hypatias were.

"Oh," she said, "it's a long story; I don't know how to tell long stories the way you do. You must realize that a thousand thousand years ago, in a powerful and distant city, there lived a wise and virtuous woman named Hypatia. She had a school of philosophy, which means love of wisdom. But in that city also some bad men lived, who were called Christians; they did not fear the gods, they felt hatred towards philosophy and they particularly could not tolerate the fact that a female should know the truth. One day they seized Hypatia and put her to death amid horrible tortures. Now some of the younger of her female disciples were spared, perhaps because they were believed to be ignorant maidens who were with her only to serve her. They fled, but the Christians by now were everywhere, and the girls had to journey a long time before reaching this place of peace. Here they tried to keep alive what they had learned from their mistress, but they had heard her speak when they were still very young, they were not wise as she had been, and they didn't remember clearly all her teachings. So they told themselves they would live together, apart from the world, to rediscover what Hypatia had really said. Also because God has left shadows of truth in the depths of the heart of each of us, and it is a matter only of bringing them forth, to shine in the light of wisdom, as you free the pulp of a fruit from its skin."

God, the gods, which if they were not the God of the Christians were necessarily false and treacherous...But what was this hypatia saying? Baudolino wondered. However, it mattered little to him, for him it was enough to hear her and he was already prepared to die for her truth.

"Tell me one thing at least," he interrupted her. "You are the hypatias, in the name of that Hypatia: this I can understand. But what is your name?"

"Hypatia."

"No, I mean you—yourself—what are you called? To distinguish you from another hypatia . . . I'm asking: what do your companions call you?"

"Hypatia."

"But this evening you will go back to the place where all of you live, and you will meet one hypatia before the others. How will you greet her?"

"I will wish her a happy evening. That's what we do."

"Yes, but if I go back to Pndapetzim, and I see, for example, a eunuch, he will say to me: Happy evening, O Baudolino. You will say: Happy evening, O . . . what?"

"If you like, I will say: Happy evening, Hypatia."

"So all of you then are called Hypatia."

"Naturally. All hypatias are called Hypatia, no one is different from the others, otherwise she wouldn't be a hypatia."

"But if one hypatia or another is looking for you, just now when you are absent, and asks another hypatia if she has seen that hypatia who goes around with a unicorn named Acacios, how would she say it?"

"Just as you did. She is looking for the hypatia who goes around with a unicorn named Acacios."

If Gavagai had given him such an answer, Baudolino would have been tempted to slap him. But not with Hypatia: Baudolino already was thinking how marvelous the place must be, where all the hypatias were called Hypatia.

"But it took several days, Master Niketas, for me to understand what the hypatias really were. . . ."

"So you saw more of each other, I imagine."

"Every day, or almost. I couldn't do without seeing her and listening to her: this shouldn't surprise you, but it surprised me, and filled me with infinite pride, as I understood that she, too, was happy to see me and listen to me. I was . . . I was like a child again who seeks

422

its mother's breast, and when the mother is not present, he weeps for fear she will never come back again."

"It happens also to dogs with their masters. But this matter of the hypatias arouses my curiosity. Because perhaps you know, or don't know, that Hypatia really did exist, even if it was not a thousand thousand years ago, but, rather, eight centuries, and she lived in Alexandria in Egypt, when the empire was ruled by Theodosius and then by Arcadius. She really was, we are told, a woman of great wisdom, learned in philosophy, in mathematics, and in astronomy, and even men drank in her every word. In the meantime our holy religion had triumphed in all the territories of the empire. There were still some unruly people who were trying to keep alive the thought of the pagan philosophers, such as the divine Plato, and I will not deny that they were doing good, transmitting also to us Christians the learning that would have been lost otherwise. But one of the greatest Christians of the time, who later became a saint of the Church, Cyril, a man of great faith but also of great intransigence, considered Hypatia's teaching contrary to the Gospels and unleashed against her a horde of ignorant and enraged Christians, who didn't even know what she was preaching, but now considered her, with Cyril as witness, dissolute and a liar. Perhaps she was slandered, even if it is also true that women should not meddle in divine questions. In sum, they dragged her into a temple, stripped her naked, killed her, massacred her body with sharp shards of broken vessels, and put her corpse on a pyre.... Many legends sprang up about her. They say she was very beautiful, but had taken a vow of virginity. One young man, her disciple, fell madly in love with her, and she showed him a cloth with the blood of her menses, telling him that only this was the object of his desire, not beauty itself.... In reality, what she taught no one has ever known exactly. All her writings were lost; those who had preserved her spoken thought had been killed, or had tried to forget what they had heard. Everything we know of her has been handed down to us by the holy fathers who condemned her, and, honestly, as a writer of history and chronicles, I tend not to give too much credence to words that an enemy puts into the mouth of an enemy."

They had other meetings and many conversations. Hypatia would talk, and Baudolino hoped her learning was extensive, infinite, so he would never stop hanging on her lips. She answered all of Baudolino's questions, with intrepid sincerity, never blushing: nothing for her was restricted by any sordid prohibition, all was transparent.

Baudolino finally dared ask her how the hypatias, after so many centuries, perpetuated themselves. She answered that at every season the Mother chose some of them who would procreate, and she accompanied them to the fecundators. Hypatia was vague about these; naturally, she had never seen them, nor had she ever seen the hypatias destined for the rite. They were led to a place, at night, they drank a potion that inebriated and dazed them, they were fecundated, then they returned to their community, where those who remained pregnant were tended by their companions until the birth: if the fruit of their womb was male, it was returned to the fecundators, who would bring it up as one of themselves; if it was female, it remained in the community and grew up as an hypatia.

"To be joined carnally," Hypatia said, "like animals, who have no soul, is only a way of multiplying the error of creation. The hypatias sent to the fecundators accept this humiliation only because we must continue to exist, to redeem the world from that error. Those who have undergone fecundation remember nothing of that act, which, if it were not performed in the spirit of sacrifice, would alter our apathy...."

"What is apathy?"

"The state in which every hypatia lives and is happy to live."

"What is the error of creation?"

"Why, Baudolino," she said, laughing with innocent amazement, "does it seem to you that the world is perfect? Look at this flower, look at the delicacy of the stem, look at this kind of porous eye that triumphs in its catch of the morning dew as in a shell, look at the joy with which it offers itself to this insect that now is sucking its juice . . . Isn't it beautiful?"

"It is indeed beautiful. But, in fact, isn't it beautiful that it is beautiful? Isn't this a divine miracle?"

"Baudolino, tomorrow morning this flower will be dead, in two days it will be rotten. Come with me." She led him into the brush and showed him a mushroom, its red crown striped with yellow flames.

"Is this beautiful?" she said.

"It is beautiful."

"It's poisonous. Anyone who eats it, dies. Do you consider a creation perfect when death is hiding in it? You know that I, too, would be dead one day, and I, too, would be rotten matter, if I were not dedicated to God's redemption?"

"God's redemption? Explain . . ."

"Surely you're not a Christian, too, Baudolino, like the monsters of Pndapetzim? The Christians who killed Hypatia believed in a cruel divinity who had created the world, and, with it, death, suffering and—even worse than physical suffering—the sickness of the soul. Created beings are capable of hating, killing, of making their fellows suffer. You can't believe that a just God could have destined his children to this misery. . . ."

"These things are done by unjust men, and God punishes them, while saving the good."

"But then why would this God have created us, only to expose us to the risk of damnation?"

"Why? Because the supreme good is the freedom to do good or evil, and, to give his children this supreme good, God must accept the fact that some of them will make bad use of it."

"Why do you say that freedom is good?"

"Because if they deprive you of it, if they put you in chains, if they will not allow you to do what you wish, you suffer, and therefore the absence of freedom is an evil."

"You can turn your head so that you can look behind you, but can you really turn it until you can see your own back? Can you enter that lake and remain under water until evening, I mean really under water, without ever sticking your head out?" she asked, laughing.

"No, because if I tried to turn my head completely, I would break my neck, if I remained under water it would prevent me from breathing. God created me with these restrictions to prevent me from doing myself harm."

"Then you say that he has deprived you of some freedoms for a good end, is that right?"

"He took them from me so that I would not suffer."

"Then why has he given you the freedom to choose between good and evil, with the risk that you may then suffer eternal punishments?"

"God gave us freedom thinking that we would use it well. But there was the revolt of the angels, which brought evil into the world, and the serpent tempted Eve, so now we all suffer from original sin. It isn't God's fault."

"And who created the rebel angels and the serpent?"

"God, of course, but before they rebelled the angels were good, as he had made them."

"Then it was they who created evil?"

"No, they committed it, but it existed before, as a possibility of rebellion against God."

"So it was God who created evil?"

"Hypatia, you are clever, sensitive, quick, you can conduct a *disputatio* much better than I, even though I studied in Paris. But don't say such things to me about the good God. He cannot wish evil."

"Certainly not. A God who wishes evil would be the contrary of God."

"So?"

"So God found evil beside him, without wishing it, as the dark part of himself."

"But God is the totally perfect being!"

"Of course, Baudolino. God is the greatest perfection that can exist, but if you only knew what hard work it is to be perfect! Now, Baudolino, I'll tell you who God is, or, rather, what he is not."

She truly was afraid of nothing. She said: "God is the Unique, and he is so perfect that he does not resemble any of the things that exist or any of the things that do not; you cannot describe him using your human intelligence, as if he were someone who becomes angry if you are bad or who worries about you out of goodness, someone who has a mouth, ears, face, wings, or that is spirit, father or son, not even of himself. Of the Unique you cannot say he is or is not, he embraces all but is nothing; you can name him only through dissimilarity, because it is futile to call him Goodness, Beauty, Wisdom, Amiability, Power, Justice, it would be like calling him Bear, Panther, Serpent, Dragon, or Gryphon, because whatever you say of him you will never express him. God is not body, is not figure, is not form; he does not have quantity, quality, weight, or lightness; he does not see, does not hear, does not know disorder and perturbation; he is not soul, intelligence, imagination, opinion, thought, word, number, order, size; he is not equality and is not inequality, is not time and is not eternity; he is a will without purpose. Try to understand, Baudolino: God is a lamp without flame, a flame without fire, a fire without heat, a dark light, a silent rumble, a blind flash, a luminous soot, a ray of his own darkness, a circle that expands concentrating on its own center, a solitary multiplicity; he is...is..." She paused, seeking an example that would convince them both, she the teacher and he the pupil. "He is a space that is not, in which you and I are the same thing, as we are today in this time that doesn't flow."

A faint flame trembled on her cheek. He was silent, frightened by that incongruous example, but how could he consider incongruous any addition to a list of incongruities? Baudolino felt the same flame piercing his chest, but in his fear for her embarrassment, he stiffened, not allowing a single muscle of his face to betray the stirrings of his heart, nor his voice to tremble, and asked, with theological firmness: "But...creation then? And evil?"

Hypatia's face resumed its roseate pallor. "Then the Unique, because of his perfection, through generosity of himself, tends to expand, to widen in ever broader spheres of his own fullness; he is, like a candle, victim of the spreading light, the brighter it grows the more it melts. Yes, God liquefies in the shadows of himself, becomes a throng of divine messengers, Eons that have much of his power, but in a form already weaker. There are many gods, demons, Archons, Tyrants, Forces, Sparks, Stars, and what the Christians call angels or archangels....But they are not created by the Unique, they are an emanation of him."

"Emanation?"

"You see that bird? Sooner or later it will generate another bird through an egg, as a hypatia can generate a child from her womb. But, once generated, the creature, whether hypatia or little bird, lives on its own, survives even if the mother dies. Now think, on the contrary, of fire. Fire does not generate heat: it emanates it. Heat is the same thing as fire; if you were to put out the fire, the heat would also cease. The heat of the fire is very strong where the fire is born, and it becomes gradually weaker as the flame becomes smoke. So it is with God. As he gradually expands from his own dark center, he somehow loses vigor, and he loses more and more until he becomes viscous and insensitive matter, like the shapeless wax of the melting candle. The Unique could not wish to emanate so far from himself, but he cannot resist this dissolving of himself into multiplicity and disorder."

"And this God of yours cannot dissolve the evil that...that forms around him?"

"Oh, yes, he could. The Unique constantly tries to reabsorb this sort of breath that can become poison, and for seventy times seven thousand years he has succeeded continually to make his residue return into nothingness. The life of God was a regulated breathing, he panted without effort. Like this: listen." She breathed in the air, vibrating her delicate nostrils, then exhaled the breath from her mouth. "One day, however, he was unable to control one of his intermediary powers, which we call the Demiurge, and which is perhaps Sabaoth or Ildabaoth, the false God of the Christians. This imitation of God, through a mistake, or through pride, or through ignorance, created time, where before there had been only eternity. Time is an eternity that stammers. You understand? And with time, he created fire, which gives heat but also risks burning everything; water, which quenches thirst but also drowns; earth, which nourishes the grasses but can become avalanche and suffocate them; air, which lets us breathe but can become hurricane.... He did everything wrong, poor Demiurge. He made the sun, which gives light, but can scorch meadows; the moon, which succeeds in dominating night for only a few days, then grows thinner and dies; the other celestial bodies, which are splendid but can emit baleful influences, and then the creatures endowed with intelligence, but unable to understand the great mysteries; the animals, who are sometimes faithful and sometimes threaten us; the vegetables, which feed us but have brief life; the minerals, without life, without soul, without intelligence, condemned never to understand anything. The Demiurge was like a child, who messes in the mud to imitate the beauty of a unicorn, and what comes out looks more like a mouse!"

"So the world is a sickness of God?"

"If you are perfect, you cannot fail to emanate yourself; if you emanate yourself, you become sick. And you must try to understand that God, in his fullness, is also the place, or non-place, where the opposites are confounded, isn't he?"

"The opposites?"

"Yes. We feel heat and cold, light and darkness, and all those things that are one contrary to the other. Sometimes we do not like the cold, and to us it seems bad compared to heat; but sometimes the heat is too great, and we want coolness. We are the ones who, confronted with opposites, believe, as our whim, our passion takes us, that one of them is good and the other evil. Now, in God opposites are reconciled and find reciprocal harmony. But when God begins to be emanated, he can no longer control the harmony of the opposites, and this is broken and they fight with one another. The Demiurge has lost control of the opposites, and has created a world where silence and noise, yes and no, one good against another good fight among themselves. This is what we feel is evil. "

Warming to her argument, she moved her hands like a little girl who, speaking of a mouse, imitates its form, or, naming a tempest, draws whirlwinds in the air.

"You speak of the errors of creation, Hypatia, and of evil, but as if none of it touched you, and you live in this wood as if everything were beautiful like you."

"If evil itself comes from God, there must be something good in evil. Listen to me, because you are a man, and men are not used to thinking in the right way of everything that is."

"I knew it. I also think wrong."

"No, you just think. And thinking isn't enough; this isn't the right way. Now: try to imagine a spring that has no source and spreads out into a thousand rivers, without ever going dry. The spring remains calm always, cool and clear, while the rivers flow towards different places, and become murky with sand, become congested among rocks, and cough, strangled; and sometimes they run dry. Rivers suffer greatly; did you know that? And yet, however muddy the rivers or the streams may be, they are still water, and come from the same source as this lake. This lake suffers less than a river because in its clarity it recalls better the source from which it is born, a pond full of insects suffers more than a lake or a stream. But all in some way suffer because they would like to return whence they came, and they have forgotten how."

Hypatia took Baudolino by the arm, and made him turn towards the wood. As she did this, her head moved close to his, and he sensed the vegetal perfume of those tresses. "Look at that tree. What flows in it, from the roots to the last leaf, is the same life. But the roots are strengthened in the earth, the trunk grows sturdier and survives all the seasons, whereas the boughs tend to turn brittle and break, the leaves last a few months and then fall, the buds live a few weeks. There is more sickness in the fronds than in the trunk. The tree is one, but it suffers as it expands, because it becomes many, and in multiplying, it is weakened."

"But the fronds are beautiful; you yourself enjoy their shade...."

"You see, Baudolino? You, too, can become wise. If these fronds didn't exist, we wouldn't sit here and talk about God; if the wood didn't exist, we would never have met, and this perhaps would be the worst of evils."

She said this as if it were bare, simple truth, but Baudolino felt his chest pierced once again, unable or unwilling to reveal his tremor.

"Then explain this to me: how can the many be good, at least to some degree, if they are a sickness of the Unique?"

"You see, Baudolino? You, too, can become wise. You said, to some degree. In spite of error, a part of the Unique has remained in each of us thinking creatures; and also in each of the other creatures, from animals to dead bodies. Everything that surrounds us is inhabited by the gods: plants, seeds, flowers, roots, springs, each of them, though suffering at being only a bad imitation of the thought of God, could wish for nothing save to be united with him. We must find again the harmony between opposites, we must help the gods, we must revive these sparks, these memories of the Unique which lie still buried in our spirit and in things themselves."

Twice Hypatia had casually said that it was beautiful to be with him. This encouraged Baudolino to return.

One day Hypatia explained to him what they did to revive the divine spark in all things, because these things sympathetically referred to something more perfect than they, not directly to God, but to his

431

less extenuated emanations. She led him to a spot near the lake where some sunflowers grew, while lotus flowers spread over the water.

"You see what the heliotrope does? It moves following the sun, seeks it, prays to it, and it's too bad you still don't know how to listen to the murmur it makes in the air as it fulfills its circular motion in the arc of the day. You would realize that it sings its hymn to the sun. Now look at the lotus: it opens at sunrise, offers itself completely at the zenith, and closes when the sun goes away. It praises the sun, opening and closing its petals, as we open and close our lips when we pray. These flowers live in sympathy with the planet and therefore retain a part of its power. If you act upon the flower, you will act upon the sun, if you can act upon the sun, you can influence its action, and from the sun be joined with something that lives in sympathy with the sun, and is more perfect than the sun. This doesn't happen only with flowers; it happens with stones and with animals. Each of us is inhabited by a lesser god, who tries to connect us, through the more powerful, to our common origin. We learn from infancy to practice an art that allows us to act on the major gods and reestablish the lost bond."

"What does that mean?"

"It's easy. We learn to weave together stones, herbs, odors, perfect and godlike, to form—how can I say it to you?—some vessels of sympathy that condense the strength of many elements. You know, a flower, a stone, even a unicorn, all have a divine character, but by themselves they are unable to evoke the greater gods. Our compounds, thanks to art, reproduce the essence that one wants to evoke, they multiply the power of each element."

"And then—when you have evoked these greater gods?"

"That point is only the beginning. We learn to become messengers between what is above and what is below, we prove that the current in which God emanates himself can be retraced, only a short way, but we show nature that this is possible. The supreme task, however, is not to connect a sunflower with the sun, it is to connect ourselves with our origin. This is where ascesis begins. In the beginning, we learn to behave in a virtuous manner, we do not kill living creatures, we try to spread harmony among the beings that are around us, and in doing this, we can revive hidden sparks everywhere. You see these blades of grass? They are now yellowed, and are drooping to the ground. I can touch them and make them vibrate again, make them feel what they have forgotten. Look: little by little, they regain their freshness, as if they were just now springing from the earth. Yet this is not enough. To revive this blade of grass, it suffices to exercise the natural virtues, achieve perfection of sight and hearing, vigor of body, memory, and facility for learning, refinement of manners, through frequent ablutions, lustral ceremonies, hymns, prayers. You make a step forward by cultivating wisdom, strength, temperance, and justice, and finally you arrive at acquiring the purifying virtues: we try to separate the soul from the body, we learn to evoke the gods—not to speak of the gods, as the other philosophers did, but to act upon them, causing rains to fall through a magic sphere, setting amulets against earthquakes, testing the divinatory powers of tripods, animating statues to obtain oracles, summoning Asclepius to heal the sick. But you have to be careful: in doing this we must always avoid being possessed by a god, because in that case we become unruly and agitated, and therefore move away from God. We must learn to do this in the most absolute calm."

Hypatia took Baudolino's hand; he kept it motionless so as not to end that sensation of warmth. "Baudolino, perhaps I am making you believe I am already far advanced in ascesis, like my older sisters. . . . If you only knew, on the contrary, how imperfect I still am. I still become confused when I put a rose in contact with the superior power who is its friend. . . . And, you see? I still talk a great deal, and this is a sign that I am not wise, because virtue is won in silence. But I speak because you are here, and you must be instructed, and if I instruct a sunflower, why shouldn't I instruct you? We will reach a more perfect stage when we are able to be together without speaking; it will be enough to touch each other and you will understand all the same. As with the sunflower." She stroked the sunflower, in silence. Then, in silence, she began stroking Baudolino's hand, and said only, at the end: "You feel?"

The next day she spoke to him of the silence cultivated by the hypatias, in order, she said, for him to learn it too. "You have to create an absolute calm, all around you. You remain alone, remote from everything we have thought, imagined, and felt; you find peace and serenity. Then we will no longer experience wrath or desire, sorrow or happiness. We will have moved out of ourselves, rapt in absolute solitude and profound calm. We will no longer look at things beautiful and good; we will be beyond goodness itself, beyond the chorus of virtues, like someone entering the sanctum of the church, leaving behind the statues of the gods, as his vision is no longer of images but of God himself. We must stop invoking intermediary powers; passing beyond them, we will overcome the flaw, in that retreat, in that inaccessible and holy place, we will arrive beyond the race of the gods and the hierarchies of the Eons, all these things will now be in us as memory of something we have cured of its sickness of being. That will be the end of the journey, the loosening of every bond, the flight of one, now alone, towards the Only. In this return to the absolutely simple we will no longer see anything, except the glory of the darkness. Soul and intellect drained, we will arrive beyond the realm of the mind; in veneration we will rest there, as if we were a sun rising, with closed pupils we will gaze at the sun's light, we will become fire, fire in that darkness, and along paths of fire we will complete our arc. And, at that moment, when we have traveled against the current of the river, and have proved not only to ourselves but also to the gods and to God that one can move against the current, we will have healed the world, killed evil, made death die, we will have dissolved the knot in which the fingers of the Demiurge were entangled. We, Baudolino, are destined to heal God, to us his redemption has been entrusted; we will bring back, through our ecstasy, all creation in the very heart of the Unique One. We will give the Unique One the strength to take that great breath that enables him to absorb into himself the evil he has exhaled."

"You do it? Some one of you has done it?"

"We are waiting to succeed in it; all of us have been preparing ourselves, for centuries, so that one of us will succeed. What we have learned, since childhood, is that it's not necessary for all of us to achieve this miracle: it's enough if one day, even in another thousand years, just one of us, the chosen one, reaches the moment of supreme perfection, in which she feels one with her own remote origin, and the miracle will be achieved. Then, proving that from the multiplicity of the suffering world it is possible to return to the Unique, we will have given back to God peace and security, the strength to recompose himself in his own center, the energy to resume the rhythm of his own breath."

Her eyes were glistening, her complexion was as if warmed, her hands almost trembled, her voice had a heartbroken tone, and she seemed to be imploring Baudolino also to believe in that revelation. Baudolino thought that perhaps the Demiurge had made many errors, but the existence of this creature made the world an intoxicating place, sparkling with every perfection.

He could not resist, he boldly took her hand and grazed it with a kiss. She made a kind of start, as if she had experienced something unknown. "You, too, are inhabited by a god." Then she covered her face with her hands, and Baudolino heard her murmur, stunned: "I have lost. . . . I have lost my apathy. . . ."

She turned and ran towards the wood, without another word, without looking back.

"Master Niketas, at that moment I realized that I loved as I had never loved, but again loving the one woman who could not be mine. One woman had been taken from me by the sublimity of her station,

435

the other by the baseness of death, now the third could not belong to me because she was dedicated to the salvation of God. I moved away, I went to the city, thinking that perhaps I should never return. I felt almost relieved the next day, when Praxeas told me that, in the eyes of the inhabitants of Pndapetzim, I was surely the most authoritative of the Magi: I enjoyed the confidence of the deacon and I was the one the deacon wanted at the command of that army that the Poet was now training so well. I couldn't evade that invitation, a rupture in the group of the Magi would have made our situation untenable in the eyes of everyone, and all were by now so passionately devoting themselves to preparing for war, that I accepted—also so as not to disappoint the skiapods, the panotians, the blemmyae, and all those other fine people of whom I had become sincerely fond. Above all, I thought that, in dedicating myself to this new venture, I would forget what I had left behind in the wood. For two days I was taken up with a thousand duties. But as I worked hard, I was distracted, terrified by the idea that Hypatia might have come back to the lake and, not finding me there, would think that her flight had offended me, that I had decided never to see her again. I was distraught by the idea that she was distraught and wanted never to see me again. If that was so, I would have followed her trail, I would have ridden to the place where the hypatias lived. What would I have done? I would have abducted her, I would have destroyed the peace of that community, making her understand what she could not understand, or else—no—would I have seen her intent on her mission, now free from her moment, her infinitesimal moment of earthly passion? But then, had that moment existed? I relived her every word, her every movement. Twice, to illustrate how God was, she had used our encounter as an example, but perhaps it was only her way, childish, innocent, of making what she was saying comprehensible to me. Twice she had touched me, but as she might have touched a sunflower. My mouth on her hand had made her tremble, I knew, but that was natural: no human mouth had ever grazed her, for her it had been like stumbling over a root and

436

losing for an instant the composure she had been taught; the moment had passed, now she thought of it no more. . . . With my friends I discussed war measures, I had to decide where to deploy the Nubians and I didn't even understand where I was myself. I had to shake off that anguish, I had to know. For this, I had to put my life, and hers, in the hands of someone who would keep us in contact. I had already had ample proof of Gavagai's devotion. I spoke to him in secret, making him swear many oaths; I told him as little as possible but enough for him to go to the lake and wait. The good skiapod was truly generous, wise, and discreet. He asked me little, I believe he understood much; for two days he returned at sunset to tell me he had seen no one, and he was saddened, seeing me turn pale. The third day he arrived with one of those smiles of his that looked like a crescent moon and told me that, while he was waiting, lying blissfully under the umbrella of his foot, that creature had appeared. She had confidently approached him, eager, as if she were expecting to see someone. With emotion she had received my message ('She seems much to want to see you,' Gavagai said, with a certain malicousness in his voice) and made me understand that she would return to the lake every day, every day ('she said two times'). Perhaps, Gavagai commented slyly, she too had long awaited the Magi. I had to remain in Pndapetzim the next day also, but I attended to my duties as general with an enthusiasm that amazed the Poet, who knew how disinclined I was to arms, and I communicated the enthusiasm to my army. I seemed to be master of the world, I could have faced a hundred White Huns without fear. Two days later, I returned, trembling with fear, to that fateful place."

34

Baudolino discovers true love

"In those days of waiting, Master Niketas, I experienced conflicting emotions. I burned with the desire to see her, I feared I would never see her again, I imagined her prey to a thousand dangers; in short I felt all the sensations proper to love, but I did not feel jealousy."

"Didn't it occur to you that the Mother could have sent her to the fecundators just at that time?"

"That suspicion never crossed my mind. Perhaps, knowing to what extent I was now hers, I thought that she was so entirely mine that she would have refused to let others touch her. I pondered this at length, afterwards, and I was convinced that perfect love leaves no room for jealousy. Jealousy is suspicion, fear, and slander between lover and beloved, and Saint John said that perfect love casts out all fear. I felt no jealousy, but at every moment I tried to summon up her face, and I failed. Yet, during our meetings, I had done nothing but stare at her face, nothing else...."

"I have read that this is what happens when one feels intense love...." Niketas said, with the embarrassment of a man who had perhaps never felt such an overwhelming passion. "Hadn't that happened to you with Beatrice and with Colandrina?"

"No, not in a way to make me suffer so. I believe that with Beatrice I cultivated the very idea of love, which did not need a face, and
to me it seemed then a sacrilege to make any effort to imagine her
carnal features. As for Colandrina, I realized—after having known
Hypatia—that with her it had not been passion, but, rather, gaiety,
tenderness, very intense affection: what I might have felt, God forgive
me, for a daughter, or a younger sister. I believe it happens to all those
who fall in love, but in those days I was convinced that Hypatia was
the first woman I had truly loved, and certainly that is true, even now,
and forever. I then learned that true love dwells in the triclinium of
the heart, and finds there calm, alert to its own most noble secrets,
and rarely returns to the chambers of the imagination. For this reason it cannot reproduce the corporeal form of the absent beloved. It
is only love of fornication, which never enters the sanctum of the
heart, and feeds only on voluptuous fantasies, that manages to reproduce such images."

Niketas remained silent, controlling, with some effort, his envy.

Their reunion was shy and touching. Her eyes shone with happiness, but she immediately, modestly lowered her gaze. They sat down
on the grass. Acacios grazed peacefully nearby. The scent of the flowers around them was stronger than usual, and Baudolino was feeling
as if he had barely touched some *burq* with his lips. He didn't dare
speak, but he determined to do so because the intensity of that silence would have drawn him to some untoward action.

He understood only then why he had heard that true lovers, at
their first love meeting, turn pale, tremble, and are silent. It is because, since love dominates the realms of both nature and spirit, it at-
tracts to itself all their forces, however it may move. Thus, when true
lovers meet, love disturbs and almost petrifies all the functions of the
body, both physical and spiritual: whence the tongue refuses to speak,
the eyes to see, the ears to hear, and every limb shirks its proper duty.
This means that, when love delays too long in the depths of the heart,

the body, deprived of strength, wastes away. But at a certain point the heart, in the impatience of the ardor it feels, almost casts out its passion, allowing the body to resume its usual functions. And then the lover speaks.

"So it is," Baudolino said, without explaining what he was feeling and what he was understanding, "all the beautiful and terrible things you have told me of are what the first Hypatia has handed down to you...."

"Oh, no," she said. "I told you that our ancestresses fled, having forgotten everything Hypatia had taught them except the duty of knowledge. It is through meditation that we have increasingly discovered the truth. During all these thousands of years each of us has reflected on the world surrounding us, and on what she felt in her own spirit, and our awareness has been enriched day by day, and the task is not yet done. Perhaps in what I have told you there were things that my companions had not yet understood, but I have understood them, in trying to explain them to you. So each of us becomes wise, training her companions in what she feels, and, acting as teacher, she learns. Perhaps if you weren't here with me, I would not have clarified certain things to myself. You have been my demon, my beneficent archon, Baudolino."

"But are all your companions as clear and eloquent as you, my sweet Hypatia?"

"Oh, I am the least of them. Sometimes they tease me because I can't express what I feel. I still have to grow, you see. But these days I have felt proud, as if I possess a secret they don't know, and—I can't say why—I preferred it remain secret. I don't really understand what is happening to me; it's as if... as if I preferred to say things to you rather than to them. Do you think this is bad, that I am untrue to them?"

"You're true to me."

"With you it's easy. I think that with you I'd say everything that passes through my heart. Even if I weren't yet sure it is right. You

440

know what has happened to me, Baudolino, in these days? I have dreamed of you. When I woke in the morning, I thought it was a beautiful day because you were somewhere. Then I thought the day was bad because I didn't see you. It's strange: we laugh when we are happy, we weep when we suffer, and now I laugh and I weep at the same moment. Can I be ill? Yet it is a very beautiful illness. Is it right to love one's own illness?"

"You are my teacher, my sweet friend." Baudolino smiled. "You mustn't ask me, also because I believe I have your same illness."

Hypatia reached out and again lightly touched his scar. "You must be a good thing, Baudolino, because I like to touch you, as I like to touch Acacios. Touch me, too. Perhaps you can waken some spark that is still in me, that I don't know."

"No, my sweet love. I'm afraid of hurting you."

"Touch me here, behind my ear. Yes, like that, again . . . Perhaps, through you, something good can be called up. You must have somewhere the mark that binds you to something else. . . ."

She put his hands under her dress, she ran her fingers over the hair on his chest. She moved closer, to nuzzle him. "You are filled with grass, good grass," she said. Then she said further: "How beautiful you are underneath here, soft like a young animal. Are you young? I don't understand the age of a man. Are you young?"

"I am young, my love, I am just born."

He was now stroking her hair and almost with violence he placed his hands behind her nape. She began giving him little flicks of her tongue on his face, licking him as if he were a kid, then she laughed, looking closely into his eyes, and said he tasted of salt. Baudolino had never been a saint; he pressed her against himself and sought her lips with his. She emitted a moan of fear and surprise, tried to withdraw, then yielded. Her mouth tasted of peaches, apricots, and with her tongue she gave his tongue little jabs, as she tasted it for the first time.

Baudolino thrust her away, not out of virtue, but to free himself of what was covering him; she saw his member, touched it with her fingers, felt that it was alive and said that she wanted it. Clearly she didn't know how or why she wanted it, but some power of the woods or the streams was prompting her, telling her what she should do. Baudolino resumed covering her with kisses, moving from her lips to her neck, then her shoulders, while he slowly slipped off her robe, baring her breasts, plunged his face between them, and with his hands continued slipping the robe down over her hips, he felt the taut little belly, he touched her navel, felt, before he was expecting it, the soft down that concealed her supreme boon. She was whispering, calling him: my Eon, my Tyrant, my Abyss, my Ogdoad, my Plerome....

Baudolino thrust his hands under the robe still concealing her, and felt that the down that had seemed to herald her sex grew thicker, covered the beginning of her leg, the inner part of the thigh, extended towards the buttocks....

"Master Niketas, I tore off her robe, and I saw: from the belly down, Hypatia had goatlike forms, and her legs ended in a pair of ivory-colored hoofs. Suddenly I understood why, concealed by her robe that touched the ground, she didn't seem to walk like someone putting down feet, but moved lightly, as if she didn't move on the earth. And I realized who the fecundators were: they were the satyrs-who-are-never-seen, with horned human heads and ram's body, the satyrs who for centuries had lived in the service of the hypatias, giving them the females and rearing their own males, the latter with their same horrible face, the former still recalling the Egyptian loveliness of the beautiful Hypatia, the ancient, and of her first pupils."

"How horrible!" Niketas said.

"Horrible? No, what I felt wasn't horror. Surprise, yes, but only for one instant. Then I decided. My body decided for my soul, or my soul decided for my body: what I saw and touched was very beautiful, because it was Hypatia, and even her ferine nature was part of her grace; that pelt, soft and curly, was the most desirable thing I had ever desired; scented of musk, those limbs of hers, hidden at first, had

442

been designed by an artist's hand, and I loved, wanted that creature with her forest balm, and I would have loved Hypatia even if she had had the features of a chimera, an icneumon, a cerastes."

So it was that Hypatia and Baudolino were united, until sunset, and when they were exhausted, they lay one beside the other, stroking each other and calling each other by the most tender appellatives, heedless of all that surrounded them.

Hypatia said: "My soul has fled like a gust of fire. . . . I feel as if I were part of the starry vault. . . ." She could not cease exploring the body of her beloved: "How beautiful you are, Baudolino. But you men are also monsters," she teased. "Your legs are long and white, without fur, and your feet are as big as two skiapods! But you are beautiful all the same, indeed, more beautiful. . . ." He kissed her eyes in silence.

"Do the females of men also have legs like yours?" she asked, frowning. "Have you felt . . . ecstasy beside creatures with legs like ours?"

"I didn't know that you existed, my love."

"I don't want you ever again to look at the legs of the females of men." He kissed her hoofs in silence.

It was growing dark, and they had to separate. "I believe," Hypatia whispered, grazing his lips again, "I will tell my companions nothing. Perhaps they wouldn't understand; they don't know that there exists also this way to rise higher. Until tomorrow, my love. Did you hear? I have called you as you called me? I will wait for you."

"In this way several months went by, the sweetest and purest of my life. I went to her every day and, when I couldn't, the faithful Gavagai acted as our go-between. I was hoping the Huns would never arrive and that this waiting at Pndapetzim would last until my death, and beyond. But I felt as if I had defeated death."

And then, one day, after many months had passed, when she had given herself with the usual ardor and they were calm again, Hypatia said to Baudolino, "Something is happening to me. I know what it is, because I've heard the confidences of my companions when they came back from their night with the fecundators. I believe I have a child in my belly."

At that moment Baudolino was filled only with an ineffable joy and kissed that belly of hers, blessed by God or by the Archons, he didn't much care which. Then he became worried: Hypatia wouldn't be able to conceal her condition from the community; what would she do?

"I will confess the truth to the Mother," she said. "She will understand. Someone, something decided that what the others do with the fecundators I would do with you. It was right, according to the good part of nature. She won't be able to reproach me."

"But for nine months you will be held by the community, and afterwards I will never be able to see the infant that is born."

"I will come here for a long time still. It will take many days before my belly is very swollen and everyone realizes. It's only in the last weeks that we won't see each other, when I will tell the Mother everything. As for the child, if it's a male it will be given to you, and if female, it will be none of your concern. So nature wills."

"So wills that asshole of a Demiurge of yours and those half-goats you live with!" Baudolino cried, beside himself. "The child is mine, female or male as may be!"

"How beautiful you are, Baudolino, when you fly into a rage, even though you never should," she said, kissing his nose.

"Don't you realize? After a hypatia has given birth, she never sees the fecundator again. Isn't this, in your hypatias' view, what nature wants?"

She had realized as much only at this moment, and she began to cry, with little moans, as when she made love, her head bowed on the chest of her man, as she clasped his arms and he felt her throbbing breast against him. Baudolino caressed her, spoke tender words into her ear, and then made what seemed to him the only sensible suggestion: Hypatia should flee with him. At her frightened look, he told her that, in doing so, she wouldn't be betraying her community. She had simply been designated with a different privilege, and her duty became different. He would take her to a distant kingdom, and there she would create a new colony of hypatias, she would simply have made more fertile the seed of their remote mother, she would carry her message elsewhere, except that he would live at her side and would found a new colony of fecundators, in the form of man, as the fruit of their viscera would probably be. In running away you're not doing anything evil, he told her; on the contrary you are spreading good....

"Then I will ask permission of the Mother."

"Wait. I don't know yet what sort of person this Mother is. Let me think. We'll go to her together. I'll be able to convince her, give me a few days to think up the right way."

"My love, I don't want never to see you again." Hypatia was sobbing. "I'll do what you wish, I will pass as a female of men, I will come with you to that new city you have told me of, I will behave like the Christians, I will say that God had a son who died on a cross. If you are not here I don't want to be a hypatia any more!"

"Calm yourself, beloved. I'll find a solution, wait and see. I had Charlemagne made a saint, I rediscovered the Magi, I'll find a way to keep my bride!"

"Bride? What's that?"

"I'll teach you in time. Go now, it's late. We'll see each other tomorrow."

"There was no tomorrow, Master Niketas. When I went back to Pndapetzim, they all came rushing towards me: they had been seeking me for hours. All doubt was gone: the White Huns were arriving, at the far horizon you could glimpse the dust cloud raised by their horses. They would reach the edge of the plain of ferns by the first light of dawn. So we had only a few hours left to organize our defense.

445

I went at once to the deacon, to announce that I was assuming command of his subjects. Too late. Those months of anxious waiting for the battle, the effort it had cost him to remain standing and participate in the undertaking, perhaps even the new vigor that I had infused into his veins with my stories: all had hastened his end. I was not afraid to remain close to him as he was breathing his last, indeed, I clasped his hand as he bade me farewell and wished me victory. He told me that, if I were to win, I would perhaps be able to reach the kingdom of his father, and therefore he begged me to do him a last service. As soon as he was dead, his two veiled acolytes would prepare his corpse as if it were that of a priest, anointing his body with those oils that would imprint his image on the linen in which he would be wrapped. I was to take that portrait to the Priest, and pale as he might seem, he would show himself to his adoptive father less destroyed than he was. He died a little later, and the two acolytes did what had to be done. They said the sheet would require some hours to become impregnated with his features, and they would then roll it up and place it in a case. They shyly suggested I inform the eunuchs of the death of the deacon; I resolved not to do so. The deacon had invested me with the command and thanks to that distinction the eunuchs would not dare disobey me. They had somehow to collaborate in the war, preparing the city to receive the wounded. If they were to know immediately of the deacon's death, at the very least they would have troubled the spirit of the fighters, spreading the fatal news, and distracting them with funeral rites. At most, treacherous as they were, they might immediately assume supreme power and at the same time upset all the Poet's defense plans. To war then: I said to myself. Even though I had always been a man of peace, now it was a matter of defending the child that was to be born."

35

Baudolino against the White Huns

They had studied the plan for months, down to the slightest detail.
If the Poet, in training his troops, had proved himself a good captain,
Baudolino had revealed gifts as a strategist. Immediately, at the edges
of the city, rose the tallest of those hills like heaps of whipped cream,
which they had observed on arriving. From up there you dominated
the entire plain, as far as the mountains to one side, and beyond the
expanse of ferns. From there Baudolino and the Poet would direct the
movements of their warriors. Beside them, a select troop of skiapods,
trained by Gavagai, would allow rapid communication with the various squads.

The ponces would be dispersed in different parts of the plain,
ready to perceive, with their highly sensitive ventral member, the ad-
versary's movements and to send, as had been agreed, smoke signals.

In front of all the others, almost at the far edge of the plain, the
skiapods were to wait, under the command of Porcelli, ready to
emerge suddenly, confronting the invaders with their fistulas and
their poisoned darts. After the enemy columns had been caught off
guard by that first impact, behind the skiapods the giants would appear, led by Aleramo Scaccabarozzi known as Bonehead, destroying

the invaders' horses. But, the Poet urged, until they received the order to go into action, the giants were to advance on all fours.

If a part of the enemy forces were to get past the deployment of giants, then the pygmies would enter action under Boidi from one side of the plain, and, from the other the blemmyae led by Cuttica. Driven in one direction by the hail of the pygmies' arrows, the Huns would move towards the blemmyae and, before discerning them in the grass, the defenders could slip under the enemies' horses.

Each, however, was to avoid running great risk. They were to inflict severe losses on the enemy, but confine their own to the minimum. In fact, the real backbone of the strategy was the nubians, who were to wait, in formation, in the center of the plain. The Huns would surely win the first skirmishes, but they would be already reduced in number when they came up against the nubians, and would be covered with wounds, their horses prevented by the high grasses from moving rapidly. At this point the bellicose Circoncellions would be ready, with their mortiferous clubs and their legendary contempt for danger.

"Right. Strike and run," Boidi said. "The truly insuperable barrier will be the fine Circoncellions."

"And you," the Poet urged, "after the Huns have passed, must immediately re-form your ranks and deploy in a semicircle at least half-a-mile long. So if the enemy falls back on that childish trick of theirs, pretending to retreat in order to encircle their pursuers, you will be the ones to squeeze them between your pincers, as they run right into your arms. Most important: not one of them must remain alive. A defeated enemy, if he survives, sooner or later will plot revenge. Then if some survivor manages to escape, you and the nubians head towards the city. There the panotians are ready to fly against him, and a surprise like that is something no enemy can withstand."

The strategy had been so designed that nothing was left to chance, and at night the cohorts crowded into the center of the city and proceeded, by the light of the first stars, towards the plain, each preceded by its own priests and chanting in its own language the Pater Noster, with a majestic sonorous effect that had never been heard, not even in Rome in a most solemn procession:

Mael nio, kui vai o les zael, aepseno lezai tio mita. Veze lezai tio tsaeleda.

O fat obas, kel binol in süs, paisalidumöz nemola. Komönöd monargän ola.

Pat isel, ka bi ni sielos. Nom al zi bi santed. Klol alzi komi.

O baderus noderus, ki du esso in seluma, fakdade sankadus, hanominanda duus, adfenade ha rennanda duus.

Amy Pornio dan chin Orhnio viey, gnayjorhe sai lory, eyfodere sai bagalin, johre dai domion.

Hai coba ggia rild dad, ha babi io sgymta, ha salta io velca…

Last to file by were the blemmyae, as Baudolino and the Poet were questioning each other about their delay. When they did arrive, each was bearing above his shoulders, bound beneath the armpits, an armature of reeds at the top of which a bird's head was placed. With pride, Ardzrouni said that this was his latest invention. The Huns would see a head, would aim at it, and the blemmyae would be upon them, unharmed, in a matter of seconds. Baudolino said the idea was a good one, but they should hurry, because they had only a few hours to reach their position. The blemmyae did not seem embarrassed at having acquired a head, indeed; they swaggered as if they were wearing a plumed helmet.

Baudolino and the Poet, with Ardzrouni, climbed up the rise from which they were to direct the battle, and they awaited the dawn. They sent Gavagai with the front line, ready to keep them informed about what was happening. The brave skiapod ran to his battle station, with the cry of "Long live the most holy Magi, long live Pndapetzim!"

The mountains to the east were already glowing in the first solar rays when a wisp of smoke, fanned by the alert ponces, warned that the Huns were about to appear on the horizon.

And they did appear, in a long frontal line, so that from the distance it looked as if they were not advancing, but swaying or jerking, for a time that seemed very long to all. They realized the enemy was advancing only because, increasingly, the invaders were unable to see the hoofs of their horses, already concealed by the ferns from those who were watching at a distance, until the Huns were suddenly close to the hidden ranks of the first skiapods, and all expected, in a moment, to see those brave skiapods come out into the open. But time passed, the Huns advanced farther into the plain, and it was clear that something odd was happening down there.

Whereas the Huns by now were quite visible, the skiapods still showed no signs of life. It seemed that the giants, ahead of schedule, were rising, emerging, enormous, from the vegetation, but, instead of confronting the enemy, they threw themselves into the grass, engaged in a struggle with what ought to have been the skiapods. Baudolino and the Poet, from afar, couldn't really understand what was happening, but it was possible to reconstruct the stages of the battle, step by step, thanks to the courageous Gavagai, who sped like lightning from one end of the plain to the other. Through some atavistic instinct, when the sun rises, the skiapod is led to lie down and to shield his head with his foot. And so the assault troops had done. The giants, even if they were not exactly quick-witted, had sensed that something was going wrong, and had started goading them; but, following their heretical habit, they called them shit-monsters, Arian Excrement.

"Skiapod good and loyal," Gavagai said in despair, as he reported the news, "but won't take insults from cheese-eating heretics; you try to understand!" In short, first a rapid theological and verbal scuffle broke out, then a hand-to-hand fight, and the giants quickly got the upper hand. Aleramo Scaccabarozzi known as Bonehead had tried to detach his one-eyed fighters from that insane confrontation, but they had lost their minds and pushed him away with shoves that sent him flying ten yards off. So they didn't realize that the Huns were by now on top of them, and what followed was a massacre. Skiapods fell and giants fell, even if some of the latter tried to defend themselves, grabbing a skiapod by the foot and using him, in vain, as a bludgeon. Porcelli and Scaccabarozzi flung themselves into the fray, each to inspire his own troops, but the Huns surrounded them. Our friends defended themselves, bravely wielding their swords, but they were soon pierced by a hundred arrows.

Now the Huns could be seen driving their way forward, crushing the grasses, amid the victims of their slaughter. Boidi and Cuttica, at opposite sides of the plain, could not understand what was happening, and Gavagai had to be sent to them so they could accelerate the lateral intervention of the blemmyae and the pygmies. The Huns found themselves assaulted from opposite directions, but they had an inspired idea: their vanguard advanced beyond the forces of the fallen skiapods and giants, the rear guard withdrew, and so pygmies on the one hand and blemmyae on the other hurled themselves against each other. The pygmies, seeing those fowls' heads appear from the weeds, unaware of Ardzrouni's ruse, started shouting: "The cranes! The cranes!" and, believing they were confronting their age-old enemy, they forgot about the Huns and riddled the blemmyae host with arrows. Now the blemmyae were defending themselves against the pygmies and, believing themselves betrayed, were shouting: "Death to the heretics!" The pygmies, thinking the blemmyae had turned traitor, and hearing themselves branded with heresy, whereas they considered themselves the sole custodians of the true faith, cried in turn: "Kill the ghosters!" The Huns fell on that brawl and dealt deathblows, one by one, to their enemies, who were still striking one another. Gavagai now reported that he had seen Cuttica trying to arrest the enemies single-handed. But then, overwhelmed, he had fallen under the hoofs of their horses.

Boidi, at the sight of his dying friend, believed both forces lost, leaped on his horse, and tried to ride beyond the nubian barrier to alert them, but the ferns blocked him, as, for that matter, they also made difficulties for the advance of the enemies. With difficulty, Boidi reached the nubians, took his position behind them, and incited them to move, in one body, towards the Huns. But once he found them, thirsting for blood, in front of him, the doomed Circoncellions followed their nature, or, rather, their natural propensity for martyrdom. They thought the moment of sublime sacrifice had arrived, and it was best to hasten it. One after another, they fell to their knees, imploring: "Kill me, kill me!" The Huns could hardly believe their luck; they drew their short, finely honed swords and began slicing off heads of the Circoncellions who crowded around them, stretching their necks and invoking the purifying bloodbath.

Boidi, shaking his fist against the sky, turned and fled towards the hill, reaching it just before the plain burst into flames.

In fact, Boron and Kyot, from the city, warned of the danger, thought to make use of the goats that Ardzrouni had prepared for that stratagem of his, futile in full daylight. They had the tongueless push hundreds of animals, their horns afire, into the plain. The sea of grass was being transformed into a sea of flames. Perhaps Boron and Kyot had thought the flames would confine themselves to drawing a fire barrier, or would drive back the enemy cavalry, but they hadn't considered the direction of the wind. The fire gained strength, but it was spreading towards the city. This development surely favored the Huns, who had only to wait until the grasses were burned, the ashes cool, and then they would have the path free for their final gallop. But, one way or another, it arrested their advance for an hour. The Huns, however, knew they had time. They confined themselves to taking positions at the edges of the fire and, raising their bows to the sky, they shot so many arrows that the sky was darkened, and the arrows fell beyond the barrier, since the Huns couldn't know if other enemies were awaiting them.

One arrow fell, hissing from above and struck the neck of Ardzrouni, who dropped to the ground with a stifled cough, blood issuing from his mouth. Trying to put his hands to his neck and extract the arrow, he saw them gradually covered with whitish patches. Baudolino and the Poet bent over him and whispered to him that the same thing was happening to his face: "You see? Solomon was right," the Poet said to him, "a remedy did exist. Perhaps the Huns' arrows are soaked in a poison that for you is an antidote, and dissolves the effect of those black stones."

"What do I care if I die white or black?" Ardzrouni gasped, and he died, still of uncertain color. More arrows were now falling, thick and fast, and the hill had to be abandoned. They fled towards the city, with the stunned Poet, who said: "It's all over. I gambled a kingdom and lost. We can't expect much from the endurance of the panotians. Our only hope lies in the time the flames grant us. Let's collect our things and escape. To the west the path is still free."

Baudolino, at that moment, had only one thought. The Huns would enter Pndapetzim and would destroy it, but their mad dash would not stop there; they would press on, towards the lake, and invade the wood of the hypatias. He had to reach it before them. But he couldn't abandon his friends, he had to find them, they all had to collect their belongings, some provisions, prepare for a long flight. "Gavagai! Gavagai!" he shouted, and at once he saw his faithful friend at his side. "Run to the lake, find Hypatia—I don't know how you'll do it, but find her, tell her to be ready. I'll be coming to rescue her!"

"I not know how to do but I find her," the skiapod said and shot off.

Baudolino and the Poet entered the city. News of the defeat had already arrived. Females of every race, with their babes in arms, were running at random through the streets. The terrified panotians, thinking that they now knew how to fly, were jumping into the void. But they had been taught to glide downward, not to hover in the sky, and they quickly found themselves on the ground. Those who desperately tried to flap their ears to move in the air, plummeted, exhausted, and were dashed against the rocks. They found Colandrino, desperate at the failure of his training, Solomon, Boron, and Kyot, who asked news of the others. "They are dead, peace to their spirits," the Poet said angrily. "Hurry! To our quarters," Baudolino cried, "and then to the west!"

When they reached their lodgings, they gathered up everything they could. Going down in great haste, opposite the tower they saw a bustle of eunuchs, loading their belongings on some mules. Praxeas, livid, confronted the friends. "The deacon is dead, and you knew it," he said to Baudolino.

"Dead or alive, you would flee all the same."

"We are leaving. When we reach the pass, we will set off an avalanche, and the path to the Priest's kingdom will be closed forever. Do you want to come with us? If so, you must accept our terms."

Baudolino didn't even ask him what those terms were. "What do I care about your damned Prester John?" he shouted. "I have more important things to think about. Come, friends!"

The others remained dumbfounded. Then Boron and Kyot admitted that their real aim was to find Zosimos again and the Grasal, and Zosimos surely had not yet reached the kingdom and would never arrive there now: Colandrino and Boidi said they had come with Baudolino and they would go with Baudolino; Solomon observed that his ten tribes could be on either side of those mountains, so for him all directions were good. The Poet didn't speak; he seemed to have lost all will, and another had to take the reins of his horse to lead him away.

As they were about to flee, Baudolino saw one of the deacon's two acolytes coming towards him. The man was carrying a case. "It's the sheet with his features," he said. "He wanted you to have it. Put it to good use."

"Are you also fleeing?"

The veiled man said: "Here or there; if a there exists, for us it will be the same. The fate of our master awaits us. We will stay here and infect the Huns."

———

Just outside the city, Baudolino saw a horrible sight. Towards the blue hills some flames were flickering. Somehow, since morning, over several hours, a part of the Huns had begun circling the scene of the battle, and they had already reached the lake.

"Quickly!" Baudolino cried, in despair. "Over there, all of you! Gallop!" The others didn't understand. "Why over there, when they are there already?" asked Boidi. "This way, why not? Perhaps the only escape path remains to the south."

"Suit yourselves. I'm going," Baudolino shouted, beside himself. "He's lost his mind," Colandrino said, imploring the others: "We must follow him to make sure he does himself no harm."

But by now Baudolino was far ahead of them, and, with Hypatia's name on his lips, he was heading for sure death.

After half an hour's furious gallop, he stopped, glimpsing a swift form coming towards him. It was Gavagai.

"You be easy," Gavagai said to him. "I seen her. Now she safe." This beautiful news was soon to be transformed into a source of desperation, because this is what Gavagai said: the hypatias had been warned in time of the Huns' arrival, and, in fact, by the satyrs, who had come down from their hills and collected them, and when Gavagai arrived they were already leading the hypatias away, up there, beyond the mountains, where only the satyrs knew how to move, and the Huns would never be able to reach them. Hypatia had waited till the last, as her companions tugged at her arms, hoping for news of Baudolino, and she was unwilling to leave before learning of his fate. Hearing Gavagai's message, she became calm and, smiling through her tears, said to tell him good-bye for her. Trembling, she charged Gavagai to tell Baudolino to flee, because his life was in danger; sobbing, she gave him her last message: she loved him, and they would never see each other again.

Baudolino asked Gavagai if he was crazy, he couldn't let Hypatia go into the mountains, he wanted to take her with him. But Gavagai said it was now too late, and before he could get there, where, for that matter, the Huns were now masters, as everywhere, the hypatias would be beyond reach. Then, mastering his respect for one of the Magi, and putting a hand on his arm, he repeated Hypatia's last message; she would also wait for him, but her first duty was to protect their child: "She said, I forever have with me someone who recalls to me Baudolino." Then, looking up at him, Gavagai asked: "You made child with that female?"

"None of your business," Baudolino said, ungratefully. Gavagai remained silent.

Baudolino was still hesitating when his companions joined him. He realized that he could explain nothing to them, nothing they could understand. Then he tried to convince himself. It was all so rational: the wood was now conquered land, the hypatias had fortunately gained the hills where their salvation lay, Hypatia had rightly sacrificed her love of Baudolino to love of that yet-to-be-born creature he had given her. It was all so heartbreakingly sensible, and there was no other possible choice.

"I had been warned, after all, Master Niketas, that the Demiurge had done things only halfway."

36

Baudolino and the rocs

"Poor, unhappy Baudolino," said Niketas, so moved that he forgot to savor the pig's head, boiled with salt, onions, and garlic, that Theophilactus had preserved throughout the winter in a little keg of sea water. "Once again, every time you happen to conceive a passion for something true, fate punished you."

"After that evening we rode for three days and three nights, never stopping, never eating or drinking. I learned later that my friends performed miracles of cleverness to elude the Huns, who could be encountered anywhere within a range of many miles. I let them lead me. I followed them, and I thought of Hypatia. It's right, I told myself, that it has gone like this. Could I really have taken her with me? Would she have adapted to an unknown world, removed from the innocence of the wood, the familiar warmth of her rites, and the company of her sisters? Would she have renounced being one of the elect, called to redeem the divinity? I would have transformed her into a slave, a wretch. And further, I never asked her age, but perhaps she could have been my daughter twice over. When I abandoned Pndapetzim, I was, I believe, fifty. To her I had appeared young and vigorous, because I was the first man she had seen, but in truth I was approaching old age. I could have given her little, while taking from her everything. I tried to convince myself that things had gone as they had to go. They had to go in a way that left me unhappy forever. If I accepted this, perhaps I would find my peace."

"You weren't tempted to turn back?"

"Every moment, after those first three mindless days. But we had lost our way. The path we had taken wasn't the one by which we had arrived; we made infinite twists and turns, and crossed the same mountain three times, or perhaps they were three different mountains but we were no longer able to distinguish them. The sun alone wasn't enough to orient us, and with us we had neither Ardzrouni nor his map. Perhaps we had circled the great mountain that occupies half of the tabernacle, and we were at the other end of the land. Then we were left without horses. The poor animals had been with us since the beginning of the journey, and had aged with us. We hadn't been aware of this, because in Pndapetzim there were no other horses with which to compare them. Those last three days of precipitous flight exhausted them. Little by little they died, and for us it was almost a blessing, because they had the good sense to leave us, one after the other, in places where we found no food, and we ate their flesh, what little remained clinging to their bones. We continued on foot, and our feet were covered with sores. The only one who never complained was Gavagai, who had never needed horses, and who had on his foot a callus two inches thick. We literally ate locusts, and without honey, unlike the sainted fathers. Then we lost Colandrino."

"The youngest..."

"The least experienced of us. He was looking for food among the rocks; he thrust his hand into a treacherous crevice, and was bitten by a snake. He had just enough breath to tell me good-bye, whispering that I should remain faithful to the memory of his beloved sister, my most beloved wife, so that I would at least make her live in my memory. I had forgotten Colandrina, and once again I felt an adulterer and a traitor, both to Colandrina and to Colandrino."

"And then?"

"Then all goes dark. Master Niketas, I left Pndapetzim, according to my calculations, in the summer of the year of Our Lord 1197. I arrived here at Constantinople last January. Between those dates there were then six and a half years of emptiness, an emptiness in my spirit and perhaps in the world."

"Six years wandering in deserts?"

"One year, or two: who could keep track of time? After the death of Colandrino, months later perhaps, we found ourselves at the foot of some mountains we didn't know how to scale. Of the twelve who had set out, six of us remained, six men and a skiapod. Our clothes in tatters, our bodies wasted, burned by the sun, we had nothing left but our weapons and our knapsacks. We said to ourselves that perhaps we had reached the end of our journey, and it was our fate to die there. Suddenly we saw coming towards us a squad of men on horseback. They were sumptuously dressed, bearing shining arms, with human bodies and dogs' heads."

"They were cynocephali. So they do exist."

"By God's truth. They questioned us, barking; we didn't understand; the one who seemed their leader smiled—it may have been a smile, or a snarl, that bared his sharpened teeth—he gave an order to the others, and they bound us, in single file. The made us cross the mountain along a path that they knew; then, after some hours' march, we descended into a valley surrounded on all sides by another mountain, very high, with a powerful fortress circled by birds of prey that, even from a distance, seemed enormous. I remembered Abdul's old description, and I recognized the fortress of Aloadin."

So it was. The cynocephali made them climb tortuous steps dug into the stone up to that impregnable refuge, then brought them into the castle, where, amid towers and keeps, they could glimpse hanging gardens, and catwalks barred by sturdy gratings. They were handed over to other cynocephali, armed with scourges. Moving along a corridor, Baudolino caught sight, through a window, of a kind of courtyard amid very high walls, where many young men were languishing in chains, and he remembered how Aloadin trained his henchmen to crime, bewitching them with the green honey. Led into a sumptuous hall, they saw an old man, who seemed a centenarian, seated on embroidered cushions: he had a white beard, black eyebrows, and a grim gaze. Alive and powerful when he had captured Abdul, almost half a century earlier, Aloadin was still there controlling his slaves.

He looked at the newcomers with contempt, obviously realizing that these wretches were not good enough for enrollment among his young assassins. He didn't even speak to them. He made a bored gesture to one of his servants, as if to say: Do as you please with them. His curiosity was aroused only by the sight of the skiapod behind them. He motioned him to move, gestured to him to raise his foot above his head, and laughed. The six men were taken away, and Gavagai was left with him.

Thus began the long imprisonment of Baudolino, Boron, Kyot, Rabbi Solomon, Boidi, and the Poet, their feet always bound by a chain, which ended in a stone ball. They were employed in servile tasks, sometimes washing the tiles of the floors and walls, sometimes turning the wheels of the mills, sometimes bidden to carry quarters of ram to the rocs.

"They were flying beasts," Baudolino explained to Niketas, "as big as ten eagles put together, with a hooked, sharp beak that in a few instants could strip away the flesh of an ox. Their claws had talons that seemed the prow of a warship. They moved restlessly in a huge cage set on a turret, ready to attack anyone, except one eunuch, who seemed to speak their language and who kept them in order, moving among them as if he were among the chickens in his coop. He was also the only one who could send them out as Aloadin's messengers:

he would place on one of them—at the neck and along the back—some sturdy thongs that he ran beneath their wings, to the thongs he attached a basket, or another weight, then he opened a shutter, issued a command to the bird thus equipped, and only that one could fly out of the tower and vanish in the sky. We saw them also return. The eunuch let them in, and detached from their harness a bag or a metal cylinder that apparently contained a message for the lord of the place."

At other times the prisoners spent days and days in idleness, because there was nothing to do; sometimes they were assigned to serve the eunuch who carried the green honey to the young men in chains, and with horror they saw those faces, devastated by the dream that consumed them. If not the dream, then a subtle listlessness devoured the prisoners, who whiled away the time constantly telling one another the vicissitudes they had shared. They recalled Paris, Alessandria, the lively markets, the serene stay among the Gymnosophists. They talked about the Priest's letter, and the Poet, more gloomy every day, seemed to repeat the deacon's words as if he had heard them: "The suspicion that consumes me is that the kingdom does not exist." Who spoke of it to us, in Pndapetzim? The eunuchs. To whom did the messengers, sent to the Priest, return? To them, to the eunuchs. Had those messengers really gone out? Did they really return? The deacon had never seen his father. Everything we learned, we learned from the eunuchs. Maybe it was all a plot of the eunuchs, who were mocking the deacon, and us, and White Huns existed...." Baudolino told him to remember their companions who had died in battle, but the Poet shook his head. Rather than remind himself that he had been defeated, he preferred to believe he had been the victim of a spell.

Then they went back to the death of Frederick, and each time they invented a new explanation to make that inexplicable death comprehensible. It had been Zosimos, that was clear. No, Zosimos had stolen the Grasal, but only afterwards: someone, hoping to gain possession of the Grasal, had acted beforehand. Ardzrouni? Who could know? One of their slain companions? What a ghastly thought. One of the survivors? But in such misfortune, Baudolino said, must we also suffer the torment of reciprocal suspicion?

"As long as we were traveling, excited by the search for the kingdom of the Priest, we were not seized by these doubts; each helped the other in the spirit of friendship. It was captivity that made us snarl; we couldn't look one another in the face, and for years we hated one another in turn. I lived withdrawn into myself. I thought of Hypatia, but I was unable to remember her face. I remembered only the joy she gave me; at night my restless hand might stray to the hair of my sex, and I dreamed of touching her fleece that wafted the scent of moss. I could arouse myself because, if our spirit was delirious, our body was gradually recovering from the effects of our peregrinations. Up there they did not feed us badly, we received abundant food twice a day. Perhaps this was the way that Aloadin, who never admitted us to the secrets of his green honey, kept us calm. In fact, we had regained strength but, despite the hard tasks we were forced to perform, we were growing fat. I looked at my prominent belly and said to myself: You're beautiful, Baudolino; are all men beautiful like you? Then I would laugh like an idiot."

The only moments of consolation were when Gavagai visited them. Their excellent friend had become Aloadin's jester, amusing him with his unpredictable movements, performing little services for him, flying through rooms and corridors to carry out his orders. He had learned the Saracen language, he enjoyed great liberty. He brought his friends some delicacies from the lord's kitchen, kept them informed about the events of the fortress, or the dogged struggles among the eunuchs to gain the favor of the master, or the murderous missions on which the young dreamers were dispatched.

One day he gave Baudolino some green honey, but just a little, he

said, otherwise he would be reduced to the state of those bestial assassins. Baudolino took it, and enjoyed a night of love with Hypatia.
But towards the end of the dream her features changed: she had agile
legs, white and comely as those of the females of men, and a goat's
head.

Gavagai informed them that their weapons and their knapsacks
had been thrown into a closet, and he would be able to find them
again if they were to attempt an escape. "Really, Gavagai, do you
think we can escape one day?" Baudolino asked him. "I believes yes.
I believes many good ways to escape. I only have to find best. But you
become fat like eunuch, and if you fat, you run bad. You have to
move body, like me, you put foot over head and you become light."

Foot over head, no. But Baudolino realized that the hope, even
vain, of an escape would help him bear imprisonment without going
mad, and so he prepared himself for the event, moving his arms,
bending his knees dozens and dozens of times until he fell, exhausted,
on his rotund belly. He urged his friends to do the same, and with the
Poet he pretended to wrestle; sometimes they would spend an entire
afternoon trying to throw each other to the floor. With the chain at
their feet it wasn't easy, and they had lost the agility of bygone days.
Not only because of prison. It was age. But it did them good.

The only one who had totally forgotten his body was Rabbi
Solomon. He ate very little, so he was too weak for the various tasks,
and his friends did his share. He had no scroll to read, no implement
for writing. He spent hours repeating the name of the Lord, and
every time it had a different sound. He had lost his remaining teeth,
now he had only gums, left and right. He chomped his food and
spoke with a hiss. He was convinced that the ten lost tribes could not
have remained in a kingdom half made up of Nestorians, who could
be tolerated, because like the Jews they believed that Mary, good
woman though she was, could not have generated any god; but the
other half were idolaters, who increased or diminished the number
of divinities at will. No, he said, disconsolate, perhaps the ten tribes

passed through the kingdom, but then resumed their wandering; we Jews are always seeking a promised land, provided it be elsewhere, and now who knows where they are, perhaps only a few steps from this place where I am ending my days, but I've given up all hope of finding them. Let us bear the trials that the Holy One, always blessed be his name, sends us. Job saw worse."

"He had lost his mind. You could see that. And Kyot and Boron also seemed mad to me, always disputing. Pondering the Grasal that they would find again—indeed, now they thought it would cause itself to be found by them—the more they talked of it, the more its virtues, already miraculous, became super-miraculous, and the more they dreamed of possessing it. The Poet kept repeating: Just let me get my hands on Zosimos, and I'll become master of the world. Forget Zosimos, I said: he didn't even reach Pndapetzim; maybe he was lost along the way, his skeleton is turning to dust in some dusty place, and his Grasal has been taken by nomad infidels who maybe use it to piss in. Be silent! Boron said to me, blanching."

"How were you able to free yourselves from that inferno?" Niketas asked.

"One day Gavagai came and told us he had found the way to escape. Poor Gavagai, he too had aged: I have never known the life span of a skiapod, but he no longer preceded himself like a lightning bolt. He arrived like thunder, a little late, and at the end of his run he was panting."

This was the plan: armed, we had to surprise the eunuch guarding the rocs, force him to fit them out as usual, but in such a way that the thongs, instead of being fastened to their packs, were tied to the belts of the fugitives. Then he was to give the birds the order to fly to Constantinople. Gavagai had spoken with the eunuch, and had learned that he often sent the rocs to that city, to an agent there who lived on a hill near Pera. Both Baudolino and Gavagai understood

Saracen and could verify that the eunuch was giving the right command. Once they reached their destination, the birds would land on their own. "Why I not think of this before?" Gavagai asked himself, comically striking his head with his fists.

"Fine," Baudolino said, "but how can we fly with a chain on our leg?"

"I find file," Gavagai said.

At night Gavagai had found their weapons and packs, and had brought them to their sleeping quarters. Swords and daggers were rusted, but the friends spent nights cleaning them and sharpening them, rubbing them against the stones of the walls. They had the file. It wasn't anything special, and they had to spend weeks cutting into the rings that circled their ankles. They succeeded. Beneath the cracked rings they passed a cord, bound to the chain, and as they shambled around the castle, they appeared shackled as always. A close look would have revealed the deceit, but they had been there so many years that nobody paid any attention, and the cynocephali by now considered them domestic animals.

One evening they learned that the next day they would have to remove some sacks of spoiled meat from the kitchen and take them to the birds. Gavagai alerted them: this was the opportunity they had been awaiting.

Next morning they went to collect the sacks. Acting as if they were doing this reluctantly, they passed through their quarters, slipped their weapons amid the meat. They arrived at the cages, where Gavagai was already present, amusing the eunuch keeper with his somersaults. The rest was easy. They opened the sacks, slipped out their daggers, put all six of them to the keeper's throat (Solomon looked at them as if what they were doing mattered nothing to him), and Baudolino explained to the eunuch what he was to do. It seemed there weren't enough harnesses, but the Poet hinted at cutting off the ears of the eunuch: he had already had more than enough cut off, and he declared himself ready to cooperate. Seven birds were prepared to bear the weight of seven men, or, rather, six men and a skiapod. "I want the strongest one," the Poet said, "because you"—and he turned to the eunuch—"unfortunately can't stay here or else you'll give the alarm, or shout at your beasts to come back. Another rope will be tied to my belt, and you'll dangle from that. So my bird must bear the weight of two people."

Baudolino translated, the eunuch declared himself happy to accompany his captors to the end of the world, but he asked what would then become of him. They assured him that once in Constantinople, he could go on his way. "And hurry up," the Poet ordered, "because the stink of this cage is unbearable."

But it took almost an hour to arrange everything properly. Each hung himself carefully from his own raptor, and to his belt the Poet fastened the strap that would bear the eunuch. The only one still not bound was Gavagai, who was watching from the corner of a corridor, making sure no one came to spoil things.

Someone did come. After a long time the guards were surprised to note that the prisoners, sent to feed the birds, had not returned. A group of cynocephali arrived at the end of the corridor, barking with concern. "Dog-heads coming!" Gavagai cried. "You leave right away!"

"Right away my foot," Baudolino cried. "Come, we'll have time to strap you up!"

It wasn't true, and Gavagai knew it. If he fled, the cynocephali would reach the cage before the eunuch could open the shutter and make the birds fly. He shouted to the others to open the cage and leave. In the sacks of meat he had also slipped his fistula. He seized it, along with the three remaining darts. "Skiapod die, but always true to most holy Magi," he said. He lay on the floor, raised his foot over his head, which he lowered as he put the fistula to his mouth, blew, and the leading cynocephalos fell dead. While the others were drawing back, Gavagai had time to fell two more of them; then he was left without darts. To restrain the attackers, he held the fistula as if he

466

were still about to blow into it, but the deceit was short-lived. The monsters were upon him and ran him through with their swords.

Meanwhile the Poet had stuck his dagger a short distance into the chin of the eunuch, who, shedding his first blood, had realized what was being asked of him and, though made clumsy by his trappings, he managed to open the shutter. When he saw Gavagai die, the Poet shouted: "It's finished. Away! Away!" The eunuch gave a command to the rocs, who flung themselves into the air and rose in flight. The cynocephali were entering the cage at that moment, but their rush was arrested by the remaining birds, enraged by the confusion, who began pecking at the newcomers.

All six were in full flight. "Did he give the command for Constantinople?" the Poet asked Baudolino in a loud voice, and Baudolino nodded yes. "Then we don't need him anymore," the Poet said. With one slash of his dagger he severed the strap that bound the eunuch to him, and the eunuch plunged into the void. "Now we'll fly better," the Poet said. "Gavagai is avenged."

"And so we flew, Master Niketas, high above desolate plains marked only by the wounds of rivers dried up since time immemorial, cultivated fields, lakes, forests. We clung to the feet of the birds, because we feared the harnesses wouldn't support us. We flew for a time I cannot calculate, and the palms of our hands were bleeding. We saw flowing beneath us expanses of sand, lush fertile lands, meadows, and mountain peaks. We flew under the sun, but in the shadow of those long wings that beat the air above our heads. I don't know how long we flew, even at night, and at an altitude surely denied even to the angels. At a certain point, below us we saw, in a deserted plain, ten hosts—so it seemed to us—of people (or were they ants?) proceeding almost parallel towards God knows where. Rabbi Solomon began shouting that they were the ten lost tribes and he wanted to join them. He tried to make his bird descend, pulling on its feet, trying to direct its flight as with the ropes of a sail or the bar of a rudder, but the bird became enraged, freed itself from his grasp and tried to claw his head. Solomon! don't be an asshole, Boidi shouted at him. They're not your people; they's just ordinary nomads going they don't know where! Wasted breath. Seized by a mystical madness, Solomon grew so agitated that he freed himself from his harness, and fell, or, rather, flew, arms wide, through the heavens like an angel of the Almighty, may his name always be blessed, but an angel attracted by a promised land. We saw him grow smaller until his form was confused with those of the ants down below."

After more time had passed, the rocs, faithful to the order received, arrived within sight of Constantinople, its domes glowing in the sun. They landed where they were supposed to land, and our friends freed themselves from their bonds. One man, however, perhaps the sycophant of Aloadin, came towards them, amazed by this descent of too many messengers. The Poet smiled at him, gripped his sword, and gave a flat blow to the head. *"Benedico te in nomine Aloadini,"* he said seraphically, while the man fell down like a sack. "Whoosh! Whoosh!" he then cried at the birds. They seemed to understand the tone of his voice, rose in flight, and disappeared on the horizon.

"We're home," Boidi said happily, though he was a thousand miles from his home.

"Let's hope our Genoese friends are still somewhere around," Baudolino said. "We'll hunt for them."

"You'll see, our Baptist's heads will still come in handy," the Poet said, who seemed suddenly rejuvenated. "We're back among Christians. We've lost Pndapetzim, but we can conquer Constantinople."

"He didn't know," Niketas commented with a sad smile, "that other Christians were already doing just that."

37

Baudolino enriches the treasures of Byzantium

"As soon as we tried to cross the Golden Horn and enter the city, we realized that we were in the strangest situation we had ever seen. It wasn't a besieged city, because the enemies, though their ships were lying offshore, were encamped at Pera, and many of them were strolling around the city. It wasn't a conquered city, because along with the invaders wearing the cross on their chests, soldiers of the emperor were seen in the city. In short, the crusaders were in Constantinople, but Constantinople wasn't theirs. And when we found my Genoese friends, who were the same ones you later lived with, not even they could explain clearly what had happened or what was about to happen."

"It was hard to understand also for us," Niketas said with a sigh of resignation. "And yet one day I will have to write the history of that period. After the sorry outcome of the expedition for the reconquest of Jerusalem attempted by your Frederick and the kings of France and England, more than ten years later the Latins had chosen to try again, under the leadership of great princes like Baudouin of Flanders and Boniface of Monferrato. But they needed a fleet, and they had one built by the Venetians. I've heard you speak scornfully of the greed of the Genoese, but, compared to the Venetians, the people of Genoa are generosity personified. The Latins got their ships, but they didn't have the money to pay for them, and Dandolo, the Venetian doge (fate had decreed that he should also be blind, but among all the blind men in this story he was the only farsighted one), asked that, in payment of their debt, before going to the Holy Land, they help subdue Zara. The pilgrims agreed, and that was the first crime, because you don't put on the cross to then go and conquer a city for the Venetians. Meanwhile, Alexius, brother of that Isaac Angelus who had deposed Andronicus to take over power, had had him blinded, exiled him to the coast, and proclaimed himself basileus."

"That much the Genoese told me at once. It was a confused story, because Isaac's brother had become Alexius III, but there was also an Alexius, son of Isaac, who had managed to flee, reaching Zara, now in Venetian hands, where he asked the Latin pilgrims to help him regain the throne of his father, promising, in return, assistance in the conquest of the Holy Land."

"It's easy to promise what you don't yet have. Alexius III, for that matter, should have realized that his empire was at risk. But, even if he still had his eyes, he was blinded by ignorance, and by the corruption surrounding him. Imagine: at a certain point he wanted to have more warships built, but the guardians of the imperial forests would not allow trees to be cut down. On the other hand, Michael Xiphlinus, general of the army, had already sold off sails and rigging, rudders and other parts of the existing ships, to fill his coffers. Meanwhile, at Zara the young Alexius was hailed as emperor by those peoples, and in June of the previous year, the Latins arrived opposite the city. One hundred ten galleys and seventy ships transporting a thousand men-at-arms and three thousand foot soldiers, with shields on the vessels' flanks and banners in the wind and standards on the foc's'les, paraded through the strait of Saint George, with trumpets blaring and drums rolling, and our men were on the walls to watch the spectacle. Only a few hurled stones, but more to make noise than to do harm. Only when the Latins tied up directly opposite Pera did that madman Alexius III send out the imperial army. But it, too, was only a parade; in Constantinople we lived in a kind of somnolence. Perhaps you know that the entrance to the Horn was defended by a great chain that joined one bank to the other, but our forces defended it poorly: the Latins broke the chain, entered the port, and disembarked the entire army before the imperial palace of the Blachernae. Our army came out from the walls, led by the emperor; from the ramparts the ladies watched the show and said that our men seemed angels, with their beautiful armor gleaming in the sun. They realized something was going wrong only when the emperor, instead of engaging in battle, went back into the city. They understood it even better a few days later, when the Venetians attacked the walls from the sea and some Latins managed to scale them and set fire to the nearest houses. My fellow citizens began to understand after this first fire. What did Alexius III do then? During the night he loaded ten thousand gold pieces on a ship and abandoned the city."

"And Isaac returned to the throne."

"Yes, but by now he was old and also blind, and the Latins reminded him he was to share the empire with his son, who had become Alexius IV. With this boy the Latins had established some pacts of which we were still ignorant: the empire of Byzantium returned to Catholic and Roman dominion, the basileus gave the pilgrims one hundred thousand silver marks, provisions for a year, ten thousand horsemen to march on Jerusalem, and a garrison of five hundred knights in the Holy Land. Isaac realized that there wasn't enough money in the imperial treasury, and he couldn't go and tell the clergy and the people that suddenly he was placing himself under the pope of Rome. Thus a farce began that lasted for months. On the one hand, Isaac and his son, to collect money, sacked the churches; their men, with axes, cut out the images of Christ, and after stripping them of their ornaments, threw them in the fire, and melted down anything they found made of gold or silver. On the other hand, the Latins, ensconced at Pera, ran freely on this side of the Horn, sat at

471

Isaac's table, lorded it over the whole city, and did everything to delay their departure. They said they were waiting to be paid down to the last penny, and the man who was most insistent was Doge Dandolo for his Venetians, but truly I believe that here they had found Paradise, and they were blissfully living at our expense. Not content with taxing the Christians, and perhaps to justify their delay in engaging the Saracens of Jerusalem, some of them went to loot the houses of the Saracens who were peacefully living here in Constantinople, and in this conflict they set the second fire, in which I also lost the most beautiful of my houses."

"And the two emperors didn't protest to their allies?"

"At this point they were both hostages in the hands of the Latins, who had made Alexius IV their puppet. Once, when he was in their camp, amusing himself like any ordinary man-at-arms, they took the golden hat from his head and put it on their own heads. Never had a basileus of Byzantium been so humiliated! As for Isaac, he was turning into an idiot. Among gluttonous monks, he raved that he would become emperor of the world and would regain his sight. . . . Until the populace rose up, and elected Nikolas Kannabos basileus. A good man, but by then the strong man had become Alexius Doukas Murzuphlus, supported by the leaders of the army. So it was easy for him to seize power. Isaac died of a heart attack, Murzuphlus had Kannabos beheaded and Alexius IV strangled, so he became Alexius V."

"Yes! We arrived just in those days when nobody knew any longer who was in command, whether it was Isaac, Kannabos, Murzuphlus, or the pilgrims; and we couldn't tell, when someone spoke of Alexius, whether he meant the third, the fourth, or the fifth. We found the Genoese still living where you also found them, while the houses of the Venetians and the Pisans had been burned in the second fire, and they had withdrawn to Pera. In this unfortunate city, the Poet decided that we had to rebuild our fortunes."

———

When anarchy rules, the Poet said, anyone can make himself king. Meanwhile, we had to find some money. The five survivors were tattered, filthy, without resources. The Genoese welcomed them with good heart, but said that a guest is like fish and stinks after three days. The Poet washed himself carefully, trimmed his hair and beard, borrowed some decent clothes from our hosts, and one fine morning went out to collect news in the city.

He came back at evening and said: "Starting today Murzuphlus is basileus; he's done away with all the others. Apparently, to make himself look good to his subjects, he wants to provoke the Latins, and they consider him a usurper, because they had made their agreements with poor Alexius IV, rest in peace, young as he was, but obviously he was doomed to end badly. The Latins are waiting for Murzuphlus to make a misstep; for the present they continue getting drunk in the taverns, but they are well aware that sooner or later they will kick him out and put the city to the sack. They already know which gold objects are found in which churches, they also know that the city is full of hidden relics; however, they know that relics are not toys, and their leaders will want to seize them for themselves and take them home to their cities. But since these Greeklings are no better than they are, the pilgrims are wooing this one and that, to secure for themselves now, and on the cheap, the most important relics. Moral of the tale: the man who wants to make his fortune in this city sells relics; one who wants to make his fortune when he's back home, buys them."

"Then the moment has come for us to bring out our Baptist's heads!" Boidi said, hopefully.

"Boidi, you're just talking because you have a mouth," the Poet said. "First of all, in a single city, you could sell one head at most, because then the news spreads. In the second place, I've heard there's already one Baptist's head in Constantinople, and maybe even two. Suppose we'd already sold both, and we turn up with a third: they'll cut our throats. So, as to Baptist's heads: nothing doing. But looking for relics takes time. The problem isn't finding them: it's making them, identical to those that exist, though no one has yet discovered them. As I was moving around I heard some talk of Christ's purple cloak, the reed and the pillar of the flagellation, the sponge soaked in gall and wormwood that was offered to Our Lord as he died, only now it's dry, and the crown of thorns. A case which once contained a piece of the bread consecrated at the Last Supper, some hairs from the Lord's beard, the seamless garment of Jesus that the soldiers diced for, the mantle of the Madonna ..."

"We have to imagine which are the easiest to counterfeit," Baudolino said, pensive.

"Exactly," the Poet said. "You can find a reed anywhere, a pillar is best forgotten because you can't sell it quietly."

"But why risk copies, when somebody might find the real relic, and our buyers of the fakes would want their money back?" Boron said sensibly. "Think how many relics could exist. Think for example of the twelve baskets from the multiplication of the loaves and fishes; breadbaskets can be found anywhere; you just have to dirty them a bit, to make them look old. Think of the axe with which Noah built the ark; there must be an axe around here that our Genoese have thrown away because the blade is chipped."

"Not a bad idea," Boidi said. "Go to the cemeteries and you'll find the jawbone of Saint Peter, and the left arm—not the head—of Saint John the Baptist, to say nothing of the remains of Saint Agatha, of Lazarus, or the prophets Daniel, Samuel, Isaiah, the skull of Saint Helen, a fragment of the head of Saint Philip Apostle."

"If it comes to that," Pevere said, attracted by the wonderful prospect, "we only have to rummage around a bit in the cellar, and I'll easily find you a fragment of the Bethlehem manger, very tiny, so there's no telling where it really came from."

"We'll make relics whose like they've never seen before," the Poet said, "but we'll remake the ones that already exist, because they're the ones everybody's talking about, and the price goes up every day."

For a week the house of the Genoese was transformed into a humming workshop. Boidi, stumbling in the sawdust, found a nail from the Holy Cross. Boiamondo, after a night of horrible pains, tied some string to a rotten tooth, pulled it out easily, and there was a tooth of Saint Anne. Grillo dried bread in the sun and put some crumbs into certain boxes of aged wood that Taraburlo had just fashioned. Pevere had convinced them to give up the notion of the loaves-and-fishes baskets because, he said, after a miracle like that the crowd would have surely divided them up, and not even Constantine would have been able to put them back together. Selling just one, they wouldn't make a great impression, and it was in any case difficult to pass them, secretly, from hand to hand, because Jesus had fed so very many people, and he can't have used a little basket you could hide under a cloak. Well, so much for the baskets, the Poet said, but you've got to find me Noah's axe. Of course, Pevere replied, and one appeared, its blade now resembling a saw, the handle all charred.

After which our friends dressed up like Armenian merchants (the Genoese by now were prepared to finance the venture) and began roaming slyly among taverns and Christian camps, dropping a hint, referring to the difficulties of the matter, raising prices because they were risking their life, and things like that.

Boidi came back one evening saying that he had found a Monferrato knight who would take Noah's axe, but he wanted a guarantee that it was the real thing. "Oh, of course," Baudolino said, "we'll go to Noah and ask him for a certificate with his seal."

"And did Noah know how to write?" Boron asked.

"Noah knew only how to down bottle after bottle of the best," Boidi said. "He must have already been drunk as a skunk when he loaded the animals onto the ark; he overdid it with the mosquitoes but forgot the unicorns; that's why you don't see any more of them."

"Oh, you can see them still," Baudolino murmured, suddenly losing his good humor.

Pevere said that in his travels he had learned a bit of the Jews' writing, and with a knife he could carve one or two of their curlicues on the handle of the axe. "Was Noah a Jew, or not?" He was a Jew, yes, a Jew, the friends confirmed: poor Solomon, it's just as well he's no longer here; otherwise God knows how he would suffer. But Boidi then managed to sell the axe.

On certain days it was hard to find buyers, because the city was in an uproar, and the pilgrims were suddenly recalled to their camp, in a state of alert. For example, there was a rumor that Murzuphlus had attacked Philea, down the coast, the pilgrims had intervened in compact formations, there had been a battle, or perhaps a skirmish, but Murzuphlus had taken a good beating and they conquered his standard with the Virgin, which his army carried as its banner. Murzuphlus returned to Constantinople, but told his men not to confess this shame to anyone. The Latins discovered his reticence, and then one morning they sailed a galley of theirs right in front of the walls, with the banner in full view, as they made obscene gestures to the Romei, such as jabbing fingers or clapping their left hand on their right arm. Murzuphlus cut a sorry figure, and the Romei sang rude songs about him in the streets.

In short, between the time it took to make a good relic and the time it took to find the right gull, our friends had gone from January to March, but, what with the chin of Saint Eobanus today and the tibia of Saint Cunegonde tomorrow, they had put together a goodly sum, refunding the Genoese and refurbishing themselves properly.

"And this, Master Niketas, explains the presence, over these past days, of so many duplicate relics in your city, until only God Himself knows which are genuine. On the other hand, put yourself in our shoes: somehow we had to survive, between the Latins, always ready to steal, and your Greculi, excuse me, your Romans, ready to defraud them. Basically, we defrauded the defrauders."

"Ah well," said Niketas, resigned, "perhaps many of these relics will inspire holy thoughts in barbarianized Latins, who will find them again in their barbarian churches. Holy the thought, holy the relic. The ways of the Lord are infinite."

At this point they could be calm and could set out again for their homelands. Kyot and Boron by now had renounced the recovery of the Grasal, and of Zosimos with it; Boidi said that, with this money, in Alessandria he would buy some vineyards and end his days like a gentleman. Baudolino had fewer ideas than any of them: now that the search for Prester John had ended, and Hypatia was lost, living or dying mattered little to him. But not the Poet: he had been seized by fantasies of omnipotence, he was distributing the things of the Lord through the world universe, he could start offering something not to miserable pilgrims, but to the mighty who led them, gaining their favor.

One day he came to report that in Constantinople was the Mandylion, the Face of Edessa, an inestimable relic.

"What's this mandolin?" Boiamondo asked.

"It's a little cloth to wipe your face with," the Poet explained, "and it has the face of Our Lord impressed on it. Not painted, impressed, by virtue of nature: it's an image, *acheiropoieton,* not made by the hand of man. Abgar V, king of Edessa, was a leper, and he sent his archivist Hannan to invite Jesus to come and cure him. Jesus couldn't go, so he took this cloth, wiped his face, and left his features imprinted on it. Naturally, on receiving the cloth, the king was cured and was converted to the true faith. Centuries ago, while the Persians were besieging Edessa, the Mandylion was flown over the walls of the city, and it was saved. Then the emperor Constantine acquired the cloth and brought it here, where it was first in the church of the Blachernae, then in Saint Sophia, then in the chapel of the Pharos. And this is the true Mandylion, even if they say others exist: at Camulia in Cappadocia, at Memphis in Egypt, and at Anablatha near Jerusalem. Which is not impossible, because Jesus, in his life, may have wiped his face several times. But this one is surely the most wondrous of all because on Easter day the face changes according to the hour: at dawn it takes on the features of the newborn Jesus, at the third hour those of Jesus a boy, and so on, until at the ninth hour it appears as Jesus adult, at the moment of the Passion."

"Where did you learn all these things?" Boidi asked.

"A monk told me. Now this is a genuine relic, and with an object like this we can return to our homes and receive honors and prebends, we have only to find the right bishop, as Baudolino did with Rainald for his three Magi. Up till now we've sold relics, now's the moment to buy one—the relic that will make our fortune."

"And who are you going to buy the Mandylion from?" Baudolino asked wearily, nauseated by now at all this simony.

"It's already been bought by a Syrian I spent an evening drinking with; he works for the duke of Athens. But he told me that this duke would give the Mandylion and God knows what else besides, if he could acquire the Sydoine."

"Now you'll tell us what the Sydoine is," Boidi said.

"They say it might have been in Saint Mary's in the Blachernae, the Holy Shroud, the one with the image of the whole body of Jesus. They talk about it in the city, they say it was seen by Amalric, the king of Jerusalem, when he visited Manuel Comnenius. But others told me that it had been left in the keeping of the church of the Blessed Virgin at the Bucoleon. But nobody has ever seen it, and if it was there, it disappeared, nobody knows how long ago."

"I can't see what you're getting at," Baudolino said. "Somebody has the Mandylion, yes. And this somebody would trade it for the Sydoine, but you don't have the Sydoine, and I would be revolted if we fabricated here an image of Our Lord. So?"

"I don't have the Sydoine," the Poet said. "But you do."

"Me?"

"Remember when I asked you what was in that case that the deacon's acolytes gave you before we fled from Pndapetzim? You told me

478

it was the image of that poor man, imprinted on his winding sheet, just after he died. Show it to me."

"You're crazy! It's a sacred charge. The deacon entrusted me with it so I could give it to Prester John!"

"Baudolino, you're past sixty, and you still believe in Prester John? We've had living proof that he doesn't exist. Let me see the thing."

Reluctantly Baudolino took the case from his sack, removed a roll, and, unfolding it, revealed a cloth of large dimensions, motioning to the others to push aside tables and stools because it required much space to spread it out on the floor.

It was an actual sheet, very large, which bore a double impression of the human form, front and back. A face could distinctly be seen, the hair falling to the shoulders, mustache and beard, closed eyes. Touched by the grace of death, the unhappy deacon had left on the cloth an image of serene features and a powerful body, on which one could see only with difficulty the uncertain signs of wounds, bruises, or sores, the traces of the leprosy that had destroyed him.

Baudolino stood there, moved, and recognized that, on that linen, the dead man had regained the stigmata of his mournful majesty. Then he murmured: "We can't sell the image of a leper, and what's more a Nestorian, as that of Our Lord."

"First of all, the duke of Athens doesn't know," the Poet replied, "and we have to sell it to him, not to you. Second, we're not selling it, we're trading it; so it's not simony. I'm going to find the Syrian."

"The Syrian will ask you why you're making the trade, seeing that a Sydoine is infinitely more precious than a Mandylion," Baudolino said.

"Because it's harder to carry out of Constantinople in secret. Because it's too valuable, and only a king could allow himself to buy it, whereas for the Face we can find purchasers of less importance, but ready to pay on the spot. Because if we offered the Sydoine to a Christian prince he would say that we stole it here, and he'd have us hanged, whereas the Face of Edessa could be the Face of Camulia or of Memphis or of Anablatha. The Syrian will understand my reasoning, because we belong to the same race."

"All right," Baudolino said, "you pass this cloth on to the duke of Athens, and I don't give a damn if he takes home an image that isn't of Christ. But you know that this image for me is far more precious than the one of Christ, you know what memories it has for me, and you can't make an illicit trade of something so venerated. . . ."

"Baudolino," the Poet said, "we don't know what we'll find back there when we go home. With the Face of Edessa we'll get an archbishop on our side, and our fortune is made again. And anyway, Baudolino, if you hadn't carried this shroud away from Pndapetzim, by now the Huns would be wiping their ass with it. This man was dear to you; you told me his story while we were wandering through the deserts and while we were prisoners, and you mourned his death, so futile and forgotten. Well, his last portrait will be venerated somewhere like that of Christ. What more sublime sepulcher could you wish for a dead man you loved? We are not humiliating the memory of his body, but, rather, we're—how can I say it, Boron?"

"We're transfiguring it."

"Yes."

"Perhaps it was because in the chaos of those days I had lost the sense of what's right and what's wrong, perhaps I was just tired, Master Niketas. I consented. The Poet went off to trade the Sydoine, ours, or, rather, mine, or, rather, the deacon's, for the Mandylion."

Baudolino started laughing, and Niketas couldn't understand why.

"The trick. We learned of it that evening. The Poet went to the tavern he knew, made his infamous bargain, to get the Syrian drunk he got drunk himself, he came out, was followed by someone who was aware of his dealings, perhaps the Syrian himself—who, as the Poet said, was of his same race—he was attacked in an alley, beaten half to death, and he came home, more drunk than Noah, bleeding, bruised, without Sydoine and without Mandylion. I wanted to kick the life out of him, but he was a finished man. For the second time he had lost a kingdom. In the days that followed we had to force him to eat. I told myself I was glad that I had never had too many ambitions, if the defeat of one ambition could reduce a man to that state. Then I admitted that I, too, was the victim of many frustrated ambitions, I had lost my beloved father, I had not found for him the kingdom, I had lost forever the woman I loved . . . In short, I had learned that the Demiurge had done things halfway, whereas the Poet still believed that in this world some victory is possible."

At the beginning of April our friends became aware that Constantinople's days were numbered. There had been a very dramatic quarrel between the doge Dandolo, erect at the prow of a galley, and Murzuphlus, who rebuked him from the shore, ordering the Latins to leave his lands. It was clear that Murzuphlus had gone mad and the Latins, if they chose, could swallow him with one gulp. Beyond the Golden Horn the preparations in the pilgrims' camp could clearly be seen, and on the decks of the ships at anchor there was a great bustle of sailors and men-at-arms making ready for the attack.

Boidi and Baudolino said that, since they had a bit of money, this was the moment to leave Constantinople, because, when it came to defeated cities, they had already seen more than enough. Boron and Kyot agreed, but the Poet asked for a few more days. He had recovered from his setback and obviously wanted to exploit the last hours to make his final coup, though what that was he didn't even know himself. He was already beginning to have a madman's look in his eyes, but, of course, there's no arguing with madmen. They contented him, saying it was enough to keep an eye on the ships to understand when the moment came to head inland.

The Poet was gone for two days, and that was too long. In fact, on the Friday morning before Palm Sunday, he still hadn't come back and the pilgrims had begun to attack from the sea, between the

Blachernae and the Evergete monastery, more or less in the area known as Petria, north of the walls of Constantine.

It was too late to pass beyond the walls, now manned on all sides. Cursing their vagabond companion, Baudolino and the others decided it was better to lie low with the Genoese, because that district didn't seem threatened. They waited, and hour by hour they learned the news from Petria.

The pilgrims' ships were bristling with obsidional constructions. Murzuphlus was positioned on a little hill behind the walls with all his chiefs and courtiers, and banners, and trumpeters. Despite that show, the imperials were fighting well; the Latins had assayed various assaults but had always been thrown back, with Greeklings cheering from the walls, and baring their behinds to the defeated, while Murzuphlus swaggered as if he had done everything himself, ordering the trumpets to sound victory.

Thus it seemed that Dandolo and the other leaders had given up the idea of taking the city, and Saturday and Sunday passed quietly, even though all remained tense. Baudolino seized the opportunity to comb Constantinople thoroughly, trying to find the Poet, but in vain.

It was Sunday night when their companion returned. His gaze was even wilder than before; he said nothing, and set to drinking silently until the next morning.

It was at the first light of dawn on Monday that the pilgrims resumed the attack, which lasted all day; the ladders of the Venetian ships were successfully attached to some towers on the walls, the attackers entered; no, it had been only one, a giant, with a turreted helmet, who frightened the defenders and set them fleeing. Or else, some landed, found a bricked-up postern, destroyed it with blows of a pick, making a gap in the wall, yes, but they were driven back, though some towers had already been conquered. . . .

The Poet paced back and forth in the room like a caged animal, he seemed anxious for the battle somehow to be resolved, he looked at Baudolino as if to tell him something, then gave up, and studied with grim eyes the movements of his other three comrades. At a certain point news came that Murzuphlus had fled, abandoning his army, the defenders had lost the little courage remaining to them, the pilgrims had broken through, passed the walls: they didn't dare enter the city because darkness was falling, so they set fire to the first houses, to flush out any hidden defenders. "The third fire, in the space of a few months," the Genoese groaned, "but this isn't a city any more; it's become a heap of dung to be burned when it's too high!"

"Damn you," Boidi shouted at the Poet. "If it hadn't been for you we'd have been out of this dunghill! What now?"

"Now you shut up, and I know why, all right!" the Poet muttered to him.

During the night the first glow from the fire was visible. At dawn Baudolino, who seemed to be sleeping, though his eyes were open, saw the Poet approach first Boidi, then Boron, and finally Kyot, and whisper something in each ear. Then he vanished. A little later Baudolino saw Kyot and Boron conferring, taking something from their packs before leaving the house, trying not to wake him.

Still later, Boidi came to him and shook his arm. He was aghast: "Baudolino," he said, "I don't know what's going on, but they're all crazy here. The Poet came to me and said these very words: I've found Zosimos, and now I know where the Grasal is, don't try to be smart, take your Baptist's head and be at Katabates, in the place where Zosimos received the basileus that time, by this afternoon, you know the way. What's this Katabates? What basileus was he talking about? Didn't he tell you anything?"

"No," Baudolino said. "On the contrary, it seems he wants to keep me in the dark. And he was so confused that he didn't remember it was Boron and Kyot who were with us, years ago, when we went to capture Zosimos at Katabates, not you. Now I want to get a clear picture."

He looked for Boiamondo. "Listen," he said to him, "remember the evening, many years ago, when you took us to that crypt underneath the old monastery of Katabates? Now I have to go back there."

"If that's what you want. You have to reach that pavilion near the church of the Holy Apostles. Maybe you can get there without finding the pilgrims, who probably haven't got there yet. If you come back, it will mean I'm right."

"Yes, but I should arrive there without arriving there. I mean: I can't explain it to you, but I have to follow—or precede—someone who will take that same road, and I don't want to be seen. I remember there are many tunnels underneath. Can you get there by some other way?"

Boiamondo began laughing. "If you're not afraid of the dead ... You can enter from another pavilion near the Hippodrome, and I think you can still get there from here. Then you proceed underground for quite a way, and you're in the cemetery of the monks of Katabates, which nobody knows still exists, but it does. The cemetery tunnels lead to the crypt, but if you like, you can stop before then."

"Will you take me?"

"Baudolino, friendship is sacred, but my skin is even more sacred. I'll explain it all to you carefully; you're a smart boy and you'll find the way by yourself. All right?"

Boiamondo described the road to take, gave him also two well-resinated pieces of wood. Baudolino went back to Boidi and asked him if he was afraid of the dead. Not me, he said; I'm afraid only of the living. "This is what we'll do," Baudolino said to him. "You take your Baptist's head and I'll accompany you there. You'll go to your appointment and I'll hide a bit earlier, to find out what that madman has on his mind."

"Let's go," Boidi said.

At the moment they were leaving, Baudolino thought for an instant, then went back and took his own Baptist's head, which he wrapped in a rag, and put under his arm. Then he thought again, and into his belt he thrust the two Arab daggers he had bought at Gallipolis.

38

Baudolino settles scores

Baudolino and Boidi reached the Hippodrome area as the flames of the fire were coming closer; they forced their way through a crowd of terrified Romei, who didn't know which way to escape, because some shouted that the pilgrims were coming from this direction, others from that. The two found the pavilion, forced a door locked by a weak chain, entered the underground passage, lighting the torches they had been given by Boiamondo.

They walked for a long time, because obviously the passage led from the Hippodrome to the walls of Constantine. Then they climbed some dank steps, and began to smell a deathly stink. It wasn't the smell of recently dead flesh; it was, so to speak, the smell of a smell, smell of flesh that had rotted and then somehow dried up.

They entered a corridor (and could see others opening out to right and left along its course), in whose walls a series of niches opened, inhabited by a subterranean population of the almost living dead. They were dead, no doubt about that, those fully dressed beings, who stood erect in their recesses, supported perhaps by iron spikes that held their backs; but time seemed not to have completed its work of destruction, because those dry, leather-colored faces, in which empty sockets gaped, often marked by a toothless grin, gave an impression of life. They were not skeletons, but bodies apparently drained by a force that from inside had dried and crumbled the viscera, leaving intact not only the bones but also the skin, and perhaps part of the muscles.

"Master Niketas, we had come upon a network of catacombs where for centuries the monks of Katabates had placed the corpses of their brothers, without burying them, because some miraculous conjunction of the soil, the air, and some substance that dripped from the tufa walls of that labyrinth preserved them almost intact."

"I thought they didn't do that any more, and I didn't know anything about the Katabates cemetery, a sign that this city still retains some mysteries that none of us knows. But I had heard tell of how certain monks in the past, to assist the work of nature, let their brothers' corpses steep among the tufa humors for eight months, then extracted them, washed them with vinegar, exposed them to the air for a few days, dressed them, and replaced them in their niches, so that somehow the balsamic air of that setting would ensure their dried immortality."

Proceeding along that line of deceased monks, each dressed in liturgical vestments, as if they were still to officiate, kissing gleaming ikons with their livid lips, Baudolino and Boidi glimpsed faces with taut, ascetic smiles, others to which the devout survivors had pasted beards and mustaches to make them look hieratic as in the past, their eyelids closed so they would seem asleep, still others with the head now reduced to a mere skull, but with hard, leathery bits of skin attached to the cheekbones. Some had been deformed by the centuries, and appeared like prodigies of nature, fetuses clumsily taken from the maternal womb, inhuman beings on whose contracted forms unnatural, arabesqued chasubles appeared, the colors now dulled, dalmatics that you would have thought embroidered but were gnawed by the work of the years and by some worm of the catacombs. From still others the clothing had fallen, now crumbled by the centuries, and beneath the shreds of their vestments appeared scrawny little bodies, the ribs covered by an epidermis taut as the skin of a drum.

"If it was piety that conceived that sacred representation," Baudolino said to Niketas, "the survivors were impious, as they had imposed the memory of those deceased as a constant, looming threat, in no way meant to reconcile the living with death. How can you pray for the soul of someone who is staring at you from those walls, saying I am here, and I will never move from here? How can you hope for the resurrection of the flesh and the transfiguration of our earthly bodies after the Last Judgment, if those bodies are still there, decaying day after day? I, unfortunately, had seen corpses in my life, and at least I could hope that, dissolved into the earth, one day they might dazzle, beautiful and rubicund as a rose. If, up there on high, after the end of time, people like this would be moving about, I said to myself, then better Hell that burns here and hacks there. In Hell, at least it should resemble what happens in our world. Boidi, less sensitive than I to mortality, tried to lift those vestments to see the state of the pudenda, for if somebody shows you such things, how can you complain if somebody else thinks of those other things?"

Before the network of passages ended, they found themselves in a circular place, where the vault was perforated by an airshaft that revealed, up above, the afternoon sky. Obviously, at ground level, a well served to give air to that place. They put out the torches. No longer illuminated by the flames, but instead by that livid light diffused among the niches, the monks' bodies seemed even more disturbing. They gave the impression that, touched by daylight, they were about to rise again. Boidi made the sign of the cross.

Finally, the corridor they had taken ended in the ambulacrum behind the columns that encircled the crypt where, the last time, they had seen Zosimos. Glimpsing some lights, they approached, on tiptoe. The crypt was as it had been before, illuminated by two lighted tripods. Only the circular basin used by Zosimos for his necromancy was missing. In front of the iconostasis Boron and Kyot were already waiting, nervous. Baudolino suggested to Boidi that he arrive, emerging between the two columns flanking the iconostasis, as if he had followed the same route, while Baudolino himself would remain hidden.

Boidi did so, and the other two received him without surprise. "So the Poet explained to you how to get here," Boron said. "We think he said nothing to Baudolino; otherwise why all the secrecy? Do you have any idea why he wants us to meet?"

"He talked about Zosimos, and the Grasal; he made some strange threats."

"Us, too." Kyot and Boron agreed.

They heard a voice, and it seemed to come from the Pantocrator of the iconostasis. Baudolino noticed that the eyes of the Christ were two black almonds, a sign that behind the icon someone was watching what went on in the crypt. Though distorted, the voice was recognizable, and it was the Poet's. "Welcome," the voice said. "You don't see me, but I see you. I am armed with a bow, I could easily shoot you before you can escape."

"But why, Poet? What have we done to you?" Boron asked, frightened.

"What you have done you know better than I. But we must get to the point. Enter, wretch." A stifled moan was heard, and from behind the iconostasis a groping form appeared.

Though time had passed, though that man dragging himself forward was withered and bent, though his hair and beard had now become white, they recognized Zosimos.

"Yes, it's Zosimos," the Poet's voice said. "I came upon him yesterday, by pure chance, while he was begging in a lane. He's blind, his limbs are bent, but it's Zosimos. Now, Zosimos, tell our friends what happened to you when you fled from Ardzrouni's castle."

Zosimos, in a whining voice, began his narration. He had stolen the head in which he had hidden the Grasal, he had fled, but he had not only never possessed but had never seen any map of Cosmas, and he didn't know where to go. He wandered until his mule died, dragged himself through the most inhospitable lands of the world, his eyes—seared by the sun—now made him confuse east with west, and north with south. He happened upon a city inhabited by Christians, who succored him. He said he was the last of the Magi, because the others had achieved the peace of the Lord and lay in a church in the distant West. He said, in hieratic tone, that in the reliquary he was carrying the Holy Grasal, to be delivered to Prester John. His hosts had somehow heard tell of both, they prostrated themselves before him, carried him in solemn procession into their church, where he began sitting on an episcopal seat, every day dispensing oracles, giving advice on the handling of things, eating and drinking his fill, surrounded by the respect of all.

In short, as the last of the most holy Kings, and keeper of the Holy Grasal, he became the maximum spiritual authority of that community. Every morning he said Mass, and at the moment of the elevation, besides the sacred host, he displayed his reliquary, and the faithful knelt, saying they could smell celestial perfumes.

The faithful also brought lost women to him, so he could lead them back to the straight path. He told them that God's mercy is infinite, and he summoned them to the church when evening had fallen, to spend with them, he said, the night in continuous prayer. Word spread that he had transformed those lost souls into so many Magdalenes, who devoted themselves to his service. During the day they prepared for him the choicest foods, brought him the most exquisite wines, sprinkled him with scented oils. At night they kept vigil with him before the altar, Zosimos said, so the following morning he appeared with his eyes hollow from that penitence. Zosimos had finally found his Paradise, and decided he would never leave that blessed place.

Zosimos now heaved a long sigh, then passed his hands over his eyes, as if in that darkness he could still see a most painful scene. "My friends," he said, "whatever thought that comes to you, you must always ask it: are you on our side or do you come from the enemy? I forgot to follow that holy maxim, and to the entire city I promised that, for Holy Easter, I would open the reliquary and finally display the Grasal. On Good Friday, alone, I opened the case, and in it I found one of those disgusting death's heads that Ardzrouni had placed there. I swear I had hidden the Grasal in the first reliquary on the left, and that was the one I took before running away. But someone—surely one of you—had changed the order of the reliquaries, and the one I took didn't contain the Grasal. A man who is hammering an iron bar first thinks what he wants to make of it: a sickle, a sword, or an axe. I decided to remain silent. Father Agatone lived for three years with a stone in his mouth, until he was able to practice silence. So to all I said that I had been visited by an angel of the Lord, who had told me there were still too many sinners in the city, hence no one was yet worthy to see that holy object. The evening of Holy Saturday I spent, as every honest monk must, in mortifications, excessive, I think, because the next morning I felt exhausted, as if I had passed the night, God forgive me even the very thought, amid libations and fornications. I officiated, staggering, and, at the solemn moment when I was to display the reliquary to the devout, I stumbled on the top step of the altar, tumbling down. The reliquary slipped from my hands, and as it struck the ground, it opened, and all could see it contained no Grasal, but, rather, a dried-up skull. There is nothing more unjust than the punishment of the just man who has sinned, my friends, because the worst of sinners is forgiven the last of his crimes, but the just man is not even forgiven his first. Those devout people felt they had been defrauded by me, who until three days before, God is my witness, had acted in perfect good faith. They fell upon me, tore off my clothes, beat me with clubs that broke my legs forever, and my arms and back, then they dragged me into their tribunal, where they decided to tear out my eyes. They drove me out of the gates of the city, like a mangy cur. You don't know how much I suffered. I wandered, begging, blind and crippled. And crippled and blind, after long years of wandering, I was picked up by a caravan of

Saracen merchants who were coming to Constantinople. The only pity I received was from the infidels, may God reward them and not damn them as they would deserve. I returned a few years ago to this my city, where I have lived by begging, and luckily a good soul one day led me by the hand to the ruins of this monastery, where I can recognize the places by touch, and since then I have been able to spend the nights without suffering the cold, the heat, or the rain."

"This is the story of Zosimos," the Poet's voice said. "His condition bears witness that, at least this once, he is sincere. So another one of you, seeing where Zosimos had hidden the Grasal, changed the position of the heads, to allow Zosimos to hasten to his ruin, and to deviate any suspicion. But he who has taken the correct head is the same who killed Frederick. And I know who it is."

"Poet!" Kyot cried. "Why are you saying this? Why have you summoned only us three, and not also Baudolino? Why didn't you tell us anything up there at the house of the Genoese?"

"I called you here because, through a city invaded by the enemy, I couldn't drag along with me this excuse for a man. Because I didn't want to speak in front of the Genoese, and especially not in front of Baudolino. Baudolino is no longer a part of our story. One of you will give me the Grasal, and then the rest will be up to me."

"What makes you think Baudolino doesn't have the Grasal?"

"Baudolino can't have killed Frederick. He loved him. Baudolino had no interest in stealing the Grasal, he was the only one among us who really wanted to take it to the Priest in the name of the emperor. Finally, try to remember what happened to the six heads that remained after Zosimos ran away. We took one each: I, Boron, Kyot, Boidi, Abdul, and Baudolino. Yesterday, after I found Zosimos, I opened mine. Inside was a smoked skull. As for Abdul's, as you will recall, Ardzrouni had opened it to put the skull between his hands as an amulet, or whatever, at the moment Abdul was dying, and now it's with him in the grave. Baudolino gave his to Praxeas; he opened it in front of us, and there was a skull inside. So three reliquaries remain, and those are yours. The three of you. Now I know which of you has the Grasal, and I know he knows. I also know that the possessor does not possess it by chance, but because he planned everything from the moment he killed Frederick. But I want him to have the courage to confess to us all that he has deceived us for years and years. After he has confessed, I will kill him. So make up your minds. Let him who must speak, speak. We have reached the end of our journey."

"Here something strange happens, Master Niketas. From my hiding place, I was trying to put myself in the place of my three friends. Let us suppose that one of them, whom we will call Ego, knew he had the Grasal, and was guilty of something. He would have told himself that, at this point, the best thing was to risk all, seize his sword or his dagger, dash off in the direction from which he had come, flee until he reached the cistern, and then the sunlight. This, I believe, is what the Poet was expecting. Perhaps he didn't yet know which of the three had the Grasal, but that escape would reveal it. Now let us imagine that Ego was not sure of having the Grasal, because he had never looked into his reliquary, and yet he did have something on his conscience concerning the death of Frederick. Ego therefore would have waited, to see if someone else who knew he had the Grasal would make a leap towards flight. Ego therefore was waiting, without making a move. But he could see that the others weren't moving either. So, he thought, none of them has the Grasal, and none of them feels he is at all worthy of suspicion. Therefore, he had to conclude, the one the Poet has in mind is me, and I must escape. Puzzled, he put his hand to his sword, or dagger, and started to take a first step. But then he saw that each of the others was doing the same thing. He stopped again, suspecting that the other two felt more guilty than he. This is what happened in that crypt. Each of the three, each thinking like the one I have called Ego, first remained still, then took one step, then stopped again. And this was the obvious sign that none of them was sure of having the Grasal, but that all three had something with which to reproach themselves. The Poet understood this perfectly, and explained to them what I had understood and have now explained to you."

The voice of the Poet said: "Wretches, all three of you! Each of you knows he is guilty. I know—I have always known—that all three of you tried to kill Frederick, and perhaps all three of you killed him, so the man died three times. That night I left the guardroom very early, and was the last to come back in. I was unable to sleep, perhaps I had had too much to drink. I urinated three times in the courtyard, I stayed outside so as not to disturb all of you. While I was outside, I heard Boron come out. He took the steps towards the lower level, and I followed him. He went into the room with the machines, approached the cylinder that produces the vacuum, worked its lever, a number of times. I couldn't understand what he wanted, but I understood the next day. Either Ardzrouni had confided something to him, or he had understood on his own, but obviously the room in which the cylinder created the vacuum, the room in which the chicken had been sacrificed, was the very one where Frederick was sleeping, where Ardzrouni used to rid himself of the enemies he hypocritically received as guests. You, Boron, turned that lever until in the emperor's room the vacuum had been created, or, at least, since you didn't believe in the vacuum, until that air was dense, where you knew candles were extinguished and animals were suffocated. Frederick felt unable to breathe; at first he thought of a poison, and took the Grasal to drink the antidote it contained. But he fell to the ground lifeless. The next day you were ready to steal the Grasal, exploiting the confusion, but Zosimos was ahead of you. You saw him, and you saw where he hid it. It was easy for you to change the position of the heads and, at the moment of leaving, you took the right one."

Boron was covered with sweat. "Poet," he said, "you saw clearly. I was in the room with the pump. The debate with Ardzrouni had aroused my curiosity. I tried to work it, not knowing—I swear— what room it affected. But, for that matter, I was convinced that the

493

pump couldn't function. I gambled, true, but it was all in play, with no murderous intentions. And anyway, if I had done what you say I did, how can you explain the fact that in Frederick's room the wood in the fireplace had all burned to ashes? If the vacuum could actually be created, and kill someone, in the vacuum no flame would burn...."

"Forget the fireplace," the stern voice of the Poet said. "For that there is another explanation. Just open your reliquary, if you're so sure it doesn't contain the Grasal."

Boron, muttering that God could strike him if he had ever had any thought of having the Grasal, furiously cut the seal with his dagger, and from the case a skull rolled to the floor, smaller than those which had been seen so far, perhaps because Ardzrouni had not hesitated to violate the graves even of children.

"You don't have the Grasal. Very well," the Poet's voice said, "but this does not absolve you of what you have done. Now we come to you, Kyot. You went out just afterwards, with the manner of someone who needs some air. But you needed quite a lot, since you went all the way to the ramparts, where the mirrors of Archimedes were. I followed you, and I saw you. You touched them, you operated the short-distance one, as Ardzrouni had explained to us, you tilted it in a way that was not random, because you devoted great attention to it. You set the mirror so that, with the sun's first appearance, it would concentrate those rays on the window of Frederick's chamber. So it went, and those rays kindled the wood in the fireplace. By then the vacuum created by Boron had given way to new air, after so much time, and the flame could be fed. You knew what Frederick would do, waking half-stifled by the smoke from the fireplace. He would believe himself poisoned and would drink from the Grasal. I know, you also drank from it, that evening, but we didn't watch you carefully enough as you were replacing it in the ark. Somehow you had bought poison at the Gallipolis market, and you let a few drops fall into the cup. The plan was perfect. Only you didn't know what Boron had done. Fred-

494

erick had drunk from your poisoned cup, but not when the fire was kindled. It was much earlier, when Boron was cutting off his air."

"You're mad, Poet," Kyot cried, pale as a corpse. "I know nothing of the Grasal. Look, now I'll open my head. . . . Here, you see? There's a skull!"

"No, you don't have the Grasal. All right," the Poet's voice said, "but you don't deny having moved the mirrors."

"I wasn't feeling well, as you said, and I wanted to breathe the night air. I played with the mirrors, but may God strike me here and now if I knew they would light the fire in that room! You mustn't think that in these long years I have never thought of that imprudence of mine, wondering if it were not my fault that the fire was lighted and if this didn't have something to do with the emperor's death. Years of horrible doubt. In a way you have relieved me, because you tell me that in any case at that point Frederick was already dead! But as for the poison: how can you say such an outrageous thing? That evening I drank in good faith, I felt like a sacrificial victim. . . ."

"You're all a flock of innocent lambs, eh? Innocent lambs who for fifteen years have lived with the suspicion of having killed Frederick. Isn't that true also for you, Boron? But let's come to our Biodi. At this point you're the only one who can have the Grasal. That evening you didn't go outside. Like all the others, you found Frederick lying on the floor in his room the next morning. You weren't expecting it, but you seized the occasion. You had been brooding over it for some time. For that matter, you were the only one who had a reason to hate Frederick, who, before the walls of Alessandria, had killed so many of your companions. At Gallipolis you said you had bought that ring with cordial in its mount. But no one saw you while you were dealing with the merchant. Who can say it really contained a cordial? You had long been ready with your poison, and you realized this was the right moment. Perhaps, you thought, Frederick is only unconscious. You poured the poison into his mouth, saying you wanted to bring him round, and only afterwards—afterwards, mind you—did Solomon realize he was dead."

"Poet," Boidi said, sinking to his knees, "if you only knew how many times over these years I have asked myself if that cordial of mine was by chance poisonous. But now you tell me Frederick was already dead, killed by one of these two, or by both. Thank God."

"It doesn't matter," the Poet's voice said, "what matters is the intent. But as far as I'm concerned, you will answer to God for your intentions. I want only the Grasal. Open the case,"

Boidi tried to open the reliquary, trembling; three times the sealing wax resisted his efforts. As he bent over that fatal receptacle, Boron and Kyot moved away from him, as if he were by now the designated victim. At his fourth try the case opened, and once again a skull appeared.

"By all the damned saints!" the Poet cried, emerging from behind the iconostasis.

"He was the very portrait of rage and madness, Master Niketas, and I no longer recognized him as my old friend of the past. But at that moment I remembered the day when I went to look at the reliquaries, after Ardzrouni had suggested we take them with us, and after Zosimos, unknown to us, had already hidden the Grasal in one of them. I took a head in my hand, the first from the left if I recall properly, and I observed it carefully. Then I set it down. Now I was reliving that moment of almost fifteen years before, and I saw myself as I placed the head to the right, the last of the seven. When Zosimos came down to flee with the Grasal, remembering he had put it in the first head to the left, he had taken that one, which was actually the second. When we divided the heads on leaving, I was the last to take mine. Obviously it was Zosimos's. You will remember that, not saying anything to the others, I had kept with me Abdul's head after his death. Later, when I gave one of the heads to Praxeas, apparently I gave him Abdul's, and I realized it even then, because it opened easily, since the seal had already been broken by Ardzrouni. So, for almost fifteen years, I had carried the Grasal with me, not knowing it. By then I was so sure that I didn't even need to open my head. But I did, trying not to make any noise. Even behind the column in the darkness I could see that the Grasal was there, set in the case, with the cup facing forward and the base emerging, rounded like a skull."

Now, as if he had been possessed by a demon, the Poet was grabbing each of the other three by his clothes, covering them with insults, shouting that they were not to try to make a fool of him. Baudolino then left his reliquary behind the column and emerged from his hiding place. "I am the one who has the Grasal," he said.

The Poet was taken by surprise. He blushed violently and said: "You've lied to us, all this time. And I believed you were the purest of us all!"

"I haven't lied. I didn't know, not until this evening. You are the one who mistook the counting of the heads."

The Poet stretched his hands towards his friend and said, his mouth foaming: "Give it to me!"

"Why to you?" Baudolino asked.

"The journey ends here," the Poet repeated. "It has been an unfortunate journey, and this is my last chance. Give it to me, or I'll kill you."

Baudolino took a step back, clutching his hands around the hilts of his two Arabian daggers. "You would be capable of that—for this object you killed Frederick."

"Nonsense," the Poet said. "You just heard these three confess."

"Three confessions are too many for one murder," Baudolino said. "I could say that, even if each of them had done what he said, you let them do it. It would have been enough if, when you saw that Boron was about to turn the vacuum lever, you had prevented him. It would have been enough if, when Kyot moved the mirrors, you had warned Frederick before sunrise. You didn't. You wanted someone to kill Frederick so you could then profit from it. But I don't believe that

497

any of these three poor friends caused the death of the emperor. Hearing you speak behind the iconostasis, I remembered the head of Medusa that made audible in Frederick's chamber what was being murmured in the stairwell below. Now I will tell you what happened. Even before we set out on the expedition to Jerusalem, you were chomping at the bit and wanted to leave for the kingdom of the Priest, with the Grasal, by yourself. You were only awaiting the right opportunity to be rid of the emperor. Then, of course, we would have gone with you, but obviously for you we didn't represent a concern. Or perhaps you thought you could do what Zosimos, ahead of you, did. I don't know. For some time I should have realized that you were dreaming on your own, but friendship had clouded my intellect."

"Go on." The Poet sneered.

"I will go on. In Gallipolis, when Solomon bought the antidote, I remember very well that the merchant offered us also an identical phial that, however, contained poison. Coming out of that emporium, we lost sight of you for a bit. Then you reappeared, but you were without money, and you told us you had been robbed. Instead, while we were wandering about the market, you had gone back there and bought the poison. It can't have been difficult for you to exchange Solomon's phial with yours, during the long journey through the land of the sultan of Iconium. The evening before Frederick's death it was you who, in a loud voice, advised him to provide himself with the antidote. So you prompted our good Solomon, who offered his—or, rather, your—poison. You must have had a moment of terror when Kyot offered to taste it, but perhaps you already knew that the liquid, taken in a small dose, had no effect, and it was necessary to drink it all in order to die. I believe that during the night Kyot had such need of air because that tiny sip had upset him, but of this I'm not sure."

"And what are you sure of?" the Poet asked, still sneering.

"I am sure that, before you saw Boron and Kyot in action, you already had your plan in mind. You went into the hall where the circular stair was, in whose central aperture one spoke to be heard in

Frederick's room. For that matter, you yourself have demonstrated again this evening the fact that this game pleased you, and as I heard you speak from behind there, I began to understand. You approached the ear of Dionysus and called Frederick. I believe you passed yourself off as me, trusting in the fact that a voice, moving from one floor to another, would arrive distorted. You said you were me, to be more credible. You warned Frederick: we had discovered that someone had put poison in the food, perhaps you said one of us was beginning to suffer horrible pains and Ardzrouni had already unleashed his killers. You told him to open the ark and drink Solomon's antidote immediately. My poor father believed you, he drank, and he died."

"A fine story," the Poet said. "But what about the fireplace?"

"Perhaps it really was kindled by the rays from the mirror, but only after Frederick was already a corpse. The fire had nothing to do with it, it was not a part of your plan; but whoever did kindle it helped you confuse the situation. You killed Frederick, and only now have you helped me understand it. Curse you. How could you commit this crime, this parricide against the man who was your benefactor, only out of your thirst for glory? Didn't you realize that you were once again stealing another's glory, as you had done with my poems?"

"That's a fine one," Boidi said, laughing, having now recovered from his fear. "The great poet had his poems written by somebody else!"

This humiliation, after the many frustrations of those days, along with the desperate determination to have the Grasal, drove the Poet to his last excess. He drew his sword and flung himself on Baudolino, shouting: "I'll kill you! I'll kill you!"

"I've always told you I was a man of peace, Master Niketas. I was flattering myself. In reality, I'm a coward; Frederick was right, that day. At that moment I hated the Poet with all my soul, I wanted him dead, and yet I didn't think of killing him, I wanted only for him not to kill me. I leaped back towards the columns, then I took the passage by which I had come. I was escaping in the darkness, and I heard his threats as he chased me. The passage had no light, groping your way ahead meant touching the corpses in the walls. When I came to a side passage to the left, I rushed in that direction. He followed the sound of my footsteps. Finally I saw a light, and I found myself below the shaft opening where I had passed before. It was now evening, and miraculously I saw the moon over my head, illuminating the place where I was, and casting silvery glints on the faces of the dead. Perhaps it was they who told me it is impossible to deceive your own death, when it is panting at your heels. I stopped. I saw the Poet arrive; he covered his eyes with his left hand, to block the sight of those unexpected guests. I grabbed one of the rotting robes and pulled hard. A corpse fell between me and the Poet, raising a cloud of dust and of tiny cloth fragments that dissolved as they touched the ground. The head of that corpse had snapped from the trunk and rolled at the feet of my pursuer, directly under the moon's beam, displaying its horrid smile. The Poet stopped for an instant, terrified, then he gave the skull a kick. On the other side, I grabbed two more cadavers, pushing them straight at his face. Get this death away from me, the Poet cried, as flakes of dried skin swirled around his head. I couldn't keep up that game forever; I would have fallen beyond the luminous circle and would have been plunged again into darkness. I clutched my two Arabian daggers in my hands, and held the blades straight out in front of me, like a beak. The Poet flung himself against me, his sword raised, grasped with both hands, to slice my head in two, but he stumbled over the second skeleton, which had rolled in front of him. He attacked me, I fell to the ground, supporting myself on my elbows; he was upon me, while the sword slipped from his hands. . . . I saw his face above mine, his bloodshot eyes above my eyes, I smelled the odor of his anger, the sweat of a beast as it claws its prey, I felt his hands clutch my neck, I heard the grinding of his teeth. . . . I reacted instinctively, I raised my elbows and dealt him two blows, one on either side, against his flanks. I heard the sound of tearing cloth, I had the impression that, in the center of his viscera, the two blades met. Then I saw him blanch, and a trickle of blood came from his mouth. His brow touched mine, his blood dripped into my mouth. I don't remember how I extricated myself from that embrace. I left the daggers in his belly, and I shrugged aside that weight. He slipped to my side, his eyes open, staring at the moon high above, and he was dead."

"The first person you killed in your life."

"And, pray God, the last. He had been the friend of my youth, the companion of a thousand adventures, for more than forty years. I wanted to weep. Then I remembered what he had done and I would have liked to kill him again. I stood up, with difficulty, because I had begun my killing when I no longer had the agility of my better years. I groped my way to the end of the passage, gasping, and reentered the crypt. I saw the other three, pale and trembling. I felt myself invested again with my diginity as a ministerial and adoptive son of Frederick. I should not show any weakness. Erect, with my back to the iconostasis, as if I were an archangel among archangels, I said: "Justice is done, I have dealt death to the murderer of the holy and Roman emperor.""

Baudolino went to collect his reliquary, took out the Grasal, showed it to the others, as if it were a consecrated host. He said only: "Does any one of you want to make a claim?"

"Baudolino," Boron said, unable to keep his hands still, "I've lived more this evening than in all the years we've spent together. It is certainly not your fault, but something has broken between us, between me and you, between me and Kyot, between me and Boidi. Just now, if only for a few instants, each of us ardently wished that the guilty party were one of the others, to put an end to a nightmare. This is no longer friendship. After the fall of Pndapetzim we've remained together only by accident. What united us was the search for that object you are holding in your hand. The search, I say: not the object. Now I know that the object remained always with us, but this didn't prevent us from rushing again and again towards our destruction. I realized this evening that I must not have the Grasal, or give it to anyone, but only keep alive the flame of the search for it. So you must keep that cup, which has the power of moving men only when it can't be found. I'm leaving. If I can get out of the city, I will, as soon as possible, and I will start writing about the Grasal, and my only power will lie in my story. I will write of knights better than we, and my reader will dream of purity and not of our flaws. Farewell to all of you, my remaining friends. Not infrequently it has been beautiful to dream with you." He vanished along the way he had come.

"Baudolino," Kyot said, "I believe Boron has made the best choice. I'm not learned, as he is, I don't know if I would be able to write the story of the Grasal, but surely I'll find someone I can tell it to, so he can write it. Boron is right, I will remain faithful to my search of so many years if I can impel others to desire the Grasal. I will not even speak of that cup you are holding in your hand. Perhaps I will say, as I said once, that the Grasal is a stone, fallen from heaven. Stone, or cup, or spear: what does it matter? What counts is that nobody must find it, otherwise the others would stop seeking it. If you will listen to me, hide that thing, so that no one will kill his own dream by putting his hands on it. And as for the rest, I too would feel uncomfortable moving among you, I would be overwhelmed by too many painful memories. You, Baudolino, have become an avenging angel. Perhaps you had to do what you have done. But I don't want to see you again. Farewell." And he, too, went out of the crypt.

Then Boidi spoke, and after so many years he spoke again in the language of Frascheta. "Baudolino," he said, "I don't have my head in the clouds like those two, and I don't know how to tell stories. The idea of people going around looking for something that doesn't exist makes me laugh. The things that count are the things that do exist, only you mustn't let everybody see them because envy is a nasty beast. That cup there is something holy, believe me, because it's simple like all holy things. I don't know where you're going to put it, but any place, except the one I'm now going to say, would be the wrong one. Now listen to my idea. After your poor Papa Gagliaudo died, bless his soul, you'll remember that everybody in Alessandria started saying if someone saves our city we'll raise a statue to him. Now you know how these things go: there's plenty of talk and nothing comes of it. But, going around selling grain, I found in a little crumbling church near Villa del Foro, a beautiful statue from God knows where. It's of a bent old man, holding his hands over his head with a kind of millstone resting on them, a construction stone, maybe, a great cheese wheel—who knows what?—and he seems to be bent double because he can hardly hold it up. I said to myself an image like that meant something, even if I didn't rightly know what it meant, but you know how it is: you make a statue and then others figure out what it means, whatever seems to work. Well, look at this: I said to myself then, this could be the statue of Gagliaudo, you stick it over the door or on the side of the cathedral, like a little column with that stone on his head like a capital, and it's the spitting image of him bearing the weight of the whole siege. I carried it home and I put it in my barn. When I talked about it with others, everyone said it was a really good idea. Then there was the business when, if you were a good Christian, you set off for Jerusalem, so I went along with it, because it seemed like God knows what. What's done can't be undone. Now I'm going home, and after all this time you'll see what a fuss they'll make over me, those of us who are still alive, and for the youngsters I'll be the one who followed the emperor to Jerusalem, and who has more stories to tell around the fire at evening than master Virgil himself, so maybe before I die they'll even make me consul. I'm going home; without saying anything to anyone, I'll go into the barn, find that statue, somehow I'll make a hole in that thing he has over his head, and I'll stick the Grasal into it. Then I'll cover it with mortar, put back the stone chips so nobody can see even a crack, and I'll carry the statue into the cathedral. We'll set it up, fitting it nicely into the wall, and there it stays per omnia saecula saeculorm, and nobody will pull it down, and nobody can see what your father is carrying on his head. We are a young city, and without too many bees in our bonnet, but the blessing of heaven can never harm anybody. I will die, my children will die, and the Grasal will always be there, to protect the city, and nobody will know. It's enough if the good Lord knows. What do you say?"

"Master Niketas, that was the right fate for the cup, also because, though for years I had pretended to forget it, I was the only one who knew where it really came from. After what I had just done, I didn't know myself why I was in the world, since I had never done one thing right. With that Grasal in my hands I would just have committed more mistakes. Good old Boidi was right. I would have liked to go back with him, but what would I do in Alessandria among a thousand memories of Colandrina, and dreaming of Hypatia every night? I thanked Boidi for that beautiful idea. I wrapped the Grasal in the rag I had brought it in, but without the reliquary. If you have to travel, and maybe come up against bandits, I said to him, a reliquary that looks like gold will be stolen at once, whereas they wouldn't even touch a common bowl. Go with God, Boidi, may he help you always. Leave me here, for I need to remain alone. So he also left. I looked around, and I remembered Zosimos. He had gone. When he escaped I don't know, he had heard that one wanted to kill the other, and by then life had taught him to stay away from trouble. Groping, he who knew those places from memory, had slipped off, while we had quite different matters to occupy us. He had done all sorts of things, but he had been punished. Let him continue begging in the streets, and may the Lord have mercy on him. And so, Master Niketas, I retraced my way along the corridor of the dead, stepping over the corpse of the Poet, and I climbed back into the light of the fire near the Hippodrome. What happened to me immediately afterwards you know: it was immediately afterwards that I met you."

39

Baudolino stylites

Niketas was silent. And Baudolino, too, was silent, seated with his hands open on his lap. As if to say: "That's all."

"There is something in your story," Niketas said at a certain point, "that doesn't convince me. The Poet formulated imaginary accusations against your companions, as if each of them had killed Frederick, and then they were false. You believed you could reconstruct what happened that night but, if you have told me everything, the Poet never said that was how things really went."

"He tried to kill me!"

"He had gone crazy, that is clear: he wanted the Grasal at any price, and to have it he had convinced himself that its possessor was the murderer. All he could think of you was that, having it, you had kept it hidden from him, and this was enough for him to pass over your dead body to take that cup from you. But you never said that he was the murderer of Frederick."

"Well, who was it then?"

"You all went on for fifteen years thinking that Frederick's death was a pure accident...."

"We stuck to that belief so that we wouldn't have to suspect one another. And then there was the ghost of Zosimos: we had a guilty party."

"That may be. But, believe me, and I am a man who in imperial palaces has witnessed many crimes. Even if our emperors always enjoyed showing foreign visitors strange machines and miraculous automata, I never saw anyone use those machines to kill. Listen: you will remember that when you mentioned Ardzrouni to me the first time, I said I had known him in Constantinople, and that one of my friends from Selymbria had been to his castle once or twice. He is a man, this Paphnutius, who knows much about Ardzrouni's diabolic tricks, because he himself has constructed similar things for the imperial palaces. And he knows well the limitations of these deviltries, because once, in the days of Andronicus, he promised the emperor an automaton that would spin in place and unfurl a banner when the emperor clapped his hands. He constructed it, Andronicus displayed it to some foreign envoys during a banquet, he clapped his hands, the automaton didn't budge, and Paphnutius's eyes were gouged out. I'll ask him if he would like to come and pay you a visit. Actually, exiled here in Selymbria, he is bored."

Paphnutius came, led by a boy. Despite his misfortune, and his age, he was a keen and lively man. He conversed with Niketas, whom he hadn't seen for some time, and then asked how he could be of help to Baudolino.

Baudolino told him the story, first summarily, then in greater detail, from the Gallipolis market to the death of Frederick. He couldn't avoid referring to Ardzrouni, but he concealed the identity of his adoptive father, saying he was a Flemish count, very dear to him. He didn't even mention the Grasal, but spoke only of a goblet studded with precious stones, to which the murdered man was greatly attached, a thing that could arouse the envy of many. As Baudolino narrated, Paphnutius interrupted him every now and then. "You're a Frank, aren't you?" he asked, and explained that his way of pronouncing certain Greek words was typical of those who lived in Provence. Or: "Why do you keep touching that scar on your cheek, while you talk?" And to Baudolino, who by now believed his blindness was counterfeit, he explained that at times his voice lost its sonority, as if he were passing his hand before his mouth. If, as many do, he were touching his beard, he wouldn't have covered his mouth. Therefore he must be touching his cheek, and if someone touches his cheek it's because he has a toothache, or has a wart or a scar. Since Baudolino was a man of arms, the scar hypothesis seemed the most rational.

Baudolino completed his tale, and Paphnutius said: "Now you would like to know what really happened inside the locked room of the emperor Frederick."

"How do you know I was talking about Frederick?"

"Come now, everyone knows the emperor drowned in the Calykadnus, a few feet from the castle of Ardzrouni, who, for that matter, then immediately disappeared, because his prince Leo wanted to chop off his head, holding him responsible for not having guarded adequately that most illustrious guest. I had always been amazed that your emperor, so accustomed to swimming in rivers, as everyone said, had let himself be swept away by the current of a trickle like the Calykadnus, and now you are explaining many things to me. So then, let's try to see this clearly." He spoke without irony, as if he were truly following a scene that was unfolding before his spent eyes.

"First of all, we can eliminate any suspicion that Frederick died because of the machine that creates the vacuum. I know that machine; first of all, it acted on a small windowless room on the upper floor, and not surely in the room of the emperor, where there was a flue and God knows how many other apertures where air could enter at will. In second place, the machine itself couldn't work. I tested it. The inner cylinder didn't occupy perfectly the outer cylinder, and there, too, air could come in all over the place. Mechanics more expert than Ardzrouni tried, centuries and centuries ago, experiments of the kind, without results. It was one thing to construct the sphere that turned or the gate that opened thanks to heat: these are tricks known since the times of Ctesibius and Hero of Alexandria. But the vacuum, dear friend: absolutely not. Ardzrouni was vain, he liked to amaze his guests, and that's all there was to it. Now we come to the mirrors. The burning of the Roman ships by the great Archimedes is consecrated by legend, but we don't know if it's true. I've touched Ardzrouni's mirrors: they were too small, and crudely ground. Even assuming they were perfect, one mirror sends solar rays of some power at high noon, not in the morning, when the sun's rays are weak. Moreover, the rays would have had to pass through a window with colored panes, and so you see that your friend, even if he had trained one of those mirrors on the emperor's chamber, would have achieved nothing. Are you convinced?"

"Let's move on to the rest."

"Poisons and antidotes...You Latins are truly ingenuous. Could you imagine that in the Gallipolis market they could sell potent substances such as even a basileus can manage to possess only through trusted alchemists, paying their weight in gold? Everything sold there is false; it serves for the barbarians who come from Iconium, or the Bulgar forest. In the two phials they showed you was fresh water, and whether Frederick drank the liquid from the phial belonging to your Jewish friend or from the one belonging to your friend called the Poet, the result would have been the same. And the same can be said for the portentous cordial. If such a cordial were to exist, every strategist would stock up on it, to animate and drive his wounded soldiers back into battle. For that matter, you told me the price at which they sold you those marvels: it was so ridiculous that it was hardly worth the trouble to take the water from the fountain and fill the phials. Now let me tell you about the Dionysius ear. I have never heard that Ardzrouni's device worked. Tricks of this kind can succeed when the distance between the aperture into which you speak and the one from which the voice emerges is very short, as when you cup your hands around your mouth, to make yourself heard a bit farther away. But in the castle, the passage from one floor to the next was complicated, twisting and winding, between thick walls. . . . Did Ardzrouni allow you to test his device?"

"No."

"You see? He showed it to his guests, he boasted of it, and that's all. Even if your poet had tried to speak with Frederick, and Frederick had been awake, he would have heard at most a vague mumbling from the Medusa's mouth. Perhaps sometimes Ardzrouni used this artifice to frighten someone he had sent to sleep up there, to make him believe the castle housed ghosts, but no more than that. Your Poet friend can't have sent any message to Frederick."

"But the empty cup on the floor, the fire in the fireplace . . ."

"You told me that Frederick didn't feel well that evening. He had ridden all day under the sun of those lands, which burns and is bad for those who are not used to it; he had spent days and days in battle and incessant peregrinations. . . . He was surely tired, weak, perhaps he was seized by a fever. What do you do if you feel chills during the night? You try to cover yourself up, but, if you have fever, you feel the chills even under the blankets. Your emperor lighted the fire. Then he felt still worse; he was gripped by the fear of having been poisoned, and he drank his useless antidote."

"But why did he feel still worse?"

"There I'm no longer certain, but if you think rationally, it's obvious there can be only one conclusion. Describe that fireplace to me again, so that I can see it well."

"There was some wood on a bed of dry twigs, there were some boughs with aromatic berries, and then chunks of a dark substance, I believe it was charcoal, but covered by something oily. . . ."

"It was naphtha or bitumen, which is found, for example, abundantly in Palestine, in the sea they call Dead, where they believe water is so dense and heavy that if you enter that sea you don't sink, but float like a boat. Pliny writes that this substance is so kin to fire that when it approaches wood, it kindles it. As for the charcoal, we all

509

know what it is if, as Pliny says, it is derived from oaks, by burning some fresh boughs in a cone-heaped pile, sheathed in damp clay, in which some holes have been made to release all the humidity during the combustion. But sometimes it is made from other woods, whose virtues we do not always know. Now many physicians have observed what happens to one who inhales the fumes of a bad charcoal made even more dangerous by its union with certain types of bitumen. It gives off poisonous gases, far more subtle and invisible than the smoke normally emitted by a lighted fire, which you try to dispel by opening the window. You don't see these fumes; they spread and, if the space is closed, they stagnate. You could become aware of them because, when they come in contact with the flame of a lamp, they color it blue. But generally when one does become aware, it is too late, that maleficent breath has already devoured the pure air around him. The unfortunate who inhales that mephitic air feels a great heaviness of the head, a ringing in the ears, his breath becomes labored, and his sight is clouded.... Good reasons to believe you've been poisoned, and to drink an antidote, and this is what your emperor did. After you have realized these symptoms, if you don't immediately leave the infected place, or someone doesn't drag you away, worse happens. You feel overcome by an immense drowsiness, you fall to the ground, and to the eyes of whoever finds you, you will seem dead, not breathing, without bodily warmth, no pulse, your limbs stiffened, and an extreme pallor on your face.... Even the most expert doctor will think he is seeing a corpse. We know of people who have been buried in this condition, whereas it would have sufficed to treat them with cold cloths on the head and foot baths, rubbing the whole body with oils that stimulate the humors."

"You—" Baudolino said, his face as pale as Frederick's that morning, "you are telling me that we believed the emperor dead, and he was alive?"

"Almost certainly yes, my poor friend. He died when he was thrown into the river. The icy water somehow began to revive him,

510

and that too would have been a good treatment, but, still unconscious, he started breathing, swallowed the water, and drowned.
When you pulled him to shore, you should have seen if he had the
look of a drowned man...."

"He was bloated. I knew it couldn't be so, and I thought it was an
impression, from the sight of those poor remains scratched by the
stones of the river...."

"A dead man doesn't become bloated remaining under water. It
happens only to a living man who dies under water."

"Then Frederick fell victim to an extraordinary and unknown fit,
and wasn't killed?"

"His life was taken, to be sure, but by whoever threw him into the
water."

"But I did that!"

"It is truly a shame. I can hear that you are distressed. Calm yourself. You acted, believing you were doing good, and surely not to
cause his death."

"I did cause him to die!"

"I do not call this killing."

"But I do!" Baudolino cried. "I drowned my poor father while he
was still alive! I..." He turned even more pale, murmured a few dis-
jointed words, and fainted.

He came to as Niketas was putting cold cloths on his head.
Paphnutius had left, perhaps feeling guilty for having revealed to
Baudolino—to show how well he could see things—a terrible truth.

"Now try to remain calm," Niketas said to him, "I understand
that you are distraught, but it was an accident. You heard Paphnutius;
anyone would have thought the man was dead. I too have heard of
cases of apparent death that deceived every doctor."

"I killed my father," Baudolino kept repeating, shaken now by a
feverish tremor, "unknowing, I hated him, because I had desired his
wife, my adoptive mother. I was first an adulterer, then a parricide,

and carrying this leprosy in me, I befouled with my incestuous seed the purest of virgins, making her believe that that was the ecstasy I had promised her. I'm a murderer, because I killed the Poet, who was innocent...."

"He was not innocent, he was driven by a relentless desire; he was trying to kill you, you defended yourself."

"I accused him unjustly of the murder I myself had committed, I killed him rather than recognize that I should punish myself. I have lived my whole life in falsehood, I want to die, to plunge into Hell and suffer for all eternity...."

It was futile to try to calm him, and nothing could be done to heal him. Niketas had Theophilactus prepare an infusion of somniferous herbs and made Baudolino drink it. A few minutes later Baudolino sank into the most restless sleep.

When he woke up the next day, he refused the cup of broth that was offered him, went outside, sat under a tree and there remained in silence, his head in his hands, for the whole day, and the next morning he was still there. Niketas decided that in such cases the best remedy is wine, and convinced him to drink wine in abundance, as if it were a medicine. Baudolino remained in a state of continuous torpor under the tree for three days and three nights.

At dawn of the fourth morning Niketas went to look for him, and he was gone. He searched the garden thoroughly and the house, but Baudolino had vanished. Fearing he might have decided to commit a desperate act, Niketas sent Theophilactus and his children to look for him through all Selymbria and in the surrounding fields. Two hours later they returned, shouting to Niketas to come and see. They took him to that meadow just outside the city where, entering, they had seen the column of the eremites of the past.

A group of curious bystanders had collected at the foot of the column, pointing upwards. The column was of white stone, almost as tall as a two-story house. At the top it widened into a square balcony, surrounded by a parapet made of rough posts and a banister, also in stone. A little pavilion stood in the center. The space extending from the column was very scant; to be seated on the balcony, one had to allow one's legs to dangle, and the pavilion could barely contain a crouching, huddled man. His legs hanging, Baudolino was seated up there, and it could be seen that he was naked as a worm.

Niketas called him, shouted to him to come down, tried to open the little door at the foot of the column that, as in all similar constructions, opened on a circular staircase that led up to the balcony. But the door, though shaky, had been barred from inside.

"Come down, Baudolino! What are you doing up there?"

Baudolino answered, but Niketas couldn't hear clearly. He asked others to go and find him a sufficiently high ladder. He was given one, he painfully climbed it, and found himself with his head against Baudolino's feet. "What do you want to do?" he asked again.

"Stay here. Now my expiation begins. I will pray, I will meditate, I will annihilate myself in silence. I will try to achieve a solitary distance from every opinion and imagination, to feel neither wrath nor desire, nor even reasoning or thought, to free myself from every bond, to return to the absolutely simple so as no longer to see anything, except the glory of darkness. I will drain soul and intellect, I will arrive beyond the kingdom of the mind; in the darkness I will complete my journey along paths of fire...."

Niketas realized Baudolino was repeating things heard from Hypatia. To such a degree this unhappy man wished to flee every passion, he thought, that he is isolated up here seeking to become equal to her whom he still loves. But Niketas didn't say this. He asked only how Baudolino thought to survive.

"You told me that the eremites lowered a basket on a string," Baudolino said, "and the faithful placed there as alms the scraps left from their table, or, better still, left uneaten by their animals. And a bit of water, even if it is possible to suffer thirst and wait until, now and then, the rain falls."

Niketas sighed, climbed down, had someone find a basket with a string, filled it with bread, cooked greens, olives, and pieces of meat; one of Theophilactus's sons threw the string up, Baudolino caught it, and drew up the basket. He took only the bread and olives, and gave back the rest. "Now leave me, I beg you," he cried to Niketas. "What I wanted to understand, telling you my story, I have understood. We have nothing more to say to each other. Thank you for having helped me arrive where I am."

Niketas went to see him every day. Baudolino greeted him with a gesture, and remained silent. As time went by, Niketas realized it was no longer necessary to take him food, because word had spread in Selymbria that, after centuries, another holy man had isolated himself on top of a column, and everyone went there, to stand below and bless himself, putting in the basket something to eat and drink. Baudolino pulled up the string, kept for himself what little he needed for that day, and crumbled the rest for the many birds that had taken to perching on the banister. They were his only interest.

Baudolino stayed up there all summer without uttering a word, burned by the sun, and though he often withdrew into the pavilion, tortured by the heat. He defecated and urinated obviously at night, over the balustrade, and his feces could be seen at the foot of the column, tiny as a goat's. His beard and hair kept growing, and he was so dirty that it could be seen and, also was beginning to be smelled, from down below.

Niketas twice had to be absent from Selymbria. In Constantinople, Baudouin of Flanders had been named basileus, and the Latins were little by little invading the whole empire, but Niketas had to look after his property. Meanwhile, in Nicaea, the last bulwark of the Byzantine empire was being constructed, and Niketas was thinking he should move there, where they would need a counsellor of his experience. Therefore it was necessary to make approaches and prepare for that new, very dangerous journey.

Every time he came back, he saw an ever-thicker crowd at the foot of the column. Some had thought that a stylite, so purified by his constant sacrifice, could not help but possess profound wisdom, and they would climb the ladder to ask his advice and solace. They told him of their misfortunes, and Baudolino would answer, for example: "If you are proud, you are the devil. If you are sad, you are his son. And if you worry over a thousand things, you are his never-resting servant."

Another asked his advice on settling a dispute with his neighbor. And Baudolino said: "Be like a camel: bear the burden of your sins, and follow the steps of him who knows the ways of the Lord."

Yet another complained that his daughter-in-law could not bear a child. And Baudolino said: "Everything a man can think about, what is under the sun and what is above the sky, is vain. Only he who perseveres in the memory of Christ is in the truth."

"How wise he is," they said, and left him a few coins, going off, filled with consolation.

Winter came, and Baudolino was almost always huddled inside the pavilion. Rather than listen to long stories from those who came to him, he began foreseeing them. "You love a person with all your heart, but at times you are overcome with the suspicion that this person does not love you with equal warmth," he would say. And the visitor would say: "How right you are! You have read my soul like an open book! What must I do?" And Baudolino would say: "Be silent, and do not measure yourself."

To a fat man, who arrived after climbing up with great effort, he said: "You wake every morning with an aching neck, and you have trouble pulling on your boots." "That's right," the man said, with wonder. And Baudolino said: "Don't eat for three days. But do not take pride in your fasting. Rather than become proud, eat meat. It is better to eat than to boast. And accept your pains as a toll for your sins."

A father came and told him that his son was covered with painful sores. Baudolino answered: "Wash him three times a day with water

515

and salt, and each time say the words 'Virgin Hypatia, take care of your child.'" The man went off, and a week later he came back, saying the sores were healing. He gave Baudolino some coins, a pigeon, and a flask of wine. All cried miracle, and the sick went to the church, praying: "Virgin Hypatia, take care of your child."

A poorly dressed man with a grim face climbed the ladder. Baudolino said to him: "I know what's wrong with you. In your heart you bear rancor towards someone."

"You know everything," the man said.

Baudolino said to him: "If someone wants to return evil for evil, he can hurt a brother with the simplest gesture. Keep your hands always behind your back."

Another came with sad eyes and said to him: "I don't know what my sickness is."

"I know," Baudolino said. "You are slothful."

"How can I be cured?"

"Sloth appears the first time when you notice the slowness of the movement of the sun."

"And then—?"

"Never look at the sun."

"Nothing can be hidden from him," the people of Selymbria were saying.

"How can you be so wise?" one man asked him. And Baudolino said: "Because I hide myself."

"How can you hide yourself?"

Baudolino held out his hand and showed his palm. "What do you see before you?" he asked. "A hand," the man answered.

"You see I know well how to hide myself," Baudolino said.

Spring returned. Baudolino was increasingly dirty and hairy. He was covered with birds, who swarmed to peck the worms that had begun to inhabit his body. Since he had to nourish all those creatures, people filled his basket frequently during the day.

516

One morning a man on horseback arrived, breathless and covered with dust. He said that, during a hunting party, a nobleman had clumsily shot an arrow and had struck the son of his sister. The arrow had entered the son's eye and had come out from his nape. The boy was still breathing, and that nobleman asked Baudolino to do whatever could be done by a man of God.

Baudolino said: "The task of the stylite is to see his thoughts arrive from the distance. I knew you would come, but you have taken too much time, and you will take just as long to go back. Things in this world go as they must go. I must tell you that the boy is dying at this moment, or rather, he is already dead. May God have mercy on him."

The knight went home, and the boy was already dead. When the news was known, many in Selymbria cried that Baudolino had the gift of clairvoyance and had seen what was happening miles away. But not far from the column there was the church of Saint Mardonius, whose priest hated Baudolino, because for months the offerings of his regular parishoners had been diminishing. This priest took to saying that Baudolino's miracle didn't amount to much. Anybody could work such miracles. He went to the foot of the column and shouted to Baudolino that, if a stylite wasn't even capable of removing an arrow from an eye, it was as if he had killed the boy himself.

Baudolino answered: "Concern with pleasing humans causes the loss of all spiritual growth."

The priest threw a stone at him, and immediately some other fanatics joined in flinging stones and clods at the balcony. They hurled stones all day, as Baudolino huddled in the pavilion, his hands over his face. They went off only when night had fallen.

The next morning Niketas went to see what had happened to his friend, but never saw him there again. The column was deserted. He went home, uneasy, and found Baudolino in Theophilactus's room. He had filled a barrel with water and with a knife he was scraping away all the filth he had accumulated. He had roughly cut his beard and hair. He was tanned by the sun and the wind; he didn't seem to have lost much weight, but it was hard for him to remain erect and he moved his arms and shoulders to loosen the muscles of his back.

"You saw for yourself. The one time in my life I told the truth and only the truth, they stoned me."

"It happened also to the apostles. You had become a holy man, and you let such a little thing discourage you?"

"Maybe I was expecting a sign from heaven. Over these months I have accumulated no small number of coins. I sent one of Theophilactus's sons to buy me some clothes, a horse, and a mule. My weapons must still be somewhere around this house."

"So you are going away?"

"Yes," he said, "staying on that column, I have come to understand many things. I have understood that I sinned, but never to achieve power and wealth. I understand that, if I want to be forgiven, I must pay three debts. First debt: I promised to have a stone raised to commemorate Abdul, and for this I kept his Baptist's head. The money has come from elsewhere, and that is better, because it hasn't come from simony but from the donations of good Christians. I will find again the place where we buried Abdul, and I will have a chapel built."

"But you don't even remember where he was killed."

"God will guide me, and I know the map of Cosmas from memory. Second debt: I made a sacred promise to my good father Frederick, not to mention to Bishop Otto, and until now I haven't kept it. I must reach the kingdom of Prester John. Otherwise I will have spent my life in vain."

"But you have had living proof that it doesn't exist!"

"We had proof that we hadn't reached it. That's different."

"But you realized that the eunuchs were lying."

"That perhaps they were lying. But Bishop Otto could not lie, or the voice of tradition, which declares the Priest is somewhere."

"But you are no longer young as when you tried the first time!"

"I am wiser. Third debt: I have a son, or a daughter, back there. And Hypatia is there. I want to find them, and protect them, as is my duty."

"But more than seven years have passed!"

"The child will now be over six. Is a child of six perhaps no longer one's child?"

"But it could be a male, and therefore a satyr-that-is-never-seen!"

"And it could be a little Hypatia. I will love that child in any case."

"But you don't know where the mountains are, the place where they have taken refuge!"

"I will search for them."

"But Hypatia could have forgotten you; perhaps she won't want to see again the man with whom she lost her apathy."

"You don't know Hypatia. She is waiting for me."

"But you were already old when she loved you, now you will seem ancient to her!"

"She has never seen younger men."

"But it will take you years and years to go back to those places, and to go beyond!"

"We people of Frascheta have heads harder than birds'."

"But how do you know you will live to the end of your journey?"

"A journey makes you younger."

There was nothing to be done. The next day Baudolino embraced Niketas, his whole family, and his hosts. With some effort, he mounted his horse, leading behind him a mule with many provisions, his sword hanging from his saddle.

Niketas saw him disappear into the distance, still waving his hand, but not looking back, heading straight for the kingdom of Prester John.

40

Baudolino is no more

Niketas went to visit Paphnutius. He told him everything, from start to finish, from the moment he encountered Baudolino in Saint Sophia, and everything Baudolino had narrated to him.

"What must I do?" he asked.

"For him? Nothing. He is going towards his destiny."

"Not for him, for myself. I am a writer of histories. Sooner or later I will have to set myself to putting down the record of the last days of Byzantium. Where will I put the story that Baudolino told me?"

"Nowhere. The story is all his. And anyway, are you sure it is true?"

"No. Everything I know I have learned from him, as from him I learned that he was a liar."

"Then you see," the wise Paphnutius said, "that a writer of histories cannot put his faith in such uncertain testimony. Strike Baudolino from your story."

"But at least during the last days we had a story in common, in the house of the Genoese."

"Strike also the Genoese; otherwise you'd have to tell about the relics they fabricated, and your readers would lose faith in the most sacred things. It won't cost you much to alter events slightly; you will say you were helped by some Venetians. Yes, I know, it's not the truth, but in a great history little truths can be altered so that the greater truth emerges. You must tell the true story of the empire of the Romans, not a little adventure that was born in a far-off swamp, in barbarian lands, among barbarian peoples. And, further, would you like to put into the heads of your future readers the notion that a Grasal exists, up there amid the snow and ice, and the kingdom of Prester John in the remote lands? Who knows how many lunatics would start wandering endlessly, for centuries and centuries?"

"It was a beautiful story. Too bad no one will find out about it."

"You surely don't believe you're the only writer of stories in this world. Sooner or later, someone—a greater liar than Baudolino—will tell it."

Translator's Note

As always, and with undiminished gratitude, I want to thank the author for his generous and invaluable assistance, and our editor, Drenka Willen, for her sensitive reading of the text and her cogent suggestions and stimulating questions. I owe a great deal also to my friends at Bard College: my colleagues Bruce Chilton, Frederick Hammond, Robert Kelly, William Mullen, Karen Sullivan, and my former students Ezer Lichtenstein and Jorge Santana, who cheerfully tamed my recalcitrant computer.

—W.W.

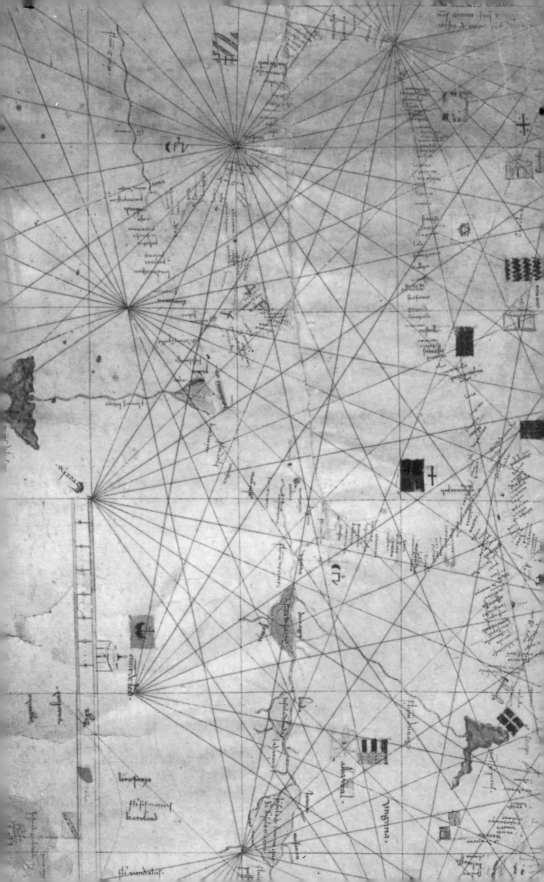